She played and sang

Manchester University Press

She played and sang

Jane Austen and music

Gillian Dooley

Manchester University Press

The right of Gillian Dooley to be identified as the author of this work has been asserted in accordance with the Copyright, Designs and Patents Act 1988.

Published by Manchester University Press
Oxford Road, Manchester M13 9PL
www.manchesteruniversitypress.co.uk

British Library Cataloguing-in-Publication Data
A catalogue record for this book is available from the British Library

ISBN 978 1 5261 7010 1 hardback

First published 2024

The publisher has no responsibility for the persistence or accuracy of URLs for any external or third-party internet websites referred to in this book, and does not guarantee that any content on such websites is, or will remain, accurate or appropriate.

Typeset
by Cheshire Typesetting Ltd, Cuddington, Cheshire

Contents

Contents

Introduction

The question of taste: did Jane Austen like music?

Jane Austen's surviving letters make intriguing reading. It is easy (and not uncommon) to lift passing remarks and quote them as evidence for all kinds of biographical details. It has been proposed, for example, that Austen disliked music. In May 1801, when Austen had just moved to Bath with her parents, she met Mrs and Miss Holder, mother and daughter. She wrote, 'It is the fashion to think them both very detestable, but they are so civil, & their gowns look so white & so nice ... that I cannot utterly abhor them, especially as Miss Holder owns that she has no taste for Music' (*Letters*, p. 88). On the other hand, in August 1805 she described meeting a Miss Hatton, who had 'little to say for herself. ... Her eloquence lies in her fingers; they were most fluidly harmonious' (*Letters*, p. 107). How can we reconcile these two opinions:

seeming to approve of one woman for being unmusical, and another for being musical?

Six years later she wrote to her sister Cassandra of a Miss Harding: 'an elegant, pleasing, pretty looking girl, about 19 I suppose, or 19 & ½, or 19 & ¼, with flowers in her head, and Music at her fingers ends. – She plays very well indeed. I have seldom heard anybody with more pleasure' (*Letters*, p. 189). This is the remark of a music-lover. How does it tally with her description in 1813 of Sir Brook Bridges's second wife, whom she first met in November 1813 at a concert in Canterbury, and liked 'for being in a hurry to have the Concert over & get away' (*Letters*, p. 251)?

It might not be possible to explain away all these contradictions, but, as Samantha Carrasco points out, 'the care and attention that Jane spent on her musical studies' reinforces the fact that music was important to her. Also, she continues, 'as we also know Jane was a satirist, her written comments taken out of context could easily be misconstrued'.[1] The best chance we have is to take them in the context of the rest of the correspondence, of the surviving memoirs, of her novels and other writings, and, above all, of her music collection.

Why does it matter whether or not she liked music? After all, Austen's fame is not as a composer of music but as a composer of narratives. She was not even writing poetry, which is arguably more allied to musical forms than prose. Why is it important that she was an amateur musician who spent some of her leisure hours playing the piano and singing music much of which, unlike her own works, is almost completely forgotten today? It was just a hobby, after all, one might argue. She was not a professional musician, only an amateur.

In this book I will offer several possible answers to this question. One reason is that her musical practice provides

Introduction

background for the music that appears as part of the lives of the characters in her novels. Knowing about music in Austen's own life helps readers understand her characters' cultural and social milieu – what would be expected of a young musician in a domestic setting, providing entertainment for family and friends and meaningful occupation for her leisure time. Another is the light Austen's musical knowledge throws on her familiarity with political and social currents, such as the war with France, the national importance of the Navy, and the relative popularity of British music and music from continental Europe. More broadly, it provides a detailed example to music historians of the place of music in the life of a woman of Austen's generation and class in England.

However, for me the most important reason to explore the music in Austen's life is the rhetorical link between writing and making music, especially given the musicality of her prose. Her knowledge of the theatre has been explored by several scholars, and it is no accident that many of the pieces of music in her collection had their origin in theatrical productions of some kind. But all music expresses and explores a range of emotions and subjective states of mind, sometimes beyond the capacity of written language, often adding depth and meaning to lyrics that are in themselves unremarkable.

I am not the first to suggest a rhetorical influence flowing from Austen's musical practice to her writing. Robert K. Wallace, in his book *Jane Austen and Mozart*, concludes that 'the classical and neoclassical values of balance, equilibrium, proportion, symmetry, clarity, restraint, wit, and elegance that are typical of Austen's novels and of Mozart's piano concertos are typical as well of the music that Austen played on her square piano'.[2] Wallace's interesting thesis is that in learning these piano sonatas by composers such as Pleyel, Schobert and Hoffmeister, 'Austen assimilated the principles of what we now call the classical style in music', and these principles fed into the structure of her novels.[3] I would go further and suggest that the kinds of rhetorical gestures in music – especially in song – that convey emotional states and situations could have influenced her writing. Knowing the language of music from the inside allowed Austen to enrich her prose with its rhythms and gestures. To illustrate this assertion, in Chapter 8 I compare the rhetoric of a multi-movement ballad setting by Tommaso Giordani of the narrative poem 'Lucy and Colin ' with selections from Austen's prose in *Sense and sensibility*, focusing in particular on passages which describe scenes that correspond in some way to the incidents described in the ballad.

Austen did not aspire to be a well-known musician in the way she was celebrated even during her lifetime as a novelist. Nevertheless, there can be no doubt that music was a significant part of Austen's life. Jeanice Brooks writes:

> Considering Austen's music as the practice of an artistic discipline rather than a trivial pastime can open new perspectives on the intellectual landscape she inhabited, which was shaped by musical as well as literary currents: it is significant that intelligent conversation between Austen's characters – as in the example of Anne Elliot and Captain Harville – very frequently involves music as well as books. ... Equally importantly, songs provided opportunities for critical reading through performance: Austen was not a silent reader of the texts that entered her life through music, but a performer who engaged with the affective claims of materials produced by male poets and composers.[4]

4

Introduction

She gave voice to these song texts in music, and, importantly, she also gave voice to non-musical literature, her own and that of others. Reading aloud was a common activity in the family circle. It was mentioned often in the letters, referred to in the novels and recalled by her younger relatives in their memoirs. She was said to be a compelling reader as well as an engaging singer.

The art of singing is akin to rhetoric. According to Robert Toft, 'Several writers from the period declare that singing should be based directly on speaking and that singers should use the orator as a model'.[5] This comes as no surprise to a singer, or indeed any musician. Music is an act of communication and rhetoric is as integral to musical performance as it is to reading aloud and acting. Austen understood the importance of attentive and skilful reading to do justice to the text being read. I examine the relation between reading aloud and music in some detail in my recent article 'Jane Austen: the musician as author'.[6]

The question of aesthetic taste and its connection with moral worth was a continuing debate throughout the eighteenth century. Hermione Lee writes that correlating them was a 'habit of thought of which Jane Austen was both aware and wary. Firmly accepting the fundamental idea of a relationship between taste and morality, she was thoroughly satirical of the excesses to which that idea could lead'.[7] As a discriminating listener, Austen knew the pleasure to be gained from both good reading and from good playing and singing. As an author, she brings all these qualities into her novels to make distinctions between her characters: aesthetic rather than moral distinctions. Consider Edward Ferrars. Early in *Sense and sensibility*, Marianne Dashwood complains to her mother that there is 'something wanting' in Edward: 'how spiritless, how tame was Edward's manner in reading to us last night! … I could hardly keep my seat. To hear those beautiful lines which have frequently almost driven me wild, pronounced with such impenetrable calmness, such dreadful indifference!' (*SS*, pp. 17–18). Marianne is, in the early part of this novel, almost a caricature of the heroine of sensibility, while her sister Elinor is all 'sense', and is not concerned about Edward's unromantic tendencies, and Edward is none the worse as a moral being for his aesthetic failings. If anyone is being satirised here, it is Marianne, for her excessive sensibility, which soon leads her to fall in love so disastrously with John Willoughby.

In *Mansfield Park* the dynamics are different but there are similar elements. Fanny Price, although superficially very different from Marianne, is also, in her way, a heroine of sensibility. She must repress her feelings more than Marianne does, but she has similar passionate feelings about poetry – she quotes William Cowper, the poet that Edward had been reading so woodenly in *Sense and sensibility* (*MP*, p. 56). Fanny is entranced by the performances of the Crawford siblings: by Mary playing the harp, and by Henry reading Shakespeare. However, she can distinguish between rhetorical skill, in music and drama, and what we might call moral worth, in a way that Marianne cannot. She sees the faults of the brother and sister, despite their attractions. Of course, the situation is more complicated than this brief summary can encompass. The debate about taste and morality, still current during Austen's time, can be traced in all of Austen's mature work.

A more important quality for Austen, both in her novels and in her personal relations, was sincerity, the opposite of affectation. 'Elinor was neither musical, nor affecting to be so' (*SS*, p. 250).

Introduction

The telling phrase is 'nor affecting to be so'. Affectation is always a target for Jane Austen's satire, and the clear message here is that Elinor knows herself and her tastes, and makes no pretence to like what she has no interest in. Elinor has her faults, but she is not a target for satire in *Sense and sensibility*. Tactful herself, while Marianne is not, Elinor can discriminate between tact and insincerity in other characters. She can see and contrast Lady Middleton's insincere praise of Marianne's musical performance with Colonel Brandon's response, which is to pay 'only the compliment of attention' (*SS*, p. 35). Austen's remarks about music in her letters show a similar attitude. She praises Miss Holder for her honesty in admitting that she has no taste for music, and Lady Bridges for her unaffected, no-nonsense wish to go home after the concert she had attended. On the other hand, she enjoys the performances of Miss Hatton and Miss Harding on her own account. It is not by whether they are musical or not that she assesses these women. It is by whether or not they are honest and unaffected about music.

The surviving collection of music that belonged to her shows that Austen would have been a reasonably accomplished pianist and singer, and, along with other sources, shows that she sustained her musical practice throughout her life. Jon Gillaspie writes, in a summary of Austen's musical handwriting, 'Perhaps the most noticeable quality of Jane Austen's mature music calligraphy is its almost modern, practical quality; it is the fairhand of an accomplished musician and is clearly prepared for her own use'.[8]

The relationship that a practising musician has with music in general is not usually a simple one. As with any field of knowledge and expertise, the more a musician knows about music, the more discriminating she is likely to be. She will develop her own tastes in repertoire. She will favour music in some settings over others. In a letter from Bath of 2 June 1799, Austen wrote to her sister that she and her companions were going to attend the King's birthday gala in Sydney Gardens on 4 June: 'I look forward with pleasure, & even the Concert will have more than its' usual charm with me, as the Gardens are large enough to get pretty well beyond the reach of its sound' (*Letters*, p. 43). (The author's original text has been preserved throughout the book).

I take this as the statement of a musical woman who prefers to have a choice about whether to listen to a particular piece of music or a particular performance in a particular time or place. Few musicians in my experience enjoy loud music in restaurants, or piped music in supermarkets. They like to enjoy music on their own terms, and to be able to choose when and where they experience it. As for Austen's own musical taste, I conclude in a recent article that 'Although the evidence is somewhat mixed, it appears that overall Austen personally favored songs that were musically less complex and virtuosic and that allowed the singer to convey the meaning of the words more directly to her audience',[9] and this appears to be supported by the detailed examination of the music collection in the following chapters.

The social uses of music

In Austen's letters and novels we can infer something of her attitude to music in various settings. One scene in *Sense and sensibility* shows an unexpected use for music not as a pleasure in itself but as cover for a private conversation: Elinor is able to talk to Lucy Steele privately only under cover of Marianne's playing, in the midst of the Middletons' oppressively sociable family party. In this case, the music being played is not in itself important.

James Johnson writes that 'musical experience is never just musical. Beyond the particular negotiation between the listener and the music, it also implies a performance space, with its own particular personality, and a unique historical moment, with its styles of expression and political preoccupations. All public expression of musical response – even silence – is inevitably social.'[10] Then, as now, music performed in private settings carried with it different social expectations and norms from music in public venues among strangers. Even so, the social pressure which 'classical music' audiences are under to listen in silence was not so ubiquitous in Austen's time. When we read of Colonel Brandon paying Marianne 'only the compliment of attention' when she plays, or of Mr Darcy listening intently to Elizabeth's performance, it is unusual: on both occasions the hostess continues to talk during the music, which Austen implies is somewhat ill-mannered but was obviously not socially unacceptable.

In his book *The Haydn economy* Nicholas Mathew examines in some detail 'various idealist tropes, now almost banal in their familiarity' that arose with Romanticism around the beginning of the nineteenth century: 'the caprice of fashion versus the eternal truths of art, tainted diversions versus pure works, slaves of time versus the free appreciators of timeless value, the value of commodities versus the value of art'.[11] These attitudes to the arts are now so embedded in our culture that it can be shocking to read comments such as Austen makes to Cassandra about the musicians hired (whom she calls 'hirelings') to perform at a private party in 1811, who 'gave great satisfaction by doing what they were paid for, & giving themselves no airs' (*Letters*, p. 183).

Also, in London, public concerts and operas were not routinely given the full attention – or socially imposed silence – usual with present-day classical music or theatre audiences. Michael Burden quotes a mid-eighteenth-century visitor from Oxford who attended Drury Lane: 'Good Heavens, what a Noise or Catcalls, Hissing, Hollowing and Fighting … Are these the Men who are to be Judges of a poetical Performance?'[12] Burden comments that

> it was certainly more restless than the audience we might encounter today at an opera performance. This restlessness was probably not unrelated to the length of the evening, for the arrangement of the bill at both the playhouses and the opera house meant that an evening at an opera performance ran for several hours, and by the latter part of the eighteenth century four hours seems to have become usual.[13]

One can imagine many reasons for this restlessness, especially if it was socially acceptable. Intervals were shorter than is usual in today's theatres. Burden's intriguing article concentrates on the opportunities for what we might call a 'comfort stop'. In other cases, audience members might need to stretch their legs after sitting for a long period, and, since long intervals were not available for socialising, moving about the auditorium might also be an opportunity to talk with friends in the audience. Austen herself recounts that, sitting with her brother Henry in a private box at the Lyceum Theatre in September 1813, she was able finally to pin him down and ask him about his plans for the following month – travelling to Godmersham, their brother Edward's estate in Kent, for a couple of days of pheasant shooting (*Letters*, pp. 217–18). She was staying with him at the time, but he was so busy during the day that she had barely had three minutes to catch up with him.

Introduction

Austen does not often mention details like these in her letters or her novels, as they would have been taken for granted by her contemporary readers. There is a scene in *Persuasion* where Anne Elliot is at a public concert in Bath with her family. Captain Wentworth is also at the concert, but Anne is obliged to sit with her family. Her cousin Mr Elliot sits beside her and they share a concert programme. He asks her, during 'an interval succeeding an Italian song', to translate the words. This happens 'towards the close' of the 'first act' of the concert (*P*, p. 186), so it is not 'the interval' as we would understand the term, but a break between songs. Given the length of the conversation between the cousins and other incidents that follow before 'the performance was re-commencing, and she was forced to seem to restore her attention to the orchestra' (*P*, p. 188), this break would have needed to be at least five minutes long, and probably more. This would be very unusual in a modern concert. Possibly artistic licence has stretched this 'interval' for the purposes of the narrative, or perhaps its length would have been normal at that time.

Captain Wentworth is described as standing and moving around during the performance, while Anne is hemmed in both physically and by social convention. This is a pivotal scene, emotionally intense, and not only seen but also felt through Anne's consciousness. When reading the novel, these circum-stantial details seem unimportant, such is the pull of the nar-rative. During the first half of the concert, before the passage I have described, the music Anne hears is enjoyable because 'her mind was in the most favourable state for the entertainment … it was just occupation enough' (*P*, p. 186). Music has brought the characters together in a public setting. The performance protocols and the arrangement of the room provide the social boundaries which constrain Anne and dictate how the other characters may behave. However, music is not in itself the focus of this scene. As in the scene from *Sense and sensibility* discussed above, music is part of the social situation described but is not intrinsically significant.

Music also plays a part in the moral life of Austen's characters. For example, in *Emma*, our heroine has neglected her music studies in her younger days, but comes to regret the fact in later years. After the evening of the Coles' party when she and Jane Fairfax have both played, 'she did unfeignedly and unequivocally regret the inferiority of her own playing and singing. She did most heartily grieve over the idleness of her childhood' (*E*, p. 231). The echoes of the Anglican liturgy here are clear and must surely be deliberate. I am thinking especially of the General Confession from the communion service: 'We do earnestly repent, and are heartily sorry for these our misdoings; The remembrance of them is grievous unto us; The burden of them is intolerable.' This ability to admit her faults to herself is one sign of Emma's increasing maturity. One could argue that her music practice is more a matter of anxiety about the way she is perceived by others, especially in relation to Jane Fairfax. However, it is important that her social standing remains what it always has been: what is new is her own consciousness of not measuring up to that standard.

Austen was not romantic or sentimental about music. She listened with pleasure when the performance was to her taste but felt no compunction about escaping beyond earshot if it was not. I suspect she would not have sat and listened to Mary Bennet's 'long concerto' in *Pride and prejudice* if she had a chance to get away (*PP*, p. 25). At times a musical performance was more a social occasion than an aesthetic experience for her – which is not a criticism. Music brings people together, and the communal aspect is important. One goes to a concert to hear music and also to spend time with friends. Sometimes the musical aspect is less compelling than the social: not every performance is memorable in itself. In November 1813 she wrote to Cassandra in anticipation of the concert at Canterbury where she met Lady Bridges, saying that she expected to enjoy it, 'as I am sure of seeing several that I want to see. We are to meet a party from Goodnestone, Lady B. Miss Hawley & Lucy Foote – & I am to meet Mrs Harrison, & we are to talk about Ben & Anna' (*Letters*, p. 249). She was especially keen to meet Mrs Harrison, the sister of her late friend Anne Lefroy who had died in a riding accident in 1804. Mrs Lefroy's son Ben had recently married Austen's niece Anna. Reporting on the concert afterwards, she conveyed her impressions of Lady Bridges and Mrs Harrison, with whom she had 'a very comfortable little complimentary friendly Chat' (*Letters*, p. 251). She wrote nothing at all about the music, either because it was unremarkable or because she thought it would not interest Cassandra.

Anna believed that 'nobody could think more humbly of Aunt Jane's music than she did herself' (*Memoir*, p. 183). However, she continued to practise the piano in the last years of her life, as Anna's younger sister Caroline recalled, and this is corroborated by the fact that she continued to copy music into her manuscript books until about 1816. She played and sang partly for her young relatives, but it must also have been an important activity in her own creative life: as Brooks writes, she was 'a performer who engaged with the affective claims' of the music she played,[14] even if she was playing alone with no one listening. How this might influence her own creative practice is considered later in the book, most explicitly in Chapters 7 and 8.

Austen, Shakespeare and the music of the theatre

As early as 1847 George Henry Lewes referred to Austen as 'a prose Shakspeare'.[15] Much has been written about Austen and Shakespeare, comparing them as literary artists and analysing passages in the novels where Shakespeare is mentioned, and more generally there has been important work by Penny Gay and Paula Byrne linking Austen with the theatrical traditions of her time. The connection between Shakespeare, Austen and music might appear more tenuous since there is actually little Shakespearean music among her surviving collection, but, given the nexus between music and theatre – both performing arts of which Austen was a discerning audience as well as a practising exponent – I include her interactions with Shakespeare in this survey of music in her life and work.

In Chapter 5 I refer to the Shakespearean productions for which Thomas Arne wrote songs, sometimes but by no means always setting Shakespeare's original texts, and the relative absence of Shakespearean lyrics among Austen's music is discussed in Chapter 6. Austen would have heard some of these Shakespeare songs at the theatre and elsewhere. But beyond this, music is integral to many of Shakespeare's plays and the text of any great writer has its own musical qualities. Thus it is interesting to consider Austen's own relationship with the playwright who was then, as now, commonly regarded as the greatest of all English writers.

I recall when I was a teenager, about the same time as I was first reading and enjoying Austen, being transfixed by a television production of *Hamlet*. I remember clearly that the language was affecting me as if it were music. I could not now say who the actors were, or what production it was, appearing on Australian television on a Sunday afternoon in the early 1970s, but it was mesmerising.

From Austen's descriptions of the Shakespeare (and indeed other theatrical) productions she attended, I believe that she was seeking the same sort of experience, analogous to hearing music played with expression and skill, and rarely finding it, in either case. Writing to her niece Anna in November 1814, she described an evening at the theatre in London. The play was *Isabella, or the fatal marriage* by David Garrick, and the title role was taken by Eliza O'Neill. Austen wrote, 'I do not think she was quite equal to my expectations. I fancy I want something more than can be. Acting seldom satisfies me. I took two pocket handkerchiefs but had very little occasion for either' (*Letters*, p. 283).

This kind of detailed evidence for Austen's experiences of the theatre is patchy, depending on surviving letters and other accounts which survive by chance as much as design. When it comes to Shakespeare, we might conclude that *Hamlet* was not Austen's favourite play. In April 1811 she and Henry were disappointed to miss out on seeing *King John* when *Hamlet* was offered instead, and they tried to change their tickets for a performance of *Macbeth* (*Letters*, p. 181), but they then decided not to attend that play either. This might be surprising: to a modern audience *Hamlet* and *Macbeth* would usually be preferred to *King John*, which is now one of Shakespeare's least performed plays.

However, there was a very specific reason for Austen's wish to see *King John*. A little later she wrote of her disappointment in not seeing Sarah Siddons: 'I should particularly have liked seeing her in Constance, and could swear at her with very little difficulty for disappointing me' (*Letters*, p. 184). Constance is the character played by Siddons in the production of *King John*, while she was not appearing in the substituted production of *Hamlet*. The last of Siddons's celebrated appearances in the title role had been six years earlier in Dublin – and in fact she never played the role in London. She apparently had played Lady Macbeth in the performance they missed, but had not been expected to, and Henry had therefore decided against buying the tickets. Siddons's health was declining and presumably this was the cause of the last-minute changes in her appearances. Lady Macbeth would be her last role before her formal retirement in June 1812.

Hamlet is mentioned in passing in *Sense and sensibility* – after Willoughby's departure, Mrs Dashwood exclaims, 'We never finished Hamlet, Marianne; our dear Willoughby went away before we could get through it' (*SS*, p. 85). Perhaps Austen intended an intertextual reference – a parallel between the predicaments of Marianne and Ophelia, both abandoned by their lovers. Both young women express their grief in music. Ophelia 'sings a series of popular ballads before the Queen and King of Denmark' in her 'mad scene',[16] while Marianne, 'unable to talk', 'nourish[es]' her grief at the piano. 'She played over every favourite song that she had been used to play to Willoughby, every air in which their voices had been oftenest joined, and sat at the instrument gazing on every line of music that he had written out for her, till her heart was so heavy that no further sadness could be gained' (*SS*, p. 83). Marianne avoids Ophelia's tragic fate, but they both resort to singing when language alone is not adequate to express their feelings.

There are several more substantial references to Shakespeare's history plays in Austen's 'History of England', completed in late 1791. As Lesley Peterson writes in her introduction to the

Juvenilia Press edition of *Sir Charles Grandison*, 'she playfully treats these plays as authoritative sources of historical fact, in order both to satirize them as unreliable and to celebrate the dramatist's power of invention'. One example Peterson gives is that 'she cites as historical fact two soliloquies, and lengthy ones at that', and she points out that 'in highlighting these speeches, Austen ... reveals her appreciation of the soliloquy as a particularly inventive dramatic genre. She acknowledges its appeal to the imagination, its effectiveness at constructing character and engaging the audience, and its power to linger in memory.'[17] These qualities are precisely those of a well-crafted song, whether written for the theatre or not, and there are many examples of such songs among Austen's music collection.

When Shakespeare is read aloud in *Mansfield Park*, Austen describes the scene as minutely as some of the musical performances in that novel. Henry Crawford reads from *Henry VIII* and Fanny cannot prevent herself from being entranced:

> in Mr. Crawford's reading there was a variety of excellence beyond what she had ever met with. The King, the Queen, Buckingham, Wolsey, Cromwell, all were given in turn; for with the happiest knack, the happiest power of jumping and guessing, he could always alight at will on the best scene, or the best speeches of each; and whether it were dignity, or pride, or tenderness, or remorse, or whatever were to be expressed, he could do it with equal beauty. It was truly dramatic. His acting had first taught Fanny what pleasure a play might give, and his reading brought all his acting before her again. (*MP*, p. 337)

After the reading, Edmund compliments Henry by saying that he must know the play well to have read it with such understanding. Henry replies, 'I do not think I have had a volume of Shakespeare in my hand before, since I was fifteen. – ...

But Shakespeare one gets acquainted with without knowing how. It is part of an Englishman's constitution.' Edmund replies that 'To know him in bits and scraps, is common enough; to known him pretty thoroughly is, perhaps, not uncommon; but to read him well aloud, is no everyday talent' (*MP*, p. 338). In my article on men and music in Austen, I claim that Henry 'might as well be singing – he is reading not just for sense, but for "beauty" and drama, and Fanny is responding to him in much the same way as Edmund does when Mary makes music'.[18] Henry's talent, which both Fanny and Edmund admire, although Fanny will not admit it, is extraordinary. Susan Allen Ford, in an article about elocution in *Mansfield Park*, notes in her discussion of this passage 'the somatic and even erotic effect that reading can have'. She goes on, 'Indeed, reading and speaking may have consequences unintended by the elocutionists arguing for their national utility'.[19] But Fanny's admiration for Henry as an actor will not unseat her devotion to Edmund.

There is no doubt that Austen knew Shakespeare as well as, or better than, Henry Crawford. Of all the Shakespeare plays, there is more direct evidence for Austen's familiarity with *The Merchant of Venice* than any other play. She referred to the play in a letter to Cassandra in June 1811: 'Your answer about the Miss Plumtrees, proves you as fine a Daniel as ever Portia was; – for I imagined Emma to be the eldest' (*Letters*, p. 194). This is a reference to Shylock's speech to Portia in Act 4, scene 1 of the play: 'A Daniel come to judgement! Yea, a Daniel! O wise young judge, how I do honour thee!' Nevertheless, she does not appear to recognise an allusion to *Merchant* made by the musical apothecary Charles Haden. In a letter to Cassandra of 24 November 1815 from Henry's home in London, she wrote, 'I have been listening to dreadful insanity. It is Mr Haden's firm beleif that a person not musical is fit for every sort of Wickedness. – I ventured to assert a little on the other side, but wished the cause in abler hands' (*Letters*, p. 300).

Haden was probably quoting from the conversation between Lorenzo and Jessica in praise of music which includes the lines,

> The man that hath no music in himself,
> Nor is not mov'd with concord of sweet sounds,
> Is fit for treasons, stratagems and spoils;
> The motions of his spirit are dull as night,
> And his affections dark as Erebus:
> Let no such man be trusted.[20]

It seems odd that Austen did not connect Haden's words with this eloquent passage. Perhaps she did recognise the allusion – and assumed Cassandra would as well – but was keen to dispute the implication. It is possible, too, that the quotation that seems obvious to me and to others – Deirdre Le Faye makes the connection in her edition of Austen's letters – was not in fact used by Haden and his 'firm belief' was expressed in his own words, with no reference to Shakespeare.

In March 1814 she was in London and went with her brother Henry and their niece Fanny to see the play, with Shylock played by the great new sensation Edmund Kean. She told Cassandra, 'Places are secured at Drury Lane for Saturday, but so great is the rage for seeing Keen that only 3rd or 4th row could be got' (*Letters*, p. 256). She was 'quite satisfied with Kean' and could not fault him, but even his excellence did not redeem the evening, with the other parts 'ill filled & the Play heavy' (*Letters*, p. 257). A good play cannot redeem poor performances, any more than great music can be enjoyed when played badly.

Outline of this book

The importance of music in Jane Austen's life and work has been the subject of a range of books and articles since Patrick Piggott's 1979 book *The innocent diversion*.[21] I have published several articles and book chapters on the subject since 2010. Some of that material is incorporated (with acknowledgement) into this book, and some is referenced. My work is informed by a lifetime of thinking about music in Austen's novels, sparked by a discussion with a high-school English teacher which led, twenty-five years later, to an Honours thesis on the subject at Flinders University in 1995. In addition I have become increasingly familiar over the past fifteen years with the Austen family music books. In 2007 I began curating and performing in concerts drawing on this repertoire, and between 2017 and 2021 I catalogued the individual items in the music books for the University of Southampton library catalogue.[22]

I hope in this book to bring together these three strands of my engagement with music and Austen: the literary readings, the historical and musicological research, and the intimate, embodied knowledge of the music Austen knew and performed. Because I am more of a singer than a pianist and have become more familiar with many of the songs, my work tends to dwell more on the vocal music than the purely instrumental pieces. Songs also have the advantage of combining music and words and so are more susceptible to thematic discussion.

There are more than five hundred individual items catalogued in the Austen family music books collection, and many of them are associated more directly with other members of Jane Austen's extended family than with Austen herself. Samantha Carrasco's work analyses the collection as a whole in

Introduction

various useful ways.[23] However, while alongside her own books among the collection there are albums which belonged to relatives she visited and with whom she shared music, there are others that Austen would not have known at all. In Chapter 1, therefore, I have concentrated on the music which is most directly connected with Austen herself: mainly the manuscript copies of sheet music that she created, and also the printed music that carries her ownership marks. I survey the manuscripts by dividing them into various categories: the types of music included, the composers and song lyricists who appear most often and the gender breakdown of the creators of these works.

In Chapter 2 I firstly look beyond the music collection to the musical relationships Austen developed over her lifetime, as evidenced by her correspondence and the memories of her younger relatives. I then return to the music books to see what additional information can be gleaned by looking at them as physical and cultural objects. Some show signs of collaboration between family members, and in this section of the chapter I look at Austen's relationship with each of the owners or creators of these volumes.

Chapters 3 and 4 are based on previously published work, and both place Austen's life and musical activities within a historical context. Chapter 3 deals with the French Revolution, which is directly reflected in three songs among her manuscripts, and more broadly with Britain's ongoing conflict with France throughout her lifetime. Chapter 4 is based on my contribution to a fascinating book project which examines family life in all its varieties and manifestations during the early modern period of European imperial expansion. My chapter concerns songs aimed at members of the British Navy and their

21

families, many examples of which are drawn from the Austen family music books.

Theatre was an important part of Austen's life in various ways, and much of the music she played and sang had its origins in the theatre. The composer Thomas Augustine Arne was such a dominant figure in English theatre in the eighteenth century that I devote the whole of Chapter 5 to his theatrical career and how his work is represented in Austen's collection.

Chapter 6 concerns the songs of the British Isles more generally, whether Scottish, Irish or English, as they are represented in Austen's collection. Many of these songs are at least notionally in the folk tradition, which is a slippery term that defies definition.

The final two chapters both put the music in Austen's collection alongside her literary works. In Chapter 7 I take the songs which she is likely to have copied and played during her teenage years and compare them in various ways with her juvenilia – as rhetorical influences, as targets for satire or as models for the songs she included in her own playlets. And lastly, in Chapter 8, I consider the possibility that a narrative ballad, set to music as 'Colin and Lucy', might have had some influence on the structure and rhetoric of *Sense and sensibility*. This is not so much a serious factual proposition as a demonstration of the potential links between musical experience and literary sensibility.

In the Conclusion I revisit some themes from earlier in the book and look at them in a slightly different light. I discuss the categories of professional and amateur in the context of Austen's literary and musical practice, and the different implications of those terms at the time. I explore the question of how the material culture of music – actual instruments, sheet music

Introduction

and so on – appears in the novels, looking particularly at the inclusion in *Emma* of specific musical facts which are otherwise absent from her fiction, and the historical and cultural implications of the range of instruments mentioned in the novels. Lastly I describe the four songs that her relatives recalled hearing her sing towards the end of her life, in memories recorded half a century after her death.

As an appendix I have included a detailed list of the items in Austen's own handwriting, including titles, composers, lyricists and category, with brief notes on each piece.

1

The Jane Austen music manuscripts

The Austen family music books

The Austen family music books are a mixed collection of printed and manuscript music that belonged to several members of the extended Austen family. There are more than five hundred separate playable pieces of music in the eighteen albums that are available on the Internet Archive.[1]

Four of the surviving music books contain manuscripts in Austen's hand. Two are the kinds of music manuscript books which were commercially available in the 1790s, with blank pre-ruled pages. The decorative title page of one of these is labelled by hand 'Juvenile songs and lessons', with a note added below, in smaller writing, reading 'for young beginners who don't know enough to practise'. This is delightful, but slightly misleading. There is no vocal music in this album, so no 'songs', and although there are some relatively simple pieces of music there are also some substantial and demanding pieces such as reductions of operatic overtures which are well beyond the skill of a 'young beginner'.

The other of the commercially printed manuscript books, dating from the late 1780s and just labelled 'Songs and duetts', may have been started earlier but seems to have overlapped with the 'Juvenile songs and lessons' volume, as it also includes pieces of music dating from the mid-1790s. 'Songs and duetts' is more aptly named. All but one of the thirty-seven items in it are vocal works. Most of them are solo songs with keyboard accompaniment, but some are duets and some have other instrumental parts as well.

These two books were bought as blank manuscript books and filled in sequentially, and the dates of their contents overlap. It seems that Austen deliberately kept one book for instrumental music and one for vocal music. It is not known exactly when the albums were bought: they would have been stocked by music shops during the late 1780s and 1790s but there is no evidence to date them more precisely. Similarly, there is little information available about the sources of the music Austen copied. We might speculate that items which also appear in other albums in the wider family collection might have been shared – and some of these possibilities are mentioned in Chapter 2 – but nothing can be established definitely.

The third album is a scrapbook-style volume, where items are not necessarily still in the order they were inserted. It contains a mixture of printed music and manuscripts which range in date throughout Austen's lifetime.

The fourth album dates from a later period, and begins with a printed edition of a sonata by Muzio Clementi, followed by an assortment of manuscripts. It contains theatre songs, children's songs, dances and even some hymns. It was probably compiled during Austen's adult years.

There is a further volume that was not included in the digitisation project which has recently come into the possession of the Blackie House Library and Museum in Edinburgh. This album belonged to Elizabeth Austen but includes four songs copied in Jane Austen's hand, which I mention at the end of this chapter.

In this chapter I will introduce the 160 or so pieces of music that Austen copied by hand into these four albums. Although these pieces are by no means the only music that Austen would have played and sung, the fact that she took the trouble to copy it by hand might indicate a more committed relationship with a piece of music, as it were. As Kathryn L. Libin writes, 'In many ways the manuscript music is the most compelling, since it represents the collective diligence and individual skills of women bent on acquiring and playing music'.[2] That said, printed music was expensive, and spending money on a musical score is also a sign of its value to the owner. Other printed scores might have been received as gifts from relatives or friends, which bestows another kind of value. However, without an external source of information, printed sources rarely reveal the kind of personal and idiosyncratic attitude to works that copied manuscripts often do.

It is difficult to be absolutely certain about the identity of the copyists of all the manuscripts. Two of the four manuscript books are entirely in Austen's handwriting, whereas the other two certainly contain a variety of hands, some of them very similar, and opinions as to their copyists have varied. On the whole I have relied on those who had access to the physical manuscripts, since during this project I have been able to access them only via their digital copies online. For each volume in the Internet Archive collection a useful summary of Resource Information is provided, prepared by the experts at the University of Southampton when uploading the digitised collection.

Another factor to be considered is the kinds of music which Austen might have copied instead of buying the printed score: there might be a tipping point between the monetary cost and the time it takes to make a copy of any particular piece of music. Some of the songs Austen copied consist of the bare outline: sometimes just a melody with no written accompaniment at all, although she might write the words out more fully. 'The Marseilles March' and 'Chanson Béarnoise' are examples that I discuss in Chapter 3. Sometimes, on the other hand, great care is taken to copy a printed score, with all the details including dynamic markings.

Among the printed music there is a greater proportion of more complex instrumental music, such as complete sonatas, piano arrangements of overtures, sets of themes and variations, and two sets of Scottish songs (Bremner and Ramsey, from the 1750s) along with some cantatas and arias. Nevertheless, there are examples of all these forms among the manuscripts as well – four complete piano sonatas, several operatic overtures and so on; and some of the printed vocal music, in particular, is very sketchy, either intended to be sung unaccompanied or relying on the accompanist to improvise harmonies.

The fact is that our knowledge of Austen's musical practice is incomplete and much of it relies on conjecture. In Chapter 2 I look more closely at other sources of information such as letters and memoirs to find traces of the ways music was shared with her family circle. I was surprised to discover that only one of the four songs that her younger relatives and friends specifically recall her singing in their much later years is found among her surviving manuscripts. The others are present in the wider music collection, but not necessarily in copies that Austen would have originally owned or even had access to. This is one illustration among many of the importance of not assuming too much from the remnants of her music that survive.

Little of this music is still in print today, and most of it is on, or beyond, the fringes of the current classical music repertoire. Given that Austen was presumably writing it out for her own purposes, she frequently omitted details such as the composer or even the title, or gave titles which do not match any extant printed source. Thus some of it has been impossible to identify at all, or to attribute to a composer. Sometimes I have been able to find the lyrics of a song elsewhere but not the music. Very occasionally a melody is familiar from a different context, but many of these pieces would be lost to posterity if they did not appear in Austen's collection. This is not always a matter for regret: there is no denying that some of this music is not particularly memorable or valuable in its own right. However, among the songs that I have come to know over the past fifteen years there are some very beautiful works, some that are purely joyous, some very moving and some very amusing, and it is a delight to be able to share them with audiences. The practice of performing 'Jane Austen' concerts provides a minor way of reviving the music of neglected composers of the period, as well as giving a sense of Austen's own sound world – the music she would have imagined her characters hearing and performing, and the music she played for her own enjoyment.

In this chapter I will begin by discussing the overall contents of these four albums, the types of music represented and some of the composers and lyricists whose works appear in Austen's manuscript copies. I will then look at each of the albums separately to see what different patterns of music consumption and sharing they exhibit throughout Austen's lifetime. Firstly, however, I will explain the basis for my analysis of the collection, the cataloguing project I undertook from 2017 to 2021.

The Austen family music books cataloguing project

Relying on my professional library training, I was able to create for the University of Southampton Library online catalogue individual records of the Austen family music books collection, digitised by the University in 2015 and made available on Internet Archive. Before I completed the project in 2021, there was no detailed online catalogue of the individual items in the collection, although each of the volumes had been expertly catalogued by staff in the University of Southampton Library.

In this project I have been building on work done by these colleagues and other researchers. Ian Gammie and Derek McCulloch published *Jane Austen's music* in 1996. It is a seminal reference work, but it includes only about half of the available music from the Austen family (consisting of the item numbers beginning CHWJA in Appendix 2, which are held at Jane Austen's House in Chawton). I have also been given a copy of an unpublished catalogue of the Jenkyns volumes, held in a private collection, compiled by Jon A. Gillaspie (now Nessa Glen) in 1987. Samantha Carrasco, in her thesis *The Austen family music books and Hampshire music culture, 1770–1820*, includes as an appendix a list of 548 pieces of music in the seventeen volumes available in 2012, sorted by composer where possible, based on the work of these previous cataloguers.[3] Carrasco's thesis can be accessed online via the University of Southampton. The only book which has been added to the collection since then and included in the digitisation project is CHWJA/19/9, a book of dance music belonging to Austen's young nieces Louisa and Cassandra that she would not have been familiar with.

Over the decades since the preparation of these important catalogues, which involved much research in British libraries and archives, a vast amount of historical information has become available online, including many institutional and crowd-sourced archives of music-related material. Many of the print sources that the earlier compilers used, such as the *British union catalogue of early music* and the *Répertoire international des sources musicales*, are now available in various forms online and allow far more options for searching, including by melody. New sources such as IMSLP/Petrucci and the Traditional Tune Archive have appeared, and the easy availability of international library catalogues makes searching for printed scores much easier. These developments have made this project possible for me, based in Australia.

It is an indication of the ephemeral nature of much of this music that, even so, many of Austen's manuscripts cannot be identified at all, and others can only be tentatively identified, and many more cannot be dated with any exactness. One complicating factor during the project was, of course, the Covid-19 pandemic, which prevented me from travelling overseas from Australia after 2019, so I had no physical access to the European libraries where some possible sources are listed. In any case the cataloguing and identification of this music is still a work in progress. Digitised music collections continue to be made available online, and items added to existing databases, so new information may yet come to light.

Types of music

It is important to note that, in the analysis of Austen's manuscripts that follows, I am treating each of these 160 or so musical items with equal weight – whether they cover a quarter of a page or five pages; whether they are simple strophic songs or multi-movement sonatas.

Roughly three-fifths of the manuscripts (ninety-five) are vocal music – mostly for solo voice, although there are eleven vocal duets and about the same number of pieces for three or more voices. These ensemble pieces are mostly able to be sung by a soloist with accompaniment if no other singer is available. Almost all of these have accompaniments laid out for keyboard, sometimes with the voice on a separate line above the keyboard part but more commonly with the vocal part sharing the right-hand keyboard part. Although Austen did not always copy it out, in the printed versions of these songs there is often an optional part provided for a violin or a flute. More often there is another version of the melody arranged or transposed for the German flute and/or guitar. These appear to be alternative versions, rather than parts to be combined with the voice and keyboard performance. The vocal range is generally on the high side – a soprano could sing most of the songs, even if they may have been written for a male singer. Sometimes a celebrity performer is mentioned on the sheet music but often enough it is not known who would have sung the role in public performance.

It is difficult to be exact about any of this, but looking at the rough distribution of song types, we find that about one-third

of them originate in theatrical productions of various kinds –
whether they are French operas or English plays. Twelve are
children's nursery songs, all of which are in the volumes compiled from the mid-1790s onwards when Austen had visiting
nieces and nephews to entertain. There are about eight that
can be assigned that slippery term 'folksong' (see Chapter 6),
and, apart from one or two religious part-songs and the French
national anthem, the rest are stand-alone secular songs of the
kind that perhaps might be expected in a Georgian drawing
room during an evening's entertainment – mostly love songs
of various kinds, with a sprinkling of songs on historical subjects, or affecting character pieces like 'Ellen the Richmond
primrose girl' or 'The match girl' – or, indeed laments such
as Stephen Storace's 'Captivity'. Many of the folk and theatre
songs would take their places alongside these stand-alone songs,
while some of them might not be thought suitable for 'polite'
company. Charles Dibdin's theatre songs are often humorous
in a somewhat unsubtle way and even include profanities, while
the directness of the sexual suggestion in some of the Scottish
songs might rule them out.

The remainder of the manuscripts are copies of instrumental
music, and this almost always means music for keyboard solo.
Of the roughly sixty-four pieces, there are about twenty-four
which are dances of various kinds, including some folk dances
arranged for piano.

There are about a dozen marches among the manuscripts,
usually honouring recent celebrities such as the Duke of York
or the Austrian Grenadiers, and about the same number of theatrical pieces – overtures to operas, incidental music from plays
and so on. The remaining twenty-five or so are what we might
think of as concert or chamber music, much of which would

have been written or arranged for the domestic market. There are, as previously noted, four complete sonatas, of various competence ranging from a Haydn masterpiece to an unattributed and inexpert work, and some sonata movements. There is a 'pot-pourri'[4] by the German composer Daniel Steibelt, along with about ten sets of variations on various themes, usually existing melodies from the folk or theatre repertoire, or other well-known songs. There are two sets of variations on 'God save the king', one by Johann Christian Bach (the youngest son of Johann Sebastian), which is an excerpt from one of his harpsichord concertos. Many of the themes of these works are, or were thought to be, Scottish songs which, as Roger Fiske points out, were hugely popular outside Scotland in the eighteenth century and were often of dubious authenticity. In any case 'there can never be a "correct" version of a Scotch Song tune'.[5] In *Pride and prejudice* piano-playing characters perform unspecified Scottish airs, to 'vary the charm' for their audience. I will explore the implications of this more fully in Chapter 6.

Composers

Johann Baptist Cramer (1771–1858), mentioned in passing in *Emma*, is distinguished by being the only composer named in any of the novels. Cramer was born in Mannheim but came to England as a child and made his career in London. He is best known today for his Études for piano, which are still in print. The only composer named in the letters, as far as I can see, is James Hook,[6] unless you count Austen's disapproving remarks about Fanny's music master 'Mr Meyers', probably Philippe-Jacques Meyer (1737–1819), who was also a composer and author of harp method books.[7] She more often refers in her letters to pieces of music, including dance tunes and songs that she hears, and musical theatre and operas that she attends, without naming the composers.

All of these composers – Cramer, Hook and Meyer – are represented in the Austen music collection, Cramer by some printed piano pieces, Meyer by a song and a piano piece in her hand, and Hook by several songs including one, 'The wedding day', in Austen's hand. Two songs by Hook also appear in Austen's handwriting in the manuscript book from Godmersham known as 'Rice 1', which will be discussed later in this chapter and in Chapter 2. However, other composers appear more often among her own manuscripts, as I will show below.

About one-third of the pieces of music among Austen's manuscripts have not been traced to any composer or arranger. Sometimes this would be because they were published anonymously either as folk music or by someone who did not wish their identity known, such as the 'Gentleman of Oxford' who is said to have written 'Seaton Clifts'. More often it is the result of the obscurity of the music and the lack of surviving scores in public collections. As often as not, Austen did not name the composer, and very occasionally she made an incorrect attribution. We usually have no way of knowing what her source was, and she may have replicated the mistakes of other copyists.

Most of the composers represented in Austen's collection were her contemporaries. In her lifetime, it was the exception rather than the rule to play music written in previous centuries. Only a few composers from the early to middle eighteenth century are to be found in the Austen family collection as a whole, some of them in books which had been passed down from earlier generations of musicians to their younger relatives.

The Austen music manuscripts

In any case, of the hundred manuscript items for which I have been able to make an attribution, about two-thirds are by composers whose works appear only once among the manuscripts and nine by composers who appear twice. Eight occur more frequently, and I will look at them more closely. These are, in order of frequency:

Samuel Arnold (6)
Stephen Storace (5)
William Shield (4)
Thomas Arne (4)
Charles Dibdin (4)
Michael Kelly (4)
Muzio Clementi (3)
Wolfgang Amadeus Mozart (3)

It is interesting, given our views of the dominance of foreign composers in England at this period, that only two of these eight were not British. There has been an assumption among generations of music historians that English music had declined since the glory days of Purcell in the late seventeenth century and would not revive until the twentieth century. This is something of a circular argument, as so much of the music by British composers is never heard today and this period is best known in western music for the ascendancy of the great German and Austrian masters, including Handel and Haydn, who were extremely influential in England, increasingly, in retrospect, overshadowing the careers and contributions of composers like these.

Samuel Arnold (1740–1802) was an eminent and active composer and musician in his time. He was organist at the Chapel Royal from 1783 and at Westminster Abbey from 1793. He was involved in the Handel commemoration in 1784 and edited the first comprehensive edition of Handel's works.[8] He is buried in Westminster Abbey. Alongside his liturgical music commitments, he was a co-founder of the Glee Club and wrote for the theatre. The list of his works in *British musical biography* is impressive in its scope and extent, although at least some of the 'musical dramas &c.' listed there are 'medley operas' or plays containing a few songs, rather than through-composed operas in the Italian style.[9]

The six Arnold pieces in Austen's manuscript book all come from stage works. Three are from George Colman the Younger's play *The mountaineers*, which was performed at the Theatre Royal, Haymarket, in 1794. Two are solo songs, and one a duet. *The mountaineers* is a comedy loosely based on the character of Cardenio in Cervantes's *Don Quixote*. Set in Granada under the rule of the Moors, it concerns relations between Christian and Muslim characters. These three songs all involve the character Agnes and her Moorish lover Sadi, who run away together. Another song from the same play, 'Oh happy tawny moor', is to be found among the printed music collection of Elizabeth Austen née Bridges.

These three items, along with Arnold's 'The poor little gypsey' from another of Colman's plays, appear in the early 'Songs and duetts' album within a few pages of each other. One of the other songs, 'In the dead of the night', was written for Mrs Inchbald's play *The wedding day*, also from 1794, although the words were written by John Hall-Stevenson and published in 1770. The sixth, 'Sure 'twould make a dismal story', is from Miles Peter Andrews's 1780 play *Fire and water*, and according to Gammie and McCulloch is the only song from this play that was published, along with the libretto. This song is a morale-boosting duet recommending fidelity to returned military husbands, discussed in some detail in Chapter 4.

Stephen Storace (1762–1796) was born in London, the son of an Italian musician. He and his sister, the singer Anna Selina Storace (known as Nancy), lived in Vienna in the 1780s and were friends with Mozart. Nancy sang the role of Susanna in the premiere of Mozart's *Marriage of Figaro*. In 1787 the siblings, along with the Irish musician Michael Kelly, also on Austen's duplicates list, travelled back to London and between them contributed much talent to the London stage.

Storace had perhaps the most idiosyncratic style of any English composer of Austen's time. He was equally adept at comedy and pathos – his beautiful song 'Captivity' is one of my personal favourites from Austen's collection, with its starkly moving portrait of Queen Marie Antoinette awaiting her fate at the hands of the French revolution. I discuss this song at greater length in Chapter 3. Storace's harmonic style could almost be called minimalist: he often refrains from modulating when expected, for example, but writes in this sometimes very direct and simple style to great effect, perhaps influenced by the aesthetic of Christoph Willibald Gluck.

The other four songs by Storace among Austen's manuscripts are all from the comic opera (really a play with songs) *The siege of Belgrade*, another cross-cultural scenario, with Turkish characters and Serbian peasants caught up in the historical events in Belgrade in 1789, which was presented at Drury Lane in 1791. 'The sapling oak' is sung by the Serbian peasant Anselm and is an allegory for the political liberation from the Turks that he is hoping for. 'Of plighted faith' is a letter duet set in a scene of similar duplicity and complexity as that between Susanna and the Countess in *The marriage of Figaro*, and uses a similar 'dictation' model. The other two items are an aria and a duet by a combative pair of lovers who marry, then part, then reconcile in true comic-opera style.

William Shield (1748–1829) was another versatile and prolific composer of the period. He was composer to the Covent Garden Theatre from 1778 to 1797, and later became the Master of the Royal Music. The four songs of his that Austen copied are all from different music theatre works. 'Her hair is like a golden clue' appears to be copied from the published vocal score of *Robin Hood* (1784), and 'Sweet transports' is from *Rosina* (1783). These two songs, however, are copied out consecutively, the first headed 'Sung by Mr Johnstone' (a tenor, playing Edwin) and the second 'Sung by Mrs Billington' (a soprano). Elizabeth Billington did not originally play the part of Rosina but seems to have taken it on in the early 1790s, while the Irish actor and singer John Henry Johnstone was the original Edwin. Both songs are sung by lovers bidding farewell – they could almost form a dialogue, even though they are from different works.

It is tantalising to try and reconstruct the circumstances in which Austen had access to these two scores in the early 1790s, and decided to copy them. How did she hear them at first, and why did she choose these two from all the songs in these operas? Were the scores available at a circulating library, or did they belong to a relative? There is another copy in the collection of 'Her hair is like a golden clue' which might actually *give* a clue, since it is probably in the handwriting of her cousin Eliza de Feuillide and Austen's copy is very similar in its annotations. Eliza visited Steventon regularly during those years, including in 1792. There is little firm evidence of Austen attending professional theatrical performances in her teens, but she and Eliza, despite their fourteen-year age difference, were close and

The Austen music manuscripts

Eliza's London life certainly included theatre-going. On her visits she would have described what she had seen to her young cousin, and no doubt shared songs that she had particularly enjoyed. (Perhaps the same might have happened in the case of Arnold's *The mountaineers* and her sister-in-law Elizabeth, who had a printed copy of another song from the play.)

Another of these Shield compositions is the song 'The heaving of the lead', a sentimental account of a sailor arriving home to his loving family. It comes from the 1792 Covent Garden production *Hartford Bridge, or the skirts of the camp* and is discussed more fully in Chapter 4. And lastly, Shield is credited as the arranger of a duet, 'From night to morn I take my glass'. The original composer of the song is not known and it does not appear to be a theatrical piece. It is another rather sentimental song – a lover tries to drown his sorrows but even drinking all night will not allow him to forget his Chloe.

There are several other songs by Shield in the broader Austen family music collection, including a setting of a verse by Robert Burns, 'The thorn', to which is added a soppy second verse that blunts the piquancy of Burns's lyric and entirely negates its sexual innuendo. On the other hand, Shield's most famous song is probably 'The ploughboy', a great work of political satire, with words by John O'Keeffe, that was later arranged by many composers including Benjamin Britten. The former probably belonged originally to Henry Austen's second mother-in-law, Mrs Jackson, but the printed music of the latter is in Austen's own scrapbook.

Thomas Arne (1710–1778) was the greatest of the English theatre composers of the Georgian period, a colleague and rival of Handel (though somewhat younger). There are four of his works among Austen's manuscripts, including the overture to his opera *Artaxerxes* and three arias from the masque *Comus*. His works endured and were performed for decades after his death, well into the nineteenth century, and he is so important in the musical and theatrical world of England in Austen's day that I have devoted the whole of Chapter 5 to him.

Charles Dibdin (1745–1814) is a fascinating character who did not work easily with others, despite his success as a singer and one of the most prolific songwriters of his age. He presented one-man shows in a series of venues in London and was known for his abilities as an entertainer, usually writing both words and music of his songs. His songs were often comic, but in whatever vein he wrote he was adept at word-setting, crafting songs to create vivid characters, usually in the first person, often telling a story, as in 'The lucky escape', or making satirical social commentary, as in 'The joys of the country'. 'The soldier's adieu' is a florid and romantic song of the genre indicated by the title: given its context among his other songs on the same concert programme it was probably intended to be as satirical as the rest. These three songs from 1790 and 1791 are all in Austen's early manuscript book: his style of comedy shares many features with that on display in Austen's juvenilia – comic hyperbole and reversals are common in both, and I compare several examples in Chapter 7. The fourth Dibdin song in Austen's manuscript book is an early work, from the 1768 play *Lionel and Clarissa*, but there are also several of his songs among her printed music. Dibdin was particularly famous for his sea songs, as will be seen in Chapter 4. We have no record of Austen ever attending one of Dibdin's famous 'Entertainments': it was Charles Dibdin Junior who wrote *The farmer's wife*, with music by Henry Bishop, which an Austen family party attended in London in March 1814.

The Austen music manuscripts

Michael Kelly (1762–1826), born in Dublin, like the Storace siblings spent time in Vienna and knew Mozart there. On his return to London with the Storaces he wrote extensively for the theatre.

It is probably of some significance that the two theatre pieces for which he wrote the music that are represented in Austen's manuscript book were both presented at the Theatre Royal in Bath when Austen was living there. Penny Gay discusses the possible influences of these two shows, *The castle spectre* (by Matthew 'Monk' Lewis) and *Blue Beard, or female curiosity* (by George Colman), on *Northanger Abbey*. She points out that these two plays, the former of which 'verged on being a self-conscious parody of every element characteristic of Gothic drama', were the two 'staple' Gothic plays from 1799–1805,[10] a period that coincides with Austen's visits to, and residence in, Bath. Gay writes, 'we know that Austen saw the latter piece (on Saturday 22 June 1799), and it is not unlikely that she saw the former'.[11] This appears all the more likely since three pieces from Kelly's score of *The castle spectre* (along with another piece of incidental music by a different composer) are included sequentially in her later manuscript book. The Kelly pieces are all vocal, two of them involving the chorus, while the music from *Blue Beard* is a march arranged for keyboard. These two plays were also presented in London at Drury Lane in the late 1790s.

It is somewhat unusual to find a concentration of music which is so closely tied to a particular theatrical production among Austen's manuscripts. Apart from the song 'Megen oh oh Megen ee', which could be performed out of context, there is a 'Spectre's song', eight bars long, and the 'Jubilate on the ghost's retiring', a simple choral piece of a mere four bars consisting of two chords. Once again the question arises as to why she collected these pieces, which seem to have little significance outside the play. Could it be that she anticipated being involved in a private theatrical performance of the play, or another in which they could be inserted? Her niece Fanny records in her diary that in 1805 Austen acted in private theatricals when she was visiting the family at Godmersham. To complicate things a little more, a song from *Blue Beard* is also in Austen's later manuscript book but in an unidentified hand – certainly not hers.

However, her interest in Michael Kelly's music was broader than this. His song 'No, my love, no', or 'The wife's farewell', from the play *Of age tomorrow*, is one of the four songs her younger relatives recalled her singing in her last years.

Muzio Clementi (1752–1832) is perhaps thus far the composer who might be most familiar to modern music-lovers, especially those who have learned the piano. His sonatinas were standard fare on music syllabi in the late twentieth century.

Born in Rome, Clementi studied music from an early age and his studies took him to England in his teenage years. He was based there throughout his career, but he toured Europe frequently and in 1781 in Vienna he famously engaged in a musical competition with Mozart for the entertainment of Emperor Joseph II. In later years he started a publishing firm and also manufactured pianos. (The square piano on display at the Jane Austen House Museum at Chawton is a Clementi, although it is not known what brand of piano she bought when she settled there, or what eventually happened to that piano.)

The three manuscript items by Clementi are all from *Twelve waltzes for the piano forte with an accompaniment for the tamburino & triangle*, Opus 38, published in 1798. They are reasonably substantial compared with some of the other dances among the manuscripts, covering two or three pages each, and Clementi is credited as the composer of the first waltz. The percussion parts are included in Austen's manuscript – perhaps a young relative might have enjoyed accompanying her aunt.

The preceding item in this album is a printed copy of a piano sonata also by Clementi, a two-movement work in F major, Opus 26, which was published in 1791.

Wolfgang Amadeus Mozart (1756–1791), the last on this list of 'multiple' composers, has, by comparison, a minor role in Austen's musical world. The first appearance his music makes among Austen's manuscripts is in her album titled 'Juvenile songs and lessons for young beginners who don't know enough to practise'. There are two short waltzes on page 34 of this book, neither of them identified beyond the title 'Waltz', and the second turns out to be arranged from 'Die Schlittenfahrt' (The sleigh ride), the trio section of the third of a set of three German dances (K. 605) published in 1791, Mozart's last year. It is only sixteen bars long – it would take less than a minute to perform it. The next piece of music in the album, probably coincidentally, is 'The Duke of York's new march: performed by the Coldstream Regiment', which is a condensed version, arranged for piano solo, of Figaro's aria 'Non piu andrai' from *The marriage of Figaro*. There is no indication that Austen was aware of the origin of the melody.

The other Mozart item among her manuscripts is a 'duettino' from his opera *La clemenza di Tito*. It bears no title or attribution, and occupies just one page of one of the later manuscript books. It does, however, appear to be complete and is copied carefully with the piano accompaniment included. Several editions of this duet were published in London in the early years of the nineteenth century.

In the later decades of the eighteenth century Franz Joseph Haydn (1732–1809) was far better known in London than Mozart. Adjacent to the Mozart duet in Austen's album are three of Haydn's English canzonets, in a hand which has been attributed to Elizabeth Austen, née Bridges, Edward's wife. It is very similar indeed to Austen's own handwriting, although as I said I defer to those who have worked directly with the manuscripts. In any case, the presence of these songs, even if copied in Elizabeth's handwriting, in Austen's manuscript book indicates that she knew them and perhaps sang them. The one item by Haydn in that album that has been judged to be copied by Austen is a complete three-movement piano sonata in C major, Hob. 16, no. 35, which was first published in 1780. However, in Austen's earlier manuscript book there is a song, 'William', by Thomas Billington, that uses the melody of the first movement of this sonata to set a sentimental lyric about a young woman awaiting the return of her lover William. This song was published in 1787 in London, predating Haydn's first visit to England in 1791.

By a Lady

This period was, of course, not a particularly propitious time for female composers, although they certainly existed. In Austen's manuscript music only three appear, two of them famous historical figures and the third a complete unknown.

Queen Marie Antoinette is said by some to have written the song 'Pauvre Jacques', in collaboration with the Marquise de Travenet, one of her attendants – opinions vary as to which wrote the words and which the music, and indeed whether the attribution is correct. I discuss this in some detail in Chapter 3.

The Austen music manuscripts

Georgiana Cavendish, the Duchess of Devonshire, wrote the music of the song 'Silent sorrow', with words by Richard Brinsley Sheridan, which appears in *The stranger*, the translation of a play by August von Kotzebue – also the author of *Lovers' vows*, the play which features in *Mansfield Park*.[12] And there is a plaintive little dirge titled 'My Phillida' by Miss Mellish, about whom nothing has come to light.

Looking beyond the Jane Austen manuscripts, we find four other female composers among the several hundred men whose work is included in the Austen music collection. There are two songs by Harriett Abrams (copies of one of which appear in two different books belonging to different sisters-in-law). There is the song 'The blue bells of Scotland' by the well-known actor and singer Dorothea Jordan. A set of six keyboard sonatas by Maria Hester Park, née Reynolds, is the most substantial work by a female composer and appears among the printed music of Elizabeth Austen. Lastly, there is a song which was inserted into the play *The secret*, by Edward Morris, and sung by Jordan, attributed to 'A Lady of Fashion', who presumably preferred to remain anonymous.

Lyricists

The habit of attributing a song to a composer without crediting a lyricist persists to this day. Sometimes the opposite is the case, but, unless the words are by an eminent poet, as often as not they are not acknowledged. Given that in any song the words are as basic an element as the melody, and given Austen's literary interests, already very active during her teenage years when she was copying many songs, it might be expected that she would pay attention to the words as much as to the music. In a few cases she has indeed taken much more care to copy the words of songs, without taking so much time over the music, but that is not always the case. As I have said, among Austen's manuscripts there are many pieces of music without basic information as to authorship of either music or words – it was her personal working collection and not intended to be a record for posterity. However, the print versions of many of these songs lack such basic information as well, and only by searching the words in poetry databases and digitised book collections have I been able to identify the lyricists of some of them. Overall, I have been able to establish the authorship of the words of about two-thirds of the songs and other vocal pieces – which is, incidentally, a similar proportion to the composers of both instrumental and vocal music that I have identified, as mentioned above. I have discovered five female lyricists among Austen's manuscripts, or six if Miss Mellish wrote the words as well as the music of 'My Phillida'. The song 'Why tarries my love?' is by the Romantic poet Susanna Blamire; the novelist and playwright Frances Brooke wrote the libretto of William Shield's opera *Rosina* in which the song 'Sweet transports' appears. Amelia Opie, author and anti-slavery campaigner, wrote the lyrics to two songs: 'The Hindoo girl's song'[13] and 'Lost is my quiet' – the latter set to a traditional melody which is better known today as 'Ye banks and braes of Bonny Doon'. I have mentioned Marie Antoinette's companion the Marquise de Travenet above as the possible lyricist of 'Pauvre Jacques'. And finally, the lyrics of the song 'The mansion of peace', composed by Samuel Webbe, are attributed in one of the print editions to 'A Lady'. The proportion of women among the lyricists I have identified among Austen's manuscripts is therefore slightly higher than among the composers, though still only about ten per cent.

Many of the lyricists who appear multiple times are librettists of operas or stage works which have been discussed above – James Cobb, George Colman, Matthew 'Monk' Lewis, for example. Charles Dibdin wrote both words and music to most of his songs, especially later in his career. An interesting case is that of Thomas Moore (often, in his publications, referred to as 'Thomas Moore the Poet'). Moore made it his life's work to bring Irish folk songs to the same kind of prominence in English cultural life as Scottish songs had enjoyed throughout the eighteenth century, and Austen collected five of his lyrics, set either to traditional Irish melodies or to new music by himself or another composer. Moore is featured in Chapter 6, where I also consider the one song by Robert Burns in Austen's manuscript collection. There is also one song with words by John Gay, author of *The beggar's opera*, and it is discussed in Chapter 5.

There are, perhaps surprisingly, no Shakespeare lyrics among her manuscripts – in fact, the only Shakespeare lyric among her surviving personal collection is the printed copy of William Jackson's setting of 'Take, oh take those lips away' from *Measure for measure*, one of his *Twelve canzonets* Opus 9. The only other Shakespeare lyric in the whole of the Austen family music collection is Haydn's English canzonet 'She never told her love', from *Twelfth night*, which is not a song but part of a speech. There are songs which appeared in eighteenth-century performances of Shakespeare's plays, but the words are not by him. The subject of Shakespeare and music in the Georgian period is discussed in Chapter 5.

The manuscript albums

Juvenile songs and lessons (for young beginners who don't know enough to practise) [Catalogue no. CHWJA/19/02]

This manuscript book was printed by London music publishers Longman and Broderip, who were in business 1779–1798, and was probably produced before 1794. The pieces that appear at the beginning of this album were copied from reasonably complex music published in the early 1790s, and Austen may have been playing the piano since her school days, so was not a 'beginner' at this stage – a beginner could not have played these pieces. We could speculate that some Lady Catherine de Bourgh-like person had made a remark about 'young beginners not knowing enough to practise' and Austen felt compelled, mischievously, to record the insult on the title page of her manuscript book. The term 'lesson' implies that these pieces of music had 'an educational motive', as Percy Scholes notes in *The Oxford companion to music*, although Austen sometimes uses 'lesson' simply to mean a piece of instrumental music for a one or two instruments, and Scholes writes that the term is equivalent to 'suite' or 'partita' in the seventeenth and eighteenth centuries.[14]

This collection of keyboard pieces contains much music which would be enjoyable to play and within the capacity of a dedicated amateur pianist. The contents appear to date from the early 1790s to around 1806 or slightly later – though dating music at this period is a very imprecise art. Publishers frequently failed to include dates on printed scores and although they often asserted that they had claimed copyright by entering their publications at Stationers' Hall, thus recording the publication date for posterity, they had not always done so, to the frustration of music researchers in ensuing centuries.

Jeanice Brooks suggests that this manuscript book, when new, might have been a gift from Austen's cousin Eliza de Feuillide, a notion that seems strengthened by the fact that the title is written in a different hand from the teasing subtitle, which appears to be in Austen's own hand. Also, the first and third items are copied from a French periodical publication that Eliza owned which survives as part of the family collection.[15] These are both opera overtures, arranged for keyboard or harp.

Another four pieces in this book are also from theatrical productions of various kinds: another overture, from Thomas Arne's English opera *Artaxerxes*, a suite from a ballet by Joseph Mazzinghi titled *Les trois sultanes*, the March from Michael Kelly's *Blue Beard*, and a set of variations on a melody titled 'To fair Fidele's grassy tomb'. This last piece is an illuminating example of eighteenth-century theatrical practice. The lyrics (which do not appear in this manuscript) are by the poet William Collins and were set by Thomas Arne to be included in a production of Shakespeare's *Cymbeline* in November 1744 (although it was *Cymbeline* 'altered by Theophilus Cibber').[16]To take this set of variations one remove further from Shakespeare, the melody in Austen's manuscript book is not that of Arne's song. I have been unable to identify the composer.

The categories into which I have divided these pieces are somewhat arbitrary, and some overlap in untidy ways. I have already discussed 'The Duke of York's new march' above. It is Mozart in disguise, originating in his opera *The marriage of Figaro*. In the Mozart opera, the music has military connotations, as the hapless young Cherubino is being banished to military service and in this aria, 'Non piu andrai', Figaro is (somewhat unkindly) teasing him by singing this rousing march tune, with words often translated as 'Now your days of philandering are over'. In the context of Austen's collection it is a march played by the Coldstream Regiment, so has lost its operatic connotations and become an actual military march.

At the time marches were popular items in an amateur musician's repertoire. In this book, along with the Mozart and Michael Kelly marches with their stage connections, and the 'Marseilles march', there are eight other marches. As well as 'The Duke of York's new march' we have 'The Duke of York's march', which is an extract from a longer work titled 'The siege of Valenciennes' by Matthew Peter King, commemorating an event that occurred in 1793. There is 'The Austrian retreat', and 'The Austrian Grenadiers' quick march', also from the 1790s. Another piece, placed later in the manuscript book, seems to be copied from the version for piano and flute of 'The nightingale: a favorite military rondo as performed at Brighton by the Royal South Glocester Band' published after 1806. Although this is not explicitly a march, that fact that it has military connections and is in a quick 2/4 tempo implies that it could be regarded as one. Other marches have little information attached in the manuscript and are difficult to identify. But their presence reminds us that during Austen's lifetime Britain was at war almost continuously; this fact will be further explored in Chapters 3 and 4. No further marches appear among Jane Austen's other manuscripts.

A similar proportion of pieces are dances of one kind or another, including, perhaps surprisingly for this period, some waltzes. Allison Thompson writes that 'while country dances in waltz time began to appear in English dance collections around 1799, the turning waltz … did not become generally popular in England until after the Peace Celebrations of 1814'.[17] Percy Scholes writes, 'The dance was almost universally opposed as improper, but from about the period of Waterloo onwards swept over Europe and America'.[18] Thompson quotes several contemporary sources that engage in the debate about waltzing in England.[19] Those whose opposing opinions were recorded were either the jealous lovers of the female partners in a waltz who felt that the dance allowed other men to take liberties, or the authors of advice manuals for young women. The very fact that these opinions were voiced suggests that the waltz was already common and the opposition was therefore not universal at all: as Erin Helyard notes, 'conduct books may have been to a large extent written against prevailing practice, rather than neatly reflecting it'.[20] However, Thompson also points out that it is implied that the 'irresistible waltz' played by Mrs Weston in *Emma* (Volume II, Chapter 8) accompanied a 'longways country dance set in waltz time, not waltzing in pairs', which would have been more controversial,[21] There are several waltz tunes from the 1790s in the 'Juvenile songs and lessons' album, but it seems likely that they were played to accompany country dances rather than the 'turning waltz' that was not widely danced in England until late in Austen's lifetime.

There are also some even more exotic items, such as a 'Polonese Russe' by the Polish composer Osip Kozlovskiĭ; an unidentified piece titled 'Fandango e los gigangas from Thicknesse's tour', presumably collected on a trip to the continent by Ann Thicknesse (née Ford), who is variously described as a singer, a viola da gamba and guitar player, and a performer on the musical glasses; and a Périgourdine, which is 'an old

French dance in a quick six-in-a-measure time; the dancers sang the tune. Its native home was Périgord.'[22] This last item has intrigued some scholars, since a trusted servant in Henry Austen's household, Mlle Bigeon, a fellow émigré from France with Eliza, married a M. Perigord in 1805. Austen knew Mrs Perigord well. Perhaps that connection prompted the addition of this item, about three-quarters of the way through the book. It is not a well-known dance form, and I have not been able to find this particular example in any other source. The other dances are a strathspey by Nathaniel Gow, and a cotillon which has not been identified.

Figure 1.1 'Nos Galen' (i.e. Nos Galan) in Austen's manuscript book of instrumental music 'Juvenile songs and lessons for young beginners who don't know enough to practise'

The Austen music manuscripts

There are, perhaps surprisingly, not many instrumental versions of Scottish dances in this book, which dates from a period when Austen would probably have been playing for her relatives to dance. There are, however, several sets of variations on folk melodies, Scottish, Irish and Welsh, which would have been intended for listening (or background music) rather than dancing. Sometimes these tunes are recognisable under another name. For example, the Welsh melody 'Nos Galen' is the tune to which we sing the Christmas carol 'Deck the halls with boughs of holly'. Two of these sets of variations are arranged for piano duet: it is not known with whom she would have played them: perhaps, as they appear later in the album, with Fanny, or even, perhaps, with Eliza. And finally there are two full sonatas, one by Mazzinghi and the other by Sterkel, and a 'pot-pourri' by Daniel Steibelt.

Songs and duetts [Catalogue number CHWJA/19/03]

The book inscribed 'Songs and duetts' on its decorative title page probably dates from the early 1790s, like 'Juvenile songs and lessons', and Austen was still adding to it at least until 1801, when the latest datable item was published. Inset at the top of the elaborate frame printed on the title page is the head of a young man, smiling rather sardonically – perhaps intended to represent Apollo. After the words 'Songs and duetts' (in Austen's writing) are a few words which have been erased and which to my knowledge have not been deciphered.

All but one of the pieces in the album titled 'Songs and duetts' are indeed a song or a duet: there is one instrumental piece, a dance from the Belgian composer André Grétry's 1783 opera *Caravane de Caire*. Three French operatic pieces also appear in this album – although two of them are, in fact, by the Italian composer Giovanni Paisiello, who spent some time in Paris. These French versions of Italian operatic pieces (one aria and one duet) are almost certainly copied from music belonging to Eliza. At least one of them also appears in a French music periodical that Eliza owned. The third comes from a different Grétry opera, *Richard the Lion Heart.*

Another four French songs are scattered through the volume, which might suggest that Austen enjoyed an ongoing musical bond with her cousin. Two of these are love songs, but they could hardly be more different. In 'Sous un berceau de jasmin', a young man finds delight in the prospect of a life of wedded bliss with his 'belle endormie' – 'sleeping beauty'. In complete contrast, the singer in 'Plus ne veux jamais m'engager' is thoroughly disillusioned and wishes to have nothing further to do with love. Neither of these songs can be definitely attributed to a composer, though I have found the poem 'Plus ne veux jamais' in a later book of poetry, ascribed to a poet named Heurtier about whom nothing is known. The other two French songs are both explicitly political, and are discussed in Chapter 3.

One of the songs in this album is in Italian, the charming 'Arietta Veneziana', about a beautiful young woman in a gondola. It is not known who wrote the melody but it remains a popular Italian song today. The other twenty-eight songs in this album are in English.

Many – more than one-third – of these are songs from theatrical productions of one kind or another. There are three or four folk songs – depending, of course, on the definition of that term. Four are duets, and there is also an unaccompanied Catch – or round – for three voices, with words beginning

'Joan said to John'. This is an amusing piece, somewhat of an antidote to many of the love songs in which the character of the singer (even if they were presumably often sung by women) is very often a man of a sentimental disposition. Austen's inclusion of 'The Irishman', another entertaining and suggestive song, has given rise to speculation about a possible connection to Tom Lefroy, the young Irishman Austen flirted with in January 1796. In Chapter 6 I discuss these English-language songs in some detail, and in Chapter 7 the focus is on the songs that date from the period when Austen was writing her juvenilia, comparing themes and rhetorical qualities across the two genres.

It is an eclectic collection, reflecting the musical culture of the day but also Austen's own taste: humour she would have shared, pathos she would have mocked, but also sheer infectious joy in songs like James Hook's 'The wedding day', simple longing in 'Somebody' and genuine depth of feeling in Thomas Carter's 'Oh Nancy'.

Songs [Scrapbook of manuscript and printed vocal and keyboard music, c. 1775 – c. 1810 – Catalogue number CHWJA/19/07]

The album simply titled 'Songs' is usually referred to as a scrapbook, because the items are not all in a fixed order and some loose sheets have been added after the original contents page was compiled. It was not originally a blank manuscript book like the previous two albums, but is a collection of loose items which has been bound together. In the Resource Information on Internet Archive, the physical characteristics of the book are explained:

> The volume is similar in some ways to binder's volumes in the collection, but here stubs in the binding enable the removal and addition of different items, which are glued into the stubs rather than being bound into the spine. ... The book contains manuscript items (solo vocal, vocal ensemble and keyboard) in a variety of hands, inserted randomly between prints of vocal and keyboard music. Printed items were published from c. 1780 – c. 1805, with most datable items appearing in print in the 1790s. Not all items in the book are included in the index, suggesting that music continued to be inserted after the index was compiled.[23]

The index, written on the inside front cover, contains twenty-seven numbered items plus two unnumbered entries for 'manuscript songs'. Jane Austen's signature is visible between the lines of the index, which was obviously compiled at some time after the book was bound and she took possession of it. All this information points to a certain fluidity in the composition of this book over time.

As it currently stands, the album contains around fifty-two pieces of music – depending what is counted – and twenty-five of them are manuscripts in Austen's hand. The manuscripts are copied from music published in roughly the same period as the two volumes described above. The reason for their inclusion in this scrapbook rather than in the bound manuscript albums may be happenstance: these pieces might have been encountered in a situation where Austen did not have her manuscript book with her, and when she was able to obtain single sheets of manuscript paper to make her copies.

Some of the music is quite scrappily written, possibly in a hurry. In some of the pieces the music appears to be in a different hand from the words. An unidentified 'Cossack dance' appears upside-down on the reverse of the song 'Since then I'm doomed' – this must surely have been a case of using a piece of manuscript paper that was handy. The song comes from the 1792 play *The spoilt child* by Isaac Bickerstaff which may have been performed in private theatricals at Godmersham: Fanny records in her diary on 30 July 1805 that 'Aunts C. & Jane, Anna, Edwd George Henry William & myself acted "The Spoilt child" & "Innocence Rewarded"'.[24]

Gillian Dow believes that the play acted by the family would have been not the Bickerstaff play but a translation of Stéphanie-Félicité de Genlis's play *L'enfant gatée*. She discusses the question in some detail in a recent article in *Persuasions*. Her doubt arises from the reputation of the actress and singer Dorothea (Dora) Jordan, whose liaison with the Duke of Clarence rendered her 'not respectable'. The play, she argues, 'lost respectability through its association with her', and it would therefore be unlikely that it would have been chosen to be acted within the family, including the children ranging in age from twelve-year-old Fanny and her cousin Anna down to the seven-year-old William.[25] On the other hand there was music written or sung by Dora Jordan in both Austen's own music manuscript collection and albums belonging to Fanny's mother Elizabeth, including this song, 'Since then I'm doomed', from the Bickerstaff play.

Dow is certainly on firm ground when she writes that Austen knew Genlis's work, but a remark she made in a letter of March 1816 to her ten-year-old niece Caroline (Anna's younger sister) implies that she did not like it: 'You seem to be quite my own niece in your feelings towards Mde de Genlis. I do not think I could even now, at my sedate time of Life, read *Olimpe et Theophile* without being in a rage' (*Letters*, p. 310). I think we cannot say with any certainty which play they performed in 1805 – the one by Bickerstaff or the one by Genlis – but, if it was the former, it would be wonderful to know who took the part of Little Pickle, the role played by Dora Jordan on stage. Little Pickle is the child of the title, and he sings this song when banished from his home after baking his aunt's pet parrot in a pie, a scenario which could have been created by Austen herself in her teenage years. The song itself was an arrangement of a melody drawn from Antoine Baudron's original setting of 'Je suis Lindor', from Beaumarchais's play *The barber of Seville*.

There are two copies of the song 'Susan', which is a setting of three verses from John Gay's ballad 'Sweet William's farewell to Black-eyed Susan'. One of them is on the bottom half of a page on the reverse of the song 'Pauvre Jacques', with a Scottish folk song occupying the top half of the page. The other copy of 'Susan' appears earlier in the current order but is more complete and a little more carefully copied. It also includes all three verses while the other copy has only one, and it has nothing on the reverse side. Perhaps it was copied more carefully at a later date, or perhaps the other copy was made quickly for a specific purpose, using the back of the 'Pauvre Jacques' which happened to be at hand. 'Pauvre Jacques' is likely to have been copied from Eliza de Feuillide's copy of *Feuilles de Terpsichore*, published in Paris in about 1792. I have been unable to find the melody of this version of 'Susan' in print, although there are manuscript versions in other contemporary music collections. In Chapter 5 I speculate that this song might be a surviving remnant from Thomas Arne's lost cantata setting of Gay's poem.

Another mysterious item is the song 'Hither, love, thy beauties bring'. Austen has written it out carefully, acknowledging the composer, and her manuscript is the only source for the combination of these words and this melody that I have found. The music is by the harp virtuoso Jean Baptiste Krumpholtz: it is a theme from the Romanza in his Harp Concerto Opus 9, no. 6. This melody was used for a song published in about 1794 titled 'The nuns complaint', based on words from a novel by Mary Robinson.[26] However, the words in Austen's manuscript are to be found, set to a different melody, in a collection of songs composed by John Ross, with words by 'Mr Rannie'.[27] Did Austen set these words to this tune? Not necessarily, but the possibility cannot be entirely discounted until another copy of the song is found.

Overall, the Austen manuscripts in this book are a mixture of songs and instrumental pieces. There are three short dances, and one nursery rhyme, 'Goosey goosey gander', set by Samuel Wesley, another eminent English composer of the time. There are two other French songs, including Benoit Pollet's amusing dialogue 'Le refus', which appears here without title: the first line is 'Laisse là sur l'herbette'. Another comic song is the Scottish folk song 'I ha'e laid a herring in salt', in which an increasingly impatient farmer tries to woo a bride. The outcome is left uncertain but the scenario would surely have amused Austen.

This book also contains the only item in the collection that is in Latin. Titled 'The prayer of the Sicilian mariners', it begins with the Latin words 'O sanctissima! O piissima dolce virgo Maria'. A Sicilian source for this hymn has not been positively identified but it has since become widespread as a tune for several hymns, and for the anthem 'We shall overcome'.

[Untitled volume – Catalogue number Jenkyns 03]

This volume, like the last, has an index to the contents written on the inside front cover, continued on the first flyleaf, which is signed 'C. E. Austen' – presumably Jane's sister Cassandra Elizabeth. The first piece in the album is a printed edition of a sonata by Muzio Clementi, but the rest of the book is all in manuscript. According to the Resource Information for the Internet Archive, written by Jeanice Brooks and her colleagues and based on a familiarity with the physical book, 'There is no evident logic to the binding order, and the contents do not always align with paper type (that is, the copying of a musical item often extends over a change to a new batch or leaf of paper.)'[28] However, the order of the items in the book matches that in the index, with just a couple of omissions, so it is not a scrapbook like the 'Songs' album.

Once again there are mysteries associated with this book. The contents page is said to be 'a good match' for Cassandra's hand,[29] which is somewhat unexpected, given that, as discussed in Chapter 2, it has generally been considered that Cassandra did not share Jane's interest in music. It is possible that she compiled the index after Jane's death, when she was lending the music to young relatives. This would also perhaps explain the fact that her signature appears on the flyleaf. However, the index is incomplete: it stops at item 58, the 'Hindoo girl's song', and sixteen more items follow this song in the album, several of them in Jane Austen's handwriting, so it seems more likely that the index was compiled before they were added.

In all, of the seventy-four pieces of music in this book, sixty-one appear to be in Austen's hand.[30] These include several of the items discussed above – works by Thomas Arne,

The Austen music manuscripts

Michael Kelly, Thomas Moore and Muzio Clementi, and the Haydn piano sonata. I also mentioned the anonymous piano sonata that has not been identified. It looks rather impressive on the page, with extended semiquaver runs and sequences of chords jumping across several octaves, but when played is awkward and repetitive, with some musical infelicities such as failing to resolve the cadence of the Andante in the root position. However, it is copied carefully, and covers eight pages of manuscript. In the margin at the beginning of the third movement is a pen and ink sketch of a woman in profile, wearing a cap, hair in ringlets. The music does seem to be in Austen's hand, although some of the annotations are in different script. This sonata remains a mystery. It is clearly not the work of a professional musician, but otherwise there is little information about its authorship.

Among the acknowledged composers, there are some names that seemed strangely familiar to me. Piccinni – was he not the composer of *La bohème* and *Madame Butterfly*? But no, that was Giacomo Puccini, and the composer of the opera *La buona figliuola* from which Austen copied the overture into her album was Niccolo Piccinni, an eighteenth-century opera composer from Bari, in southern Italy. *La buona figliuola* (1760) was based on Samuel Richardson's novel *Pamela*. Perhaps that explains why Austen was interested in the piece. A printed copy of a version for keyboard duet appears in one of her other albums.

A set of piano variations on the song 'On ne saurait trop embellir' is attributed to Holst. Surely, though, the Holsts (Gustav and Imogen) were twentieth-century composers? Gustav is most famous for writing *The planets*. It turns out that this Holst was Gustav's great-grandfather, Matthias, who appears to have been a musician busy in the London scene, publishing many sets of variations and other keyboard pieces. He was in fact the composer of the melody of 'The nightingale', mentioned above as a 'favorite military rondo': Holst wrote it 'for the German Theatre' and it was published in about 1805 by Longman and Broderip.[31]

When indexing this manuscript book I was intrigued to come upon three songs which have been copied from *A Tour through Germany: particularly along the banks of the Rhine, Mayne, etc.* by Wilhelm Render, published in London in 1801. In the printed version the German words are given with an unattributed English translation. Austen does not include the German words. These are songs that Render collected on his travels: a 'Freemason's song', a song titled 'Love and wine' about how life is not worth living in the absence of both, and 'Rhenish wine', enthusiastically recommending the consumption of the best wine in copious quantities. There is a copy of the German version of 'Love and wine' in the scrapbook volume, although it does not appear to be in Austen's writing. Although there is instrumental music by German or Austrian composers in the music books – Austen's own and the whole collection generally – there is almost nothing else in the way of German songs – many French songs, some Italian, but the songs are predominantly British in origin, and it was unexpected to come upon what are, frankly, German drinking songs among Austen's manuscripts.

Immediately following these songs in the album are some of Thomas Moore's Irish songs. But preceding the German songs is another interesting item which appears to be closer to home for Austen. Thomas Shell was a musician in Bath, active in the 1790s, and composed not only *Twenty new psalms*, sung at 'the Rev'd Dr Randolph's Chapel, Laura Street, Bath' (1801), but also a Morning Hymn, with matching Evening Hymn, which is in Austen's manuscript book – although opinions differ as to whether the handwriting actually belongs to Jane rather than Cassandra or someone else. This is one of very few pieces of sacred music in her collection and it is tempting to think that she copied it because she knew Thomas Shell, or knew of him. Thomas Shell died in April 1801, apparently at an early age, leaving behind a young family. He had been involved in the Sydney Gardens concerts that the Austens had attended on earlier visits. When they moved to Bath from Steventon, the Austens leased a house at 4 Sydney Place, not far from Laura Place, from the end of May 1801.

This is not only one of very few pieces of religious music in the collection but also one of very few choral pieces – which I imagine is because Austen was not herself a chorister – indeed, it would have not been usual for a woman to sing in an Anglican choir at this period. The music in parish churches, as opposed to cathedrals, at this time was, according to Erik Routley, 'grey and spiritless', consisting of 'a metrical psalm or two sung' by the congregation 'to one of the half-dozen tunes they knew'.[32] Even that might have been beyond the resources of some churches. Adrienne Bradney-Smith writes that organs were rarely found in country churches. She has found some evidence for communal music-making in Hampshire in the nearby parish of Hannington, but 'the possibility of congregational singing at St Nicholas', the little church where Jane's father was incumbent, remains purely conjecture'.[33] The situation is likely to have been different in Bath. Nevertheless, the reason for the inclusion of this hymn in Austen's otherwise predominantly secular collection is something I have discussed with Shell's descendant, Janet Shell, who is also a musician and has collected information about her ancestor on her web page.[34] Did Austen know Shell from earlier visits to Bath? Did she hear about his early death and take an interest in the music for that reason? Despite these fascinating speculations, we have agreed that we will never know the answers to these questions.

All but one of the nursery rhymes in Austen's manuscript collection appear in this album. It was common (and presumably lucrative) for composers of the time to publish collections of nursery rhymes, usually with new melodies and often set for vocal duos or trios. Most of the English nursery rhymes among the manuscripts are unattributed and the only one which uses the tune familiar today is 'Dickory, dickory dock'. They appear towards the middle of the book and were probably copied by Austen to sing for the amusement of her young nieces and nephews. In addition, along with the waltzes discussed earlier in this chapter, there are six dances in Austen's hand in this album, most of them Scottish. These might also have been collected with her young relatives in mind.

On the last few pages of this book there are three instrumental pieces which it has been suggested are in Fanny Knight's handwriting: 'The black dwarf', 'Nicol Jarvie' and 'The slave'. These three pieces could all be tentatively dated to 1816. A visit to Chawton with her father, Edward, in April and May 1816 was the last time Fanny saw her aunt Jane.[35] Perhaps Fanny had brought the songs with her from London, where she had been visiting her Uncle Henry, and copied them into Austen's manuscript book. At the foot of the second-last page of the album, immediately following 'Nicol Jarvie', is a little dance in Austen's hand titled 'The Waterloo', which may be the last piece of music she ever copied. Overleaf, on the last page of this manuscript book is Thomas Kelly's 'An evening hymn' in a different handwriting again, not yet identified. (This is not to be confused with the earlier Morning and Evening Hymns by Thomas Shell.) The published versions of the hymn have two verses, but the manuscript includes a third verse, beginning 'Here midst pain and grief we languish', which I have been unable to find anywhere else. This verse is added in the bottom left corner of the page, as if as an afterthought. The order and placement of these manuscripts invites further specula-tion. Was this final item, a hymn suitable for a funeral, copied into the book after Austen's death, and perhaps the third verse composed by one of her family members as a tribute to her?

Songs, duets and glees [Catalogue number Rice 1]

This album is not included in the 2015 digitisation project by the University of Southampton. Along with Rice 2 (which is all copied in the handwriting of Edward and Elizabeth's second daughter, Lizzy) it is held in the Blackie House Library and Museum in Edinburgh. Rice 1 is a collection of glees, catches, vocal duets and songs in several contemporary hands. The evi-dence suggests that it was bound from loose sheets after 1810. Gillaspie writes that this book 'is unique in containing examples of all the female musicians in the Austen family in Jane Austen's generation (Jane Austen, Eliza Hancock [Mrs Henry] Austen and Elizabeth Bridges [Mrs Edward] Austen as well as juvenile examples of the musical calligraphy of Jane's two nieces, Fanny and Lizzy Austen Knight'.[36] Most of the music is copied by Elizabeth Austen (Edward's wife), with a concentration of items later in the volume copied, perhaps after her death in 1808, by Fanny and Lizzy.

She played and sang

There are four items in Jane Austen's hand in this book.
Two are by James Hook: 'The Cheshire tragedy' and 'Hail,
lovely rose', both from 'a musical farce' titled *Catch him who can*,
from 1806. Three other songs from the same play are copied on
either side of these two songs, in the handwriting of her sister-
in-law Elizabeth. A copy of another Hook song, 'The wedding
day', appears in Elizabeth's handwriting later in the album: this
song is also in Austen's 'Songs and duetts' album. The third of
Austen's manuscripts in Rice 1 is a song titled 'No riches from
his scanty store' by Johann Georg Graeff with words by Helen
Maria Williams, and the fourth is a hymn, 'Before Jehovah's
awful throne' by Martin Madan. As this book appears to have
belonged to Elizabeth, it seems unlikely that Austen was copying these items purely for her own purposes, from her own
inclinations. She might have been doing Elizabeth a favour
by finishing a copying task for her. As is suggested in Austen's
letter to Cassandra of January 1799, she might have previously
copied music for Elizabeth: she wrote 'Elizabeth is very cruel
about my writing Music; – and as punishment for her, I should
insist upon always writing out all hers for her in future, if I were
not punishing myself at the same time' (*Letters*, p. 33).

At least one of the two items in this book to which Eliza contributed seems to confirm this pattern of working co-operatively:
another hymn by Martin Madan, the copy of which had been
begun by Elizabeth and completed by Eliza.

Many other titles in this book are familiar from other albums
in the digitised collection, which might be evidence of sharing
music between the extended family. Examples are songs by
John Wall Callcott, Thomas Moore and Giovanni Paisiello,
and Georgiana Cavendish's lovely song 'Silent sorrow', which
is also in Austen's scrapbook.[37]

Austen's printed music

In addition to the music she copied by hand and the print music in the mixed albums, Austen owned three volumes made up solely of a variety of printed music, collected and bound after publication. Details of the bindings and annotations of these albums are available on the Internet Archive page for each volume.

Two of these albums contain instrumental music: sonatas and sonatinas by German composers such as Ignaz Pleyel, Johann Franz Xaver Sterkel, Johann Schobert (not Franz Schubert) and Karl Stamitz; a collection of opera overtures by Italian composers; and Kotzwara's programmatic sonata 'The Battle of Prague'. There is some overlap between the repertoire in these two books and Elizabeth Austen's collection of printed keyboard music, whether by coincidence or arising from a shared interest. Some of these pieces are orchestral works arranged for keyboard, sometimes with other instruments *ad lib.*, by composers working in England, but there is not a great deal of original instrumental music by English composers. An exception is William Evance of Durham, whose 'Concerto for the harpsichord or piano forte with accompanyments' appears alongside Pleyel's Overture. One remarkable item is a keyboard duet by John Marsh that combines two original fugues with Handel's Hallelujah chorus from *Messiah* and part of his coronation anthem 'Zadok the priest'.

The other album of printed music bearing Austen's signature is of vocal music, and this has more decided connections with the British Isles. There are twelve 'canzonets' for vocal duet by William Jackson (1730–1803), from Exeter. Jackson, according to Gammie and McCulloch, was 'proudly English' and 'resented the furore and adulation that accompanied Haydn's visits'.[38] There are two sets of Scottish songs, containing thirty and twenty-six songs respectively, published by Robert Bremner: all these publications will be discussed at more length in Chapter 6. The final item in this book is by Tommaso Giordani, who was born in Naples but made his career in England and Ireland. His cantata 'Colin and Lucy' is a setting of a poem by Thomas Tickell. In Chapter 8 I make a detailed comparison of the rhetoric of this piece with Austen's *Sense and sensibility*, as an example of the kind of reading which can arise from placing a poem and its musical setting alongside a work of narrative fiction.

Conclusion: Austen's musical taste

These music albums raise as many questions as they answer. Why, for example, did Austen copy 'The Marseilles march' (a version of the French revolutionary anthem, which became 'La Marseillaise') into her manuscript book, alongside 'Captivity', Stephen Storace's moving lament for Queen Marie Antoinette?

Judgements on Austen's musical taste have inevitably been based on assessments of these music books. Patrick Piggott (in *The innocent diversion*) wrote that 'it would be idle to pretend that many of the songs and piano pieces which Jane Austen copied with such care and labour into her books are of a good musical standard, ... too many of the items in her collection being no more than superficially pretty and sometimes rather worse than that'.[39] Robert Wallace observes that 'Piggott's judgement of Austen's musical taste ... seems to have been reached by imposing the musicological standards of the 1960s and 1970s upon the material of the 1790s as if it were material of the 1810s'.

The 1790s, as he points out, was her formative musical decade, and 'In England this was not the decade of Beethoven' – or even Mozart.[40]

In any case, we cannot be sure that the music she copied gives a faithful and comprehensive picture of her taste in music, because there could be a variety of reasons for the choices she made: she could need a particular song for a specific occasion, perhaps, or it might have words which she thought would amuse a young relative. Copying music from a friend's collection could be an obligation of friendship, just as today music-lovers might share recordings on iTunes. Or it could simply be a matter of what was both available and within her capability as a performer. And what survives definitely did not comprise her whole music collection. Still, this material is worth studying for the positive information it provides as well as for the possibilities it allows. There is much 'pretty' music (whether superficial or not, *pace* Piggott) but also much really beautiful and moving music which would otherwise be totally unknown today.

2

Jane Austen's musical relationships

Austen's correspondence and the memoirs

Music seems to have been in some ways a private pleasure in Jane Austen's life – in fact, reading the memoirs written long after her death by her brother James's children, one could perhaps conclude that for her, like Anne Elliot in *Persuasion*, she had no one to share her love of music: 'In music she had been always used to feel alone in the world' (*P*, p. 47). Her niece Caroline wrote that she 'was never induced (as I have heard) to play in company', and practised the piano before breakfast so as not to disturb the other members of the Chawton household, as 'none of her family cared much for it' (*Memoir*, p. 170). But few musicians like to practise in public, and if she had the choice she might well do her scales and Cramer études in private.

Austen's letters give a somewhat different impression. She shared musical information and jokes with her family and friends and planned to play country dances for her young relatives. Decades later some of them recounted memories of hearing her sing, although this might indeed have been only within the family circle, not 'in company'. The Austen family music books throw yet more light on the sharing of music within the family, with copies in Jane's manuscript books made from printed music in the collections of her extended family. As Jeanice Brooks notes, 'Several books include material associated with more than one user', and 'overlapping material traces create the impression of a conversation through and about music that involved a wide circle of family and friends'.[1] Austen copied music into her sister-in-law Elizabeth's album, as mentioned in Chapter 1, and so did other family members. This is an example of co-operation within the family circle, but music copying could be 'a mark of friendship or courtship',[2] as can be seen in *Sense and sensibility*, where Marianne mourns Willoughby's absence by sitting 'at the instrument gazing on every line of music that he had written out for her, till her heart was so heavy that no further sadness could be gained' (*SS*, p. 83). There is no direct evidence of a similar scenario in the Austen family albums, although not all the musical handwriting in the books has been securely identified.

Cassandra

Austen's sister Cassandra, who was her best friend and with whom she lived all her life, is generally thought to have been radically uninterested in music. It is disconcerting, however, to look critically at the evidence for this belief. If we take the statements in the letters regarding music at their face value, after all, we will be very confused as to Austen's own attitude to music, as suggested in the Introduction.

She played and sang

When Cassandra's planned trip to London in 1801 was post-poned, Austen's letter praising her 'noble resignation of Mrs Jordan and the Opera House' sounds ironic (*Letters*, p. 71).[3] Fifteen years later, in September 1816 when Cassandra was staying at the spa town of Cheltenham, Jane wrote, 'Success to the Pianoforte! I trust it will drive you away' (*Letters*, p. 322). I suspect that Cassandra had complained about hearing too much of someone playing the piano in their lodgings, and Jane was jocularly hoping it would shorten her visit and bring her home sooner. We cannot be sure exactly what she meant: apart from the fact that Cassandra's letters do not survive, there is much left unsaid between these two closest of friends and sisters. And two references in twenty years of correspondence are, after all, not much to go on.

On the other hand, Jane writes to Cassandra quite often about music she has heard, giving details of performers and titles of pieces of music. Sometimes this is information to be passed on to someone, often their niece Fanny – but not always. Late in 1808, when they were about to set up their new per-manent household in Chawton, she wrote to Cassandra, 'yes, yes, we will have a pianoforte, as good as can be got for thirty guineas, and I will practice country dances, that we may have some amusement for our nephews and nieces, when we have the pleasure of their company' (*Letters*, p. 161). This sounds like a response to a sympathetic query. Perhaps Cassandra did in fact share Austen's idiosyncratic tastes in music – neither of them was keen on Italian opera, but music at home to share with the family was welcome.

Austen also made musical jokes and references which she clearly expected Cassandra to understand. In February 1807, when they were both living in Southampton and Cassandra was on an extended visit to Edward and his family at Godmersham, she wrote that she was sorry to hear that Cassandra's return was to be delayed. She added, however, that it was 'no use to lament. I never heard that even Queen Mary's Lamentation did her any good' (*Letters*, p. 118). 'Queen Mary's lamentation' was a Scottish folk song, and Austen had an arrangement of it by Tommaso Giordani among the manuscripts in her music collection. She clearly assumes that Cassandra will recognise the reference. And in 1811 she drew on an extended musical metaphor to characterise their niece Anna.

Anna with variations[4]

On 25 April 1811 Jane Austen relayed some news of Anna to her sister in a long gossipy letter. Anna was staying at Chawton with Mrs Austen and Martha Lloyd at the time; Jane was in London with Henry and Eliza, and Cassandra was at Godmersham with Edward and Elizabeth:

> My Mother & Martha both write with great satisfaction of Anna's behaviour. She is quite an Anna with variations – but she cannot have reached her last, for that is always the most flourishing and shewy – she is at about her 3d or 4th which are generally simple and pretty. (*Letters*, p. 184)

I had always thought this was a clever musical joke and not much more. Austen was familiar with the very popular genre of variations on a theme (often a folk melody) set for piano solo, ubiquitous at the time and well-represented in her surviving music collection. However, when browsing through the catalogue of the works of Jan Ladislav Dussek I noticed that in 1792 he had published 'Anna with variations' – or, to give its full title (in the Dublin edition), 'Anna: A favorite Scotch song with variations for the piano forte composed by J. L. Dussek'.[5] The Dussek variations are not to be found in any of her surviving music books.

This Scottish folk song, which is more usually titled 'Shepherds I have lost my love', was well known at the time, appearing in musical arrangements by several other composers including Joseph Haydn and Ignaz Pleyel. Austen would have been familiar with the tune – she had a copy of an arrangement for piano duet by Thomas Billington in one of her composite volumes of printed music. The song lyrics are not included in the Dussek and Billington versions, but Austen might still have known them.

> Shepherds, I have lost my love;
> Have you seen my Anna?
> Pride of ev'ry shady grove,
> Upon the banks of Banna!
> I for her my home forsook,
> Near yon misty mountain;
> Left my flock, my pipe, my crook,
> Greenwood shade, and fountain.
> Never shall I see them more
> Until her returning;
> All the joys of life are o'er,
> From gladness chang'd to mourning.
> Whither is my charmer flown?
> Shepherds, tell me whither?
> Ah! Woe for me, perhaps she's gone
> For ever and for ever.

Dussek's set of variations on this rather wistful song follows the very common pattern noted by Austen in her letter. It begins with the Air – the tune, in a straightforward arrangement for keyboard solo. This is followed by five variations on the tune, each with its own character – the score I have, which was published by Hime in Dublin, contains many dynamic markings, some indicating quite dramatic contrasts, and there is also a great degree of rhythmic complexity, which alters the speed and brilliance of the different sections. Variation Four is the most 'simple & pretty', as Austen suggests. It is set at a lower pitch with the melody stated simply over a ruminative, chromatic bass line, while Variation Five, the last, is 'the most flourishing and shewy', covering a wider range of the instrument with octaves in the right hand and a long elaborate cadenza passage written out in the second-last bar.

Among Austen's surviving poems is one she wrote about her niece Anna – nobody knows exactly when – which begins:

> In measured verse I'll now rehearse
> The charms of lovely Anna
> And, first, her mind is unconfined
> Like any vast savannah. (*Memoir*, p. 75)

Austen's witty verse continues for seven stanzas, praising in extravagant geographical (and affectionately ironic) similes Anna's fancy, her wit, her judgement and her charms. She compares her to Lake Ontario and the Niagara Falls as well as the vast American savannah.

Obviously the subject of the poem, beyond being a young woman named Anna, is quite different from that of the song. But what is striking is that the metre and rhyme scheme of Austen's verse are similar to the Scottish song, so it could readily be sung to the same tune. It is not an unusual form, but it is not common among Austen's small clutch of poems.

She played and sang

The text of Austen's poem survives only in the memoir written years after her death by Anna's younger brother James
Edward Austen-Leigh, and he does not provide a date. Deirdre
Le Faye speculates that it might have been written in 1810.
Austen expressed concern for her niece's behaviour and disposition in several letters around this time. In 1809 Anna had
become engaged to the Rev. Michael Terry, twice her age.
Anna was at the time sixteen years old and her parents for-
bade the match. In early 1810 Mr Terry re-emerged to plead
his cause, via his sister Charlotte, and Anna's father, James,
changed his mind. But after visiting her new fiancé's family
for a few days, Anna called off the engagement. In 1813 Anna
became engaged to Ben Lefroy and they were married in
autumn 1814. Well might Mr Terry have sung, 'Ah! Woe for
me, perhaps she's gone, for ever and for ever.'

Austen did not need to have known Dussek's 'Anna with
variations' to make her little musical joke to Cassandra in 1811.
Her attention might have been caught by an advertisement for
it on another piece of music, or in a magazine, or it might have
been a complete coincidence. But the fact that the musical work
existed gives us a little more context to one throwaway line
among those miracles of telegraphic compression that are Jane
Austen's letters to Cassandra.

Anna Lefroy, née Austen

Both Anna and her younger half-brother, James Edward, wrote
fiction and shared their work in progress with Austen, but neither of them seems to have shared her interest in music. There
is a slightly puzzling reference about Anna in a letter from
Austen to Fanny Knight at the time of Anna's marriage to Ben

Lefroy in 1814. It seems that the young couple had decided to buy a piano. Austen wrote, 'I was rather sorry to hear that she *is* to have an instrument; it seems throwing money away. They will wish the 24 G[uinea]s. in the shape of sheets & towels six months hence; – and as to her playing, it never can be anything' (*Letters*, p. 285). I have seen no other suggestion that Anna was at all musically inclined.

Anna did, however, offer some information about Austen's own musical history in a letter she wrote to James Edward when he was compiling his memoir in 1869:

> I believe that a music Master attended at Steventon, who also gave lessons at Ashe: but am not *certain*. Any way, nobody could think more humbly of Aunt Jane's music than she did herself; so much so as at one time to resolve on giving it up. The Pianoforte was parted with on the removal from Steventon, and during the whole time of her residence at Bath she had none. In course of time she felt the loss of the amusement, or for some other reason repented of her decision; for, when settled at Chawton she bought a Pianoforte, and practised upon it diligently – This, as I understood at the time, she found necessary in order to recover that facility of fingering, which no doubt she had once possessed. (*Memoir*, p. 183)

Anna's memory, or perhaps her knowledge at the time, was not complete. Austen might not have had a piano in Bath, but we know that Austen spent part of her scarce resources on a piano when she was living in Southampton with her mother and sister. She recorded the sum of £2 13s 6d in her end-of-year accounts for 1807 for 'Hire Piano Forte' (*Family record*, p. 145).

The 'music Master' Anna mentions is presumably George William Chard, who was during the 1790s the deputy organist at Winchester Cathedral. The only explicit evidence for their lessons is in Austen's letter to Cassandra of 1 September 1796:

> I am glad to hear so good an account of Mr Charde, and only fear that my long absence may occasion his relapse. I practise every day as much as I can – I wish it were more for his sake. (*Letters*, p. 5)

Chard obviously recovered from his affliction, despite Austen's absence of several weeks on this visit to Edward's home in Kent, as he lived on until 1849. However, his earnings from the Cathedral were modest and he died a bankrupt. Perhaps it was financial necessity that made him travel to Steventon, and possibly also to Ashe, to give private music lessons.[6]

Caroline Austen

The earliest memories recorded in Anna's 'Recollections' of 1866 provide a wonderfully vivid glimpse of the Steventon household from her own childhood, as well as her more mature – or at least later – relationship with her aunt. However, it is in her younger sister Caroline's memoir, and in letters from Austen to her young niece, that we find contemporary evidence of a genuine musical bond.

Most of what we know directly about Austen's musicianship relies on Caroline's memories, as well as letters Caroline received from her beloved aunt in her last years. She was only twelve when Austen died. Uniquely among her younger relatives, it seems, Caroline actively shared both Austen's literary and musical pursuits. Caroline was writing stories by the age of ten. Like her siblings, she would send her stories to her aunt for her opinion and receive kind encouragement and advice.

But she was apparently the only musical one in the household of the eldest Austen brother, James, and his wife Mary née Lloyd. In her *Reminiscences*, written towards the end of her life, she describes a visit in 1809, when she would have been only four years old, to the mansion of Stoneleigh, which belonged to the Leigh side of the family. She particularly remembers her pleasure at being allowed to spend as much time as she liked playing on 'an old spinet, ... old and uncared for' in the gallery. She was happy to be left alone to make music, without being 'teized' or 'wanted ... in the parlour'.[7]

On 30 October 1815 Austen wrote from Henry's London house to Caroline, who was staying with Grandmama and Cassandra at Austen's home in Chawton. She wrote that she did not yet feel 'quite equal to taking up your Manuscript' but promised to do so soon, meanwhile hoping that she was doing her piano practice. 'I trust to you for taking care of my Instrument & not letting it be ill used in any respect. – Do not allow anything to be put on it, but what is very light. – I hope you will try to make out some other tune besides the Hermit.' She ends the letter by claiming her as a 'sister-Aunt' (since Anna's first child had recently been born) – 'I have always maintained the importance of Aunts, as much as possible, & I am sure of your doing the same now' (*Letters*, p. 294).

It is not known what brand of piano Austen owned when she lived at Chawton, but it would have been a square piano, not a grand. The Ganer piano she sold when they left Steventon in 1801 was probably also a square piano. These wooden-framed early instruments are much smaller and lighter than the modern upright piano, which has a heavy iron frame. Two people can easily lift a typical domestic square piano of this period. The grand pianos of the time were also much lighter and on a smaller scale than the concert grands of today, which were developed much later in the nineteenth century. The historic instruments of the eighteenth and early nineteenth centuries are now commonly referred to by the term 'fortepiano', although that is not a word Austen used. She generally writes 'piano forte', or, commonly in the novels, just 'the instrument': the piano is so commonly associated with female musicians that further specification is not required.

The evidence suggests that Caroline had no piano at home in Steventon, which makes it all the more significant that she was able to practise her scales and 'make out the Hermit' on Jane's piano at Chawton. In February 1817 Austen replied to a letter from Caroline which had conveyed 'great News … about Mr Digweed Mr Trimmer, & a Grand Piano Forte. I wish it had been a small one, as then you might have pretended that Mr D.'s rooms were too damp to be fit for it, & offered to take charge of it at the Parsonage' (*Letters*, p. 331). Mr William Digweed lived in the Steventon manor-house, and Mr Trimmer was a lawyer in Alton – it is not clear what his part in this transaction might have been: perhaps he sold Mr Digweed the grand piano. A month later, in what would be her last letter to Caroline, Austen wrote 'I wish you could practise your fingering oftener. Would it not be a good plan for you to go & live entirely at Mr Wm Digweed's? He could not desire any other remuneration than the pleasure of hearing you practise' (*Letters,* pp. 337–8). The logical reason for Caroline being unable to practise her fingering more often is that she did not have access to a piano at home.[8]

Fifty years later in 1867 Caroline records her memories of standing by the pianoforte at Chawton Cottage and hearing her Aunt Jane play, and sometimes sing. Her account is frequently quoted:

Austen's musical relationships

> Aunt Jane began her day with music – for which, I conclude she
> had a natural taste; as she thus kept it up – tho' she had no one
> to teach; was never induced (as I have heard) to play in com-
> pany; and none of her family cared much for it. I suppose, that
> she might not trouble *them*, she chose her practising time before
> breakfast – when she could have the room to herself – She prac-
> tised regularly every morning – She played very pretty tunes, *I*
> thought – and I liked to stand by her and listen to them; but the
> music (for I knew the books well in after years) would now be
> thought disgracefully easy. (*Memoir*, pp. 170–1)

A great deal of what has been assumed about Austen's music
practice is based on this passage. The remark about 'none of
the family' caring much for music has been particularly influential, although references in Austen's letters suggest that Martha
Lloyd, Caroline's aunt on her mother's side, who also lived in
the Chawton household, was studying music during these years.
The idea of the music being 'disgracefully easy' is an interesting one. I wonder whether Caroline realised that Austen would
have been improvising accompaniments from the bare outlines
that appear on the pages of many of the music books that she
knew so well in a later time when piano accompaniments were
more usually composed and printed in full.

In her *Reminiscences* Caroline does not mention her own
musical education. Some of the comments in Austen's letters
about practising her fingering might encourage us to believe
that Austen was giving her some lessons, but Caroline explicitly writes in the passage quoted above that 'she had no one to
teach'.

In any case, there is a touching testimony to Caroline's
importance to Austen as a listener and fellow musician in a
postscript to the letter from 23 January 1817:

The Piano Forte often talks of you; – in various keys, tunes & expressions I allow – but be it Lesson or Country dance, Sonata or Waltz, *You* are really its' constant theme. I wish you cd come & see us, as easily as Edward can. (*Letters*, p. 326)

James Edward, in his late teens, was a frequent visitor to Chawton, while Caroline, not yet twelve, was not so independent.

Fanny Austen Knight, later Lady Knatchbull

Fanny, the daughter of Edward and Elizabeth Austen, was Austen's oldest niece (a few months older than Anna, also born in 1793). Fanny's diaries show that she was closer to her older aunt, Cassandra, than to Jane, and wrote to her regularly.[9] However, in 1813, the year Fanny turned twenty, Edward brought his family to stay at the Chawton great house. During the summer Fanny records '*interesting*' conversations and 'delicious' private meetings with her younger aunt. The main subject of their discussions seems to have been Mr John Plumptre, whose inconclusive romance with Fanny continued for some time and was the topic of correspondence between Jane and Fanny in November 1814.

Fanny and Jane also had music in common. Jane's letters to Cassandra register this interest in 1811 when she begins sending messages to be relayed to Fanny. From London in April 1811, she writes about the plans for a party at Henry and Eliza's house. Describing the music, she says, 'Fanny will listen to this. One of the Hirelings, is a Capital on the Harp, from which I expect great pleasure' (*Letters*, p. 180). After the event she wrote, 'The Music was extremely good – it opened (tell Fanny) with 'Prike pe parp pin praise pof Prapela' (*Letters*, p. 183) – a song that was clearly something of a joke between them. The title is actually 'O strike the harp in praise of Bragela', and this song, a trio for two sopranos and a bass by R. J. S. Stevens, can be found among the manuscript music of Fanny's mother Elizabeth Austen.

Fanny was a harpist, though it is not known when she began to learn the instrument. In the *Family record* it is noted that Fanny 'hired a harp from Chappells in New Bond Street and arranged for a music-master, Mr Meyer, to call and instruct her' when she was visiting London in November 1815. By this time she had already been learning the harp for at least a year: Austen wrote in a letter of 18–20 November 1814 that 'Miss Lloyd … desires her love. – She is very happy to hear of your learning the Harp' (*Letters*, p. 281), which implies that Fanny's harp lessons had only recently begun, and also signals Martha's interest in music. In the previous year, in July 1813, when she was staying at Chawton House, Fanny reported that 'Miss Lloyd came in the morng. to hear me play'. Presumably, as Julienne Gehrer notes in her introduction to *Martha Lloyd's household book*, she was playing the piano on this occasion, having not yet started learning the harp.[10]

In November 1813, when Austen was staying at Godmersham, they visited the Wildman family at nearby Chilham Castle. Mr James Wildman was at that time taking 'an admiring interest in Fanny',[11] and Austen acutely observed that 'Fanny & Miss Wildman played, & Mr James Wildman sat close by & listened, or pretended to listen' (*Letters*, p. 251). The potential for music to play a part in romance, often a feature of Austen's fiction, occurs again in Austen's delighted description of an evening in London when the musical Mr Haden was attending Henry, both as a medical man and as a dinner guest, in November 1815. She writes that 'from 7 to 8 the Harp' – Fanny playing and perhaps, as had happened a few days earlier, Mr Haden 'suggesting improvements' – and then at 8 o'clock two other guests arrived, sitting 'on the sopha side' with Jane and Henry, while 'On the opposite side Fanny & Mr Haden in two chairs (I *believe* at least they had *two* chairs) talking together uninterruptedly. – Fancy the scene! And what is to be fancied next?' (*Letters*, p. 301). According to the authors of the *Family record*, Cassandra was alarmed at the possibility of romance between Mr Haden, a mere apothecary, and her precious niece, and Jane had to placate her in her next letter (*Family record*, p. 206). In any event, although both aunt and niece admired Charles Haden, he remained just a friend. Fanny eventually married a widower, Sir Edward Knatchbull, MP for Kent, twelve years her senior, in 1820.

One of the letters that Fanny wrote to her aunt Jane in November 1814 about John Plumptre was smuggled in a parcel of music delivered by her father Edward: Fanny seems to have wanted to keep this correspondence a secret from Cassandra. We do not know what particular pieces of music Fanny sent on this occasion, but the fact that it was a way for the two of them to communicate in secret indicates to what extent the musical bond excluded other members of the family. In early 1817 Fanny had written again, this time about James Wildman, and Austen responded with a delighted, interested, confidential letter. Perhaps Fanny had used the same subterfuge again, as towards the end of the letter Austen writes, 'Much obliged for the Quadrilles, which I am grown to think pretty enough, though of course they are inferior to the Cotillions of my own day' (*Letters*, p. 330). The coolness of this message, taken out of context, is not reflected in the warmth of the rest of the letter. It could be just Austen's rueful acknowledgement of the passing of her now distant dancing days of twenty years earlier. The cotillon, sometimes anglicised, as in Austen's letter, to 'cotil-lion', was a French square dance for four couples. According to Allison Thompson, 'Cotillons fell out of favor in England in the 1790s but remerged [*sic*] roughly fifteen years later reconfigured into the quadrille'.[12]

As Jeanice Brooks points out, the device of sending a letter secretly by means of a parcel of music 'has obvious parallels with the transmission of Robert Martin's letter to Harriet Smith in *Emma* (ch. 7): the young farmer puts his marriage proposal into a parcel of songs that his sister Elizabeth had borrowed from Harriet for copying'.[13] Perhaps Fanny's 'admirable device' (*Letters*, p. 281) in communicating under cover of music was too good not to be used in the novel.

These are not the only instances of their sharing music. As discussed in Chapter 1, in one of the music books that contains mainly manuscripts in Austen's own handwriting, there are songs scattered through the book in different handwriting, and Fanny is probably one of the scribes.

Martha Lloyd

Fanny undertook a commission for Martha Lloyd on a trip to London in September 1813. Austen wrote to Cassandra:

> Fanny desires me to tell Martha with her kind Love that Birchall assured her there was no 2^{d} set of Hook's Lessons for Beginners – & that by my advice, she has therefore chosen her a set by another Composer. I thought she w^{d} rather have something than not. (*Letters*, p. 224)[14]

As mentioned earlier, exchanges like this seem to contradict Caroline's assertion that nobody else in the household 'cared for' music. It implies that Martha Lloyd was learning to play the piano, and probably already had a copy of James Hook's first set of *Guida di musica* intended 'for beginners on the piano forte or harpsichord'. Music had been part of Martha's life since childhood: 'Singing was part of the Lloyd home and Martha and Eliza were remembered as having particularly good voices'.[15] These traces of Martha beyond her cooking and household management are fascinating but fugitive, and most of them were recorded by Caroline Austen in her *Reminiscences*, written in the early 1870s. Martha was Caroline's aunt on her mother's side, and Caroline relates her grandparents' inferred attitude to female accomplishments: 'if music had been desired, I suppose it would not have been very easy to find an instructor. For singing, none was thought needful. If girls had good voices, they *would* sing, like the birds, by nature, so what would be the use of teaching them?'[16] Caroline remarks that she often heard 'old-fashioned people regret that such or such a one had had a singing-master – she sang so much better before!'[17] It would be interesting to know whether the Austens shared this opinion. There is reason to believe that Jane Austen had a piano teacher, but no one, to my knowledge, has ever mentioned a singing teacher.

The Austen family music collection

The Austen family music collection allows us to construct a slightly different version of Jane Austen's network of influences and relationships – not necessarily contradicting what is generally believed, but perhaps changing the emphasis. Several of the books belonged to, or are closely associated with, Austen herself, as discussed in the previous chapter, but there are others she would have known from visiting among the extended family and others still which she would probably never have seen.

When the Austens left the Steventon Parsonage in 1801, among the furniture, china and kitchen utensils offered for sale was a 'piano forte in a handsome case (by Ganer)' along with 'a large collection of music of the most celebrated composers'.[18] There is no record of what was in this music collection. However, eighteen sheet music albums survive, along with some separate sheets of music, in the Austen family music books collection, digitised by Southampton University and available on the Internet Archive.[19] It has been established that at least seven of these volumes belonged to Austen herself, but the other eleven appear to have belonged to members of her extended family. There are also two surviving volumes that belonged to the Rice family, descended from Lizzy Austen Rice, which are held in the Blackie House Library and Museum in Edinburgh.

The relationships implied in the surviving music collection are all among the female members of the family. The earliest music belonged to Ann Cawley, while other books belonged to Austen's cousin Eliza, née Hancock, who married her brother Henry in 1797; to Elizabeth Bridges, married to Edward Austen (later Austen Knight); and to Eleanor Jackson, who married Henry in 1820, after Eliza's death in 1813. The latest volumes belonged to Edward and Elizabeth's youngest two daughters, Louisa (born 1804) and Cassandra (born 1806).

Ann Cawley, née Cooper

The family link between the Austens and Ann Cawley is somewhat labyrinthine. The two Leigh sisters (whose older brother was James Leigh Perrot) both married clergymen. Jane, the elder, married the Rev. Edward Cooper; Cassandra, the younger, married George Austen and they became Jane Austen's parents.

Edward Cooper had a sister, Ann, who married Ralph Cawley in 1768. Ralph and Ann had no children of their own, and the Rev. Cawley, the principal of Brasenose College in Oxford, died in 1777. Mrs Cawley, then in her mid-forties, enters Jane Austen's story in 1783 when the young Austen sisters were sent to study with her in Oxford, along with their cousin Jane, the daughter of Edward and Jane Cooper. 'Mr. Austen's bank account shows payments to Mrs Cawley of £30 in April of that year and £10 in September 1783.'[20] It appears that Mrs Cawley was not running a school as such, but tutoring the three girls in her home.

For some reason which has not been established, she took the girls to Southampton later in 1783. Both the Austen girls caught a fever and their cousin Jane Cooper wrote to her mother with the news. Both mothers – Austen and Cooper – travelled to Southampton and retrieved the girls. Although there is a family tradition that Jane Austen 'was in grave danger',[21] the young ones all survived. But Jane Cooper the elder died, leaving her husband, Ann Cawley's brother Edward Cooper, a grieving widower with two young children.

Ann Cawley died in 1787. There are suggestions that it was her negligence that caused this chain of events. Her brother 'perhaps found himself unable to forgive her for the actions that led to the death of his beloved wife' and there may have been an estrangement between them.[22] However, he was her executor and therefore had the task of distributing her goods – including, presumably, the two music books that ended up in the Austen music collections.

Austen's musical relationships

Previously, opinions have varied as to the original owner of these two books, which appear to share the same handwriting. The collection had been arbitrarily divided up in the nineteenth century, and only half of the collection was generally available to researchers until the twenty-first century.[23] The book that was known to earlier researchers such as Patrick Piggott, and Gammie and McCulloch, had no ownership information and they assumed, presumably on the basis of its vintage, that it belonged to Cassandra Leigh, Jane's mother. However, when the collection came together again, the other book, clearly matching in handwriting, style of repertoire and vintage, was discovered to have 'Ann Cooper' written in the front. It is logical therefore to conclude that both these books were hers.[24]

Jeanice Brooks writes that these books 'were originally copied in the mid-1750s by Ann Cawley', and she brought them out again when she began teaching:

> Mrs Cawley apparently used her old music copybooks to provide musical instruction, noting dates in the early 1780s for lessons, payments and harpsichord tuning. Both books contain pages of practice music writing, some fairly accomplished, as if made by a child already reasonably skilled with a pen, while others were done by a younger writer – possibly the 7-year-old Jane – whose entries are both musically nonsensical and graphically inexpert in writing of any kind.[25]

The three girls presumably all had some musical tuition from Mrs Cawley. One could speculate that Jane Austen took to music more naturally than the other two and that the books were therefore given to her, either by Mrs Cawley or by her brother after her death. Cassandra seems not to have been a performer, whatever her attitude to music, and if Jane

Cooper were musical it seems more likely that her father, the Rev. Edward Cooper, would have given the books to her. There are of course many other possibilities among a family network like this: all we can say is that Austen is likely to have known these books and they may have introduced her to the works of Handel, Boyce, Arne and other composers from the earlier part of the eighteenth century whose music they contained.

Eliza, née Hancock, who married Austen's brother Henry

In 1792, the year Austen turned seventeen, Eliza de Feuillide, who was staying at Steventon with the Austen family, wrote to their mutual cousin Philadelphia Walter:

> Cassandra & Jane are both very much grown (The latter is now taller than myself) and greatly improved as well in Manners as in Person … They are I think equally sensible, and both so to a degree seldom met with, but still My Heart gives the preference to Jane, whose kind partiality to me, indeed requires a return of the same nature. (*Family record*, p. 71)

That this was in part a musical friendship is demonstrated by the fact that Austen borrowed some music from Eliza and copied it into her own manuscript book – a book which Eliza might have given her, as Jeanice Brooks suggests.[26] It seems that Eliza had already been responsible for introducing a piano into the Steventon household. In a letter of December 1786, Mrs Austen mentions that they have borrowed a pianoforte for 'Madame' – Eliza – who was visiting with her mother and her son Hastings: 'she plays to us every day', and, the *Family record* continues, 'thereafter one was acquired on a more permanent basis' (*Family record*, pp. 53, 55), although it is not known exactly when. What is certain is that a pianoforte made by Christopher Ganer was sold in the auction when the family left Steventon in 1801.[27] Ganer was an instrument maker based in London from the 1770s until about 1809.

In Chapter 3 ('Jane Austen and the music of the French Revolution') I discuss the probable influence of Eliza on the French music that Austen knew, and how it formed one source of her information about the events in France. At the very least it shows how Austen knew very well what was happening, despite not mentioning it explicitly in her novels.

There are two books of music that belonged to Eliza in the collection, both of music printed in France. Much of it is in the form of periodical publications dating from the 1780s, containing arrangements for harp or keyboard instruments of recent arias and instrumental music from the French theatrical works. Some of the music in these books is copied into Austen's own manuscript albums, and it is likely that at least some of the other French repertoire in her albums originated from copies belonging to Eliza.

The musical friendship between Jane and Eliza continued into adulthood. When *Sense and sensibility* was published in 1811, Eliza organised a musical party to celebrate her cousin's achievement: according to E. J. Clery,

> For Henry and Eliza, Jane's authorial debut was cause enough to celebrate. ... Jane told Cassandra that the musical party arose from a dinner invitation to a couple of their friends. It could have nothing to do with the forthcoming novel, because she had sworn the family to secrecy over her authorship. But Henry was bursting with pride.[28]

Figure 2.1 'Air du Marquis de Tulipano' by Giovanni Paisiello from Austen's manuscript book 'Songs and Duetts'

Eliza, although not in the best of health, went to great efforts to 'stage-manage' the event, decorating the house and engaging excellent musicians for the occasion. Jane, not always impressed by musical entertainment, reported to Cassandra that the music was 'extremely good ... Between the songs were lessons on the harp, or harp and piano forte together' (*Letters*, p. 183) – 'lessons' clearly, here, not having any educational connotations but simply meaning instrumental solos or duets.

Jane was staying with Henry and Eliza in London at this time, and shortly after the party they visited their French friends, the émigré Comte d'Antraigues and his family.

The son was a gifted musician, and Austen reported to Cassandra that 'Count Julien's performance is very wonderful' (*Letters*, p. 185).

Jane's fondness for Eliza was not universal within the broader family circle. There were jealousies and rivalries and rifts between the brothers and their families. Jane tried to encourage her oldest nieces to visit Eliza and befriend her, but the family prejudice, it seems, was too strong to be overcome, and, as Clery writes, Anna's refusal to visit the London household in 1811 'increased Eliza's sense of alienation from the Austen cousins who were once so dear to her. She almost never accompanied Henry on his many visits to Godmersham and when she did, she felt she was there merely on sufferance.'[29] Caroline Austen, recording Eliza's death in 1813 in her *Reminiscences*, says 'I do not remember that I ever saw her',[30] which may be another hint of a family rift between the James and Henry Austen families. Jane, however, usually seems to have been able to enjoy the company of all her relatives without taking sides in their disputes, while observing their differences in sometimes cryptic allusions in her letters to Cassandra.

Elizabeth Bridges, married to Edward Austen (later Austen Knight)

Elizabeth Bridges was born in 1773, and so was only a little older than Austen. She was the daughter of Sir Brook Bridges of Goodnestone Park, and the contents of her music collection indicates a more expensive formal education than the Austen sisters had been afforded. Elizabeth went to 'a grand girls' boarding school in Queen Square, Bloomsbury, London, known as "the ladies' Eton"', according to Valerie Grosvenor Myer. However, the main item on the curriculum was etiquette, along with 'French, music and dancing'.[31] She married Edward in 1791.

The music that survives from Elizabeth's collection consists of two books and some loose sheets. One book contains seven separately published items bound together in an album labelled 'Cembalo' – the German word for harpsichord. These are all instrumental pieces, rather than songs, including a set of six sonatas by the English composer Maria Hester Park, née Reynolds (1760–1813) and Franz Kotzwara's 'programmatic sonata' 'The Battle of Prague' – Austen also had a copy of this popular piece of programme music in her personal collection. In addition to these, the album contains pieces by Nicolo Piccinni, Ignaz Pleyel, Ernst Eichner and other European composers. However, all were published in London probably between 1767 and the early 1790s. Most of them are labelled as suitable for either the harpsichord – which by the 1790s was becoming an old-fashioned instrument – or piano-forte – the more up-to-date option that most young women would play. This confirms that these editions were published in the transitional years, when Elizabeth would have been at school. Many of the pieces are signed with Elizabeth's maiden name (Elizabeth Bridges).

The other book is later and more miscellaneous, containing mainly songs and operatic arias and duets, both English and Italian. On the inside of the front cover it is signed 'Eliz'th Austen, August 17th 1799', and all the music is copied by hand. Along with the more serious music (which includes pieces by both Mozart and Haydn) there is a set of nursery rhymes by James Hook. Elizabeth's first child, Fanny, was born in 1793, which might explain their presence. Notably, the song 'O strike the harp in praise of Bragela' by R. J. S. Stevens is in this book. This song is immortalised, as we have seen, in Jane's letter to Cassandra (from London to Godmersham) describing Henry and Eliza's party in April 1811 at which this song was performed (*Letters*, p. 183). This seems to confirm that Jane was familiar with Elizabeth's music collection, and that it was also shared with Elizabeth's daughter Fanny to the extent that this song had become something of a joke between them. Elizabeth died in October 1808, and appears to have continued to transcribe songs into this book until shortly before her death, going by the dates of publication of the items copied.

Among this miscellany is a much greater proportion of Italian vocal music than in Austen's own collection. But despite her more sophisticated education, Elizabeth was not above playing country dances for impromptu balls. Austen mentions a 'ball' at Goodnestone (Elizabeth's family's estate, near Godmersham) in September 1796 where four couples danced 'two Country Dances & the Boulangeries', and specifies that Elizabeth played one of the country dances and Lady Bridges (her mother) the other (*Letters*, p. 8). Not included in the digitisation project is another album of manuscript vocal music which belonged to Elizabeth, now known as 'Rice 1', as described in Chapter 1, which contains a miscellany of music including many composers and some items that appear elsewhere in the collection. It is recorded that 'Jane Austen visited Godmersham Park on six occasions over a fifteen-year period, from 1798 to 1813'.[32] Before 1808 she visited along with her parents and Cassandra, but in 1808 and 1813 she went alone. It was presumably during these visits that Austen copied four items into Elizabeth's album of vocal music.

However, Cassandra was a more frequent visitor at Godmersham. Anna Lefroy wrote in her 1864 memoir that Elizabeth was 'not really fond of her [Jane]; at least that she very much preferred the elder Sister [Cassandra]' (*Memoir*, p. 158). In early 1799 Jane was at home at Steventon and Cassandra was at Godmersham Park with Elizabeth and Edward. In a letter of 8–9 January Austen wrote, 'Elizabeth is very cruel about my writing Music; – and as punishment for her, I should insist upon always writing out all hers for her in future, if I were not punishing myself at the same time' (*Letters*, p. 33). This remark – shorn of any explanatory context, as is so much of the correspondence between the sisters – might trouble some readers, but of course we have no idea at all what Elizabeth's remark had been. It might have been not on the quality of the handwriting but on some other aspect entirely. And in any case, although for the most part her musical hand was neat – as neat as it needed to be for any particular purpose – she was not a flawless musical copyist.

Elizabeth's death in October 1808, following the birth of her eleventh child, was a huge shock to the family: Austen's flippant letter-writing style disappears for a few weeks afterwards. She wrote to Cassandra, who was at Godmersham, that she felt for all of them, especially Elizabeth's widower, 'for dearest Edward, whose loss & whose suffering seem to make those of every other person nothing. – God be praised! That you can say what you do of him – that he has a religious Mind to bear him up, & a Disposition that will gradually lead him to comfort' (*Letters*, p. 146). She was fond of all her brothers, but mentions Edward's happy disposition several times in her letters. Edward never remarried and died in 1852.

Eleanor Jackson, who married Henry in 1820, after Eliza's death in 1813

Eleanor Jackson was the eldest daughter of Henry and Sarah Jackson, and Sarah's brother, the Rev. J. R. Papillon, was the rector of Chawton. She probably met Jane Austen in 1812 when visiting her aunt and uncle. Austen mentions Miss Jackson in a letter to Cassandra, implying, Clery notes, 'that she seemed intelligent and capable of being witty'.[33] They met again when Jane was visiting Henry in London in October 1815, but although they clearly enjoyed each other's company they were not close friends and Clery does not mention a musical connection.

There are two books in the Austen family collections which apparently belonged to Eleanor Jackson, and which Jane Austen is not likely to have been familiar with. One of them contains printed music published between about 1795 and 1810, including two pieces of music dedicated to her mother, Sarah. According to the description on the Internet Archive, 'the book was likely bound for Eleanor, second wife of Jane Austen's brother Henry Austen, whom she married in 1820, and contains music she obtained before her marriage (including music inherited from or given by her mother)'. This book contains reprints of many songs which, although published towards the end of the eighteenth century, are by earlier composers including Handel (1685–1750) and even Henry Purcell (1659–1695), along with more recent compositions. The other book contains instrumental music, for harp or piano, solo or duet, dating from slightly later but still before her marriage to Henry.

Several of these more recent works in the song book are by composers who also feature in Austen's own music books.

It seems that, had Austen survived and got to know Eleanor better, they would have been kindred spirits, musically and in other ways.

Lizzy Austen Knight, Edward and Elizabeth's second daughter

Lizzy Austen was born in 1800, the sixth child and second daughter of Edward and Elizabeth. Her sister Marianne was born the following year. She contributed to the manuscript volume known as Rice 1 which belonged to her mother, and Rice 2 is entirely in her hand. Neither of these albums is included in the 2015 digitisation project, and they are held in the Blackie House Library and Museum in Edinburgh.[34] According to the bookseller's description, Lizzy's album contains 'approximately one hundred and fifty pieces, all in the hand of Jane Austen's niece, Elizabeth Austen Knight, including works by Auber, Haydn, Rossini, Rousseau, Sarti, and Weber, and a number of compositions by George Augusta Hill (husband of Jane's god-daughter, Louisa Austen Knight), and George Cholmeley Oxenden (brother of Mary Oxenden, a friend of Fanny and Lizzy Austen Knight). The paper is watermarked 1818.'[35] This date makes it clear that her aunt Jane would not have been familiar with this album.

However, Lizzy is mentioned several times in Austen's letters. As discussed above, she was in London with her sisters Fanny and Marianne in September 1813 and they all went to the theatre with the family party on two consecutive nights. In the following month, Jane was staying at Godmersham with the Edward Austen Knight family, and the thirteen-year-old Lizzy wrote a joint letter to her aunt Cassandra with her aunt

Jane, who began her section, 'I think Lizzy's letter will entertain you', and with good reason: Lizzy's letter is both sympathetic and amusing in a way that is reminiscent of her aunt Jane. She responds to the news she has heard from Cassandra and adds news of her own, deftly bringing in dialect words she has heard and making shrewd observations about a cast of characters obviously familiar to them both (*Letters*, p. 242).

Austen had played at least a small part in Lizzy's education. During her visit to Godmersham in 1808, Jane had helped Elizabeth, then 'imminently expecting her 11th child' (*Family record*, p. 149), by 'hear[ing] Lizzy read' (*Letters*, p. 137). Lizzy married Edward Rice in 1818, and had fifteen children. The two manuscripts books known as Rice 1 and 2 were passed down through this branch of the family.

Louisa and Cassandra Austen Knight, Edward and Elizabeth's youngest two daughters

It is also extremely unlikely that Austen had any knowledge of the collection of dances in the manuscript book of her young nieces Louisa and Cassandra. Inside the front cover is written 'Cassandra Jane Knight, October 2d, 1823' and 'Louisa Knight, April 24th, 1824'. It seems likely that the book was not in existence during Austen's lifetime, as neither hand is that of a child – Louisa and Cassandra were born in 1804 and 1806 respectively, so were in their late teens when they inscribed the book and presumably began copying.

The items in this book were not individually described in my cataloguing project because of the difficulty in identifying most of the pieces. Few have a more specific title than 'Waltz' or 'Allemande' – and interestingly, there are a couple of cotillons.

Louisa and Cassandra were the goddaughters of their aunts Jane and Cassandra respectively. Austen displays an affectionate relationship with both of them in her letters to her sister Cassandra. Writing from Godmersham in September 1813, she adds a postscript, presumably quoting their niece's own words: 'Louisa's best Love & a Hundred Thousand Million Kisses' (*Letters*, p. 228). Later, writing to Fanny in February 1817, she expresses her relief at hearing that young Cassandra 'should be so recovered!', presumably from a serious illness, and she adds 'I can easily believe she was very patient & very good. I always loved Cassandra, for her fine dark eyes & sweet temper' (*Letters*, p. 329). In the letter the senior Cassandra wrote to Fanny after Austen's death, she informed her of some bequests to be made to Fanny herself, and to 'her God-daughter Louisa', who was to have one of her gold chains. Louisa, in later life Lady George Hill, is said to have recounted to a friend that 'Miss Austen's sister Cassandra tried to persuade her to alter the end of Mansfield Park and let Mr. Crawford marry Fanny Price'. They argued about it, 'but Miss Austen stood firmly and would not allow the change' (*Family record*, p. 248). Louisa also recalled seeing Austen dressing for dinner one night at Godmersham: 'She had large dark eyes and a brilliant complexion, and long, long black hair down to her knees' (*Family Record*, p. 184). Louisa would have been eight years old at the time. Such eyewitness memories of Austen are rare and precious. However, the two young nieces do not seem to have recorded any musical memories of their aunt.

Conclusion

This network of musical memories and memorabilia provides some possible points of contact across the extended family and across generations from which we can attempt to construct a partial portrait of Austen's musical life and that of her circle. From Ann Cawley's manuscript copies of arias and harpsichord music by Handel and William Boyce, to Louisa and young Cassandra's waltzes and cotillons, the music collection as a whole presents a history of the music popular during a period of seventy or eighty years which more than encompassed Austen's life.

We cannot know with any certainty how all these musical relationships operated. Did Austen's evident liking for the music of Thomas Arne arise from her introduction to his songs by Ann Cawley? Did Louisa and young Cassandra hear about Austen's fond memories of 'the Cotillions of my own day' (*Letters*, p. 330) from their older sister Fanny, and make a point of including some of these dances, by now out of fashion and displaced by the quadrille, in their collection?

We are on firmer territory with the relations between Eliza de Feuillide and Jane, whose musical friendship is recorded in several ways, not only in their sheet music collections. But although these physical traces are eloquent, the memories recorded by Anna Lefroy and Caroline Austen in their later years allow us no doubt that music was a continuing part of Austen's life, and perhaps the letters between Caroline and her aunt are the most poignant of all: 'The Piano Forte often talks of you. ... *You* are really its' constant theme' (*Letters*, p. 326).

3

Jane Austen and the music of the French Revolution[1]

France and Britain

On 1 February 1793, when Jane Austen was seventeen, France declared war on Great Britain. The Revolutionary War turned into the Napoleonic Wars, and they continued with only a brief interval until Napoleon's final defeat at Waterloo in 1815. The Anglo-French war of 1778–1783 had taken place during her childhood, so France was the sworn enemy of Britain for well over half of Austen's lifetime.

Four years earlier, in 1789, 'forces were unleashed in France that set that nation and every nation of the western world on a different course',[2] and although she never mentioned the Revolution in her novels or her correspondence, Austen was inevitably affected by those upheavals. Kathryn Sutherland points out that 'we might say she was war-conditioned – wartime was the ordinary, everyday time of her adult life'.[3] Two of her brothers, Frank and Charles, were officers in the

Austen and the music of the French Revolution

British Navy and took part in the wars with France in Europe and the West Indies, and another, Henry, was in the militia for five years during the 1790s.

Britain's relationship with France was not, however, a simple one of enmity. In Jane Austen's life, as in the life of many of her contemporaries, France and French culture were a significant influence. Every well-educated young person would learn French. As Nicola McLelland writes,

> After the Norman conquest in 1066, French – initially the language of the conquerors and the elite who collaborated with them – became, over the course of generations, the first foreign language and language of prestige for those outside the clerical education system. Britain's continuing close ties with neighbouring France and France's cultural pre-eminence in Europe for centuries have kept French as the 'first' foreign language for most British children ever since.[4]

Noël Riley points out that even in the early nineteenth century, at 'its lowest ebb', the education of a 'lady' would typically involve learning 'to sing, play the piano or harp, to sketch and to speak French, sometimes German ... and occasionally Italian'.[5]

Despite the cultural prestige of the French language, anti-French sentiment was common enough in England at the time. James Austen, Jane's eldest brother, wrote an essay in the April 1789 issue of his magazine *The loiterer* which deprecates the animosity between the two peoples: 'I must lament the prevalence, and would diminish the force of a passion, which interrupts the harmony of nations, and damps the warmth of private friendship, which robs peace of its dearest blessings, and adds new horrors to the frowns of war'.[6]

Despite what he no doubt believed to be his enlightened views, in his essay James nevertheless reinforces many stereotypes: English thuggery versus French dishonesty; English dullness versus French frivolity and so on. Lucy Worsley notes that, although 'in 1789 many Britons ... welcomed the news of the storming of the Bastille ... within a year, doubt had set in as the consequences became clearer'. Worsley quotes Anna Seward, who had revised her initial enthusiasm: 'O, that the French had possessed the wisdom of knowing Where To Stop'.[7] As James Austen implies, in these two countries with such long-entwined histories, personal and intellectual ties between individuals across the channel were common. The Revolutionary government of France was waging war not only on foreign countries but on counter-revolutionaries within France, and sympathy with those who had a personal stake in the outcome of the extraordinary events taking place there could override – or reinforce – any ideological position.

Eliza Hancock

Austen's paternal aunt Philadelphia Hancock, with her daughter Eliza, settled in Paris in 1779. In 1781 Eliza married a 'young Captain in the Queen's Regiment of Dragoons, Jean-François Capot de Feuillide, from Nérac, in the province of Guienne', who claimed the title of 'Comte' (*Family record*, p. 34). De Feuillide fell foul of the Revolutionary government and died by the guillotine in February 1794. Eliza survived and went on to marry Jane's older brother Henry. She often stayed with the Austens during the 1780s and 1790s and Jane knew her well.

Eliza was fourteen years older than Jane. She was the dedicatee of Austen's brief 1790 juvenile 'novel in letters' 'Love and freindship'. In Chapter 2 I discuss Eliza's friendship with Jane and her place within the extended Austen family: 'Jane was much impressed by Eliza's charm and cosmopolitan vivacity, and this initial childish admiration grew into a steady and affectionate adult friendship that lasted' until Eliza died in 1813 (*Family record*, p. 54).

France in Austen's life and work

Music was important to both women, and for Austen it was a form of artistic expression that ran alongside, and in some ways intersected with, her literary career. Austen was certainly familiar with a range of French songs, but her interest in France is somewhat muted in her novels. Mary Spongberg writes that Austen's novels, unlike those of some of her female contemporaries, were 'neither complaisant nor oblivious to the events in France', documenting 'the localized effect of the Revolution as experienced by Britons, buffeted by time lags in news, the vagaries of the postal service, and a real sense of distance from the action on the Continent'. She goes on to point out that

> early observers of Austen's fiction understood her to be deliberately eschewing the literary heritage of France. As a critical tradition evolved around her in the nineteenth century however, a myth of an 'unconscious' Austen emerged. This 'unconscious' Austen lived through one of the most dramatic periods in history, yet according to her biographers had 'absolutely nothing' to say about the 'great strifes of war and policy which so disquieted Europe'.[8]

This view of Austen as 'unconscious' of wars and politics is now thoroughly discredited, to the extent that Kathryn Sutherland can write that 'Jane Austen is the first English novelist to explore the effect of contemporary war on the home front'.[9]

To become aware of this exploration in her novels takes a degree of close attention to detail, as well as some sophisticated historical awareness. For example, as Sutherland points out, *Persuasion* was written in 1815 but set in 1814 – written after, but set before, Waterloo. It is 'Austen's most time-stamped novel. … In the real and fictional summer of 1814 … peace looked secure. … The resumption of conflict, and with it the threat of loss, lie just beyond the novel's frame. In *Persuasion*, through Anne Elliot's quiet characterisation, Austen offers her most subtle domestic mediation on war's cost', ensuring (for the contemporary reader) 'the poignant understanding that, like peace, happiness is fragile and not without risk'.[10]

Warren Roberts complains about 'the paucity of biographical evidence' of Austen's knowledge of the French Revolution, given that it is mentioned neither in her correspondence nor in her fiction.[11] It is unfortunate that her music collection was not generally available to researchers in the 1970s when he undertook his study of Austen's response to the Revolutionary age. As I have suggested, clearer evidence about Austen's interest in, and awareness of, current events in France is to be found there. Paul F. Rice writes, 'rarely has the relationship between society, politics and the performing arts been closer' in Britain than in the early years of Revolutionary France.[12] As I show in Chapter 4, this relationship manifested itself in public theatres and concert halls, but was also evident in the music of the drawing room.

Doomed queens

One striking feature among the music Austen chose to write out, presumably for herself to perform, is the juxtaposition of several songs in the volume of thirty-seven items (mainly songs) dating from the early to middle 1790s – her later teenage years. No. 29 in this manuscript book is a ballad titled 'Captivity', first published in 1793. The title on the printed version is 'Captivity: a ballad supposed to be sung by the unfortunate Marie-Antoinette during her imprisonment in the Temple. The words by the Revd. Mr Jeans ... Set by Stephen Storace.'

This song is one of several composed by English musicians about Queen Marie Antoinette at the time.[13] In his lyrics, the Hampshire-based Anglican minister Joshua Jeans provided a lurid and disquieting imagining of Marie Antoinette's agony and distress before her execution in 1793, set in the first person:

> How dread the horrors of this place!
> In every treacherous guard I trace
> The dark design, the ruffian face,
> Amid this sad captivity.[14]

Later verses weep over 'my babes [who] lie hushed in sleep, In briny tears their couch I steep', and imagine 'My murdered Lord ... The headless trunk, the bosom gor'd'. The composer, Stephen Storace, was born in England of Italian parentage. He knew Mozart in Vienna, and was clearly one of Austen's favourites: several of his compositions appear among her manuscripts. Most are from comic opera and are lighter in nature: 'Captivity' is among the most moving and dramatic of his works, despite its simplicity of form. Whatever one's political views on the monarchy and the revolution might be, it is impossible to sing 'Captivity' without entering into the feelings of the woman who is expressing in such starkly effective music the predicament she finds herself in. I imagine it would be even more harrowing for someone who lived at the time these events were taking place, especially when she had close relatives who were involved.

Immediately after this ballad in Austen's music manuscript comes Tommaso Giordani's 1782 arrangement of the traditional Scottish air 'Queen Mary's lamentation', discussed in Chapter 7. The links between these two ballads, one about Queen Marie Antoinette and the other about Mary Queen of Scots, both in captivity, awaiting violent death at the hands of their political enemies, are emphasised by their juxtaposition in Austen's manuscript book. Spongberg claims that, in 'The history of England',

> while Burke predicted the disastrous fate of Marie Antoinette and sought to utilize the horror of her captivity to convince Protestant England to support Catholic France, Austen resists Burke's chivalric understanding of history, drawing attention to another ill-fated queen from France, anticipating the vindication of Mary Stuart, and other ill-fated queens, in the works of writers such as Mary Hays and Elizabeth Benger.[15]

Could the twinning of these two ballads in Austen's manuscript complicate this picture further? Storace's restrained setting of Jeans's rather melodramatic words creates a sympathetic and moving portrait of the doomed French queen, and it is at least conceivable that copying 'Captivity' into her manuscript book reminded Austen of the earlier ballad about Mary Stuart, which she then sought out and copied immediately afterwards. As Spongberg points out, in 'The history of England', Austen 'draws attention to what Burke's account of England's transition from Catholic past to Protestant present suppresses, that the violence of this transition was largely played out upon the bodies of women'.[16] The evidence of her music book seems to indicate a link in Austen's mind between these two women, and thus a link between the current violence in France and England's violent history.

Contemporary France in Austen's music collection

There is another song with a rather poignant French royal connection in Austen's scrapbook volume. The words and music of the 1789 chanson 'Pauvre Jacques' are variously attributed to Jeanne-Renée de Bombelles, Marquise de Travenet (1753–1828), or to Marie Antoinette, although they may have been by her sister-in-law Madame Elisabeth. The song was inspired by a Swiss milkmaid who looked after the cows in the queen's dairy at Versailles, daily lamenting having left her fiancé behind in Switzerland.[17]

In later life, Austen's niece Caroline remembers her often singing and playing another song in French, a romance beginning 'Que j'aime à voir les hirondelles', which survives in the family collection in a book which had belonged to her cousin Eliza de Feuillide (*Memoir*, p. 193). This 1788 song, a setting by François Devienne of a romance from the pastoral novel *Estelle et Némorin* by Jean-Pierre Claris de Florian (1755–1794), also deals with the trope of captivity and death: a swallow captured by a cruel child and kept from its faithful lover will die 'd'ennui, de douleur et d'amour'.[18]

But lest we start thinking that Austen's sympathies lie exclusively with the victims of revolutions and wars, we should consider another song in this same music book. No. 25, 'The Marseilles March', otherwise known as 'The Marseillaise', was composed in April 1792 in support of the French war against Austria. Austen wrote out not just the music, both tune and simple accompaniment, but all six of Rouget de Lisle's verses. Two versions of the 'Marseillaise' were published in London in 1792. One, 'The Marseilles March', is listed in the English Stationers' Register on 23 October. It is subtitled 'as sung by the Marseillois going to battle', with English words beginning 'Ye sons of France awake to glory'. The other, with French words, was published the following month, with the title 'Marche des Marseillois or French Te Deum'.[19] While Austen's version is titled 'The Marseilles March', the lyrics she has copied are in French, so it is uncertain from what print source she was copying.

At the time of publication, England was not yet at war with France, so there was no patriotic reason why this song should not appeal to a young English woman. Although it is not certain when Austen copied it, a song composed in 1794 appears just a couple of pages before it in the manuscript book, so it seems likely that it was copied no earlier than that, when the two countries were at war – and after her cousin's husband had been executed by the French government. Paul Rice points out that 'after 1793, a composer would have to be viewed as unpatriotic (or worse) if he composed a movement based on a French revolutionary song'.[20] What about the teenage daughter of a Hampshire clergyman who copied 'The Marseillaise' into her manuscript book?

On the other hand, we have the 'Chanson Béarnoise'. The words of this song appear in a volume titled *Justification de M. de Favras*, published in Paris in 1791. The song was included as an appendix, because it had been adduced in evidence against Favras at his trial.[21] According to Wikipedia,

Thomas de Mahy, Marquis de Favras (March 26, 1744–February 19, 1790) was a French aristocrat and supporter of the House of

Bourbon during the French Revolution. Often seen as a martyr of the Royalist cause, Favras was executed for his part in 'planning against the people of France' and is known for saying 'I see that you have made three spelling mistakes' upon reading his death sentence.[22]

The words of the first verse of the Chanson run:

Un troubadour Béarnois, les yeux inondés de larmes,
A ses Montagnards chantoit, par un refrain, source d'alarmes,
Louis le fils de Henri est prisonnier dedans Paris.[23]

Louis was not literally the son of Henri – his father was the Dauphin, Louis – but he was descended from Henry IV, who was king of Béarn and Navarre in 1589 when he succeeded to the French throne. Along with the region's loyal feelings to the king himself, there could have been another reason for their opposition to the Revolution. The Parlement de Navarre et Béarn had been created in 1620 upon the region's incorporation into France by Louis XIII, but was disbanded after the Revolution, and the people of the region were thus deprived of their autonomy by the Revolutionary government.

The interesting thing about this song is that Jane Austen copied it into her manuscript book at around the same time as the other songs I have mentioned. It is hard to date this manuscript book exactly, but the contents up to that point in the book mostly seem to come from publications before 1795, the year Austen turned twenty. Of the thirty-seven songs in this manuscript book, eight are in French, composed by André Grétry, Egidio Duni, Giovanni Paisiello and Antoine Baudron, among others. There is one song in Italian and the rest are in English. 'The Marseilles March' and the 'Chanson Béarnoise' are distinctive, however, because of their overtly political nature – and because they come from different sides of the conflict.

How did these songs come to be among the music collection of the young daughter of an English country parson? The logical presumption is that she transcribed them from copies belonging to friends or relatives. This is simple enough with the songs we know to have been printed in England, like 'Captivity' and 'The Marseilles March'. The 'Chanson Béarnoise', however, as far as I can establish, does not appear to have been published in England. Perhaps her cousin Eliza had a copy with her on one of her visits in the early 1790s. In the Favras book there is a note below the words of the song, protesting that, as the song was printed and freely available on the streets of Paris, there was nothing suspicious about the fact that it was found among Favras's papers, since anyone could have obtained a copy.[24]

It is interesting that Austen included only the tune – no bass or keyboard accompaniment – but made sure of writing out the words of nine of the verses (five of which correspond to the Favras version). As with 'The Marseilles March', she seems to have been as interested in the words as in the music – perhaps even more so.

Austen and politics

The question of Austen's political sympathies has been hotly debated over the past decades, since the myth of her quietism has been debunked. Some, like Marilyn Butler in *Jane Austen and the war of ideas* (1987) assume Tory sympathies based on her family background, while Helena Kelly more recently wrote of her as a 'secret radical' in a 2017 book of that title. As Freya Johnston writes,

Austen and the music of the French Revolution

> Austen, depicted by her immediate family as a covert, dutiful, and domestically-minded writer, has since her death been serially repackaged by critics and imitators as a conservative and a radical, a prude and a saucepot, pro- and anti-colonial, a feminist and a downright bitch. Perhaps this fluidity and adaptability spring from her reluctance to be pigeonholed.[25]

In her parodic 'History of England', written in her mid-teens, Austen displays strong sympathy for Mary Queen of Scots and equally strong odium for Queen Elizabeth. As with her religious beliefs, however, the clues about her politics in her letters are ambiguous. What she writes to one correspondent might be contradicted by something she writes – ironically or not – to another. She is known to have detested the Prince Regent, later George IV, but she had dealings with his librarian, James Stanier Clarke, and dedicated *Emma* to the Prince at his suggestion. In her published fiction she does not give voice to any political passions and prejudices she may have felt. Mary Poovey writes that 'unlike her more radical peers, Austen did not want literary writing to be a political engine'.[26] Roberts believes that she was neither a conservative nor a radical, but that 'she hoped, as a member of the gentry, of traditional landed society, to see the members of her class adjust to a world that was changing before her, but also she was aware of their shortcomings. Neither attacking nor defending her class, she examined its chances of survival.'[27]

Austen's music books show her to have been interested in songs that embody or dramatise a character or point of view, and, looking at the contents of this particular manuscript book, it is tempting to believe that the attraction of songs like this lies in the staging of particular attitudes – that is, she valued the songs for their drama and ability to convey a mood, an emotion or a situation, rather than for their adherence to a particular point of view – which is, after all, what a novelist aims for. But the very presence of such songs in her music collection also demonstrates that she was far from unaware of events across the channel.

4

'These happy effects on the character of the British sailor': family life in sea songs of the late Georgian period[1]

Music and war

During the late Georgian period in Britain life at sea, and the love lives of sailors, provided singers and songwriters with an endless source of material. These songs may have been primarily thought of as entertainment, but in this age of war with France there was an implicit political agenda behind many of them. As Mark Philp writes, during the period 1793 to 1815 'the war was linked to an unprecedented level of national mobilization in which music and song played a major role'.[2] While some songs criticised the war, others aimed to recruit volunteers and encourage courageous and 'manly' behaviour.[3] Cheap printed copies of such songs were widely available, often subsidised by the government.[4] The recurrent theme of personal lives of sailors and their families in the songs reflects the pervasive influence of the continual state of war on the lives not only of the men serving in the military but also of their lovers, wives and children. These songs often make a direct appeal to patriotic duty and present a romantic ideal of the fidelity of both men and women.

The conflict between the Navy's voracious need for highly mobile manpower during this period of war and colonial expansion, and the social stability represented at home by marital fidelity and family cohesion, was not lost on the authorities. The utility of popular music in reconciling these aims was perceived at the highest levels. In 1803 the musician Charles Dibdin (1745–1814) was granted a government pension of £200 per annum in recognition of the importance of the songs he had been writing for decades. These songs had encouraged men to volunteer, and, equally importantly, reassured wives and sweethearts that their men would not only stay faithful while away, but would return. Dibdin's biographer, George Hogarth, writing in 1848, proposed 'that these happy effects on the character of the British sailor have been mainly caused by the Songs of Dibdin'.[5]

Songs sung on the streets and in the taverns would have reached all levels of society more readily than books and pamphlets. When songs were performed, their message could reach and influence anyone within earshot, even if they could not afford to purchase the printed ballad. As Gillian Russell writes, these songs, although often written for the theatre, were 'capable of reaching a wider audience than the usual range of playgoers, including the illiterate'.[6] However, although there were many straightforward stories of 'jolly tars' and 'old salts', there were also high-flown songs of love and duty presumably intended for the officer class.

In the first part of this chapter I look at why these ballads were important at this time, and the appeal they had to both sailors and officers, and their wives and lovers, in both the public and private spheres. In the second part, I survey a selection of songs by Dibdin and his contemporaries from music books belonging to Jane Austen and her family, to provide a 'snapshot' of the social background in which these songs were created and performed, and to consider their likely effects.

Life at sea: the Navy in the late Georgian era

During the eighteenth century, British military spending increased more than tenfold, reflecting a similar increase in military personnel. Life at sea was harsh and desertion rates were high. Mortality rates were also high. Seafaring was a perilous business in itself, due to shipwreck, drowning and disease. On top of this, as Niklas Frykman points out, 'war not only increased the demand for seamen, it also killed them by the tens of thousands'.[7] The consequences of this on the home front were profound, as large numbers of the male population of marriageable age were required to leave their families and risk their lives at sea. Marriage was the chief form of financial security for women at the time: as Jane Austen writes (perhaps not without irony) in *Pride and prejudice*, it was 'their pleasantest preservative from want' (*PP*, pp. 122–3). However, marrying a sailor or even a naval officer could mean a life of lonely destitution or hardship, especially if a woman had no family able or willing to support her.

Music has always been linked with military and maritime pursuits. There are marches and work songs, but equally societies have celebrated military victories and mourned fallen heroes in song. Folk music expresses the preoccupations of people of all classes and the most popular ballads reflect their 'anxieties

and recuperative responses'. Caroline Jackson-Houlston identifies two strands in British songs of the early nineteenth century:
'The loss of loved ones (almost always male sexual partners) ...
[and] the fear of military defeat, and even of possible invasion'.[8] While these songs were generally created by working-
class people for each other, there were 'moral and patriotic
pieces ... produced by those higher in society for propaganda
purposes'.[9] In his examination of how songs and ballads were
used to encourage men to enlist in the Navy, James Davey
points out that men who volunteered to go to sea 'were not
merely following simple narratives of unthinking duty; on the
contrary, they were individuals responding to complex motiva-
tions, community pressures and constructions of identity'.[10]

The power of song: ballads in the public sphere

As Russell writes, 'many nautical memoirs confirm [that] singing was one of the ways in which life on board a man-of-war
could be made tolerable, enlivening the sailor's recreational
moments as well as assisting him in his daily tasks'.[11]

Ballads, which would have been sung for recreation, should
be distinguished from sea shanties. Shanties are work songs,
'rhythmically fitted to the seafaring processes' and sung during
activities like 'pulling ropes or pushing the capstan', while 'the
true ballad is a narrative poem' – often, but not always, anonymous. The words of ballads (often referred to as 'songs' even
when separated from the music, or 'airs', they were set to)
were printed and sold in public places by ballad-sellers. They
often dealt with topical themes – recent news stories and current issues.[12] These broadsheets, or broadsides, were hugely

popular in the eighteenth century. 'There is a mass of evidence describing unnamed sheets being circulated, pinned up in public spaces, given out, pulled out of pockets and sung to gathering audiences'.[13] Versions of ballads which included the printed music, usually with a simple accompaniment for piano, were also printed and sold by the publishers of other types of sheet music. Several of these songs are to be found in both print and manuscript in surviving music collections, including that of Jane Austen and her extended family.

Music also played its part in more formal theatrical settings, often at this period explicitly intended to be 'loyal performances' at public events.[14] In her discussion of the representation of the 'Jolly Jack Tar' on stage, Russell argues that, while 'the naval community was far from being a group of eager students, ready to be moulded ... the theatre was profoundly important to the French wars because it became the place in which the civilian community's ambivalence in relation to its armed forces could be acted out', and nautical songs were an integral part of many theatrical performances.[15]

Given the large numbers of men employed in the Navy, it is not surprising that many ballads of this period dealt with life at sea. Isaac Land discusses the blatant misogyny of many sailors' ballads in the folk tradition. The image of the sailor with a 'wife' in every port became common as a part of the 'libertine bravado' of sailors. However, as Land argues, it was combined with 'a deep anxiety about women turning the tables and somehow playing the libertine themselves'. Men fed on 'a steady diet of misogynist song and story' were 'primed ... to vent their fury on women'.[16] Into this murky world, songwriters like Charles Dibdin intervened to create a more acceptable sailor. 'Inevitably, Dibdin's sailor would be not merely brave or fierce but also funny.' Dibdin's typical sailor is singing on his own account, not being sung about: 'He prides himself on his plain speaking, but what he speaks about are his orthodox sexual and national loyalties, which intertwine and reinforce each other'.[17] As discussed later in this chapter and also in Chapter 7, Jane Austen appears to have enjoyed his songs, since she included several of them among her personal music collection, despite – or perhaps because of – their sometimes slightly risqué humour and colourful language – reminiscent of characters like John Thorpe in *Northanger Abbey* and Mr Price in *Mansfield Park*.

Davey writes that 'politicians understood the cultural signifi-cance of ballads, and by the end of the eighteenth century radi-cal and conservative commentators alike understood that they were one way into the hearts and minds of ordinary people'.[18] The rhetoric and humour of these songs was frequently aimed squarely at the 'honest British tar'. George Hogarth wrote in 1848 that if Dibdin's portrayals of sailors had been 'coarse and literal copies, the originals would turn away in anger and dis-gust'. However, if Dibdin had gone to the other extreme and portrayed them as 'mere fancy-pieces, they would be neither understood nor cared for'. Dibdin's ballads worked because in his seafaring characters 'the sailor recognizes a brother-sailor – a being like himself, but nobler and better than himself, whom he would gladly resemble more fully'. Hogarth, like those who had granted Dibdin a government pension, recognised that, once the mariner approved of and sympathised with the 'high and generous sentiments' of these fictional characters, he could adopt them as his role models. Hogarth even suggested that, so influenced, 'His courage is no longer a brute instinct, sustained by a blind fatalism. He is calm in the midst of the battle … and yet prepared, should such be the will of Heaven, to die bravely in the cause of his country.'[19]

Yet, according to Hogarth, it is not just a sailor's conduct in battle or dealings with his 'brother-sailors' that Dibdin models so effectively, it is his personal life. As Joanne Begiato points out, 'The sailor's wife and infants and home were reshaped into the sailor's motivation to leave them: to defend and protect them and the nation'.[20] Hogarth goes so far as to claim that for the sailor, 'The image of his favourite hero stands between him and the allurements to sensual indulgence'. The hero of Dibdin's ballads focuses on 'his faithful girl, or tender wife' during the lonely midnight watch, as well as in the Saturday's carouse, when the merry crew assemble to toast their 'sweet-hearts and wives'. Although Hogarth could be critical about Dibdin's personal life and musical abilities, he had no doubt of the efficacy of Dibdin's compositions in improving the character and family life of sailors.[21]

Songs in the domestic sphere: the marriage of Matthew and Ann Flinders

These ballads were undoubtedly influential, and believed to be so, but they were not the only type of cultural product to encourage seafaring. Matthew Flinders (1774–1814), the English navigator and cartographer, whose short lifespan coincided with that of Jane Austen and who knew her brother Charles as a brother officer, claimed that it was after reading Daniel Defoe's *Robinson Crusoe* that he decided to go to sea and joined the Navy 'against the wishes' of his father.

By the time Flinders proposed marriage to Ann Chappelle in 1801, he had spent most of the preceding decade at sea. Ann had little enthusiasm for marrying a 'servant' of the sea. Her father had been a mariner and died at sea when she was four, and her mother, from a Hull seafaring family, had also lost two of her brothers to the sea. Although there was no doubting their mutual attraction, it took Matthew some persuasion, as well as some over-optimistic promises, to convince her that they had a future together. They married in April 1801 and lived together for a few weeks before Flinders left to survey the Australian coastline as commander of the HMS *Investigator*. Flinders had hoped to take his wife with him, but the Admiralty intervened and Ann stayed in England with her mother and step-father. Ann suffered deeply during their separation, which was to last nine years. In 1803, while travelling back to England, Flinders was detained by the French governor on Mauritius in the Indian Ocean for more than six years. Stranded there, Flinders worried about his wife, realising, among other things, that each year apart lessened the likelihood of their having children.

Flinders acknowledged Ann's sorrow by writing words to a tune adapted from a Haydn symphony and sending them to her in November 1805. Flinders wrote in the persona of the woman left behind: 'Why, Henry, didst thou leave me? ... Thou knew'st how much I loved thee, yet could resolve to go.' He wrote one verse, and three lines of a second, adding 'To be completed' in place of the last line.

On receiving the song, Ann responded to the implied invitation to co-authorship by finishing the second verse and adding two more, ending: 'Will comforts cheering sunshine e'er beam on this sore heart? / Yes, when we meet, my Henry, never again to part.'[22] In 1810 Flinders returned and the couple settled in London, Flinders working on various projects one of which involved the ship captained by Charles Austen, the *Namur*.

'These happy effects'

In 1812, after suffering at least one miscarriage, Ann eventually bore a daughter at the age of forty-two. Flinders died less than four years after his return when their child was only two. The story of the Chappelle–Flinders marriage was unique in its particulars, but in its general outline was common enough during these decades of war and expansion.

Sailors' songs in Austen's music collection

Flinders's musical training and level of education meant that, when he took to song to mediate in his marriage, it was in elevated poetic diction set to a melody by Haydn. The English composer Thomas Billington (1754–1832) set the words of a song, about a woman lamenting the absence of her lover William, to another Haydn tune:

> Ye cliffs! I from your airy steep look down with hope and fear
> To gaze on this extensive deep and watch if William's there.
> Sad months are past while here I breathe Love's soft and constant pray'r.

This song also ends in the prospect of a reunion:

> His promised signals from the Mast my timid doubts destroy
> What was your pain, ye terrors past, to this dear hour of Joy?

'William', first published in 1795, is known today only because Jane Austen copied it into one of her music manuscript books. The words, like those in the Flinders collaboration, stress the suffering of the woman waiting at home for her sea captain, but place more emphasis on her constancy. Written for publication, it was (at least in part) a contribution to the public conversation about the way women should behave while their men were away, while the Flinders song was a private document.

Ann Flinders wrote to express her own 'misery & alarms', her 'silent agony': she had no need to convince a reader or listener of her fidelity.

It can be assumed from its poetic register that 'William' was intended for an educated audience. The eponymous character would have been the captain or at least a high-ranking officer, since he was able to arrange a signal from the mast of his ship. Although it is certainly a narrative, it may not have been considered a ballad – defined by Davey as 'a popular song sung in the streets – as opposed to a hymn or classical song'. However, there was not a clear-cut class distinction. As Davey notes, 'ballads were not only geographically ubiquitous; they also filtered across all levels of society'.[23] Ballads were often performed at theatres to middle-class audiences, and popular songs depicting the lives and loves of the other ranks could also be part of the musical repertoire of the drawing room. Dibdin's songs, and others on similar themes by composers such as William Shield and Samuel Arnold, were thus enjoyed not only by seamen. Indeed, Dibdin boasted that his songs 'were sold in every music-shop, seen on every lady's pianoforte, and sung in every company'.[24] While he may have been exaggerating, several of his sea songs do appear in the private music collection of Jane Austen.

Austen had two brothers in the navy, Frank and Charles, and so had personal experience to draw on when writing her naval novels, *Mansfield Park* and *Persuasion*. However, the presence of these songs in her collection hints at a broader engagement with naval culture which could also have influenced her depiction of naval officers and men. Although Austen's naval connections were with the officer class – both her two naval brothers eventually became admirals – the songs in her collection range from the refined art music of 'William' to the

knockabout, though still relatively respectable, humour of ballads like those written by Charles Dibdin.

In the eighteen volumes of Austen family music books, as
we have seen, ownership of the various books has been traced
to at least five other women in her extended family. However,
Dibdin seems to have been a personal favourite of Austen's: of
the eleven Dibdin songs in the Austen music collection, nine
are in Jane Austen's own music books, either in print or copied
in her handwriting. In the remainder of this chapter, I consider
a sample of the 'sea songs' in Austen's collection particularly
from the perspective of the message they might be calculated
to convey to women respecting their behaviour in relationships
with their lovers or husbands during their absence at sea, and
on their return.

The sailor's farewell: tears and vows

One song in Austen's music scrapbook is an anonymous setting of three verses from John Gay's famous 1719 poem 'Sweet
William's farewell to Black-eyed Susan', a dramatic account
of Susan's farewell visit to her sailor lover William as his ship
is about to depart. In Chapter 5 I suggest the possibility that
this was an extract from a lost cantata by Thomas Arne. In
any case, this song strips away the narrative drama of Susan's
visit to William's ship and uses only the words that the sailor
William addresses to Susan, including a verse which confronts
head-on the popular belief in sailors' promiscuity:

Believe not what the landsmen say,
Who tempt with doubts thy constant mind,
They tell thee, sailors when away,
At every port a mistress find.

She played and sang

William is perhaps unusually eloquent for a common seaman, but elements like his appeal to Susan's fidelity, his sympathy with her tears, and his assurance that her love will keep him safe, are themes that will recur in later ballads. What is more uncommon is the frank admission of the Navy's reputation for promiscuity, and the ingenious rebuttal which concludes this verse about finding a mistress in every port: 'Yes, yes, believe them when they tell thee so, / for thou art present where so e'er I go.' One could see this as an early example almost of propaganda – attempting to persuade women that it is safe to let their lovers and husbands go to sea, as well as encouraging good behaviour on the part of the men.

One of the Dibdin ballads in Austen's earlier manuscript album, 'The soldier's adieu', first appeared in one of his London 'entertainments', titled *The wags*, in 1790, where he performed his own songs. Most of the songs in this miscellany were comic character pieces, but 'The soldier's adieu' was written to be delivered in heroic mode. Although it was obviously written about a different branch of the military service, Austen had other ideas. In her manuscript copy, she crossed out 'soldier' and substituted 'sailor' in the line 'Remember thou'rt a soldier's wife, these tears but ill become thee'. The man in question is made of sterner stuff than Susan's soft-hearted William. Verse 2 refers to the inspiration and comfort of wife and family:

My safety thy fair truth shall be as sword and buckler serving;
My life shall be more dear to me because of thy preserving:
Let peril come, let horror threat, let thund'ring cannons rattle!
I'll fearless seek the conflict's heat, assur'd when on the wings of love,
To Heav'n above thy fervent orisons are flown;

The tender prayer thou put'st up there
Shall call a guardian angel down, to watch me in the battle.

The tortuous poetic syntax, combined with a tune that manages to be both martial and florid, must have made this soldier/sailor seem amusingly pompous when set alongside the other characters in *The wags*. Dibdin varied the register and tone of his songs, and 'his amazing ability to mimic provincial accents' and people of different social classes meant he could carry the audience with him through an evening's programme containing nearly three dozen songs.[25]

'Yo heave ho', from Dibdin's 1799 show *Tour to the Land's End*, is also in the Austen music collection, in a printed copy that belonged to Eleanor Jackson, Henry Austen's second wife. The singer in this case is 'Tom Tough', a former sailor looking back on his naval career, with pride and a certain amount of boasting: 'I've seed [i.e. seen] a little service / Where mighty billows roll and loud tempests blow'. In the first verse he lists some of his commanders in order to establish his credentials: Howe, Jarvis, Duncan, Boscawen and Hawke. In the second, he shares the sorrow of parting from his love while supressing his tears in order to do his duty:

When from my love to part I first weighed anchor,
And she was snivelling seed [i.e. seen] on the beach below,
I'd like to catch my eyes sniv'ling too, d'ye see, to thank her,
But I brought my sorrows up with a Yo heave ho!
For sailors, though they have their jokes,
And love and feel like other folks,
Their duty to neglect must not come for to go.
So I seized the capstan bar, like a true honest tar,
In spite of tears and sighs sung out, Yo heave ho!

Joanne Begiato argues that 'the tar was not sanitised and civilised' during the course of the Georgian era, 'but was given feelings', allowing the construction of masculine sensibility to reach the lower ranks.[26] In voicing his impulse to tearfulness and sympathy, and then suppressing it, Tom Tough recalls Flinders's sentiments: 'When stern duty calls thee, thou couldst not but obey'. He is more forgiving than the character in 'The soldier's adieu', who exhorts his wife (in Austen's version) to 'remember thou'rt a sailor's wife, these tears but ill become thee.'

Home life: families and children

The last verse of 'Yo heave ho' adds another dimension to the sailor's lot – what happens at the end of his career:

> And now at last laid up, in decentish condition,
> For I've only lost an eye and got a timber toe;
> But old ships must expect in time to be out of commission,
> Nor again the anchor weigh with a Yo Heave Ho!
> I smoke my pipe and sing old songs,
> My boys shall well avenge my wrongs,
> My girls shall rear young sailors nobly for to face the foe.
> Then to country and king, fate no danger can bring,
> While the tars of old England sing, Yo, heave ho!
> The tars of old England sing, Yo, heave ho!

Humour, self-parody, sentiment and patriotism all play their part here. A 'timber toe' is slang for a wooden leg. The sailor's 'decentish condition' is an understatement for the loss of both a limb and an eye. But Tom Tough is a family man, with sons and daughters he has brought up – along with his wife, presumably the tearful woman he left behind in verse two – to follow his example and do their duty for 'old England'. The tune combines rollicking hornpipe-like passages with a steady march rhythm, with the words 'Yo heave ho' set on three even, affirmative beats at the end of each phrase. Although Tom Tough is not a commander like Captain Wentworth's brother officer Captain Harville in *Persuasion*, their situations and dispositions are similar. Both have been wounded at sea and have retired happily to a settled family life ashore.

The implications for wives of injured men are made explicit in a song by Samuel Arnold from the comic opera *Fire and water* (1780), in which the woman sings:

Sure 'twould make a dismal story
If when honour leads him on,
Love should slight the cause of glory,
Or disdain its wounded son.
If, his country's rights defending,
He should some disaster prove,
Duty with affection blending,
Will but more increase my love.

In Jane Austen's handwritten version of this song, which appears in her scrapbook, she perhaps misremembered or deliberately improved the second-last line to 'Pity with my passion blending'. In the opera, this brief song is sung by a woman making a case for marrying the man she chooses rather than one chosen for her. Divorced from this setting, with its simple, no-nonsense tune in common time, the song proffered a general statement about the duty of the patriotic woman to harness her affections (or indeed passions) in the patriotic cause.

A more idealised image of the sailor's return comes in William Shield's song 'The heaving of the lead' (1792). This four-square song, copied into Austen's earlier manuscript album, uses the figure of the plumbline being cast to measure the depth of the water as a ship approaches its home port, to illustrate the sailor's longing for home and domestic comforts:

And as the much-loved shore we near,
With transport we behold the roof,
Where dwells a friend or partner dear
Of faith and love a matchless proof.
The lead once more the seaman flung,
and to the watchful pilot sung,
Quarter less five! Quarter less five!

These sailors, unlike Dibdin's comic yet heroic characters, are generalised, and the commonality of their positive emotions assumed. They are equally reassuring to those waiting at home, or more realistically, perhaps, to the broader social field where a well-behaved, domesticated Navy safely embedded in a familial network of equally devoted and docile 'friends and partners' spells freedom from the kinds of social disruption which might well result from long absences and family separations.

Another song in Eleanor Jackson Austen's printed music collection, Joseph Major's 1800 ballad, 'Far o'er the western ocean', tells of a wife whose husband has been taken 'beyond the stormy sea'. He seems to have had no choice in the matter: perhaps he is an impressed sailor. The wife complains that she is subjected not just to personal sorrow but to loss of reputation:

Some say that I'm deserted,
They flout and jeer and scorn;
And slander's hounds are started,
Because I am forlorn.

However, she is not only a wife but also a mother:

My children seem forsaken
But he'll come back to me.

The wife concludes her song with a pious belief that 'the power that chastens' will bring her husband home: 'We'll twine our hearts together / A Family of Love!' This ballad, with its simple but engaging melody and straightforward modelling of a long-suffering and virtuous wife and mother, illustrates Davey's point that 'ballads are not used simply to hold a mirror up to British society'. Their purpose is to actively 'influence opinions and ideas'.[27]

Cautionary tales

One song in Austen's earlier manuscript album tells a cautionary tale, and it is cautioning *against* joining the navy. Dibdin's 'Lucky escape' (1791) is a comically hair-raising story of a ploughman who is persuaded by a friend to go to sea, leaving his 'dear' at home. He is lured by promises 'of such things / as if sailors were kings', only to find that 'I did not much like for to be aboard a ship / When in danger there's no door to creep out'. Hurricanes and battles confirm his conviction that he had been unwise 'to roam, when so happy at home'. When 'at last safe I landed, and in a whole skin', a helpful friend tells him that his father is dead and his wife has run away: 'Wives losing their husbands oft lose their good name', he moans: 'Curse light upon the carfindo[28] and the inconstant wind / that made me for to go and leave my dear behind!' But once he has expressed this remorseful sentiment, 'this very same friend' reveals that this news had been a ploy to test whether his desire to stay at home was genuine: in fact 'Dad's alive, and your wife's safe at home'. Our ploughman returns to his fields and his family – his 'wife, mother, sister and all of my friends', where 'once more shall the horn call me up in the morn', and nothing will 'e'er tempt me for to go and leave my dear behind'. It is notable that he is not only a husband but a son and a brother, embedded in a network of family relationships, with implicit mutual obligations.

She played and sang

Didbin's melody for this little morality tale is full of character and drama. Like most of Dibdin's songs, the music supports the words and allows for a full range of comic expression in performance. It certainly reinforces the importance of family values, as do 'Yo heave ho' and 'The heaving of the lead', but there is no countervailing appreciation of the bravery and endurance of Jack Tar. With its frank message of staying where you are well off, perhaps Dibdin intended to discourage impetuous decisions endangering family life.

Charles Dibdin's career appears to have declined in the early 1800s. In 1803 he wrote an 'Entertainment' called *Britons strike home*. 'Devoted as I have ever been to my public duty, it was impossible that, at the present moment, I should sleep at my post,' he wrote, presumably referring to Britain's resumption of war with France in May 1803.[29] For this Entertainment he wrote a song titled 'Victory, and George the Third', alluding to the 1695 song 'Britons, strike home' by Henry Purcell, a patriotic anthem which during the eighteenth century rivalled 'God save the king' and 'Rule Britannia' in popularity. This ballad, with its 'king and country' lyrics, perhaps composed with the idea of demonstrating Dibdin's gratitude for the government pension, 'did not catch on to any measurable degree'.[30] Although Dibdin retired in 1805 at the age of sixty, in 1808, owing to the withdrawal of his pension, 'he found himself ... compelled to resume his professional labours. ... But these endeavours terminated in failure and bankruptcy.'[31] He died in 1814 at the age of sixty-nine. The government pension may have suppressed the vitality and variety of Dibdin's characterisations of British seamen and their family relationships in favour of an attempt 'to keep up the enthusiasm against our Gallic neighbours'.[32] Songs like

'These happy effects'

'The lucky escape', encouraging men to stay home on the farm with their families, or 'Every inch a sailor', in which both the sailor and his lover perish, could have no part in this morale-boosting project.

Conclusion

It is significant that Dibdin's career took a downward turn once he directed his energies towards consciously fulfilling his duty. It seems likely that the humour, pathos and variety of Dibdin's maritime characters, and those of other composers and balladeers of the time, had a more positive effect on the morale of sailors and their families when they were not too blatant in their patriotic messages. While men would have listened to or sung many of these songs while at sea or in port, those they left behind – their sweethearts, wives, children and other family members – would have done likewise. Samantha Carrasco has remarked that 'through their musical choices and the words expressed within a song, women could immerse themselves in the world of politics, marital affairs, compassion and free expression of emotion'.[33] A lively, rousing or tender ballad, combining music and words, enjoyed actively by singing along or passively by listening to a performance, could have a powerful effect on the emotions. Likewise, a private message of love and shared pain sent by means of a song, as in the Flinders example, could do the same. Both could result in a softening of the heart, a hardening of resolve or even a change in behaviour.

Dibdin's skill at characterisation might perhaps have been the secret of his appeal to Jane Austen – and to other women who read, heard or sang his songs. Austen found the virtues of respect for women, fidelity in marriage and preference for domestic life attractive, and most of the men she portrays sympathetically have these qualities, whether they are minor characters or the destined husbands of her heroines. I am not proposing that Austen's novelistic practice was influenced in any substantial way by her familiarity with the ballads of Dibdin and his colleagues. However, in collecting, copying out and performing their songs for her own amusement (and perhaps that of her nieces and nephews), Austen was reflecting the national preoccupation with war and imperial expansion and the concern about its effect on families. In her last completed novel, *Persuasion* (first published 1818), Austen's admiration for men who go to sea is clear. All the naval characters are officers: Captain Harville, Admiral Croft, Captain Wentworth and Captain Benwick. All are quite distinct characters with different combinations of attractive qualities and virtues, but all are committed to a happy domestic life. The novel ends:

> Anne was tenderness itself, and she had the full worth of it in Captain Wentworth's affection. His profession was all that could ever make her friends wish that tenderness less; the dread of a future war all that could dim her sunshine. She gloried in being a sailor's wife, but she must pay the tax of quick alarm for belonging to that profession which is, if possible, more distinguished in its domestic virtues than in its national importance. (*P*, p. 252)

This assessment of the naval profession is not merely a passing remark: it bears the added significance of ending the novel. As Kathryn Sutherland points out, '*Persuasion* is Austen's most time-stamped novel [...] written after Waterloo' but set 'before Waterloo'. In this novel, 'through Anne Elliot's quiet characterization, Austen offers her most subtle domestic meditation on war's cost'.[34] The lives of these characters were shaped by war and politics, like countless other families of the time whose stories were reflected in and perhaps shaped by contemporary popular songs.

5

Jane Austen, Thomas Arne and Georgian musical theatre

Austen and Arne

In March 1814, when she was visiting her brother Henry in London, Jane Austen, along with other members of the family, attended a performance of Thomas Arne's 1762 opera *Artaxerxes* at Covent Garden. For Austen, Thomas Augustine Arne (1710–78) would have been a household name. Although she never mentions him in her letters or her novels, and despite his belonging to an earlier generation, Arne is a significant presence in her music manuscript books, one of the top six named composers whose work she transcribed.

Arne's reputation as a composer of vocal music has been eclipsed by German-born George Frideric Handel (1685–1759), who carved out a phenomenally successful career in Britain (with the help of royal patronage) and, as I discuss in Chapter 6, exerted extraordinary influence in the London musical scene long after his death. Even today, according to Todd

Gilman, Arne 'is largely forgotten, cowering in the shadow of Handel'.[1] Only one or two of his works are still well known: 'Rule Britannia', for example, and some of his Shakespeare songs. However, as Gilman writes, 'we should remember that Thomas Augustine Arne ... is considered the greatest native-born English opera composer of his day as well as the most popular composer of songs for the London theatre and pleasure gardens'.[2] Gilman describes 'Arne's graceful, elegant, and particularly English musical style during his youth', and points out that he later adopted 'the "modern" Italianate comic (or *galant*) musical style before many of his fellow musicians in England did'.[3] The Austen music books include examples of Arne in all these guises – from the simplest of English love songs to the most ornate Italianate arias.

Artaxerxes and opera in London

In 1814 Austen went with her brother Edward, niece Fanny and Mr John Plumptre (who was then courting Fanny) to the Theatre Royal, Covent Garden, to see *The devil to pay* – and Dr Arne's *Artaxerxes* was also on the programme. Gilman writes of Arne's *Artaxerxes* that 'by 1814 Jane Austen had seen it so many times that she had grown "very tired" of it'.[4] This is almost certainly a misreading. We do not know whether she had seen the opera before, although it had been revived many times since it premiered in 1762, but her words to Cassandra were: 'Excepting Miss Stephens I dare say Artaxerxes will be very tiresome'. And then, later that night, when she arrived home, she wrote, 'I was very tired of Artaxerxes, highly amused with the Farce, & and in an inferior way with the Pantomime that followed' (*Letters*, p. 260). While Gilman takes this as evidence that Austen had been over-exposed to this particular opera, Douglas Murray believes it shows that Austen was bored by opera in general.[5] There are several points to take into consideration here. One is how very different this opera was from what we know and expect of opera today. Michael Burden explains that

> there were three main theatres in London during the period 1660 to 1830: the Theatre Royal, Drury Lane; the Theatre Royal, Covent Garden; and the King's Theatre (also the Queen's), also known as the Opera House. All three theatres performed opera, but the first two staged mainly operas with spoken dialogue and all-sung afterpieces, while the King's Theatre was limited to all-sung Italian opera.[6]

There is no record of Austen visiting the King's Theatre. In an 1801 letter to Cassandra, she speaks with characteristic irony of her sister's 'noble resignation of Mrs Jordan and the Opera House' upon postponing her trip to London, which, as I mention in Chapter 2, I take to be anything but a literal implication that either of them would have willingly attended Italian opera (*Letters*, p. 71).

However, on her visits to London Austen often went to both the Theatres Royal to see various productions, musical and dramatic. In 1813 a family party, including three of her nieces and her brothers Edward and Henry, went to Covent Garden and saw, among other things, *Don Juan*, which was 'A tragic pantomimical entertainment' based on Thomas Shadwell's 1676 play *The libertine*.[7] Austen preferred this to all the pieces she saw during those two visits to Covent Garden in September 1813, and even perhaps beyond: 'I must say that I have seen nobody on the stage who has been a more interesting Character than that compound of Cruelty & Lust' (*Letters*, p. 221). The pantomime included 'songs, duets and chorus' and other music.

Austen, Arne and Georgian musical theatre

However, it was not an opera. She commented that '*my* delight was very tranquil' (*Letters*, p. 219), and when she summed up the two evenings' entertainment she commented that 'there was no acting more than moderate' (*Letters*, p. 221). Later that month she wrote to her brother Frank, summing up her visits to the theatre as mostly 'Sing-song and trumpery, but did very well for Lizzy and Marianne [thirteen and twelve years old respectively], who were indeed delighted; – but I wanted better acting' (*Letters*, p. 230).

Paula Byrne persuasively argues 'that Austen's comic genius was shaped by her love of theatre'.[8] On the basis of the surviving evidence, which is of course patchy, she documents the 'private theatricals' that Austen was involved in not only in her early years but as an adult, as well as the theatres, actors and plays that she was familiar with. Byrne draws attention to the wealth of evidence in the letters of familiarity with the contemporary theatre – quotations and glancing references which would be missed by most readers. She writes,

> there is enough evidence in the few surviving letters to suggest that she was utterly familiar with contemporary actors and the range and repertoire of the theatres. Her taste was eclectic; she enjoyed farces, musical comedy and pantomime, considered to be 'low' drama, as much as she enjoyed Colman and Garrick.[9]

Byrne does mention musical drama and refers to Austen's dissatisfaction with the soprano Catherine Stephens in *Artaxerxes* and *The farmer's wife*. However, Byrne does not appear to be familiar with the music collection and what we can learn from it about Austen's dramatic experiences.

John Cunningham explains the differences between stage music in Shakespeare's time, where it was integrated into the drama and belonged to the characters, and the traditions which had grown up by the mid-eighteenth century, when 'audiences … would have been unperturbed by the aural presence of an orchestra in, say, a forest. In effect, the music was more for the audience and the actors than for the characters.'[10] I suspect that Austen's dissatisfaction with many of the productions she attended sprang from this kind of theatrical convention, which interrupted the emotional impact of the dramatic narrative.

Sadly, when a new version of the Don Juan story appeared at the King's Theatre in April 1817 to alert literary London belatedly to Mozart's 'new' style of opera, it was too late for Jane Austen. Gillen D'Arcy Wood explains that, for Leigh Hunt and other literary members of his circle, '*Don Giovanni* was a conversion experience'.[11] Charles Lamb, 'on his own admission, unmusical', and Percy Bysshe Shelley, like Austen, 'so often an unhappy theatre-goer', both became 'absorbed' and 'delighted' by the opera. Wood points out that

> Mozart opera did not depend on spectacle and virtuosic singing. It did not merely 'astonish' the ears and eyes of the audience, but offered a psychological truth of character through music that required from the audience an intellectual commitment more often associated with reading the great poets.[12]

Austen commented on the mediocre acting in the performances she saw and criticised the virtuosic singer Catherine Stephens, who appeared in *Artaxerxes* and whose performance she was expecting to enjoy. Her assessment of Stephens was 'a pleasing person & no skill in acting', whose 'merit in singing is I dare say very great; that she gave *me* no pleasure is no reflection upon her' (*Letters*, p. 261). With comments like these, we can begin to build a picture of Austen's theatrical preferences. 'Not easily pleased, Jane is no novice theatergoer', write Janine Barchas and Kristina Straub.[13]

Although eighteenth-century operas contained much beautiful and expressive music, the immersive dramatic experience that we now expect from nineteenth and twentieth-century operas – and indeed from Mozart operas – was not to be found on the London stage in this period. Arias were often imported from other composers at the whim of the virtuoso performers. The Italian opera offered at the time, as Wood writes, depended on 'spectacle and virtuosic singing',[14] while the English theatre pieces, like *Don Juan*, were often plays with music added, cobbled together from previous works by various composers and authors.

Thomas Arne's *Artaxerxes*, however, is something rather different. It is a virtuosic, Italianate opera, without spoken dialogue, but written in English: one of the first *opere serie* (serious, or 'grand', operas) in English. Arne translated and adapted the libretto himself, from a work of the famous Italian poet and librettist Pietro Metastasio (1698–1782). Michael Burden writes that *Artaxerxes* 'was the most popular English Opera on the eighteenth-century London stage'. He speculates that it is not often performed today partly because of the old-fashioned style of plot which, like other 'serious' operas of the period, features 'complex debates concerning issues of personal and political morality, and have little interest for today's opera-goers who thrive on emotional indulgence'.[15]

Burden goes on to explain the plot of *Artaxerxes*, in which the character Mandane, sister of the title character, goes through several crises when her lover Arbaces is accused of murdering her father, King Xerxes, when, in fact, he was murdered by Arbaces's father Artabanes. However, as Burden explains,

Although she provides the opera's romantic interest, her reunion with Arbaces is peripheral to the resolution of the action. This turns, rather, on Artabanes' admission of responsibility for the assassination of King Xerxes, which is forced on him by a belated realisation of his love for his son. The opera's moral centre lies in the magnanimity of Artaxerxes, who banishes rather than executes the now repentant Artabanes.[16]

English audiences at the time, on the other hand, 'preferred Mandane's anguish, struggle, and joy' to the moral message Metastasio was at pains to promote.[17] It is interesting that Mandane is not mentioned at all in 'The argument' to Arne's 1762 libretto, whereas the opera itself begins with a love scene between Mandane and Arbaces.[18] The continuing success of Arne's opera can thus be partly attributed to the prominence Arne gave to the character of Mandane in his adaptation and setting of the libretto. Mandane became a celebrated role, prized by aspiring sopranos, 'and it is an indication of its status that there are some thirty-eight recorded images of singers performing it'.[19] It was still being performed in London well into the nineteenth century.

Austen might have seen *Artaxerxes* before, though there is no record of it. She knew the overture, at least, since she copied a keyboard reduction of it into her manuscript book some time after 1808. When she went to *Artaxerxes* in 1814 she expected to derive pleasure only from the performance of Catherine Stephens, who was singing the role of Mandane. Stephens was a disappointment because of her poor acting in the role which offers many of the most emotional and dramatic possibilities in the opera. Austen was unmoved by her singing, which she admitted was good and was admired by her niece Fanny and friend John Plumptre. For Austen, we gather, the music in a theatrical work needs to be a part of the emotional and dramatic action. Otherwise all is 'singsong and trumpery'. Add to this the length of the opera, with a bewildering and improbable story line explained via lengthy recitative passages and arias that, despite their beauty and variety, dissipate the already stilted narrative drive, and it is not difficult to understand that Austen, who knew so well how to create engaging and absorbing works of fiction, would find it tedious.

'Lotharia'

Gilman writes that '*Artaxerxes*, which provided another boost for Arne late in life, succeeded in no small measure because it imitated the serious Italian opera of the day, whose florid vocals took him as far from his signature and much-loved native English style as Arne could get'.[20] Indeed, the variety of music represented by the nine items by Arne in the Austen music collections provides a perfect illustration of his range. The composition of his that appears earliest in the collections is in one of the manuscript books which is believed to have belonged to Ann Cawley, Austen's early teacher and distant relative, and which seems to have become part of Austen's music library. In the manuscript book it is titled 'Lothareo set by Mr Arne', and the copy includes no lyrics, just the melody and bass line. It is a simple and charming pastoral love song, very much in the 'English style' that Gilman refers to. The lyrics, which appear among the works of Aaron Hill (1685–1750), begin:

Vainly now ye strive to charm me,
All ye sweets of blooming May.
How should empty sunshine warm me
While Lotharia keeps away?[21]

The earliest publication of this song I have been able to find is from 1749 in the *Universal magazine*. A possible clue to dating the manuscript is that Arne did not receive his doctorate from Oxford University until 1759, so, if the transcriber is accurate, it must have been created before that date, when he would still have been 'Mr Arne' rather than 'Dr Arne'.

'The Scotch air in the overture to Thomas and Sally'

Another simple pastoral song, although of a rather different character in both melody and words, is titled 'The Scotch air in the overture to *Thomas and Sally*; sung by Mr Tenducci, and Miss Brent at Vauxhall & Ranelagh, compos'd by Dr Arne'. It appears in the bound book of printed music which Austen appears to have used as a scrapbook, with manuscript items interleaved and a handwritten contents list at the front. Three items by Arne are listed on the contents page and appear in printed versions in this book, with the 'Scotch Air' listed under its opening lyrics – 'To ease his heart'.

Thomas and Sally is a 1760 opera by Arne, and this air appears, without lyrics, in the overture. Gilman writes that 'the Scotch gavotte in the overture proved so popular that Arne set it to words as the song "To ease his heart", which he promptly published as part of his collection *Vocal melody* XIII'.[22] The words are unattributed in the score, but they are based on lyrics set to a different tune in Thomas D'Urfey's 1719 collection *Wit and mirth, or pills to purge melancholy*.[23] Despite the title of the publication, the words bear no relation at all to the opera *Thomas and Sally* and concern a young man named Jocky and his lover. An interesting difference in Arne's version of this comic and saucy seduction story, related from the point of view of the woman at her spinning wheel, is that, despite her strong inclination, the young man is unsuccessful in his attempts to seduce her until 'he swore he meant me for his wife', at which point the young woman succumbs: 'And flung away my spinning wheel'.

This song is considerably more earthy than the floridly sentimental 'Lotharia'. The melody is in a solid common time, in contrast with the graceful minuet lilt of 'Lotharia', and contains characteristic 'Scotch snaps'. Austen's collection contained many Scottish songs, which is hardly surprising given their popularity during her lifetime, but this kind of down-to-earth, unromantic view of the relations between the sexes would surely have appealed to the Austen we know from her letters and from her teenage writings, even if it surfaces more rarely in her novels.

'Cymon and Iphigenia'

In the same volume as the 'Scotch air from *Thomas and Sally*' we find a print copy of Arne's English cantata 'Cymon and Iphigenia'. This cantata was first published in 1750 by Thompson and Son.[24] It was performed by Thomas Lowe at Vauxhall Gardens in the early 1750s.[25] There were many eighteenth-century editions of the cantata, and dating this particular edition is not straightforward. It is a short score, with figured bass and no indication of any instrument apart from the keyboard. Although it includes no publication details, it closely matches the copy online at the British Library printed for T. Skillern with a suggested date of 1780, rather than the Thompson and Son version, also available online at the British Library, which they suggest was published in 1753, and which covers eight pages in contrast to the crowded four of the later edition and, although still in short score, shows which parts of the accompaniment are intended for the flute to play. A note at the end of this score offers 'full parts, from the original copy'.[26]

As the number of editions testifies, this cantata remained in circulation: according to Rice it was one of Arne's most popular cantatas from this period:

> The cantata consists of six sections cast in alternating recitatives and airs. The opening recitative is of particular interest for it has several changes of metre, and includes a flute to illustrate Cymon's whistling. The final air, 'Love's a pure, a sacred Fire', is cast in triple time, and demonstrates Arne's gift for infectious melody.[27]

The text is often attributed to Dryden, although his version of the tale is an extended epic poem (based on Boccaccio) and only traces of his poem survive in these lyrics. Rice points out that Cymon, in Arne's cantata described as 'a clown', a simple rustic, is, in Dryden's version, 'a noble outcast', and that 'this change of character is in keeping with the general pastoral symbolism found in the text and makes the change of Iphigenia's heart all-the-more surprising and moving'.[28] Briefly, the story tells of Cymon discovering Iphigenia asleep and being strongly attracted to her. Iphigenia wakes in alarm but is reassured when she sees that it is only Cymon, whom she thinks of as a simple, harmless clown. Cymon declares his passion, and Iphigenia looks again, sees, instead of a clownish rustic, an attractive young man, and invites him to meet her again the following day. A greater contrast between this scenario and that in the 'Scotch Air' could hardly be imagined, even though both stories end with the union of the lovers. The music is direct and expressive, and although it is for solo voice it allows the singer to express a range of emotions and personae, including the narrative voice and the voice of each of the title characters.

'Nymphs and shepherds'

The third of the Arne songs among the printed music in this scrapbook is 'Nymphs and shepherds'. It was published in around 1765, 'Sung by Miss Brent at Ranelagh and Mrs Vincent at Vauxhall Gardens, set by Doctor Arne'. This setting is at least the second of these words that Arne composed, and possibly the third. In 1740 he composed new music to Shadwell's *Don John, or the libertine destroy'd*, replacing Henry Purcell's score, which included Purcell's famous setting of 'Nymphs and shepherds'. However, Gilman notes that 'no music survives' from this production[29] – and the version of *Don Juan* that Austen saw in 1813 had music by Gluck. Gilman later mentions that in 1761 at the King's Theatre Charlotte Brent 'sang "Nymphs and Shepherds" from *Alfred*, the 1740 masque which introduced Arne's most famous song, 'Rule Britannia'.[30] However the version in the Austen music book, first published probably in 1765, is different from the version in *Alfred*. It is possible that he composed this new setting for his favourite soprano, Charlotte Brent, either in 1761 for the King's Theatre, or later in the decade.

The words of Arne's surviving two settings of this song are different from the words in the Purcell song, and according to *The Brent, or English syren* were written by Arne himself:

> Nymphs and shepherds, come away,
> Wanton in the sweets of May.
> Trip it o'er the flowery lawn,
> Lighter than the bounding fawn.

She played and sang

Frolick buxom blyth and gay
Nymphs and shepherds, come away.[31]

The version of 'Nymphs and Shepherds' in *Alfred* is in lilting
6/8 time, and while it contains some melismatic passages it is
not especially virtuosic. The highest note is a G, well within
the normal soprano range.[32] It is shorter and simpler than the
1765 version in the Austen book, which is in 3/4 time, with a
lot of rapid passage-work in groups of four semiquavers – more
of a technical challenge than triplets – and other technical dif-
ficulties like jumps from the bottom to the top of the soprano
range – low B to high G. And it ends with a coloratura passage
in which the singer rapidly ascends through two octaves to a
high C, not once but twice. It requires formidable technique
and breath control to sing this aria effectively and was probably
written for Brent, 'to showcase [her] vocal agility', like the part
Arne wrote for her in *Love in a village*.[33]

'Susan'

There is another intriguing possibility in this scrapbook
of music. An unattributed song titled 'Susan' appears twice
among the manuscripts in the same book. The song is a setting of a part of John Gay's 1719 poem 'Black-eyed Susan', but,
while several composers set the whole poem as a ballad, Rice
writes that Arne set the poem in 1740 as a cantata, divided into
recitatives and arias and assigned to different voice types. The
three stanzas of the poem beginning 'Oh Susan, Susan, lovely
dear' would presumably have been an aria sung by the tenor.
However, the music of this cantata has been lost.[34] The strophic
song in Austen's manuscript includes the same three verses,

beginning 'Oh Susan'. Stylistically it seems quite plausible that the song in Austen's manuscript collection is by Arne: it is not in a folk idiom, but has his characteristic melodic charm – not unlike 'Lotharia', with melismatic passages decorating a melody of clarity and heartfelt simplicity. Perhaps it, and the extant manuscript copies in other music collections, also unattributed, listed in various online archives, are the only surviving records of this cantata.

Comus

Three songs from Arne's 1738 masque *Comus* are copied in Austen's handwriting into one of the manuscript music books which also contains several other hands. It is difficult to date these copies, as this volume was rebound in the twentieth century and its original order was not retained. However, immediately before the first of these songs is a copy of the nursery rhyme 'Sing a song of sixpence', which must have been the last item copied beforehand because it finishes on the top half of the page on which the Arne recitative and aria 'How gentle was my Damon's air / On every hill and every dale' begins. I suspect that these nursery rhymes were included in her collection to provide amusement for her young nieces and nephews, so it seems likely that these songs were copied into the book in the late 1790s – Anna and Fanny, the eldest of the nieces, were both born in 1793. This is perhaps supported by the fact that the piece that immediately follows, on the reverse of the last of these selections from *Comus*, is Callcott's 'Epitaph', which was not published until late 1795.

'How gentle was my Damon's air' is the first of the three items from *Comus* to be transcribed into the book, followed by

She played and sang

'Sweet Echo, sweetest nymph' and 'By the gaily circling glass'. The first is merely headed 'Dr Arne' while the other two have no title information and are identifiable by their lyrics.

Comus was Arne's first big success and the first of his scores to which he assigned an opus number, usually a sign that a composer is particularly proud of an early work: 'the title page describes it as his "Opera Prima"'.[35] It 'achieved immediate success with audiences' and 'for the rest of Arne's life scarcely a year passed without a revival of the piece'.[36] It is a lovely score, owing to 'Arne's ingenious and very modern setting, in which the composer cunningly married English folk simplicity with modish Italian *galanterie*'.[37] The sweetly plaintive recitative 'How gentle was my Damon's air' is followed by a relatively simple two-verse aria 'On every hill and every dale', in which a nymph complains of being abandoned by her lover. Although this aria appears late in the masque, in Austen's album it precedes two earlier arias, firstly the jovial tenor aria 'By the gaily circling glass', an invitation to enjoy the pleasures of the night before 'the busy Day' returns. This aria is quite short, AABB in form, and followed in the score by a dance, 'a light fantastick Round'. The third song Austen chose to copy is a more virtuosic piece. 'Sweet Echo, sweetest nymph' is a soprano aria with flute obbligato providing the echoing phrases. It is longer and more musically complex than the tenor aria, which is the previous piece of music in the masque – although there is spoken dialogue between the songs – and it completely changes the mood of bacchanal to one of enchantment. As Gilman writes, 'it is the only song in the masque that Arne through-composed',[38] as opposed to the usual pattern of multiple verses set to the same repeated melody. The first half of the aria is in a slow triple time, marked Largo in the score, changing to Allegro in common time in the second half with the addition of a trumpet to the obbligato part, as the echo is invited to 'give resounding Grace to all Heav'n's harmonies'. This is one of the musical centrepieces of the masque, ravishing to hear and providing wonderful contrast with the previous earthy music.

Comus was revived at Covent Garden in 1815, in an arrangement by Henry Bishop which included arias of Handel as well as Arne's music,[39] but I have found no evidence that Austen attended a performance of the masque. However, the *Piano-forte magazine* Volume III, no. 2 included an arrangement for piano of *Comus*. The British Library suggests a publication date of 1797 for this volume, and it is possible that Austen copied the three songs from that source: the arrangements in her manuscript seem to be in similar short-score format to the versions of other works in the publication that I have been able to view online. The *Piano-forte magazine* was published by Harrison & Co. in London between 1797 and 1802.

Sadly *Comus* languishes in obscurity now – there is no current recording and the only one I have been able to find is a vinyl LP record dating from the 1950s. It is surely time for a revival of this lovely music.

'The tout-ensemble'

In *Mansfield Park* there is a somewhat chilling conversation between Henry Crawford and his sister Mary. He confesses to her that he is 'fairly caught' by Fanny Price and intends to marry her. 'Lucky, lucky girl!' cried Mary as soon as she could speak – 'what a match for her!' She goes on to say, 'You will have a sweet little wife; all gratitude and devotion. Exactly what you deserve' (*MP*, p. 292). Throughout this conversation, it is clear how little they both understand Fanny, and how well she has succeeded in keeping her secrets, not only from the Crawfords but also from the world. Nobody but Edmund has any inkling of her inner strength and her true nature, and nobody at all realises that she is hopelessly in love with Edmund.

The Crawfords' conversation continues for some time. Mary asks,

> 'When did you begin to think seriously about her?'
> Nothing could be more impossible than to answer such a question though nothing be more agreeable than to have it asked. 'How the pleasing plague had stolen on him' he could not say. (*MP*, p. 292)

The quotation about 'the pleasing plague' comes from a poem by William Whitehead (1715–1785), which was set by several composers, including Thomas Arne. It appears in his *Second volume of lyric harmony* from 1746 as 'The tout-ensemble':

> Yes, I'm in love, I feel it now,
> And Celia has undone me;
> And yet I'll swear, I can't tell how,
> The pleasing plague stole on me.
> 'Tis not her face that love creates,
> For there no graces revel;
> 'Tis not her shape,
> For there the Fates have rather been uncivil.
> 'Tis not her air, for sure in that
> There's nothing more than common;
> And all her sense is only chat,
> Like any other woman.
> Her voice, her touch, might give th' alarm;
> 'Tis both, perhaps, or neither;
> In short, 'tis that provoking charm
> Of Celia all together![40]

Austen's choice to refer to this text in this context is telling, and it would probably have been recognised by her contemporaries. With its dismissive misogyny and insulting tone towards a woman with whom the poet is supposedly in love, it resonates with the Crawfords' superior and patronising attitude to Fanny.

The poem was set by several other composers, including Handel, under several different titles, including 'The pleasing plague', 'To Celia', 'Celia's charms' and 'The Je ne scay quoy'. Arne's version was offered at Vauxhall Gardens in 1746 and reprinted in the second volume of his later collection *Clio and Euterpe* (1758–1762). No setting of this verse is included in the surviving Austen collections, but there is no doubt that Austen knew the poem, and possibly at least one of its musical settings, given her reference in *Mansfield Park* and a fuller quotation in her teenage writings.

In 'A collection of letters', written probably in 1792, Austen's young character, an heiress named Henrietta Halton, is writing to her friend Matilda. She includes the text of a letter from her lover, Musgrove, which is full of unrestrained hyperbole and every sickly flattering image drawn from the dregs of the sentimental literature and love songs of the eighteenth century, pushed to exuberant lengths by the teenage Austen. Henrietta finds this 'a pattern for a Love-letter ... Such Sense, Such Sentiment, Such purity of Thought, Such flow of Language & such unfeigned Love in one Sheet' (*TW*, p. 145). Henrietta may not be as naive as she seems at first: she confides in her friend that 'Indeed I had always heard what a dab he was at a Love-letter' (*TW*, p. 145). She has been introduced to Musgrove by his cousin Lady Scudamore, who encourages Henrietta's enthusiasm for her impecunious relative. She later reports hearing him 'exclaiming in a most Theatrical tone –

> Yes I'm in love I feel it now,
> And Henrietta Halton has undone me –'

Henrietta responds, 'What a sweet Way ... of declaring his Passion! To make such a couple of charming Lines about me! What a pity it is that they are not in rhime!' (*TW*, p. 147). The letter reports the continuing conversation between Lady Scudamore and Henrietta, to the effect that Musgrove promises in the most affecting terms to wait until Henrietta's relatives die and they are able to marry. The whole tenor of this letter emphasises Henrietta's vanity and Musgrove's insincerity. Henrietta is clearly not aware of the poem, while Austen's reference to it, like that in *Mansfield Park* two decades later, shows that she understood it for what it was and used the intertextual reference knowingly. Her joke in the juvenilia about it not 'being in rhime' – that is, not scanning properly – gives another hint that Henrietta is not as ingenuous as she might at first seem.

It is not known why Arne chose to set this particular poem. It may just have been a lyric which he felt his tenor, Thomas Lowe, would enjoy singing. However, Rice writes that 'As seen in Arne's mature cantatas, the need for strong images that he could depict musically had become central to his musical style. It can only be presumed that Arne chose his texts based on their imagery and their appropriateness for the performer and location of the performance.'[41] In the same way, Austen appears to have been drawn to songs offering a variety of vividly portrayed characters she could inhabit while performing them, and I believe this preference resonates with her own writing practice. She tended to avoid obvious figurative imagery in her writing, as I discuss in Chapter 8. However, her skill at slipping with increasing subtlety between various narrative voices might well have been in some way prompted or encouraged by her practice of embodying varied subject positions in song.

Shakespeare songs

Given the theatrical traditions of the eighteenth-century London stage, it is quite likely that, when Austen visited the theatre to see a Shakespeare play, many of the song settings she heard would have been those of Thomas Arne. Cunningham writes of the conservatism of Georgian audiences, who were used to hearing Arne's settings of the songs even when they were interpolated from other sources.[42] Even to many twentieth-century audiences, Arne's setting of 'Where the bee sucks' would have been the most familiar.[43]

Two Arne songs with words by an unknown author (possibly Arne himself) were inserted into *The merchant of Venice*. They were 'My bliss too long my bride denies' and 'To keep my gentle Jessy'. And, on the other hand, the song 'Tell me where is fancy bred', which originated in *The merchant of Venice*, having been used in *Twelfth night* in the Shakespeare revivals of the 1740s, was firmly ensconced in that play and not usually included in *Merchant*. In March 1814 Austen went to see *The merchant of Venice*. She loved Edmund Kean as Shylock, but had her reservations about the production:

> We were quite satisfied with Kean. I cannot imagine better acting, but the part was too short, & excepting him & Miss [Sarah] Smith, & *she* did not quite answer my expectations, the parts were ill filled & the Play heavy. (*Letters*, p. 257)

Later in the same letter to Cassandra, she came back to Kean:

> I shall like to see Kean again excessively, & to see him with You too; it appeared to me as if there were no fault in him anywhere; & in his scene with Tubal there was exquisite acting. (*Letters*, p. 258)

Austen was, as we have seen, a connoisseur of acting. Whether she was aware of the composers of the songs she heard that night is not recorded. However, such is Arne's connection with Shakespeare's songs at this period that the handbill for this performance of *Merchant* attributes the song 'Haste, Lorenzo' (another interpolation) to Arne, while there seems to be no record that he set this text:[44] the surviving setting, and all references I have been able to find, attribute this song to Joseph Baildon.

Conclusion

Many of the English-born musicians in Georgian England had parallel careers in secular music and the church – among them William Jackson, Samuel Wesley and Samuel Arnold. Thomas Arne, a practising Catholic, was unable to contribute to the Church of England as a musician. He wrote a small amount of sacred music, but 'as a Roman Catholic … he had no opportunity to have his sacred works performed in the Anglican Church'.[45] It was as a secular composer of mainly vocal and dramatic music that he was most celebrated.

Gilman, in his book *The theatre career of Thomas Arne*, discusses the contemporary and continuing debates about the relative merits of Arne and Handel at length. Among several reasons for the unjust neglect of Arne's music, he mentions the circular assumption that Arne wrote 'beautiful' music, while Handel's music was 'sublime' and therefore superior. As well as writing in the more 'serious' high Baroque style rather than the new *galant* style that Arne favoured, Handel had the advantage of setting 'biblical texts for a pious and elite audience' – a Protestant audience – which lent his music further sublimity. In much of the aesthetic theory of the day, 'the musical aspect of the sublime was considered secondary to its manifestation through other art forms', in this case poetry.[46] 'Arne's beauty', on the other hand, 'was associated with comic drama and other light texts'. Gilman also notes that 'Arne was not alone among English composers in having his works treated less seriously than those of foreign musicians'.[47] This kind of judgement extends into later critiques of Jane Austen's taste in music, such as Piggott's assertion that 'too many of the items in her collection [are] no more than superficially pretty and sometimes rather worse than that'.[48] I think it is fair to assume that Austen was not unduly influenced by such judgements.

The careers of musicians, like those of most artists, rarely run smoothly in any age, and the eighteenth century was no exception. Public taste is notoriously fickle, and professional rivalries can be brutal. Even Handel, well known as a consummate business man as well as a great composer, had his challenges, while 'during a musical career that lasted almost half a century, Arne came to know abject failure as well as real success'.[49] It is telling that Deborah Rohr's book *The careers of British musicians 1750–1850* includes a whole chapter on 'The fortunes of musicians' which discusses 'the financial insecurities of musicians' and contains a long section headed 'Destitution'.[50] On the whole, however, Arne fared comparatively well during his lifetime, and, although his posthumous fortunes did not quite rival Handel's, some of his works – *Artaxerxes, Comus* and his Shakespeare songs – remained part of the standard London repertoire until well into the Victorian era.

In the broader Austen music collection, there are about twenty pieces by Handel while there are only nine by Arne. However, much of this Handel repertoire is in books Austen would not have known, and some is in the two books belonging to her teacher Ann Cawley that she seems to have inherited. It appears that she rarely sought out Handel's music for her own collection, for whatever reason: perhaps it was readily available elsewhere, or perhaps not suitable for her purposes. The Arne items in the broader collection, on the other hand, are mainly in the albums she owned or compiled. Arne died when Austen was only two years old, while most of other the composers she favoured were her contemporaries. But Arne's music perhaps remained approachable and could co-exist with the music being published and performed during her lifetime, while Handel might have seemed too grand and serious for domestic settings. In any case, there can be little doubt that she appreciated Arne's music, despite her dismissive comments on the 1814 performance of *Artaxerxes*.

The gifts of great acting, like those of musicianship, are rare, and for a connoisseur they are doubly so. Austen was a connoisseur of both. When she visited the theatre, she looked for drama and emotional impact and rarely found it. Only occasionally in her letters does she describe hearing a musician (either professional or amateur) with great pleasure, and more often complains about the length of the evening, or being unexpectedly trapped into listening to a performance. When she does enjoy it, she rarely specifies the actual music she has heard. We know that she found Arne's *Artaxerxes* tiring, and not improved by the poor acting of the cast, however skilled their musical performances might have been. Thomas Arne was certainly one of the composers whose music she liked playing and singing for her own enjoyment and that of her family and close friends – which is a different matter from enjoying a performance of the same music in a crowded, overheated drawing room, or an uncomfortable and noisy theatre.

6

Jane Austen and British song

Songs of the British Isles

Most of the songs in Jane Austen's collection are in English, though they often draw on subjects beyond the borders of England, sometimes as far away as Serbia or India, whether they are theatre pieces or stand-alone songs. Austen had many of these exotic pieces, but she had 'genuinely' English songs in her collection as well – English in the sense of being written by English composers in English, and set, implicitly, in England, or at least not dealing explicitly with exotic themes. Perhaps the greatest concentration of these is William Jackson's *Twelve canzonets*, first published in about 1770, which appear in Austen's album of printed songs.

Few musicians, even if they were born in England of English parents, were as 'proudly English' as Jackson.[1] Many incorporated various musical traditions from continental Europe, and increasingly from Scotland, in their songs – or at least they thought that was what they were doing. As Roger Fiske writes of the British folk song tradition, the term 'Scotch song' was 'commonly used in eighteenth-century England for a type of popular song, usually Scottish but not always, which from Purcell's time onwards increasingly flooded the market'.[2] In an appendix to his book *Scotland in music* Fiske lists thirty of the most enduringly popular 'Scotch songs', noting that at least five or six of them are probably English or Irish in origin. He observes that, paradoxically, 'during these lean years when, in the world of "art music", Scotland seemed to have no composers or performers worth more than a brief mention, ... the country so often permeated musical thinking in Germany, France and elsewhere'[3] – including south of the border. I hope it is clear that in this chapter I use these labels – Scottish, Irish, English and so on – without any claim for their historical or musicological accuracy, but with the meaning they tended to have in Austen's own time.

Given Austen's well-known Jacobite sympathies, it is not surprising that she felt no impulse to resist the tide from the north. Her music collection shows that she was drawn to Scottish music, and two of the four songs her young relatives remember her singing in her later years were Scottish: 'Their groves of sweet myrtle' and 'The yellow-haired laddie' – the other two being respectively French and English (by an Irish composer). Fiske proposes that one of the reasons for the popularity of Scottish songs was 'the piquancy of their Scots characteristics'.[4] Other political or ideological reasons might be adduced, but these characteristics do set them apart from the common run of pastoral love songs and help to explain their attraction for Austen. Even if they were not all genuinely Scottish, the genre of 'Scotch song' allowed non-Scottish songwriters a certain licence to include musical and lyrical elements which would be thought out of place in the English 'art' song.

'Scotch songs'

During the eighteenth century, the melodies of Scottish songs found their way into sonatas, symphonies and overtures of composers based in England, and on to the London stage in ballad operas and plays. Arrangements of the tunes multiplied: among the sets of variations on pre-existing themes in the Austen collection, Scottish traditional tunes outnumber all other sources. As discussed in Chapter 5, Thomas Arne wrote a melody for the overture to his 1760 opera *Thomas and Sally*, a gavotte-style tune with a few 'Scotch snaps', and it proved so popular that he extracted it and adapted it to some words by Thomas D'Urfey, giving the resultant song the title 'Scotch air in the overture to *Thomas and Sally*'. A copy of the printed music for this song is in Austen's scrapbook volume.

Also in her collection, alongside Jackson's *Canzonets* in the album of printed vocal music, are Allan Ramsay's two collections of 'Scots songs', 'the music taken from the most genuine sets extant' and the words written by Ramsay, published in Edinburgh in the late 1750s by Robert Bremner. This was the culmination of Ramsay's career as a poet and promoter of 'genuine' Scottish music. Earlier he had published volumes of song lyrics, indicating the tunes to be used but not including the musical notation. These last volumes were a much more useful source for music-lovers beyond Scotland who might not know the original tunes. They were simple arrangements: a bass line for the harpsichord and the melody, sometimes with a second voice part. Someone in Austen's circle bought the two sets, which were eventually bound with the Jackson *Canzonets* and, at the end of the album, the cantata by Tommaso Giordani, *Colin and Lucy*, which I discuss at length in Chapter 8. Giordani is a rather typical musician of his time. As so many were, he was well travelled, having been born in Italy in 1740, moving to London in his early twenties and eventually settling in Dublin, where he wrote settings like this: of poetry by an Englishman, set in Ireland and based on a Scottish folk ballad. He also made an arrangement for voice and string quartet of the Scottish song 'Queen Mary's lamentation', on which Austen seems to have based her manuscript version.

Fiske allows himself a bitter comment on the state of music in London at this period:

> A by-product of the long-lasting rage for Scotch Songs in London was the virtual annihilation of the English variety. [George] Thomson would have published a volume of English Songs if he could have found any; he sent Beethoven *God save the King* and *The miller of the Dee* and then gave up. Some forgotten German described England as the Land without Music, and no wonder, with Londoners for ever besotted with Scotch Songs and Tom Moore's *Irish Melodies*. No Englishman before William Chappell in the 1850s made any serious attempt to find out whether the English had any folk-songs or not. Thousands must have been lost through Scottish dominance and English indifference.[5]

Although Austen clearly knew and liked many Scottish songs (as we know from her collection and from her young relatives' memoirs) she mentions Scottish music only twice in her fiction, both times in *Pride and prejudice*. The implication in both cases is that it is being offered to lighten the mood, or to offer something more familiar or accessible to the drawing-room audience – and in both cases the Scottish music is suitable for dancing, rather than singing. Erin Helyard writes in disparaging terms of the notion of taste, in *Pride and prejudice*, as 'an attitude that only barely disguised the reality of playing simple national tunes to enliven domestic settings of courtship and family entertainment'.[6]

The first time Scottish music is mentioned in *Pride and prejudice*, the Bennet family are at Sir William Lucas's, 'where a large party were assembled' (*PP*, p. 24), including the Bingleys and Mr Darcy. Elizabeth plays and sings, but 'after a song or two, and before she could reply to the entreaties of several that she would sing again, she was eagerly succeeded at the instrument' by her sister. 'Mary, at the end of a long concerto, was glad to purchase praise and gratitude by Scotch and Irish airs, at the request of her younger sisters' (*PP*, p. 25). The younger Bennet sisters dance with some officers, while 'Mr Darcy stood near them in silent indignation at such a mode of passing the evening, to the exclusion of all conversation'. He rather impolitely replies to Sir William's enthusiastic approval of the dancing by asserting that 'Every savage can dance' (*PP*, p. 25).

On the second occasion, Elizabeth is at Netherfield visiting her sister Jane, who is ill. Miss Bingley has complied 'with alacrity' to Mr Darcy's request for music. 'After playing some Italian songs, Miss Bingley varied the charm by a lively Scotch air' (*PP*, p. 51). Darcy, hearing the change in pace, approaches Elizabeth and asks if she would like 'to seize such an opportunity of dancing a reel' (*PP*, p. 52). Elizabeth refuses, but this development alarms Caroline Bingley, who no doubt now wishes she had politely let Elizabeth play the piano. It is the moment when she begins to be jealous and starts wanting to 'get rid of Elizabeth' (*PP*, p. 52). Darcy's reaction to the dance music is in each case an indication of a stage in his descent from the lonely pedestal of pride. Music in a social setting continues to play a role in Darcy's increasing attraction to Elizabeth.[7]

On the many other occasions in the novels when a woman sings, Austen's contemporary audience would have understood the kind of repertoire she would have drawn on, including Scottish traditional songs alongside ballads from English theatre and songs from French and Italian opera. Many poets and musicians were involved in making Scottish song so popular throughout the eighteenth century, but none has had the enduring influence of Robert Burns.

Robert Burns[8]

Robert Burns and Jane Austen, while both being objects of literary idolatry today, had little in common, as Elaine Bander writes, 'except for their limited formal education, enthusiastic reading, comic wit, and unquenchable desire to write. They differed in almost every other respect: nationality, gender, class, politics, religion, temperament, and (conspicuously) sexual experience.'[9] Burns died in 1796, but his celebrity was well established and his reputation as a poet and as a philanderer lived on during Jane Austen's later years. His *Works* were published in 1800 in London by Cadell, followed in 1808 by Cromek's *Reliques of Robert Burns*, and in 1816 Wordsworth published his *Letter to a friend of Robert Burns occasioned by an intended republication of the account of the life of Burns, by Dr Currie*, an impassioned defence of Burns's reputation.

Although there can be no doubt that she knew Burns's poetry, the only surviving references to him in Austen's writings (including the surviving letters) are in *Sanditon*. Charlotte Heywood,

the heroine of the incomplete novel fragment, is confronted by
the rhapsodies of Sir Edward Denham, a devoted fan of Burns:
'I confess my sence of his Pre-eminence Miss H. – If Scott *has* a
fault, it is the want of Passion. … But Burns is always on fire,'
he enthuses (*MW*, p. 397). Charlotte's reaction is to hose him
down:

> I have read several of Burn's Poems with great delight, said
> Charlotte as soon as she had time to speak, but I am not poetic
> enough to separate a Man's Poetry entirely from his Character; –
> and poor Burns's known Irregularities, greatly interrupt my
> enjoyment of his Lines. – I have difficulty in depending on the
> *Truth* of his Feelings as a Lover. I have not faith in the *sincerity* of
> the affections of a Man of his Description. He felt & he wrote
> and he forgot. (*MW*, pp. 397–8)

This has usually been interpreted as a fairly transparent statement of Austen's own views of Burns. However, there are reasons for caution. Firstly, *Sanditon* is very much a first draft, and a
fragment at that; and though it appears *prima facie* that Charlotte
is a sensible, reliable character – 'a pleasing young woman of
two and twenty' (*MW*, p. 374) – whose opinions may coincide
with those of her author, since Austen did not write beyond the
first twelve chapters I would be reluctant to jump to any such
conclusions. And consider the context of this conversation. Sir
Edward, whose 'great object in life was to be seductive' (*MW*,
p. 405), is, not to put too fine a point on it, chatting Charlotte up:

> The Coruscations of Talent, elicited by impassioned feeling in the
> breast of Man, are perhaps incompatible with some of the pro-
> saic Decencies of Life; – nor can you, loveliest Miss Heywood –
> (speaking with an air of deep sentiment) – nor can any Woman
> be a fair Judge of what a Man may be propelled to say, write or
> do, by the sovereign impulses of illimitable Ardour. (*MW*, p. 398)

Austen and British song

Charlotte, very sensibly, decides to pour cold water on this: 'This was very fine; – but if Charlotte understood it at all, not very moral – being moreover by no means pleased with his extraordinary stile of compliment, she gravely answered "I really know nothing of the matter"' (*MW*, p. 398). And she changes the subject to the weather.

So there is not much to go on in *Sanditon*, apart from the repetition of a fairly generally held disapproval of Burns's private life, as well as an admission of 'great delight' in reading his poetry.

Turning to the Austen family music books, we find two Burns songs in Austen's manuscript book 'Juvenile songs and lessons', 'My love she's but a lassie yet' and 'My ain kind dearie', but only as sets of variations for piano solo, without their words. Although there are many other Scottish songs, only once do we find Burns's words written in Austen's hand. The song, titled by Austen 'Song from Burns', is 'Their groves o' sweet myrtle'; both a love song and a fierce statement of Scottish nationalist fervour:

> Their groves o' sweet myrtle let Foreign Lands reckon,
> Where bright-beaming summers exalt the perfume;
> Far dearer to me yon lone glen o' green breckan,
> Wi' the burn stealing under the lang, yellow broom.
> Far dearer to me are yon humble broom bowers
> Where the blue-bell and gowan lurk, lowly, unseen;
> For there, lightly tripping, among the wild flowers,
> A-list'ning the linnet, aft wanders my Jean.
>
> Tho' rich is the breeze in their gay, sunny valleys,
> And cauld Caledonia's blast on the wave;
> Their sweet-scented woodlands that skirt the proud palace,
> What are they? – the haunt of the Tyrant and Slave.
> The Slave's spicy forests, and gold-bubbling fountains,

She played and sang

The brave Caledonian views wi' disdain;
He wanders as free as the winds of his mountains,
Save Love's willing fetters – the chains of his Jean.[10]

Gillaspie (now Glen) notes that 'one unusual feature of Jane Austen's music copying is her occasional alteration of the lyrics – either to make the words applicable to the extended Austen family or to change the excessive sentiments expressed',[11] and it is with great excitement that researchers have noted a slight difference in Jane Austen's version of these lyrics. Aside from the occasional variation in spelling – 'of' for 'o'' and so on – the last line of each verse is slightly changed. In verse one, 'Jean' is altered to 'Jane', and in verse two, 'the chains of his Jean' becomes 'the charms of his Jane'. Surely here we have evidence that Austen, however much her public persona disapproved of Burns, secretly admired him, even perhaps cherished a secret fantasy of taking the place of his wife Jean in his affections.

The painstaking research of Jeanice Brooks of Southampton University has called this romantic notion into question. She has found the same alterations of these lines in another manuscript book which belonged to Mary Egerton, copied in about 1801 and currently held at Tatton Park, near Knutsford in Cheshire.[12] There is no evidence that Austen knew Mary Egerton, and it is likely that both manuscripts were copied from printed sheet music in circulation at the time, though it is difficult to confirm this as no edition of this version has been found. There are also important differences between the two versions. The reason for the change in words, presumably by an unknown editor, can only be guessed at, but one might remark that, while in verse one 'Jean' rhymes with 'unseen', in verse two 'disdain' seems to require 'Jane' rather than 'Jean'.

Brooks discusses this song at length in her article 'In search of Austen's missing songs'. She points out that, relying on the material on either side of the song, the date of copying can be narrowed to 1798 to 1808.[13] This decade takes Austen from age twenty-two to thirty-two. She may have been amused by the possibilities that the reference brought to mind, or perhaps she just liked the song: it is a robust Scottish air and the words are eloquent and pithy, with their sweeping disdain for the effete foreigner and their pride in the hardy 'brave Caledonian'. Brooks notes that Austen's version of the words, while matching the Anglicisation of the names in the last lines of each verse, in other respects 'matches the reading of more authoritative publications of Burns's poetry' than the other manuscript version.[14]

As discussed in Chapter 2, Austen's niece Caroline remembers her singing this song, among others, towards the end of her life, when she had 'nearly left off singing' (*Memoir*, p. 193). As for Austen's attitude to Burns, little can be safely assumed, beyond the fact that she had read his poetry with some enjoyment, and that she had reservations about the sincerity of the sentiments he expressed. This engaging 'Song from Burns' adds little definite information but allows a tantalising glimpse of another range of possibilities.

Thomas Moore and Ireland in song

There is even less external information about her reasons for transcribing songs of the Irish poet Thomas Moore. Moore – often known in his publications as 'Thomas Moore the Poet', is most famous today for his lyrics to songs such as 'The last rose of summer' and 'The harp that once through Tara's halls'. Born in Ireland in 1779 of an Irish Catholic family, he was already, in his twenties, becoming well known as a poet when he began working with Sir John Stevenson on a series of Irish song collections. In a letter to Stevenson quoted in the first volume of *Irish melodies*, Moore writes:

> I feel very anxious that a Work of this Kind should be undertaken. We have too long neglected the only Talent for which our English Neighbours ever deigned to allow us any credit. Our National Music has never been properly collected. ... The Task which you propose to me, of adapting Words to these Airs, is by no means easy. The Poet who would follow the various Sentiments which they express must feel and understand that rapid Fluctuation of Spirits, that unaccountable Mixture of Gloom and Levity, which compose the Character of my Countrymen, and has deeply tinged their Music. Even in their liveliest Strains we find some melancholy Note intrude, some minor Third or flat Seventh, which throws its Shade as it passes, and make even Mirth interesting. If BURNS had been an Irishman ... his heart would have been proud of such Music, and his Genius would have made it immortal.[15]

Thus began a project which continued from 1807 until 1834, beyond Stevenson's death in 1833 when Henry Bishop took over as arranger of the music. Moore's mention of Burns not only implies his profound admiration for the Scottish bard's 'genius' but also underlines the fact that Scottish song had become so prominent in European culture, partly owing to the efforts of Burns, and that this publication is intended to redress the balance in favour of Irish song.

Moore regarded music 'as the well-spring of his lyrical writing', and 'his response to music was essentially emotional', according to Una Hunt. In his *Irish melodies* 'the words grew directly out of the musical form of the airs'.[16] He would compose the poetry in his head while walking, so as to achieve the ultimate bond between lyric and music. This is an interesting and graphic illustration of the embodiment of song not just in performance but in its creation.

Austen collected five of Moore's songs in her later manuscript book. They all appear towards the end of this album and are concentrated within a few pages. The earliest by publication date, 'The wreath you wove', was published in about 1803. Moore later described this 'song' as one of his 'juvenile productions',[17] without specifying whether he wrote the music as well as the words. It seems more certain that he wrote both words and music of 'Here's the bower she loved so much', published in 1807 separately from the *Irish melodies*. The first of these is a song of unrequited love, while the second is a lament for the untimely death of a young woman.

Two others explicitly draw their melodies from the Irish folk tradition – 'Fly not yet' and 'Eveleen's bow'r'. 'Fly not yet' is from Volume 1 of *Irish melodies* and appears to be a straightforward love song, while 'Eveleen's bow'r', from Volume 2, concerns a woman who has been seduced by 'The lord of the valley' and whose honour is therefore irretrievably 'stained'. There is certainly a political element in this song, concerning not only sex, race and class but also the English ascendancy in Ireland. I discuss it briefly in the context of other songs with political subtexts in a recent article on 'The Hindoo girl's song'.[18]

Another of these songs, 'Love, my Mary, dwells with thee', was also published as a Moore lyric set to an 'ancient ballad', arranged by Stevenson, although it does not appear in the eight-volume *Irish melodies* series. A sixth Moore song appears a little later in this album, although without Moore's words (or any others): the melody is traditional Irish – 'The Dandy O' – but

Austen has titled it 'The young May moon', the title of Moore's lyric from Volume 5 of *Irish melodies*, even though she does not include the words. It is a simple arrangement for keyboard, different from Stevenson's arrangement in the Moore publication and one that I have been unable to trace elsewhere.

The placement of these songs in Austen's manuscript album, clustered together, indicates that, at some time in 1809 (when the first in her sequence was published) or thereafter, Austen encountered Moore's songs and chose to copy a selection. There is a cluster of songs from the first and second volumes of *Irish melodies* in Rice 1, in Elizabeth's hand, including 'Fly not yet' but none of the other Moore songs in Austen's album. It seems unlikely that there is a direct link, as Elizabeth died in 1808, although Fanny presumably inherited the album and continued to write in it and might have shared it with Austen on one of her later visits. However, all the songs in Austen's manuscript album appear in different sources, so it was not a matter of her coming upon them in a single publication. The items immediately preceding the first in her album are the three German songs from Render's *Tour of the Rhine*. Who can tell what the connection, if any, might be?

'Robin Adair'

Moore's *Irish melodies* are mentioned in *Emma*, the only one of her novels that specifies particular musical works or composers, while 'Robin Adair', an Irish song, is the only piece of music specifically mentioned anywhere. Peter Alexander has written a short article on the significance of this song in *Emma*, pointing out that it can be seen as one of the clues in the intricate 'detective novel' that is *Emma*'s plot.[19]

Austen and British song

'Robin Adair' features in the scene when Jane Fairfax is playing her new piano, a gift that has arrived mysteriously at the modest home she shares with her aunt, Miss Bates, and grandmother. Frank Churchill and Emma are visiting and listening to Jane play. The way Austen uses the word 'play' often implies singing as well: in this case it is not clear whether Jane is singing 'Robin Adair', with its lyrics accusing the singer's lover of acting coldly, or playing a piano arrangement of the melody such as the set of variations by George Kiallmark which is in one of the Austen family music books.

Whether the lyrics are sung by Jane or not, the Irish connection would not have been lost on Austen – or, presumably, her contemporary readers. Jane's dear friend Miss Campbell has just married an Irishman, Mr Dixon, and Jane has declined their kind offer for her to join them at his 'country seat, Balycraig' (*E*, p. 159).

Colleen Taylor has written in detail about the Irish allusions in *Emma*. Although she does not mention 'Robin Adair', she points out that one of the music books that comes with the gift of the piano is 'a new set of Irish melodies' (*E*, p. 242), which is no doubt one of Thomas Moore's eight volumes.[20] However, the song 'Robin Adair' is not in Moore's *Irish melodies*. The melody is 'Eileen Aroon', 'one of the oldest traceable tunes in all fiddle literature', according to the Traditional Tune Archive.[21] The words were written in the middle of the eighteenth century by Lady Caroline Keppel, the daughter of the Earl of Albemarle, who had been forbidden from marrying the penniless Robin Adair. Her parents eventually relented and they married.

Austen copied several other Irish melodies – or melodies she thought were Irish, or that could be either Irish or Scottish – into her various manuscript albums. An example of the confusion of these categories is the English poet Amelia Opie's 'Irish air'. Opie wrote lyrics beginning 'Lost, lost is my quiet' and set them to what she called 'a melody altered from an Irish Air'. However, this is the melody which we know today as 'Ye banks and braes of Bonny Doon', which was published by Neil Gow in 1788 as 'The Caledonian hunt's delight', and later set to words by Burns, who relates an amusing story of its origins.[22]

Contemporary English songs

However, there are also many songs in Austen's albums that are English in the sense that I outline at the beginning of this chapter. English songs by contemporary composers such as James Hook, William Shield, John Wall Callcott and Samuel Webbe are all represented among her manuscripts. As discussed in Chapter 4, there are many songs dramatising the lives of the officers and men of the British Navy and their families, including several by Charles Dibdin. And, of course, there is Jackson's set of *Twelve canzonets* in her printed volume of songs.

Jackson (1730–1803) was twenty years younger than Thomas Arne, and roughly a contemporary of Haydn. In 1791 he wrote a pamphlet titled *Observations on the present state of music in London*, complaining of the neglect of English music in favour of European compositions. He explicitly refrained from naming any particular living composer in his pamphlet, but it is fairly clear that he disliked the adulation with which Haydn was greeted on his first London visit in that year, and was unimpressed by his symphonies. He criticised the current style of singing: high notes were sung too loudly, low notes too softly. But his most bitter complaint was reserved for the reverence with which Handel was still regarded. Handel had died more than thirty years earlier, in 1759, but his music continued to hold the pre-eminent place in the Anglican churches and cathedrals to the exclusion of that of contemporary composers. In addition, as Carrasco shows, Handel's music dominated the programmes of the Hampshire 'music meetings' that included both sacred and secular music, well into Austen's lifetime. She has surveyed the period 1770–1820 and discovered that 'the majority of works performed in this fifty-year time period were by Handel'.[23] Jackson wrote,

> For ought we know, there are numbers of Composers in England who may be very worthy of notice, if they had the advantage of a public exhibition. These are prevented from shewing their abilities, by the idea that Handel alone can compose Oratorios, Anthems, &c. or that no one else can equal, much less excel, what he has done in that class of Music. But, by this prepossession, the public may be cheated out of much pleasure, and all possible improvements precluded.
>
> Let us suppose, that such an exclusive taste had formerly prevailed for the Composers of the age of Charles the First, we then should have lost Purcel; and, if no Music but Purcel's could have been heard in the reign of George the First, Handel himself would have continued unknown.[24]

Jackson is complaining not that Handel was not English but that he had been canonised to such an extent that his music was performed to the exclusion of all others; he somewhat grudgingly admits that much of Handel's music (though not all) is of good quality. His argument, though it applies to church music rather folk music, parallels Roger Fiske's lament quoted above concerning the loss of English traditional music owing to the rage for 'Scotch songs'. As Fiske wrote, despairingly, 'Some forgotten German described England as the Land without Music, and no wonder'.[25] Jackson, two centuries earlier, would probably not be surprised to read those words. Jackson himself was a well-regarded musician in his time. Gammie and McCulloch quote Michael Kelly, who visited Jackson in Exeter: 'His melodies were pure and natural, and some of his madrigals and anthems will live for ever, to the credit of the English school'.[26] Only his *Te Deum* and two or three other vocal works are in print today to represent his lifetime's output.

The *Twelve canzonets* are all duets. They could be sung by sopranos and/or tenors – the range is quite high in both parts. Their accompaniments are figured bass, designed to be improvised by the keyboard player (whether harpsichord or piano). They are all very attractive and well-crafted, with interweaving vocal lines rather than the simple chordal harmony which became more common later in the classical period. In particular Canzonet 8, 'O, Venus, hear O hear my ardent pray'r', is quite ravishing. It is, like the others, contrapuntal in structure, and although it is not florid it requires sophisticated technique to sustain the purity and flow of the vocal lines.

Canzonet 7 is a setting of Shakespeare's 'Take, oh take those lips away' from *Measure for measure*. Jackson also wrote a four-part setting of Arne's well-known melody for 'Where the bee sucks' which was still being reprinted in collections of Shakespeare songs well into the nineteenth century.

Countless composers have written settings of Shakespeare songs, but there is another Shakespearean musical connection in Austen. In the early pages of *Northanger Abbey* Austen, with characteristic irony, explains that part of Catherine's 'training for a heroine' has been reading 'all such works as heroines must read to supply their memories with those quotations which are so serviceable and so soothing in the vicissitudes of their eventful lives' (*NA*, p. 15), including Shakespeare – or at least, snatches of the plays. One of these quotations tells her 'that a young woman in love always looks –

'like Patience on a monument
"Smiling at Grief."' (*NA*, p. 16)

This phrase is from the poignant passage in *Twelfth night* when Viola, disguised as a boy, confesses her love to Duke Orsino without his realising: 'She never told her love, but let conceal-ment, like a worm in the bud, feed on her damask cheek.' This passage was set to music by Joseph Haydn in 1795 during one of his visits to London, and Elizabeth Austen copied it into her music book during the late 1790s. Austen might have been familiar with the passage via that connection, as well as from the play itself. This text is not a song in the play, however, and there was no tradition of setting it to music before Haydn com-posed his magnificent, though brief, canzonet, which was not intended for theatrical performance.

But Haydn's songs were outnumbered in Austen's personal music library by those of James Hook, Stephen Storace, William Shield and Michael Kelly, as well as Charles Dibdin. Each of these composers had their own characteristic style – Hook has ornate and melodious charm, Storace effective stripped-back drama and so on. Dibdin wrote amusing maritime ballads, as discussed in Chapter 4, but he wrote on other themes as well: Austen must have greatly enjoyed his song 'The joys of the country', as I discuss in the next chapter.

Conclusion

Jane Austen, like others in her circle, was a musician but she was not a music historian or an expert in the characteristics of national styles. She copied words and music from a range of sources, sometimes abbreviating a title, or changing it slightly; but she tended to take the description of the music she encountered on trust. The 'Prayer of the Sicilian mariners' seems to have little or nothing to do with Sicily. It was published in the mid-1790s alongside 'The Portuguese hymn on the Nativity', which Elizabeth Austen copied into her manuscript book. This hymn is the familiar Christmas carol 'O come all ye faithful', of uncertain authorship, dating from the mid-seventeenth century, which was published in London, with the Latin words beginning 'Adeste fideles', and was known as the 'Portuguese hymn' because the Duke of Leeds heard it sung at the Portuguese Embassy in 1795. Similarly, 'Scotch' and 'Irish' were used to describe folk music that could come from any part of the British Isles or further abroad. 'The Duke of York's new march' was an arrangement of a melody from an Italian opera written by an Austrian composer. Many of the songs Austen knew as English theatre pieces were actually based on melodies written by European composers for Italian or French opera.

Nevertheless, Austen's music collection shows little of the conscious bias against English music that Fiske and Jackson bemoan. As Gammie and McCulloch write, 'For general entertainment the English school of Arne, Arnold, Boyce, Hook and Jackson had more to offer than foreign entertainments'.[27] The pre-eminence of Handel applied in sacred music more than secular, and there was plenty of English music that was not displaced by the folk traditions of Scotland and Ireland. Her collection shows that she seemed to prefer 'the English school' to showy Italian opera, and although she had a few Italian songs in her repertoire they were not in a virtuosic style.[28] We have seen in Chapter 5 that she preferred sincere musicality and good acting to 'singsong and trumpery' in the theatre. In the music she chose to sing for herself, some of it in Italian, more of it in French, but most in English, there is scope for great expressiveness. This is particularly true of the four songs that she is known to have sung late in life. Each one of them is a small narrative, with opportunities for embodying the feelings of characters in a similar way that she pioneered in her fiction.

In the following two chapters I look at the way music might have influenced her as a writer, firstly in her teenage writings, where there are possible echoes or parodies of songs that she knew, and secondly in a detailed comparison of the rhetoric of the Giordani ballad *Colin and Lucy* with that of *Sense and sensibility*.

7

Juvenile songs and lessons: music culture in Jane Austen's teenage years[1]

Introduction: music and the young Jane Austen

The stories, poems and 'scraps' Jane Austen wrote in her teenage years are now well known as her 'juvenilia' – crazy, irreverent, transgressive miniatures of a wildly creative mind playing and experimenting with literature. During the same years Austen was studying music and forming a collection of songs and keyboard pieces that would stay with her throughout her life. On her return from school in 1786, a piano was bought for her and she apparently had lessons for at least the next ten years (*Family record*, p. 55). Not all the music she studied is known – some was sold with her piano when they left Steventon – but three of the manuscript books with piano music and songs copied out in her own hand include items dating from her teenage years. Her teacher, George William Chard (1765?–1849), was assistant organist at Winchester

Cathedral, and he was also involved in organising public concerts in Winchester for much of his career, as Carrasco shows.[2] Most of Austen's music is secular and much of it is vocal music. This chapter will look specifically at this music, collected during her mid to late teens, in tandem with her teenage writings.

Our view of the music of this period – the three decades straddling the eighteenth and nineteenth centuries – is now largely coloured by the ascendancy of the great composers who were active in Vienna, like Haydn, Mozart and Beethoven. As has been discussed, she knew Haydn's music, and she knew some Mozart although it was not identified. It is unlikely that she had heard of Beethoven at all. There is something oddly disconcerting about one of our greatest writers living at the same time as some of the greatest composers while being apparently unaware of their existence. But music was an important part of her life from childhood through adulthood, although the music she knew was largely different from the repertoire a music student of our time typically learns.

The Austen family music books

Kathryn Sutherland and Freya Johnson observe that Austen's juvenilia, or teenage writings, were not 'intended only for the author's private use. Rather, they were written and prepared for sociable reading and for circulation and performance among family and friends' (*TW*, p. ix). As is shown by the music shared among the family circle discussed in Chapter 2, this is also true of the music albums, some of which include not only music in different scripts but also several pieces of music which were probably shared among the family members.

What music was feeding the creative imagination of this young artist? There is no way we can be absolutely certain of what music Austen particularly liked to play and sing in her teenage years. Decades later, as we have seen, her niece Caroline recorded memories of a few songs that she sang to her as a child. But in this early period we can only guess that songs the young Austen took the trouble to copy by hand into her manuscript books might have been favourites – although it would also be revealing if she spent money on buying music, expensive at that time.

There are three music books from this period with manuscripts in Austen's hand, described in detail in Chapter 1. 'Juvenile songs and lessons' contains no vocal music, so, apart from providing a perfect title for this chapter about music and the juvenilia, this book is not of such great interest to me here, because it is in the songs, like those that appear in the second album, 'Songs and duetts', that we can most clearly see links between the teenage writings and the music that Austen was playing when she wrote them. The third album is a mixture of printed and manuscript music in various hands. About sixteen of the manuscripts in this scrapbook album are copies of music that dates from the period when Austen was writing the juvenilia.

Songs in the juvenilia

In these teenage writings, Austen occasionally includes a song lyric. In the introduction to the Juvenilia Press edition of *Frederic and Elfrida* Sylvia Hunt writes that the juvenilia are 'not only the apprentice work of a budding writer but also a commentary through parody on the ridiculous aspects of the sentimental novel'.[3] Austen's music collection shows that she was also well aware of the ridiculous aspects of the sentimental song. There are three potential song lyrics in 'Frederic & Elfrida' (1787–1790).[4] One, in the best folksong tradition, is overheard by the characters when they are out walking. A young woman is heard singing:

> That Damon was in love with me
> I once thought & beleiv'd
> But now that he is not I see,
> I fear I was deceiv'd. (*MW*, p. 5)

Although Damon is a common name for an Arcadian shepherd in this repertoire, this might almost be a direct reference to the song 'How gentle was my Damon's air' from Thomas Arne's 1738 masque setting of Milton's *Comus*, which is included in a later manuscript book and was probably not copied until the late 1790s. However, the masque itself was well known throughout this period, as I have discussed in Chapter 5, so Austen might have known it when she was a teenager. There is a comic contrast between the perfunctory commonsense of Austen's version and the plaintive agonising of the nymph in *Comus*, who wanders disconsolately around the countryside, while 'all nature does my loss deplore'.

The Epitaph in 'Frederic & Elfrida' on the death of Charlotte, who extricated herself from a tricky romantic situation by throwing 'herself into a deep stream which ran thro' her Aunts pleasure Grounds in Portland Place' – itself a ludicrous concept – and floated conveniently but impossibly to her home village, though not explicitly a song, has many possible musical models, including 'My Phillida' by Miss Mellish, which is almost silly enough in parts to have been written by the young Austen:

She played and sang

Ding dong, my Phillida is dead,
I'll stick a branch of willow at my fair Philli's head.

The narrator of 'Frederic & Elfrida' first gives Charlotte's Epitaph:

Here lies our friend who having promis-ed
That unto two she would be marri-ed
Threw her sweet Body & her lovely face
Into the Stream that runs thro' Portland Place.

And then she goes on: 'These sweet lines, as pathetic as beautiful were never read by anyone who passed that way, without a shower of tears, which if they should fail of exciting in you, Reader, your mind must be unworthy to peruse them' (*MW*, p. 9). Having thus cavalierly disposed of one of the main characters, possibly for the sole purpose of composing 'sweet … pathetic' and 'beautiful' lines on her, and directed this unexpected beam of authorial bossiness towards the unwary reader, the narrator skips off to relate the next scene, in which Rebecca's mother is persuaded at the point of a dagger to allow her to marry her fiancé forthwith. And naturally, they celebrate with a song, about Corydon buying a ribbon for Bess with which she 'made herself look very fess' (*MW*, p. 10). Corydon is a stock romantic name, like Damon, and he is the bridegroom in James Hook's delightful 1784 pastoral song 'The wedding day', included in Austen's 'Songs and duetts' manuscript book.

In 'The first act of a comedy' (1793), a mere two pages sets up a farcical plot, complete with two songs sung by 'Chloe & a chorus of ploughboys' which could have been written, a hundred years later, by W. S. Gilbert. However, the eighteenth-century English stage was teeming with knockabout musical comedies and Austen certainly saw some of them. Her music collection includes many songs from the theatre: often musically quite simple, with straightforward harmonies and tunes often borrowed from Italian opera or Scottish folk music. In the notes to the Juvenilia Press edition of 'The first act of a comedy', the significance of the 'chorus of ploughboys' is discussed in some detail: 'By selecting ploughboys as her chorus, JA seems to exaggerate how very "unmusical" these musical comedies were in comparison with the sophistication, complexity and harmony of the traditional opera style'[5] – although how familiar and sympathetic Austen was with 'traditional opera' is a moot point, as discussed in Chapter 5.

Charles Dibdin and 'The joys of the country'

In her 'Ode to pity' from 1793 Austen delights in the humour of high-flown language: 'the Paths of honour and the Myrtle Grove' – juxtaposed with the ridiculous: 'Gently brawling down the turnpike road, Sweetly noisy falls the Silent Stream'. This little comic Ode is quirky and original:

> The hut, the Cot, the Grot, & Chapel queer,
> And eke the Abbey too a mouldering heap,
> Conceal'd by aged pines her head doth rear
> And quite invisible doth take a peep. (*MW*, p. 66)

Only the teenage Austen could conceive of these lines, but they could have had any number of models. For example, Sutherland and Johnston discuss the influence of Alexander Pope and Samuel Johnson on her capacity 'to engineer comic flops, to stage a series of triumphant verbal and syntactic letdowns' (*TW*, p. xxxii). They might have added the songwriter Charles Dibdin to this duo. Four of Dibdin's songs appear in Austen's teenage repertoire, and others crop up in later volumes of her music, several of them on naval topics, as discussed in Chapter 4. In a career spanning the early 1760s to the Regency period, Dibdin often performed his own songs in a series of one-man shows in theatres around London. He developed a large repertoire of characters, varying the register and tone of his songs, from the comic to the 'pathetic' and the grandiose,[6] and 'his amazing ability to mimic provincial accents' and people of different social classes meant he could carry the audience with him through an evening's programme containing nearly three dozen songs.[7] One of the songs from his 1790 'entertainment' titled *The wags* is 'The joys of the country':

> Let bucks and let bloods to praise London agree,
> The joys of the country my jewel for me!
> Where sweet is the flower that the maybush adorns,
> And how charming to gather it, but for the thorns.
> Where we walk o'er the mountains with health our cheeks glowing,
> As warm as a toast honey when it ent snowing,
> Where nature to smile when she joyful inclines,
> And the sun charms us all the year round, when it shines.
> *Refrain:* Oh the mountains and vallies and bushes,
> The pigs and the screech owls and thrushes!
> Let bucks and let bloods to praise London agree,
> The joys of the country my jewel for me!

In this first verse, we have a comic litany of contradictions: we enjoy the maybush but for the thorns; it is warm as long as it is not snowing; the sun charms – when it shines. The refrain celebrates 'mountains and vallies and bushes' in one breath, only to come to 'pigs and the screech owls and thrushes' in the next line, in comic juxtaposition of the sublime and the ridiculous that Austen often employs in the teenage writings: in 'Love and freindship' (1790), the protagonist Laura writes:

> The place was suited to meditation. – . A Grove of full-grown Elms sheltered us from the East – . A Bed of full-grown Nettles from the West – . Before us ran the murmuring brook and behind us ran the turn-pike road. (*MW*, p. 97)

That passage in turn echoes the contradictory 'gentle brawling' of the turnpike road and the impossibility of a 'silent stream' that is 'sweetly noisy' in Austen's 'Ode to pity'.

The song continues:

> There twelve hours on a stretch we in angling delight,
> As patient as Job tho' we ne'er get a bite.
> There we pop at the wild ducks and frighten the crows,
> While so lovely the icicles hang from our cloathes.
> There wid Aunts and wid Cousins & Grandmothers talking
> We are caught in the rain as we're all out a-walking
> While the muslins and gauzes cling round each fair she
> That they look all like Venuses sprung from the sea.
> *Refrain:* Oh the mountains and vallies and bushes [etc].

In verse two, the men are hunting and fishing – this is very much a masculine song – and then the rain starts while they are out walking with female relatives, offering the delighted singer and his friends a vision of diaphanous clothing clinging to the figures of each 'fair she'. The hyperbolic world of this verse is akin to much of the juvenilia – one might think of Sir William Mountague, his 'Park well stocked with Deer', his refusal to get married on the First of September because he 'was a Shot & could not support the idea of losing such a day', and his propensity to fall 'violently in love' with every lovely young woman he sees.

The third verse adds another dimension: country hospitality.

She played and sang

Then how sweet in the dogdays to take the fresh air
Where to save you expence the dust powders your hair.
There pleasures like snowballs encrease as they roll
And tire you to death – not forgetting the Bowl,
Where in mirth and good fellowship always delighting
We agree, that is when we're not squabbling and fighting
Then wid toasts and pint bumpers we bodder the head
Just to see who most gracefully staggers to bed.
Oh the mountains and vallies and bushes,
The pigs and the screech owls and thrushes!
Let bucks and let bloods to praise London agree,
The joys of the country my jewel for me!

The jokes continue, with heavy irony that might remind us of Mary Crawford's amused horror at 'country ways', decades later, in *Mansfield Park*. Although the singer claims, in the refrain of each verse, to leave the admiration of London to 'bucks and bloods' while he seeks 'the joys of the country', his is a very urban sensibility. He notices the dust along with the fresh air, and is exhausted by 'pleasures like snowballs'. And then they visit the 'Bowl', or public house, where all is harmony, except when it's not, and they compete in drunkenness and who can 'most gracefully stagger to bed.' They are, however, somewhat more restrained than the Johnsons in Austen's 'Jack & Alice' (1787–1790), who, 'the bottle being pretty briskly pushed about … the whole party were carried home, Dead Drunk' (*MW*, p. 14).

This song was published in 1790 and the other songs around it in Austen's manuscript book are from the early 1790s. She may not have known the song at the time when she was writing the earlier juvenilia, but Austen and Dibdin both clearly relished the same comic traditions of ludicrous juxtapositions, hyperbole and mockery of masculine swaggering and drunkenness.

Austen obviously enjoyed Dibdin's well-crafted and singable songs, which she must have sung herself without any qualms about their explicitly masculine subject positions. A similar lack of regard towards established gender roles also appears in the juvenilia: in 'Frederic & Elfrida' the two title characters are introduced as 'exceedingly handsome and so much alike, that it was not every one who knew them apart' (*MW*, p. 4). Their distinguishing features are listed, but difference in sex is not one of them. And the exploits of some of her heroines are far from ladylike: 'The beautifull Cassandra' (c. 1788), for example, stealing bonnets and ices completely without compunction and striding around the streets of London for seven hours (*MW*, pp. 44–7), and Eliza, in 'Henry & Eliza' (1787–1790), escaping from prison and walking thirty miles 'without stopping' (*MW*, pp. 37–8). As Karen Hartnick writes, 'Eliza lives out the traditional male adventure – she leaves her family, travels, faces danger, demonstrates cunning and bravery, and defeats her enemies in armed battle. … Only in the juvenilia would Jane Austen allow her heroine a hero's rewards.'[8] This must have been liberating for the teenage Austen, and I am reminded of her letter to her niece Caroline from decades later, regretting that Caroline (being not only young but also female) could not visit her aunts at the cottage in Chawton as often as her older brother James Edward (*Letters*, p. 326). The letters, like the novels, often refer to the complex arrangements which had to be made if women were to travel any distance from home.

'The mansion of peace'

In many other songs in Austen's music manuscript books the singer is explicitly male, but often they have little else in common with Dibdin's comic songs. For example, 'The mansion of peace', by Samuel Webbe (1740–1816), is a highly sentimental love song in a strain which is satirised in many of the teenage pieces. In 'A collection of letters' (1792), Henrietta's lover Musgrove writes: 'Adorable Henrietta how beautiful you are! I declare you are quite divine! You are more than Mortal. You are an angel. You are Venus herself' (*MW*, p. 163). This passage shares the same strain of hyperbolic flattery as the lyrics of 'The mansion of peace':

> Soft zephyr on thy balmy wing
> Thy gentlest breezes hither bring.
> Her slumbers guard, some hand divine.
> Ah! Watch her with a care like mine.
> A rose, a rose from her bosom has strayed,
> I'll seek to replace it, replace it with art.
> But no, no no, twill her slumbers invade.
> I'll wear it (fond youth) next my heart.
> Alas, silly rose, silly rose hadst thou known,
> 'Twas Daphne that gave thee thy place.
> Thou never, no never, from thy station hadst flown.
> Her bosom's the Mansion of Peace.

This song was published in 1780 in Dublin but is the second-last song in Austen's manuscript book, so could not have been copied until after other songs from about 1794. (Despite the masculine persona, a London edition in 1790 attributed the text to 'A Lady'.) This kind of lyric was typical of the artificial and formulaic eighteenth-century poetic diction that the Romantic movement rejected. Austen's character Henrietta might be just as delighted with the inane flattery of this song as she had been with Musgrove's love letter, which exaggerates these tropes even more.

Juvenile songs and lessons

Another song is directly referenced in this letter. Henrietta's friend Lady Scudamore later reports him saying: 'Yes I'm in love I feel it now, and Henrietta Halton has undone me', which Henrietta finds 'a Sweet Way ... of declaring his Passion!' (*MW*, p. 167). These lines are adapted from a lyric by William Whitehead which was set by Thomas Arne, among others, and it is discussed at some length in Chapter 5. The tone of this piece undercuts the artificial sentimentality of songs like 'The mansion of peace' more subtly but as surely as Austen's juvenilia satirises the sentimental fiction of the period.

'For tenderness form'd'

Another staple of the sentimental repertoire of the time is what we might call the song of an innocent, and often hard-done-by, young person. In 'Henry and Eliza', Eliza sits under a tree, 'happy in the conscious knowledge of her own Excellence', and amuses herself by 'making & singing the following Lines':

> Though misfortunes my footsteps may ever attend
> I hope I shall never have need of a Friend
> as an innocent Heart I will ever preserve
> and will never from Virtue's dear boundaries swerve. (*MW*, p. 34)

The joke here is that she is far from innocent, and has been turned out of her benefactors' house because she has stolen £50. Austen very consciously subverts this genre, with which she was certainly familiar. There are several songs in this vein in Austen's music books. One is 'For tenderness form'd,' which appears as print music in the scrapbook volume. The song

comes from a 1786 play by John Burgoyne called *The heiress*.
The melody is adapted by Thomas Linley from an aria in the
Italian composer Giovanni Paisiello's score for his opera *The
barber of Seville*.

> For tenderness form'd in life's early day,
> A parents soft sorrows to mine led the way;
> the lesson of pity was caught from her eye,
> and e'er words were my own, I spoke with a sigh.
> The nightingale plunder'd, the mate widow'd dove,
> the warbled complaint of the suffering grove,
> to youth as it ripen'd gave sentiment new,
> the object still changing the sympathy true.
> Soft embers of passion yet rest in their glow,
> a warmth of more pain may this breast never know,
> or if too indulgent the blessing I claim,
> let the spark drop from reason that weakens the flame.

'For tenderness form'd' is a well-crafted and effective expression of this species of modest self-promotion. Another song in
this vein, 'Since then I'm doom'd', is more consciously satirical.
It comes from Isaac Bickerstaff's 1792 play *The spoilt child*, and
incidentally also takes its melody from a version of *The barber of
Seville*, in this case the original 1775 French stage production of
Beaumarchais's play. The lyrics begin,

> Since then I'm doom'd this sad reverse to prove,
> To quit each object of my infant care.
> Torn from an honoured parent's tender love,
> And driven the keenest storms of fate to bear.

This song is in Austen's manuscript book but probably dates
from 1792, slightly later than most of the juvenilia, and certainly later than 'Henry and Eliza', but the lyrics, with their
lavish self-pity, echo Eliza's situation more closely than 'For

tenderness form'd'. What Eliza's song and these two theatre songs share is the slightly absurd pathos of injured innocence in a self-justifying lament.

As mentioned in Chapter 1, *The spoilt child* may have been performed by Austen family members and friends at private theatricals at Godmersham in 1805 and unfortunately it is not known who, on that occasion, might have played the character of Little Pickle, who sings this song when he is banished from his home after cooking his aunt's pet parrot and serving it to her in a pie.

'Queen Mary's lamentation'

A more serious type of lament also appears in this manuscript book. There is a long tradition of a lamentation 'supposed to be written' by a historical figure, often a queen awaiting execution. The first of two lamentations in Austen's manuscript book is a ballad titled 'Captivity', first published in 1793, which is discussed in some detail in Chapter 3.

Immediately after this ballad in Austen's music manuscript comes Tommaso Giordani's 1782 arrangement of the traditional Scottish air 'Queen Mary's lamentation'.

> I sigh and lament me in vain,
> These walls can but echo my moan:
> Alas it increases my pain,
> When I think of the days that are gone!
> Through the grate of my prison, I see
> The birds as they wanton in air;
> My heart how it pants to be free,
> My looks they are wild with despair.
> Above, tho' opprest by my fate,
> I burn with contempt for my foes;

Tho' fortune has alter'd my state,
She ne'er can subdue me to those.
False woman! In ages to come,
Thy malice detested shall be;
And, when we are cold in the tomb,
Some heart still will sorrow for me.
Ye roofs! where cold damps and dismay,
With silence and solitude dwell,
how comfortless passes the day,
How sad tolls the evening bell!
The owls from the battlements cry,
Hollow winds seem to murmur around,
'O Mary, prepare thee to die:' –
My blood it runs chill at the sound.

Figure 7.1 'Queen Mary's lamentation' from Austen's manuscript
book 'Songs and Duetts'

Juvenile songs and lessons

Mary Spongberg points out that in her youthful, parodic 'History of England', written in November 1791, 'Austen rendered Mary Stuart's fate central to the history of England by mentioning her in the reign of every single Tudor monarch'.[9] 'The history of England' is, like most of Austen's teenage writing, for the most part witty and wildly satirical, but, when it came to Queen Elizabeth's crimes against Mary, Austen's wit falls away and is replaced by passionate intensity:

> what must not her most noble mind have suffered when informed that Elizabeth had given orders for her Death! Yet she bore it with a most unshaken fortitude, firm in her Mind; Constant in her Religion; & prepared herself to meet the cruel fate to which she was doomed, with a magnanimity that could alone proceed from conscious Innocence. (*MW*, p. 145)

The sentiments expressed in Austen's strongly partisan rhetoric are shared by the lyrics of 'Queen Mary's lamentation'. The words are not actually by Mary Queen of Scots: although some of her poetry does survive, in this case both the words and the tune are anonymous. The song dramatises Mary's plight, using for the most part clichéd sentimental melodramatic verse. Some lines in the second verse stand out: 'I burn with contempt for my foes', and 'False woman! In ages to come, / Thy malice detested shall be'. The implication, of course, is that the 'foes' are the English and that the 'false woman' is Queen Elizabeth. Austen's version is more explicit:

> It was the peculiar misfortune of this Woman [that is, Elizabeth] to have bad Ministers – Since wicked as she herself was, she could not have committed such extensive Mischeif, had not those vile & abandoned Men connived at, & encouraged her in her Crimes. (*MW*, pp. 144–5)

This passage threatens to tip over into absurdity, but there is no doubting Austen's strong partiality for the Stuart cause and her awareness of the historical context.

Conclusion

G. K. Chesterton wrote in his Preface to an early edition of the juvenilia that

> there is not a shadow of indication anywhere that this independent intellect and laughing spirit was other than contented with a narrow domestic routine, in which she wrote a story as domestic as a diary in the intervals of pies and puddings, without so much as looking out of the window to notice the French Revolution.[10]

However, this edition included 'The history of England', which, although often very funny, is an explicitly Jacobite text. Austen's manuscript book of 'Songs and duetts', as discussed in Chapter 3, contains within just a few pages the laments of Mary Stuart and of Queen Marie Antoinette, as well as 'The Marseillaise' and other songs with political angles both explicit and implicit, which further complicates this picture.

Austen could not have composed these high-spirited and eloquent fragments in her teenage years without a knowledge of the theatrical world of her day, or without awareness of the radical turmoil in France which had life-changing consequences for her cousin Eliza, and which threw a new light on anything which might have been thought of as normality. The contents of Austen's music collection provide further insights to the evolving picture of the historical, social and cultural milieu in which she wrote. To investigate a possible instance of linkage between her music collection and her more mature writing, the next chapter compares in detail the rhetoric of a piece of music in Austen's collection with the narrative structure and prose of *Sense and sensibility*.

8

Marianne and Willoughby, Lucy and Colin: betrayal, suffering, death and the poetic image[1]

'Lucy and Colin'

'Lucy and Colin' is a 1725 ballad by the English poet Thomas Tickell (1686–1740). In 1747 Oliver Goldsmith wrote that, in this ballad, Tickell 'seems to have surpassed himself. It is, perhaps, the best in our language in this way.'[2] Tickell's reputation has waned considerably since then: in the 1912 *Cambridge history of English literature* Thomas Seccombe called 'Lucy and Colin' 'a wooden ballad in eight and six'.[3] The 1993 edition of the *Cambridge guide to literature in English* mentions his feud with Alexander Pope and his friendship with Joseph Addison, but says 'his work is largely forgotten'.[4]

Tickell's ballad survived his death in 1740 in at least one form. In 1783 it was set to music (as 'Colin and Lucy') by Tommaso Giordani (c. 1730–1806), an Italian musician working in Dublin, in a seven-part cantata, and a copy of Giordani's setting was purchased by someone in the Austen family and bound in a volume with other music. Jane Austen knew this volume herself and at some stage owned it – her signature appears on the page facing the handwritten title page. If Austen sang this ballad, I wonder whether her embodiment of Giordani's music – playing and singing – might have affected her treatment of some of the plot elements that Tickell's florid melodrama shares with *Sense and sensibility*, a novel of complex and ambiguous power.

The outline of the ballad's story is this. Lucy, a beautiful young woman of Leinster (a province in the east of Ireland: Tickell lived much of his life in Dublin), is abandoned by her lover, Colin, for a richer woman. Lucy falls ill and as her death, and Colin's wedding day, approach she asks her friends to carry her corpse to the wedding feast and present it to Colin. They do so; Colin is immediately struck dead with remorse; and he and Lucy are buried together. Their grave becomes a site of pilgrimage for lovers and a warning for the unfaithful 'swain'.

This scenario was not invented by Tickell: there is an earlier folk ballad called 'Fair Margaret and Sweet William', with a later version, 'William and Margaret', probably written by the Anglo-Scots playwright David Mallet. Tickell's 'Lucy and Colin', when first published in Dublin, was explicitly subtitled 'A song written in Imitation of William and Margaret'.[5] An interesting twist is that, while the earlier ballad describes the spurned Margaret's ghost appearing before William at midnight and taxing him directly with his faithlessness, in Tickell's version it is not a ghost but the actual dead body of Lucy with which Colin is confronted, and the scene is his wedding, in broad daylight. This change from the supernatural to the literal imparts a certain grotesquely comic melodrama to the story. It also removes words from the confrontation. Lucy's mute corpse in itself is a sufficient rebuke to Colin to cause him to fall dead.

Whether Austen would have known the poem apart from the Giordani setting is unsure, but Tickell's reputation was not yet in eclipse by the end of the eighteenth century. The poem was included in such anthologies as Robert Dodsley's *Collection of poems in six volumes by several hands* (1758), a copy of which Austen owned, and sold for 10 shillings in May 1801 (*Letters*, p. 88). Tickell's collected poetical works were published in 1781 and 1796, and in 1788 a print by William Ward titled 'Lucy of Leinster' was published. In the absence of other evidence, however, I will assume that Austen knew the story of 'Colin and Lucy' best through Giordani's cantata.

Sense and sensibility

There are clearly parallels between Lucy and Colin's story and the abortive love plot in *Sense and sensibility*. A beautiful young woman (Lucy/Marianne) is courted and then abandoned for a richer woman. There is a confrontation. The young woman falls ill and nearly dies; her former lover (Colin/Willoughby), learning of her illness, reacts in an extreme and dramatic way. The outcomes, of course, are different: Marianne recovers and marries sensibly; Willoughby survives and returns to the wife he believes he will never love. The differences are as telling as the similarities, and they concern not only the facts but also the rhetoric of their narration, partly explained by their different genres: narrative poetry versus fiction in the comic tradition. The poem is full of figurative language and romantic imagery which is all but absent in Austen's prose.

The Tickell verse-ballad, 'Lucy and Colin', then, if Austen were familiar with it, is thoroughly recast in *Sense and sensibility*. The melodrama is undercut; the clichéd language avoided.

Marianne and Willoughby, Lucy and Colin

The aesthetic is far more prosaic. But this is not to say that the novel is not dramatic and, in its own way, theatrical. Paula Byrne points out that there are several 'quasi-theatrical devices' in the novel, like the 'set-piece' between Elinor and Lucy Steele:

> Scenes such as this, which contain pointed exchanges of dialogue and repartee, can be traced back to wit-comedies. ... But Austen's dramatic rendering of the polite quarrel in *Sense and sensibility* achieves a realistic quality that transcends the burlesque absurdities of similar comically stylised exchanges in Fielding's plays and novels.[6]

Byrne points out many possible theatrical influences on *Sense and sensibility*, including plays by Sheridan and Congreve: she notes 'specific sentimental conventions from stage comedy, devices that had been assimilated into the sentimental novel: filial defiance, romantic heroes, giddy heroines, kindly benefactors'.[7]

The fact that Austen rarely uses obviously figurative language – a fact comically underlined by Willoughby's self-criticism for using a 'hackneyed metaphor' in his confession to Elinor: 'Thunderbolts and daggers! – what a reproof she [Marianne] would have given me!' (*SS*, p. 325) – does not mean that she does not use imagery at all. Kathleen Fowler, in a discussion of *Mansfield Park*, writes that 'Austen's emblems are almost always natural metaphors, unobtrusively worked into the text'.[8] In *Mansfield Park* Fowler finds a 'natural metaphor' in the apricot tree at Mansfield Parsonage. But where are these 'emblems' to be found in *Sense and sensibility*? It is difficult to find an equivalent metaphor which operates outside the characters' consciousness. Margaret Anne Doody, in her article on 'Turns of speech and figures of mind', identifies metonymy and synecdoche as the dominant types of figuration in *Sense and sensibility*: 'the figurative problems at the center of *Sense and Sensibility* perplex intelligent minds. How to relate parts to wholes, or decide what is "part" and of which "whole"? Physical sense, "common sense", and sensibility alike may err. There is no relief in allegory.'[9]

Doody's 'intelligent minds' belong to the characters: Elinor, Marianne, Brandon. Edward's lock of hair, Lucy's love letters and Sir John Middleton's pointer pups are metonyms, stand-ins for attachments either willing or unwilling, or for friendship bestowed or withheld; but there is nothing in *Sense and sensibility* like the apricot tree at Mansfield Parsonage that occasions a tense exchange between Mrs Norris and Dr Grant. Rodney S. Edgecombe examines trees as a symbolic referent in the novel, but the way they are used in the narrative belongs to the characters, not the narrator. As Edgecombe writes, Edward and Marianne discuss the picturesque: they are both well aware of the significance of their divergent interpretations of trees in the landscape: 'Approaching the topic of trees from several angles, and with an ironized commitment that both endorses and mocks in the same breath, Austen all but fulfils a central dictum of the Picturesque, viz., that "Picturesque composition consists in uniting in one whole a variety of parts"'.[10] The kind of figurative language which is inseparable from Tickell's vein of poetry – and indeed which Austen herself sometimes uses in her rare forays into verse – is inimical to her narrative voice, except when used in quotation or, occasionally, dialogue, when a character is being self-consciously literary. This allies Austen more closely with the naturalistic rhetoric of the theatre than with the poetic diction of the eighteenth century.

But the emotional force of *Sense and sensibility* does not arise from the narrator's ironic denial of figurative language. There is a rhythm in Austen's prose which always rewards reading it aloud, and which it shares with musical phrasing: repetition, sequences and pauses are common, and remind us that Austen was herself a practising musician.

'Colin and Lucy'

Nobody, to my knowledge, has considered the possible influence of Giordani's setting of Tickell's ballad on *Sense and sensibility*. By itself, the verse is clichéd and stilted, the tone melodramatic and full of sentimental excess. However, though the musical setting is no great work of genius, the piece as a whole has an emotional impact well beyond that of the verse on its own.

The full text of Tickell's ballad is printed at the end of this chapter. Giordani has set all nine stanzas, divided into seven through-composed sections, for high voice with piano accompaniment. The first section, 'Of Leinster, famed for maidens fair', in E flat major, is marked Larghetto, and is a reasonably sedate, expository piece in common time (4/4), with an eight-bar piano introduction. Pairs of reversed sequences mimic the Liffey's 'reflection' of Lucy's face. The words 'luckless love' introduce a key change, taking the melody high into the soprano range, with a further intensification via modulation to the relative minor with 'her coral lips'. 'Oh, have you seen a lily pale' brings the melody back to the tonic key, with 'beating rains' emphasised by a run of quaver pairs tied across syllables. The pathos in the last line of this section is expressed by a succession of downward melismas on the words 'drooped' and 'slow'. The last four bars contain a short variation on melodic elements of the last line.

Despite the elevated poetic rhetoric of the lyrics, the music in this first section has more in common with the opening chapter of *Sense and sensibility*: not without dramatic intensity but in essence expository, restraining any tendency to extremes. The 'voice' is the narrator's: sympathetic but impersonal. Unlike Lucy, introduced at the beginning of the poem as 'the grace' of Leinster, which is 'fam'd for maidens fair', Marianne is not physically described in any detail until the beginning of Chapter X of *Sense and sensibility*, when we have already heard much about her temperament:

> Marianne was still handsomer [than Elinor]. Her form, though not so correct as her sister's, in having the advantage of height, was more striking; and her face was so lovely, that when in the common cant of praise, she was called a beautiful girl, truth was less violently outraged than usually happens. Her skin was very brown, but, from its transparency, her complexion was uncommonly brilliant; her features were all good; her smile was sweet and attractive; and in her eyes, which were very dark, there was a life, a spirit, an eagerness, which could hardly be seen without delight. (*SS*, p. 46)

This description, though complimentary, sounds strangely as though Marianne is being assessed against a checklist of criteria: form; face; skin; features; smile; eyes. As is so often the case in Austen, the description occurs at the point when a newly introduced character encounters Marianne: it is implicitly Willoughby's own view, since the previous paragraph ends, 'Of their personal charms he had not required a second interview to be convinced' (*SS*, p. 46). Although in both cases the young woman is unusually beautiful, the narrator's wry comment about 'the common cant of praise' is in a quite different register from Tickell's formulaic description of Lucy as the fairest among the fair. Tickell provides similar details, though not more originality: Shakespeare was already satirising 'coral lips' in Sonnet 130 ('My mistress' eyes are nothing like the sun; coral is far more red than her lips' red'). Tickell's second stanza begins:

> Oh! have you seen a lilly pale,
> When beating rains descend?
> So droop'd this slow-consuming maid,
> Her life was near an end.

Compared with Tickell's picture of Lucy's decline, the description of Marianne's physical appearance following Willoughby's defection is almost brutally unromantic, again typically conveyed via an observer, in this case her half-brother John:

> My dear Elinor, what is the matter with Marianne? – she looks very unwell, has lost her colour, and is grown quite thin. ... At her time of life, any thing of an illness destroys the bloom for ever! Her's has been a very short one! She was as handsome a girl last September, as any I ever saw; and as likely to attract the men. There was something in her style of beauty, to please them particularly. I remember Fanny used to say that she would marry sooner and better than you did. (*SS*, p. 227)

There is no romantic image of lilies beset by bad weather here, just a breathtakingly tactless calculation of Marianne's devaluation on the marriage market due to her loss of beauty. Austen's choice of John Dashwood as a mouthpiece for the description of Marianne's state is almost comically appalling, and underlines Austen's deliberate refusal of the sentimental register of the ballad's words.

Section 2 of Giordani's setting, 'By Lucy warn'd', takes us abruptly from the E flat major of the opening section to a prosaic Andante in C major, still in common time. After an eight-bar piano introduction we might, perhaps, imagine the warning voice of Sense, embodied by Elinor Dashwood, in the warning to 'easy fair' and 'perjur'd swains'. Once again, the second couplet, though its rhythmic pattern is similar to the first, is intensified by modulation and the melody moving to a higher register. A brief and florid piano solo introduces the dark omens of bell and raven, with the telling phrase 'a bell was heard to ring' in the relative minor. The ominous words come again, but set to a different, repeated scrap of melody back in C major, with repeated quavers in the right hand imitating a bell, giving it an oddly calm, trance-like effect, akin to Elinor's calm desperation by Marianne's sickbed, before this section comes to a close with a more florid figure before a perfect cadence.

But at the end of this bar, for the first time in the cantata, the piece moves positively into the minor mode for 'Full well the love-lorn maiden knew', and we are thus introduced to our heroine's 'dying words' to the 'virgins weeping round' her. This ten-bar section is almost completely set in even crotchets, one syllable to each note, like a march, with repeated mournful descending phrases to denote the dying and the weeping. The melody, repeating the last line of the stanza, ends impressively on middle C, low in the soprano register, with no harmony in the piano accompaniment for the final chord.

Marianne's actual illness at Cleveland is described in more sober, though still literal, language: 'Marianne, suddenly awakened by some accidental noise in the house, started hastily up, and with feverish wildness, cried out – "Is Mama coming?"' (*SS*, pp. 310–11). Lucy, well versed in the folklore of romantic death, hears the tolling of the bell and knows her hours are numbered. Though Marianne is quite possibly aware at some level that she is seriously ill, she is, as shown by her incoherent appeals to her mother, 'not quite herself': it is Elinor who rationally perceives her danger, and Mrs Jennings who is convinced that 'the rapid decay, the early death of a girl so young, so lovely as Marianne' is imminent (*SS*, p. 313). It is up to Mrs Jennings 'to attribute the severity and danger of this attack, to the many weeks of previous indisposition which Marianne's disappointment had brought on' (*SS*, p. 314).

John Wiltshire points out that, unlike the illness of Samuel Richardson's Clarissa Harlowe, 'Marianne Dashwood's illness … is not the generalised sickness of exacerbated sensibility'. Although 'the decline and sickness of the heroine from wounded sensibility is entailed upon Austen by her predecessors, … Marianne's sickness is articulated as a sequence of quite specific, and physiologically plausible reactions'.[11] In contrast, Lucy's illness and death, like Clarissa's, are sufficiently explained by the romantic trope of the heroine of sensibility dying simply from disappointed love: 'What Clarissa [like Lucy] actually dies of is not important'.[12]

After the doleful introduction to Lucy's speech in Section 2, Section 3, 'I hear a voice', moves back to E flat major but now in compound time, 6/8, marked Largo. The piano introduction rocks slowly back and forth on different inversions of the same E flat chord in the right hand. There is a note in the score: 'The bass notes without octaves in imitation of the tolling of a bell'. The melody introduces us to Lucy's own voice for the first time, in a sweetly lilting melody, setting the words describing her hallucinations – 'a voice you cannot hear', 'a hand you cannot see'. The word 'die' is set low in the voice, but otherwise the tune remains undramatic, repetitive and slightly ethereal. It gains intensity by moving briefly to the relative minor for the direct appeal to Colin – 'give not her thy vows' – then back to the original melody, now heard for the fourth time, when she apostrophises Colin's bride: 'Nor thou, fond Maid, receive his kiss, nor think him all thy own'. The bell in the bass accompanies all the iterations of this musical phrase.

These repetitions, like those in Section 2, have a trance-like effect. They convey acceptance, reminiscent of Marianne's speech to Elinor setting out the plan for her new life of 'rational employment and self-controul' at Barton Cottage:

> We will take long walks together every day. We will walk to the farm at the edge of the down, and see how the children go on; we will walk to Sir John's new plantations …; we will often go to the old ruins. … I know we shall be happy. I know the summer will pass happily away. (*SS*, p. 343)

There is a wistfulness in this plan, which represents for Marianne a kind of life beyond the death of her hopes of happiness. Margaret Anne Doody calls *Sense and sensibility* 'Austen's saddest novel',[13] and this passage, though looking resolutely to the future, is not devoid of sorrow. The summer which she is anticipating will not be 'the season of happiness' for her (*SS*, p. 54): that hopeful spring has passed long ago, with Willoughby's attentions. The foreboding note struck in that phrase, used so early in the novel, has always seemed to me one of the saddest in all Austen's works. She could have written, 'Marianne was happy at this time', or even 'this was *a* season of happiness', but the chill finality of the definite article rules out a return to happiness, in the same way that Lucy, on a descending arpeggio ending on a low B flat, sings with fatal certainty, sings 'In early youth I die'.

The fourth section, 'Tomorrow in the church to wed', is faster – 'poco Andante' – in 3/4 time. Lucy addresses her distraught friends with a thorough condemnation of Colin, which

explains with unexpected bluntness the reason for his abandon-
ment of her:

> Was I to blame, because his bride
> Was thrice as rich as I?

She calmly follows this with her instructions for the following
day: to present her corpse, 'in my winding-sheet', to Colin
at his wedding. A seven-bar piano introduction, including a
brisk Alberti bass passage, precedes a businesslike, wide-awake
melody, more varied than the previous section, as if her plan for
revenge on her lover and his bride has given Lucy a temporary
burst of energy. She repeats the final lines, 'he in his wedding
trim so gay' and 'I in my winding sheet' in turn, before a four-
bar piano coda reprises the last bars of the introduction.

Although these are the final words of a wronged, dying
maiden, the musical setting imparts an almost malicious glee
which seems more in keeping with the character of another
Lucy, the younger Miss Steele, in *Sense and sensibility*. The couple
in the song are, after all, 'impatient' to wed and Lucy's posthumous intervention will ruin any hope they have of being happy.
Because the man to whom Lucy Steele is engaged remains
faithful to her despite having fallen in love with Elinor, she does
not need to go to these lengths to have her revenge on him.
However, she contrives in a similarly efficient fashion to dash
Elinor's hopes of marrying Edward by producing undeniable
evidence of their engagement during their walk in the grounds
at Barton (*SS*, Volume 1, Chapter 22).

It is striking that Elinor's distress at Marianne's bedside,
though couched in far less dramatic language, without the
use of any of the paraphernalia of romantic imagery, is more
palpable than that depicted in Tickell's oddly composed and

articulate heroine and the 'virgins weeping round' her: '[Elinor] was calm, except when she thought of her mother, but she was almost hopeless; and in this state she continued till noon, scarcely stirring from her sister's bed, her thoughts wandering from one image of grief, one suffering friend to another' (*SS*, pp. 313–14).

The short fifth section of the cantata starts with high drama: 'She spoke, she died', declaimed in stark, unadorned tonic/dominant dyads, first from C up to high F, then down the octave. This section then continues, dirge-like, in F minor, with 'his wedding trim' and 'her winding sheet' again repeated, and 'she in her winding sheet' repeated again at the end, accompanied only by octaves in the piano part. This short section, only sixteen bars of 2/4, contains the most dramatic music in the whole cantata. It is simple, with no piano introduction or coda, very little rhythmic variation and short, repeated phrases.

At moments of high emotion, short exclamations are natural, as is repetition:

> 'Perhaps you mean – my brother – you mean Mrs – Mrs Robert Ferrars.'
>
> 'Mrs Robert Ferrars!' was repeated by Marianne and her mother, in an accent of utmost amazement. (*SS*, p. 360)

Though the nature of the drama is different, the static nature of this passage echoes the short, repetitive phrases of this most dramatic part of the cantata.

The sixth section, 'Then what were perjur'd Colin's thoughts', Andante in 2/4, is back in B flat major. It provides a startling contrast to the previous starkly simple section. It is florid, with Alberti bass, triplets and demisemiquavers in the right hand of the introduction. The voice of the narrator returns, telling the story in a pleasant, prosaic melody which takes on a darker tone only after Colin's 'confusion, shame, remorse, despair', moving to a minor key for 'the damps of death bedew'd his brow', and a passage of short dyadic melismas followed by dramatic pauses for 'he groan'd, he shook, he fell',[14] which is then repeated at double time, and followed by a five-bar piano coda with a descending demisemiquaver figure in the right hand representing his fall.

This passage corresponds with the meeting between Willoughby and Marianne in London, one of the most dramatic points in the novel. However, Willoughby, despite betraying 'confusion', recovers his composure, fails to groan, shake or fall, and is fated not to die but to live on, separated from Marianne, in a loveless marriage. The matter-of-fact setting of the first part of this section, containing such dramatic events related with almost ironic detachment, is perhaps akin to the narrative voice which appears from time to time in *Sense and sensibility*. 'Marianne would have thought herself very inexcusable had she been able to sleep at all the first night after parting from Willoughby' (*SS*, p. 83); or 'After a proper resistance on the part of Mrs Ferrars, just so violent and so steady as to preserve her from that reproach which she always seemed fearful of incurring, the reproach of being too amiable ...' (*SS*, p. 373). The last part of this section of the music, with short phrases punctuated by pauses, is more in the vein of the incomplete sentence interrupted by a dash which so often, as John Wiltshire writes, is used 'as a retardant intensifier, a space which the reader is invited to fill with feeling'.[15]

Lucy has no false shame about being betrayed by Colin, and she intends to make *his* shame and downfall as public as possible. Her intentions are foreshadowed earlier by the poet's injunction – 'Of vengeance due to broken vows, / Ye perjur'd swains, beware'. Her plan to confront her lover posthumously is duly carried out by her 'comrades', and Colin is immediately and fatally smitten.

When Willoughby is confronted by Marianne at a party in London, on the other hand, she is still very much alive: 'At that moment she first perceived him, and her whole countenance glowing with sudden delight, she would have moved towards him instantly, had not her sister caught hold of her.' Elinor is concerned that Marianne is betraying her feelings 'to every body present' and tries to restrain her (*SS*, p. 176). When he can no longer ignore Marianne, it seems to Elinor that he is embarrassed; 'he was evidently struggling for composure', but recovers himself and turns 'hastily away' (*SS*, p. 177). So he partakes of Colin's 'confusion' but so far there is no sign of his 'shame, remorse, despair'. These come later, when he has heard that Marianne is ill and has rushed to Cleveland from London 'to offer some kind of explanation, some kind of apology for the past' (*SS*, p. 319). He then asks Elinor to 'tell her [Marianne] of my misery and my penitence – tell her that my heart was never inconstant to her' (*SS*, p. 330). His despair – 'Domestic happiness is out of the question' – is not fatal like Colin's, and is tempered by a hope that he may 'be allowed to think that you and yours feel an interest in my fate and my actions' (*SS*, p. 332).

Section 7, 'From the vain bride', starts sombrely, but soon takes us, via a really quite lovely melody, with an unusually lyrical accompaniment, to the 'happy ending' of this tragic tale. We are back to the original E flat major, but now in serene 3/4 time. 'One mould with her beneath one sod forever he remains' soars to a high G and resolves via a pretty downward melisma to the tonic. 'The plighted maid' and 'garlands gay and true love knots' takes off again with an expansive, chromatic figure, to land again on the 'sacred green'. The piece ends with a reprise of the sombre beginning motif, warning the 'swain for-sworn' to stay away from 'this hallow'd spot', but the last few bars, 'and fear, and fear to meet him there', are ornamented with sprightly leaps which rather belie the stern warning, and are repeated in the piano coda.

Romantic reunions

Though Marianne and Willoughby both survive their separa-tion, while Lucy and Colin both die in a dramatic fashion, the implication of Tickell's ballad is that Lucy is vindicated, and as the ballad ends it effectively brings about their reunion, buried together in a romantic setting which becomes a site of pilgrim-age. They are united in death, and Lucy has her revenge on Colin and on his 'vain bride', who is left discomfited: 'the vary-ing crimson fled' from her face. Their joint grave becomes a site of pilgrimage for 'the constant hind and plighted maid', and 'perjur'd swains' are duly warned to keep away.

For Willoughby and Marianne there is no such romantic reconciliation. As Elinor says, 'she can never be more lost to you than she is now' (*SS*, p. 332). He has to 'rub through the world as well as I can' (*SS*, p. 332), while Marianne applies herself 'to a scheme of ... rational employment and virtuous self-controul' (*SS*, p. 343), until it bursts upon her that Colonel Brandon is in love with her.

> Instead of falling a sacrifice to an irresistible passion, as once she had fondly flattered herself with expecting, – instead of remain-ing even for ever with her mother, and finding her only pleasures in retirement and study, as afterwards in her more calm and

> sober judgement she had determined on, – she found herself
> at nineteen, submitting to new attachments, entering on new
> duties, placed in a new home, a wife, the mistress of a family,
> and the patroness of a village. (*SS*, pp. 378–9)

We are invited to believe that 'her whole heart became, in
time, as much devoted to her husband, as it had once been to
Willoughby' (*SS*, p. 379). They live on in defiance of the romantic odds – this is very much the point and moral of *Sense and
sensibility*. Even Willoughby was not 'for ever inconsolable. …
He lived to exert, and frequently to enjoy himself' (*SS*, p. 379).
There is verbal irony (in Marianne's 'flatter[ing] herself' that
she would die of love) and dramatic irony (in Willoughby's ability to enjoy himself despite himself) in this conclusion to their
romance.

So although the ballad of Lucy and Colin ends with death
and burial, their ending has a romantic overlay which is denied
to the love story of Marianne and Willoughby. The music to
which the conclusion is set by Giordani is lyrical and comfort-
ing, in the same way that Austen's concluding paragraphs are:
'Colonel Brandon was now as happy, as all those who best
loved him, believed he deserved to be; – in Marianne he was
consoled for every past affliction; – her regard and her society
restored his mind to animation, and his spirits to cheerfulness'
(*SS*, p. 379).

The next paragraph sounds the note of warning to the
'perjur'd swain':

> Willoughby could not hear of her marriage without a pang; and
> his punishment was soon complete in the voluntary forgiveness
> of Mrs Smith, who, by stating his marriage with a woman of
> character, as the source of her clemency, gave him reason for
> believing that had he behaved with honour towards Marianne,

he might at once have been happy and rich. That his repentance
of misconduct, which thus brought its own punishment, was sincere, need not be doubted. (*SS*, p. 379)

With this brief, soberly ironic, note, the novel draws to a close,
with the romantic hero consigned to an unromantic marriage
rather than a romantic death, and both the heroines unexpectedly married into happily compatible situations: 'among the
merits and the happiness of Elinor and Marianne, let it not be
ranked as the least considerable, that though sisters, and living
almost within sight of each other, they could live without disa-
greement between themselves, or producing coolness between
their husbands' (*SS*, p. 380). This little ironic flourish at the end
of the novel is another version of Giordani's slightly inappropri-
ate gaiety at the end of the cantata.

Whether any of the echoes from Tickell's ballad and
Giordani's cantata I have excavated in *Sense and sensibility* have
any basis in actual influence – whether there are genuine parallels to be drawn – can never be known. I only mean to state a
possibility, and after a decade of myself performing the music
from Austen's family collection, it seems to me natural that the
music she played and sang, particularly songs she played often
and whose rhythmical and melodic patterns were lodged in
both her mind and in what musicians often call their 'muscle
memory' – the bodily experience of performing certain pieces
of music – would influence the rhythms and melodies of her
writing. Although her prose is not decorated with metaphor
and hyperbole like Tickell's ballad, reading her work aloud
is not unlike singing; her prose is structured with the human
voice in mind. Its supple rhythms are more akin to the metrical
variety to be found in a well-crafted song than the humourless

'wooden … eight and six' of Tickell's verse, and her 'figures of speech' are hidden in the warp and weft of her narrative voice and the words of her characters, spoken or unspoken – and are more musical and pervasive for that reason.

Text of 'Lucy and Colin' by Thomas Tickell

I.

Of Leister [*sic*], fam'd for maidens fair,
Bright Lucy was the grace,
Nor e'er did Liffy's limpid stream
Reflect so sweet a face:
'Till luckless love and pining care
Impair'd her rosy hue,
Her coral lips and damask cheeks,
And eyes of glossy blue.

II.

Oh! have you seen a lilly pale,
When beating rains descend?
So droop'd this slow-consuming maid,
Her life was near an end.
By Lucy warn'd, of flatt'ring swains
Take heed, ye easy fair,
Of vengeance due to broken vows,
Ye perjur'd swains, beware.

III.

Three times, all in the dead of night,
A bell was heard to ring;
And shreeking at her window thrice,
The raven flap'd his wing:
Too well the love-lorn maiden knew
The solemn boding sound,

Marianne and Willoughby, Lucy and Colin

And thus in dying words bespoke
The virgins weeping round:

IV.
'I hear a voice you cannot hear
Which says I must not stay;
I see a hand you cannot see,
Which beckons me away.
By a false heart and broken vows,
In early youth I die;
Was I to blame, because his bride
Was thrice as rich as I?

V.
'Ah, Colin! give not her thy vows,
Vows due to me alone;
Nor thou, fond maid, receive his kiss,
Nor think him all thy own.
To morrow in the church to wed,
Impatient both prepare:
But know, fond maid! and know, false man,
That Lucy will be there.

VI.
'Then bear my coarse ['corse', i.e. corpse], my comrades, bear,
This bridegroom blyth to meet;
He in his wedding-trim so gay,
I in my winding-sheet.'
She spoke; she dy'd: her coarse was born,
The bridegroom blyth to meet;
He in his wedding-trim so gay,
She in her winding sheet.

VII.
Then what were perjur'd Colin's thoughts!
How were these nuptials kept!

She played and sang

The bride's men flock'd round Lucy dead,
And all the village wept.
Confusion, shame, remorse, despair,
At once his bosom swell;
The damps of death bedew'd his brow:
He shook, he groan'd, he fell.

VIII.
From the vain bride (ah bride no more!)
The varying crimson fled,
When stretch'd before her rival's coarse
She saw her husband dead.
Then to his Lucy's new made grave
Convey'd by trembling swains,
One mold with her, beneath one sod,
For ever now remains.

IX.
Oft at his grave the constant hind,
And plighted maid are seen,
With garlands gay and true-love knots
They deck the sacred green.
But, swain forsworn, whoe'er thou art,
This hallow'd spot forbear;
Remember Colin's dreadful fate,
And fear to meet him here.

Text transcribed from The tea-table miscellany or, a collection of choice songs, Scots and English, in four volumes *by Allan Ramsay (London: Millar, 1750), pp. 349–51. Internet Archive. Online. https:// archive.org/details/teatablemiscellao3rams/page/348/mode/2up. Accessed 14 November 2022.*

Conclusion

Amateur versus professional

Austen, I believe, regarded herself as an artist, but not as a professional artist. That statement buys into a whole debate about the class implications of artistic practices of various kinds during her lifetime which is beyond the scope of this book. However, Austen's implied attitude to her own literary career throws some light on the question.

She told her niece Fanny, when discussing the prospects of success of a second edition of *Mansfield Park* in November 1814, that 'tho' I like praise as well as anybody, I like what Edward calls Pewter too' (*Letters*, p. 287). Nevertheless, she was serious about keeping her identity as the author of the four novels published during her lifetime from being generally known. The first edition of *Sense and sensibility* was 'by a Lady', and each subsequent novel was 'by the author of' the previous novel. It might have been a fairly open secret, and the anonymity which carried over on to the title pages of her two posthumously published novels, *Northanger Abbey* and *Persuasion*, was certainly destroyed on the first page of Henry Austen's memoir which prefaced the publication, boldly naming Jane Austen as the author of these novels. But it was a matter of taste and of self-respect that she was not a mere professional who would publicly name herself as an artist, a 'hireling' like the musicians whom Eliza engaged to perform at her party in April 1811, of whom Austen wrote, 'all the Performers gave great satisfaction by doing what they were paid for, & giving themselves no airs,' while 'no Amateur could be persuaded to do anything' (*Letters*, p. 183).

These class distinctions are perhaps clearer in the case of music than literature, which could be created in private and did not require the professional artist to present herself personally in public. In a 2018 article that I co-authored with Kirstine Moffat and John Wiltshire, the gendered and class-based distinctions between professional and amateur musicians in Austen's novels are discussed in detail, in the context of her life and social circle. 'Music in eighteenth- and nineteenth-century Britain was certainly very class-based, as well as being divided on gender lines.'[1] Austen was an amateur musician in both the historical and the current sense of the word. Today, an amateur musician is more likely to be thought of as less skilled than a professional, and the artistry of the professional musician is admired and valued. Austen was not a virtuoso musician, but a competent pianist and singer in a private setting. To her, however, the word 'amateur' would have connotations that could be traced back to its etymological roots – one who practises an art for love rather than financial necessity. It had little to do with artistic talent or technical mastery.

Conclusion

The distress of Jane Fairfax in *Emma* at the prospect of having to use her musical training to earn a living by teaching dramatises this distinction. The vulgar Mrs Elton officiously tries to hurry her into her destined career as a governess, which Jane has, at this stage, no intention of pursuing, for reasons which become obvious only later in the novel. Mrs Elton is obnoxiously and persistently helpful and brushes aside Jane's polite but steadfast refusal to accept her help, insisting that she is being too modest:

> with your superior talents, you have a right to move in the first circle. Your musical knowledge alone would entitle you to name your own terms, have as many rooms as you like, and mix in the family as much as you chose; – that is – I do not know – if you knew the harp, you might do all that, I am very sure; but you sing as well as play; – yes, I really believe you might, even without the harp, stipulate for what you chose. (*E*, p. 301)

Emma witnesses their conversation, observing that Mrs Elton was 'judging and behaving ill', and that being overheard discussing her private affairs in company must have been 'unpleasant to Jane' (*E*, p. 299). Moreover, Mrs Elton's tactless assessment of Jane's market value on the basis of her musical talents devalues these talents as accomplishments in their own right, and as personal resources for her own fulfilment with the capacity to give pleasure to her listeners in a social setting. Music, being so closely allied to the career destined for her by her guardians and by Mrs Elton, and which she regards with horror, must give Jane Fairfax very little unmixed pleasure.

The material culture of music
in the novels

Austen's own attitude to music, as far as we can gather from the evidence external to the novels, was, at least later in her life, a fairly easy-going and relaxed one. She seems to have enjoyed playing for herself and for her immediate family circle, and often shared her observations on the performances of other musicians with those in the family who would understand them. Various aspects of music are important in most of her novels, although specific detail is rarely provided. The novels are not of course in themselves vehicles for Austen to demonstrate her factual knowledge, and it is only in *Emma* that she draws on explicit musical facts in the service of the plot.

As I mention in Chapter 1, Johann Baptist Cramer is the only composer named in any of Austen's novels. Austen presumably knew Cramer's music, and, in one of the music albums of uncertain ownership which might have belonged to her, there are two pieces by him, a divertimento, and a sonata which includes the melody of 'God save the king'. In *Emma*, an unspecified volume of Cramer's music is among the music that arrives with the mysterious gift of a piano for Jane Fairfax – Frank Churchill is being disingenuous (as usual) when he says to Emma, taking 'some music from a chair near the pianoforté', 'Here is something quite new to me. Do you know it? – Cramer' (*E*, p. 242). Cramer's *84 Études*, the first book of which was published in 1804, are still in print, but he also composed sonatas and other piano works. In the years 1810–1815, leading up to the publication of *Emma*, more than twenty new works by Cramer were registered at Stationers' Hall, including, in 1815, 'A new rondo on a favorite Irish air' and several other piano works with an Irish connection.[2] The *Études* are for advanced students and are reasonably virtuosic so might have been an appropriate gift for Jane Fairfax, although their pedagogical connotations would have been less than tactful.

Frank has also included with his ill-considered and secretive gift a volume of Thomas Moore's *Irish melodies*, discussed in Chapter 6. The piano itself is a Broadwood, and, in the scene where Frank and Emma are visiting and looking over the music, Jane is playing 'Robin Adair'. These are the only specific circumstantial references to current musical culture that Austen employs in her novels, and all are concentrated in *Emma* in relation to the mysterious present of the piano. Each of these details – the fact that the Broadwood piano was not a grand but was a good-quality, handsome, square piano; the specific sheet music that accompanies the gift; and so on – has its importance in situating the intentions, resources and generosity of the giver. We witness Frank playing a double game with Emma and Jane, pretending to Emma that he had no prior knowledge of the sheet music which he had chosen for Jane, while at the same time communicating indirectly with Jane via his comments to Emma. In order to achieve this narrative feat, Austen needed to include these specifics. In the other novels, while music may be just as important, details like these are not necessary.

Spinets, pianofortes and harps

In my 2010 article 'Musicianship and morality in the novels of Jane Austen' I discuss how Austen uses music in the narrative of all the published novels except *Northanger Abbey*. For each of the novels I chose an aspect of musicianship 'which seems particularly well illustrated by that novel'.[3] For *Sense and sensibility*, it is the question of musical taste; in *Pride and prejudice* I look at music as a female accomplishment; in *Mansfield Park* it is music in education; in *Emma* subjective attitudes to music; and in *Persuasion* music as a personal resource.

It is true that in *Northanger Abbey* music is not a major theme, and there are no characters who are musicians. However, in the first chapter the brief musical education of the heroine, Catherine Morland, is described:

> Her mother wished her to learn music; and Catherine was sure she should like it, for she was very fond of tinkling the keys of the old forlorn spinnet; so, at eight years old she began. She learnt a year, and could not bear it; and Mrs. Morland, who did not insist on her daughters being accomplished in spite of incapacity or distaste, allowed her to leave off. The day which dismissed the music-master was one of the happiest of Catherine's life. (*NA*, p. 14)

The 'old forlorn spinnet' which must have been sitting in a corner of the Morland family home, the parsonage at Fullerton in Wiltshire, brings to mind the spinet that Austen's niece Caroline discovered in the gallery at Stoneleigh in 1809, 'old and uncared for'.[4] These instruments, which are basically small harpsichords, were already out of date and unfashionable by the time Austen wrote *Northanger Abbey* in the 1790s, and positively antiquated when Caroline encountered the one in Stoneleigh. Indeed, in *Emma* Mrs Cole ruefully signals her sense of Jane Fairfax's deprivation, before the mysterious piano arrives, by saying that she, 'who is a mistress of music, has not any thing of the nature of an instrument, not even the pitifullest old spinet in the world, to amuse herself with' (*E*, pp. 215–16). Spinets are old, pitiful, forlorn and uncared for. Pianofortes, on the other hand, are modern, elegant-looking and socially desirable. One of the items that the Dashwood women retain from their formerly prosperous life at Norland is Marianne's 'handsome pianoforte' (*SS*, p. 26), which has to be brought around by sea from Sussex to Devonshire. When the Dashwoods arrive at Barton Cottage, they endeavour, 'by placing around them their books and other possessions, to form themselves a home. Marianne's pianoforte was unpacked and properly disposed of; and Elinor's drawings were affixed to the wall of their sitting room' (*SS*, p. 30). It is not clear whether Marianne's piano is a grand or a square piano, but it remains important to her not as a status symbol but as site of self-expression and emotional indulgence.

Presumably when the narrator of *Northanger Abbey* writes that Catherine's mother 'wished her to learn music', this means

Figure 9.1 The author at the Clementi square piano in Jane Austen's House Museum, Chawton, in 2023

learning to play the piano, and perhaps some rudiments of music theory. But as a child Catherine 'shirked her lessons … whenever she could' and 'hated confinement and cleanliness' (*NA*, p. 14), and no doubt applying herself to serious piano practice was a part of learning music that 'she could not bear', as well as, perhaps, the disapproval of a strict and unsympathetic music master.

Catherine, however, does become more socialised as her teenage years pass, and, the narrator announces ironically, 'from fifteen to seventeen she was in training for a heroine', the kind who appears in books that 'were all story and no reflection' (*NA*, p. 15). She learns the lines from Shakespeare that I mention in Chapter 6 along with other poetic quotations, and

> so far her improvement was sufficient – and in many other points she came on exceedingly well; for though she could not write sonnets, she brought herself to read them; and though there seemed no chance of her throwing a whole party into raptures by a prelude on the pianoforte, of her own composition, she could listen to other people's performance with very little fatigue. (*NA*, p. 16)

The clause about throwing a party into raptures 'by a prelude on the pianoforte', capped by the rider 'of her own composition' is a delicious and beautifully timed piece of prose. It also might be the only time in all of Austen's novels when the idea of a woman composing music arises. As I note in Chapter 1, a few female composers are represented within the Austen music books, but the contribution of women to music culture was overwhelmingly as performers and listeners – both equally necessary to a thriving musical culture. Being able to 'listen to other people's performance with very little fatigue' is a valuable attribute indeed.

Conclusion

The keyboard instruments were thought suitable for genteel women throughout the eighteenth century, rather than flutes or violins, which were regarded as 'unbecoming the Fair Sex'.[5] It is interesting to note that these smaller instruments were more portable than pianos and harpsichords, so apart from the unsuitable qualities that are mentioned in books of these kinds, these strictures also confine women's music-making to a domestic, indoor setting.

The harp is somewhat more portable than the piano, though not as easily carried as the flute or violin, and not to be played out of doors. In the later novels, written and set in the 1810s – *Mansfield Park, Emma* and *Persuasion* – the harp appears as a supplement and sometimes a rival to the piano. The harp – not the small celtic harp but the large, delicate instrument that was in vogue in France before the Revolution and arrived in England in the 1790s, and which evolved into the modern concert harp – was more expensive and more fashionable than the piano and it is, as Mike Parker points out, not played by any of the heroines of the novels.[6] The young harpists in the novels are Mary Crawford in *Mansfield Park* and the Musgrove sisters – who have one harp between them – in *Persuasion*. The expense of a harp is not only in the purchase price. In both these novels, moving the harp requires special arrangements involving vehicles – Henry Crawford's barouche (*MP*, p. 59) and Louisa's place in the Musgrove family carriage in *Persuasion* (*P*, p. 50) – and ready access to these vehicles is a sign of wealth.

Jane Fairfax in *Emma* is thought by Mrs Elton to be at a disadvantage without a knowledge of the harp, and Anne Elliot in *Persuasion* is a pianist, of an earlier generation than the Musgrove sisters whose more fashionable accomplishments overshadow her own more solid musicianship.[7] In the twelve chapters of *Sanditon* which Austen wrote before she died in 1817, the harp has displaced the piano in the fashionable world. The excitable entrepreneur Mr Parker is enraptured by 'the sound of a Harp ... heard through the upper Casement' of a building in the town – 'Civilization, Civilization indeed!', he exclaims (*MW*, p. 383). Austen herself did not play the harp but her beloved niece Fanny did, as well as her cousin Eliza de Feuillide. Eliza lived in France before the Revolution and, as we have seen, owned music nominally set for harp, although it could be played on the piano. She mentioned in a 1780 letter to her cousin Philadelphia Walter that she had 'both an harpsichord and harp (The latter is at present the fashionable instrument)'.[8] In June 2023 I was fortunate to be present at a concert in which Mike Parker, an expert in historic harp restoration and performance, played Eliza's harp, which he had tracked down to Belgium and restored to playable condition. It had been left there by Eliza when she fled to England during the French Revolution.

But the piano is the instrument that Austen is associated with. The piano had all but supplanted the harpsichord by the end of the eighteenth century, and the pianos she knew would have been the 'commonly encountered type': the square piano. Geoffrey Lancaster writes that only 'financially successful professional musicians and the wealthy owned grand pianos', and Austen was neither of these.[9] She loved to play for the amusement of her 'nephews and nieces, when we have the pleasure of their company', as she wrote to Cassandra in 1808 (*Letters*, p. 161). She played – but she also sang. And her voice was the instrument that stayed with her all her life, whether she used it or not. It is almost too obvious to say that a singer is her own instrument but it is worth thinking about what that means. Automata were already, in her lifetime, being invented that could play instruments, including the piano, after a fashion. But only a living being could sing: to hear singing in Austen's lifetime – before sound recording was developed – you had to be in the presence of a human being. She played and sang. Much of her music collection was vocal music that gives an idea of what she might have sung, and fifty years after her death the trace of her voice remained in the memories of some of her surviving relatives.

Austen's four last songs

In a letter to her brother James Edward of about 1870, Caroline Austen wrote that Aunt Jane 'had nearly left off singing by the time I can recollect much about her performances', but she remembered three songs (*Memoir*, p. 193). She gives a few words of each of these songs, all of which are in the wider family collection. The first is titled by Austen in her manuscript 'Song from Burns' – the only setting of Robert Burns among her manuscripts. The second is 'Oh no, my love, no', by Michael Kelly, which appears in a manuscript album not included in this digitisation project, and not in Austen's handwriting, and also among the printed sheet music of Eleanor Jackson. The third is 'Que j'aime à voir les hirondelles', a 'Romance' by François Devienne based on a text from Florian's novel *Estelle et Némorin*, which was in a book of printed music that belonged to Eliza. Caroline recalls this as 'a little French ditty in her M. S. book' (*Memoir*, p. 193). It does not appear in any of the manuscript albums currently available, and as Samantha Carrasco remarks, 'if one is to trust this recollection, then one must assume that there was another manuscript book' which has gone missing.[10]

She played and sang

In her letter to James Edward, Caroline also quotes a letter she had received in January 1870 from Fulwar William Fowle, her cousin on her mother's side: 'I well remember her singing – & "The yellow haired Laddie" made an impression upon me, which more than half a century has no power to efface' (*Memoir*, p. 194). This Scottish song appears in the publication *Thirty Scots songs for a voice & harpsichord* which is bound into a book of print music that belonged to Austen. Fowle was born in 1791, the nephew of Tom Fowle, Cassandra's fiancé. It is uncertain when he heard her sing – it is difficult to gauge exactly what he means by 'more than half a century', although it seems more likely to be towards the latter part of her life than her younger days at Steventon.

Only one of these songs – the 'Song from Burns'– is among the surviving manuscripts in Austen's hand, which I have been inclined to regard as the music with which she is most likely to have been intimately familiar. However, most of these songs would have been readily available as printed music, and, as Gammie and McCulloch point out, 'it should be emphasised that the music still preserved at Chawton survives by chance as much as by design. We cannot know with any certainty how much music Jane Austen possessed.'[11] And since she had a print copy of 'The yellow haired laddie' there would be no need for her to make a manuscript copy of it.

In concluding this study of Jane Austen and music, it seems appropriate to reflect on these four songs as audible traces of Austen's musical world. What do these songs share that drew Austen back to them at a time in her life when, in Caroline's words, she had 'nearly left off singing' (*Memoir*, p. 193)?

Musically, they are harmonically straightforward and in bright major keys, as is typical of music of this period. They all have very attractive melodies. None of them, in the versions that survive, has more than the sketchiest accompaniment. Austen's printed copy of 'The yellow hair'd laddie' in Ramsey's *Thirty Scots songs for a voice and harpsichord* has the bass line of an accompaniment plus a second voice part for a male singer, which could easily be omitted and used as the basis of a piano accompaniment. Austen would not have needed a fully notated piano part: she had the skill to improvise while she sang, and her familiarity with the songs would have made it even easier for her to play for herself.

The melodies are not undemanding, all requiring a vocal range of at least an octave and a half, and extending up to quite high notes – G or A. There are several ascending phrases covering more than an octave which require careful breath management to sing well. That said, they are not what would be called virtuosic – no fast-paced passages requiring the kind of vocal agility that opera singers of the day needed. Still, they are not songs someone would choose to sing if she were feeling tired, or ill or short of breath. They are all strophic songs – two or more verses sung to the same melody, which is also typical of the songs in Austen's collection.

Above all, what these songs require is to be sung with conviction and the clarity of diction that comes with good vocal technique. Each one of them tells a story and, as Jeanice Brooks points out, they all 'treat the topic of fidelity within different generic and stylistic frameworks'.[12] The yellow-haired laddie is a young Scottish man who is in danger of being forced to marry a woman he dislikes instead of the one he loves. This is a very common situation in the songs of the time but it is slightly unusual for a young man to be expressing these sentiments, rather than a young woman in a similar situation. The singer of the

Robert Burns song is, on the other hand, happily united with his 'Jane' (Jean in the original poem) and proudly congratulating himself on his Scottish freedom from the empty trappings of decadent foreign civilisations.

In its original context, the song 'Que j'aime à voir les hirondelles' is sung by the shepherdess Estelle, who is about to be separated from her lover, Némorin, and married to someone else. The song tells of the fate of a swallow, by nature unfettered, if captured and caged by a cruel child. Both the captured bird and her mate will die of sorrow at the loss of their love and their freedom.

Finally, 'Oh no, my love, no' comes from Thomas Dibdin's farce *Of age tomorrow*, adapted from Kotzebue's *Der Wildfang*, with music by Michael Kelly, and is the servant Maria's account of her words years earlier to her 'faithless swain' as he departs[13] – wishing he were not leaving, but protesting that she will not blame him for going 'if it gives pleasure to you'. She nevertheless asks him to remain faithful to her. Austen saw the play with her niece Fanny and other family members in Southampton in September 1807.[14] This song (with words by Matthew Lewis)[15] had been such a success in the play that it was published separately in 1805, rebranded 'The wife's farewell, or no, my love, no', and paired with 'The husband's return', for which Eleanor Jackson also owned the music. In the play the song is almost an aside, a commentary on the action and a part of the character development but having no bearing on the plot. Removed from this context and given the added weight of the word 'wife' in the title, it gains in significance, though it loses none of its satirical force.

Jeanice Brooks writes of the three songs that Caroline mentions:

Conclusion

> While the degree of emphasis and affective urgency might
> differ from singer to singer depending on performance vari-
> ables such as tempo and timbre, the vocal effort required to
> move higher into the range … would produce some effect in
> any performance – including Jane Austen's own renditions. In
> the production of increasingly heightened sentiment through
> melodic gesture, 'Que j'aime à voir les hirondelles' employs
> musical techniques similar to those we have seen in both the
> 'Song from Burns' and 'No, my love, no'. But in contrast to the
> latter, there is no irony in the relation of the song to its literary
> source.[16]

Taken together, these four songs contain both humour and
pathos, though not the broad comedy that appears elsewhere
among Austen's manuscripts in songs like 'I ha'e laid a herring in sa't', or Charles Dibdin's cheerful satire in 'The joys
of the country' and 'The lucky escape'. In the Burns song and
in the wife's farewell the humour is more in the way the sentiments are expressed – the music reinforces the point of view
in both cases, with the most emphatic parts of Burns's rhetoric
in the higher part of the voice, and in the wife's farewell, a
melody that wheedles and cycles back to the phrase 'no, my
love, no'. Learning the Kelly song and singing it to family
and friends has given me insight into its biting irony beyond
what I had gathered from reading the words on the page. The
singer has to act the role of the woman who clearly knows
her lover's intention but is determined not to put herself at a
disadvantage by openly venting her anger. The pathos is more
pronounced in the other two songs where the comic element
is absent. We do not discover the fate of the yellow-haired
laddie – will he be forced to marry the wrong woman? And
the swallows depict the dire fate of the lovers forced to part,
with no ironic overlay.

She played and sang

The gender of the implied singer in two of these songs is indeterminate, since they are in the third person. The other two are first-person accounts, one masculine, the other feminine. This is not at all unusual among Austen's vocal music. Robert K. Wallace lists 'the classical and neoclassical values of balance, equilibrium, proportion, symmetry, clarity, restraint, wit, and elegance' as 'typical ... of the music that Austen played on her square piano'.[17] I would add that when performing her vocal music she gave voice to an infinite range of subjective positions: feminine, masculine, sentimental, witty, happy, unhappy, defiant, submissive, proud, abject, petulant, noble. The classical values Wallace mentions are certainly characteristic of Austen's fiction, but so is the emotional range to be found in the songs. On the face of it most of the songs could be described as love songs, in the same way that her novels are sometimes regarded as romances. However, these 'love songs' have the capacity to express a wide range of individual human emotions and a singer is embodying those emotions each time she sings them. Katherine Larson writes, 'to attend to the airy substance of song as an acoustic, embodied, and musical phenomenon underscores the need radically to rethink the boundaries of literary form'.[18] The practice of singing and feeling the drama of each scenario cannot, I believe, have failed to influence the singer when she sat at her desk to write, and the rhetoric of music naturally flowed into the musicality of her prose.

Appendix 1

The Austen family network

Names

The Austen family, like most families of the time, economised on given names, which can present a problem when writing a book of this kind. To distinguish between various family members, I have generally referred to them by the names by which they were known within the family. I list below those who are mentioned most frequently, and the names which I use in the text. (When I quote Austen's letters and she uses different names, I have made this clear in the text.)

Children of George Austen (1731–1805) and Cassandra Austen (née Leigh) (1739–1827)

Jane Austen (1775–1817) – usually referred to as 'Austen', or 'Jane' in some contexts to distinguish her from other members of the Austen family.

James Austen (1765–1819) – referred to as 'James'; after the death of his first wife, Anne Matthew (mother of Anna) he married **Mary Lloyd**, whose sister **Martha Lloyd** (1765–1843) was a close friend of Jane Austen and lived with her in Chawton from 1809.

Edward Austen – Edward Knight from 1812 (1767–1852) – referred to as 'Edward'; he married **Elizabeth Bridges** (1773–1808) – referred to as 'Elizabeth'.

Henry Austen (1771–1850) – referred to as 'Henry'; he married (1) **Elizabeth de Feuillide (née Hancock)** (1761–1813) – referred to as 'Eliza'; (2) **Eleanor Jackson** (d. 1864) – referred to as 'Eleanor'.

Cassandra Elizabeth Austen (1773–1845) – referred to as 'Cassandra'.

Children of James Austen

Anna Austen (1793–1872, married **Ben Lefroy** 1814) – referred to as 'Anna'.

James Edward Austen Leigh (1798–1874) – referred to as 'James Edward' (note: in her letters, Austen usually calls him, as well as his uncle and a cousin, 'Edward'). James Edward added the surname **Leigh** in 1838.

Caroline Austen (1805–1880) – referred to as 'Caroline'.

Children of Edward Austen (Knight from 1812)

Frances Austen Knight (1793–1882) – referred to as 'Fanny'. Married **Sir Edward Knatchbull** 1820.

Elizabeth Austen Knight (1800–1884) – referred to as 'Lizzy'. Married **Edward Rice** 1818.

Marianne Austen Knight (1801–1896) – referred to as 'Marianne'.

Louisa Austen Knight (1804–1889) – referred to as Louisa. Jane Austen's god-daughter. Married **Lord George-Augusta Hill**, her sister Cassandra's widower, in 1847.

Cassandra Jane Austen Knight (1806–1842) – referred to as 'young Cassandra'. Married **Lord George-Augusta Hill** in 1834.

Note that this is far from an exhaustive list of the Austen family, and includes only those who are mentioned more than once in this book. Full details of the Austen family network are to be found in many books such as *Jane Austen: a family record* and *Jane Austen's letters*.

Places

Steventon parsonage (Hampshire) – The home of George and Cassandra Austen and their daughters until 1801, and afterwards of James and Mary Austen and their children.

Chawton (Hampshire) – The village in which Mrs Austen, Cassandra, Jane and their friend Martha Lloyd settled in 1809, in a house belonging to the estate of Edward Knight.

Godmersham Park (Kent) – the main residence of Edward Austen Knight and his family. They also owned the manor house at Chawton and occasionally stayed there for short periods.

Appendix 2

Annotated list of manuscripts in Jane Austen's hand

Introductory note

This list includes the items within the four albums described in Chapter 1 that are thought to be in Austen's own handwriting, plus two loose sheets which are less certainly attributed to her. The information, including the notes, is based on the catalogue records that I created 2017–2021 for the University of Southampton Library, and further information can be found by searching individual items by title or composer on the library catalogue online.[1] Links to the manuscript of each song online are provided in each of the library catalogue records.

Each entry is in the following format. '(lyricist)' is added for clarity in cases where there is no composer.

Title on MS [or first line or other description]
Composer (if known)
Lyricist (if known)

Date of published source (if known or estimated)
Type
Catalogue number in Southampton University Library
    Catalogue
      Notes

Juvenile songs and lessons (for young beginners who don't know enough to practise) [Catalogue no. CHWJA/19/02]

Ouverture des pretendus

Lemoyne, J.-B. (Jean-Baptiste), 1751–1796
1789
Theatre instrumental
CHWJA/19/02:01

> Lemoyne's opera *Les prétendus* premiered in Paris in 1789. This arrangement was printed as *Feuille de Terpsichore*, 5e. Année, no. 37, a copy of which was owned by Eliza de Feuillide (see Jenkyns 04).

Fandango e los gigangas from Thicknesse's tour

Dance instrumental
CHWJA/19/02:02

> Ann Thicknesse née Ford (1737–1824) was an English guitar and viola da gamba player.

Ouverture de Renaud d'Ast

Dalayrac, Nicolas-Marie, 1753–1809
1787
Theatre instrumental
CHWJA/19/02:03

Arranged by M. [P. P.] Blattman. This arrangement was printed as *Feuille de Terpsichore*, 4e. Année, no. 29, a copy of which was owned by Eliza de Feuillide (see Jenkyns 04). Dalayrac's opera *Renaud d'Ast* premiered in Paris in 1787.

Nos Galen
Folk instrumental
CHWJA/19/02:04

Ten variations on the Welsh tune 'Nos Galan', now used for the Christmas carol 'Deck the halls with boughs of holly'. Composer not identified.

Mrs Hamilton of Pincaitlands strathspey
Gow, Nathaniel, 1763–1831
1792
Dance instrumental
CHWJA/19/02:05

From Niel [Nathaniel] Gow, *A third collection of strathspey reels &c for the piano-forte, violin and violoncello.* Edinburgh: Stewart, 1792.

The Austrian grenadier's quick march
Military instrumental
CHWJA/19/02:06

No composer or other information given – melody unidentified.

Troop of the Coldstream Regiment of Guards
Military instrumental
CHWJA/19/02:07

No composer or other information given – melody unidentified.

The London march

Military instrumental

CHWJA/19/02:08

>Several similar MS versions (in various keys) found in RISM but no print source. A similar tune appears under this title in *Hamilton's universal tune book*, Volume 2 (Glasgow, 1846), p. 44.

March by Mr Meyer

Meyer, Philippe-Jacques, 1737–1819

Military instrumental

CHWJA/19/02:09

>The march is followed by a gigue. Source unidentified. 'Mr Meyer' is probably Philippe-Jacques Meyer, who is likely to have been the music master Fanny Knight employed in London.

Scotch air

Folk instrumental

CHWJA/19/02:10

>No composer or other information given – melody unidentified.

The Austrian retreat

Elrington, William

1795

Military instrumental

CHWJA/19/02:11

Elrington was a 'composer and flutist' who was master of the band of the First Regiment of Guards. Estimated publication date 1795.

Les trois sultanes

Mazzinghi, Joseph, 1765–1844

1796

Theatre instrumental

CHWJA/19/02:12–14

> These are numbers 12, 13 and 14 from the ballet *Les trois sultanes*. 'Performed at the King's Theatre, composed by Sigr Onorati, arranged for the Piano Forte or Harp, the Music chiefly new by I. Mazzinghi, Op. 20.' London: G. Goulding, [1796].

Sonata – Mazzinghi

Mazzinghi, Joseph, 1765–1844

Instrumental

CHWJA/19/02:15

> Keyboard sonata in G major. This particular sonata has not been found among the many Mazzinghi works in IMSLP. (Sonatas opus 2, 5, 16, 30 and 61 checked against the MS.)

Waltz

Mozart, Wolfgang Amadeus, 1756–1791 (et al.)

Dance instrumental

CHWJA/19/02:16–17

> 2 short waltzes in F major. No composers given. The 2nd Waltz on this page is arranged from 'Die Schlittenfahrt', the trio of K. 605, no. 3 by Mozart.

The Duke of York's new march: performed by the Coldstream Regiment

Mozart, Wolfgang Amadeus, 1756–1791

Military instrumental

CHWJA/19/02:18

> Gammie and McCulloch note that this arrange-
> ment for keyboard of the aria 'Non piu andrai' from
> Mozart's *Marriage of Figaro* was 'presumably transmit-
> ted via military bands and apparently still in use today'
> (p. 14).

March in blue beard – Kelly

Kelly, Michael, 1762–1826.

Theatre instrumental

1798

CHWJA/19/02:19

> Copied almost exactly from the score published as 'The
> grand dramatic romance of *Blue Beard or Female Curiosity* as
> now performing at the Theatre Royal Drury Lane with
> unbounded applause, the words by George Coleman
> the Younger Esquire, the music composed & selected
> by Michael Kelly'. Printed for Corri, Dussek & Co.,
> 1798.

German waltz

Dance instrumental

CHWJA/19/02:20–21

> 2 unidentified waltzes for solo keyboard.

Coolun with variations

Folk instrumental

CHWJA/19/02:22

> Variations on an Irish song: 'Oh! The hours I have passed in the arms of my dear'. No composer given – various print versions identified including two American editions available online.

The Duke of York's march

King, M. P. (Matthew Peter), 1773–1823

Military instrumental

1793

CHWJA/19/02:23

> Part of 'The Siege of Valenciennes for the Piano-forte or harpsichord with an accompaniment for a violin, humbly dedicated to His Royal Highness the Duke of York' by M. P. King, Opus VII.

Sonata by Sterkel

Sterkel, Johann Franz Xaver, 1750–1817

Instrumental

1784

CHWJA/19/02:24

> This is the third sonata of 'Trois sonates pour le clavecin ou piano forte avec l'accompagnment d'un violon oblige composee par J. F. Sterkel. Oeuvre XVIII', StVW 192/3, first published in Mainz c. 1784. Later published in London but undated.

Gloucester waltz on Ly [i.e. Lady] Caroline Lee

Latour, T. (Jean Theodore) (?)

Dance instrumental

CHWJA/19/02:25

No composer given. RISM has a matching incipit in an MS titled 'Lady Caroline Lee'. No source is given. Sainsbury's *Dictionary of musicians* (1824) lists 'Lady Caroline Lee's Waltz' as a composition of T. (Jean Theodore) Latour.

La Rose: cotillon
Dance instrumental
CHWJA/19/02:26
> No composer or other information given – melody unidentified.

The perigodine (Perigourdine)
Dance instrumental
CHWJA/19/02:27
> No composer or other information given – melody unidentified.

To fair Fidele's grassy tomb with variations
Collins, William, 1721–1759 (lyricist)
Theatre instrumental
CHWJA/19/02:28
> No composer given. This appears to be the same basic tune as a glee titled 'The Dirge in Cymbeline, harmonized by Mr Rauzzini. London, c. 1805'. Thomas Arne set these words for the Shakespeare season of 1740–1741, but this melody is different.

Old Robin Gray with variations
Leeves, W., Rev. (William), 1748–1828
Instrumental duet
CHWJA/19/02:29

Air and 2 variations for piano duet on 'Auld Robin Gray'. No other source found for these variations. Traditional Tune Archive attributes the melody to Rev. W. Leeves. The words (not present in this edition) were written by Lady Anne Lindsay in 1771.

March
Military instrumental
CHWJA/19/02:30

No composer or other information given – melody unidentified.

My lodging is on the cold ground: duet
Corri, Domenico, 1746–1825 (?)
1790
Instrumental duet
CHWJA/19/02:31

A published version of this tune arranged for piano duet by Domenico Corri is in the Glasgow University Library but has not been compared with the MS. The tune is that used by Thomas Moore in *Irish melodies* for his verse 'Believe me if all those endearing young charms'.

My love she's but a lassie yet: with variations – T. Powell
Powell, Thomas, 1776–1860 (?)
Folk instrumental
CHWJA/19/02:32

7 variations on the Scottish song. Print edition titled 'My love she's but a lassie yet: a favorite Scotch Air arranged with variations for the piano Forte and respectfully

dedicated to Miss E. Head by T. Powell. London, Printed
by Goulding, Phipps, D'Almaine & Co.' No date given.

My ain kind dearie: with variations by D. Corri

Corri, Domenico, 1746–1825

1795

Folk instrumental

CHWJA/19/02:33

> Air with 6 variations on the Scottish song. Earliest dates
> for this item in British Library catalogue 1795 and 1796.

The nightingale

Holst, Matthias, 1769–1854

1806

Military instrumental

CHWJA/19/02:34

> Almost identical to the version for piano and flute of
> 'The nightingale: a favorite military rondo as performed
> at Brighton by the Royal South Glocester Band' pub-
> lished by Wheatstone after 1806. The melody of this
> piece is drawn from Matthias Holst's rondo of the same
> title, 'composed for the German Theatre' and published
> c. 1805 by Longman and Broderip.

Polonese Russe

Kozlovskiĭ, Osip Antonovich, 1757–1831

1788

Dance instrumental

CHWJA/19/02:35

> No composer given in MS, but the melody matches an
> incipit in RISM for a 1788 manuscript titled 'Polonoise

par Mr Le Prince Kosloffsky', i.e. Osip Antonovich Kozlovskii.

Steibelt's 18th pot pourri with variations: air of Guardami un poco

Steibelt, Daniel, 1765–1823 / Martín y Soler, Vicente, 1754–1806

1800

Instrumental

CHWJA/19/02:36

> Steibelt's 18th pot pourri is listed in the British Library Catalogue as 'Steibelt's Eighteenth Pot-Pouri for the Piano Forte, in which is introduced Martini's Favorite Air of "Guardami un poco"' with a suggested date of 1800. A pot-pourri is 'a composition that consists of a string of favourite tunes with the slightest connecting links and no development' (Percy Scholes, *The Oxford Companion to Music*).

Overture to Artaxerxes – Dr Arne

Arne, Thomas Augustine, 1710–1778

1793

Theatre instrumental

CHWJA/19/02:37

> Piano reduction of the overture to Thomas Arne's 1762 opera *Artaxerxes*. Score closely matches 'Overture in Artaxerxes, Composed by Dr Arne. published by A. Blands Music Warehouse, 23 Oxford Street'. Bland published under this name c. 1790–1793.

Songs and duetts [Catalogue number CHWJA/19/03]

[Tis in vain Alcanzor]
Vocal duet
CHWJA/19/03:01

>No composer identified. Gammie and McCulloch's suggested identification with Tommaso Giordani's setting of 'Alcanzor and Zayda' is incorrect as the MS does not match this work in IMSLP. This is a through-composed setting of the first six lines only of the last of the 13 verses of Giordani's song. Samuel Arnold's glee 'Alcanzor: a Moorish tale' has not yet been sighted for comparison.

William – Haydn
Billington, Thomas, 1754–1832 (arranger)
1787
Vocal
CHWJA/19/03:02

>An arrangement by Thomas Billington of the Allegro con brio (first movement) of Joseph Haydn's keyboard sonata Hob. XVI/35. First published by Preston as 'William: a ballad, as sung by Sigra. Sestini, at Mr. Lacy's readings, Free Masons Hall, with universal applause' published c. 1787.

Oh Nancy
Carter, Thomas, c. 1740–1804
Percy, Thomas, 1729–1811
1773
Vocal
CHWJA/19/03:03

A printed copy of this song arranged as a duet is included in Jenkyns 05 – (Eleanor Jackson). Austen's MS has been altered to read 'Nancy'. The printed words begin 'Oh Nanny'.

The Irishman

Merry, Robert, 1755–1798 (lyricist)

1791

Vocal

CHWJA/19/03:04

> The words, headed 'None can love like an Irishman', appear in *The Gentleman's Magazine*, Volume 69 (January 1791), p. 84, quoted in a review of *The Picture of Paris* by Robert Merry.

The joys of the country – Dibdin

Dibdin, Charles, 1745–1814 (words and music)

1790

Theatre vocal

CHWJA/19/03:05

> A song from Dibdin's 'Entertainment sans souci', *The wags, or the camp of pleasure*, produced at the Lyceum in 1790.

In Lionel and Clarissa [Go and on my truth relying]

Dibdin, Charles, 1745–1814 (attrib.)

Bickerstaff, Isaac, 1735–1812

1768

Theatre vocal

CHWJA/19/03:06

> A song from *Lionel and Clarissa*, a 1768 pasticcio/opera with text by Isaac Bickerstaff. Many of the songs in this

work were composed by Charles Dibdin, while the rest were arrangements of tunes from Italian operas.

Air [Plus ne veux jamais m'engager]

Heurtier (lyricist)

Vocal

CHWJA/19/03:07

> No composer given and music is not yet identified. The words of this song appear in in *Petite encyclopédie poétique* (1804) with the title 'La Résolution', by Heurtier.

Her hair is like a golden clue, sung by Mr Johnstone – Shield

Shield, William, 1748–1829

MacNally, Leonard, 1752–1820

1785

Theatre vocal

CHWJA/19/03:08

> Copied from page 22 of score of *Robin Hood … selected & composed* by W. Shield. The words by Leo MacNally (c. 1785).

Sweet transports, gentle wishes, go. Sung by Mrs Billington in *Rosina*

Shield, William, 1748–1829

Brooke, Frances, 1745–1789

1792

Theatre vocal

CHWJA/19/03:09

> William Shield's comic opera *Rosina* was first published in 1783 and many editions followed. Early editions of

the full score give Miss Harper as the performer of this song. There are entries in the Stationers' Register for other songs from *Rosina* sung by Elizabeth Billington in 1792.

Air des Ballets de la Caravane

Grétry, André-Ernest-Modeste, 1741–1813
1783
Theatre instrumental
CHWJA/19/03:10

This is a keyboard arrangement of the 'Ballets' from Grétry's *Caravane de Caire* first performed in 1783.

Of plighted faith: a duett – Storace

Storace, Stephen, 1762–1796
Cobb, James, 1756–1818
1791
Theatre vocal duet
CHWJA/19/03:11

Duet for Catherine and Seraskier from Storace's 1791 opera *The siege of Belgrade*. Libretto by James Cobb.

The soldier's adieu – Dibdin

Dibdin, Charles, 1745–1814 (words and music)
1790
Theatre vocal
CHWJA/19/03:12

A song from Dibdin's 'Entertainment sans souci', *The wags, or the camp of pleasure*, produced at the Lyceum in 1790.

Air de *Marquis de Tulipano*: accompt. par Hausman [Je croyais ma belle]

Paisiello, Giovanni, 1740–1816

Gourbillon, Joseph-Antoine de (arranger)

1789

Theatre vocal

CHWJA/19/03:13

> The lyrics appear (with slight variations) in the libretto of *Le Marquis de Tulipano*: Opera bouffon en trois actes, et en vers blancs, parodie sur la musique de G. Poesiello (i.e. Paisiello) par C. J. A. Gourbillon (1789). The original melody is from the aria 'Credea Nina Cara' from Paisiello's opera *Il matrimonio inaspettato* (1779). 'Hausman' has not been identified.

Sous un berceau de jasmin

1793

Vocal

CHWJA/19/03:14

> A song of this name (with no composer given) is listed among the contents of *Bibliothéque des amans, ou choix de romances et chansons notées* [Partition] Paris, chez Pollet, [1793].

From night till morn I take my glass

Shield, William, 1748–1829 (arranger)

1790

Vocal duet

CHWJA/19/03:15

> Listed in *A short-title catalogue of music printed before 1825 in the Fitzwilliam Museum at Cambridge University*. Described as

'A favorite duett … the accompanyments by Mr Shield.'
Longman and Broderip: London, [c. 1790].

Duo du roi Theodore [Filles charmantes, jeunes amantes]

Paisiello, Giovanni, 1740–1816
1789
Theatre vocal duo
CHWJA/19/03:16

> This is an arrangement of a duet and chorus in Act
> 1, scene 6 & 7 of Paisiello's *Le roi Theodore a Venise* or
> *Il re Teodoro in Venezia* which appears to be copied
> from *Journal de harpe, par les meilleurs maîtres* (1789),
> a copy of which was owned by Eliza de Feuillide.
> The Italian words (1784) begin 'O giovinette
> innamorate'.

Catch [Joan said to John]

Atterbury, Luffman (?)
1800
Vocal ensemble
CHWJA/19/03:17

> This catch appears on p. 60 of *The flowers of harmony* (1800)
> attributed to Atterbury. Luffman Atterbury published a
> *Collection of catches and glees for three and four voices* in 1777.
> This volume has not been sighted to confirm whether it
> contains this catch.

De Richard Coeur de Lion [La danse n'est pas ce que j'aime]

Grétry, André-Ernest-Modeste, 1741–1813

Sedaine, Michel-Jean, 1719–1797
1785
Theatre vocal
CHWJA/19/03:18

> A song for the character Antonio (a young boy sung by soprano) from Grétry's opera *Richard Coeur de Lion* (1784/1785).

My Phillida adieu love

Mellish, Miss
1790
Vocal
CHWJA/19/03:19

> BUCEM lists four editions of this song by Miss Mellish (about whom nothing is known) from 1790 and 1800. There was also a New York edition, and it was reprinted in Alfred Moffat's *English songs of the Georgian period* (1907).

Chanson Béarnoise

1791
Folk vocal
CHWJA/19/03:20

> The words of this song appear in *Justification de M. Favras* (Paris, 1791), with a note 'Sur l'air: Eh! vraiment, ne savons-nous pas'. At the end there is a note to the effect that this song had been printed and was freely available in the streets.

Thy fatal shafts unerring move

Meyer, Philippe-Jacques, 1737–1819
Smollett, T. (Tobias), 1721–1771

1780
Vocal
CHWJA/19/03:21

> The melody in Austen's book is somewhat similar to that in Philippe-Jacques Meyer's setting of the same words in his *Twelve English songs* (1780). However, this tune is in 3/4 while Austen's version is in 4/4, and there are many other differences.

The lucky escape [I that once was a ploughman]

Dibdin, Charles, 1745–1814 (words and music)
1791
Theatre vocal
CHWJA/19/03:22

> A song from Dibdin's *Private theatricals*, produced at the Royal Polygraphic Rooms, Strand, in 1791.

From *The mountaineers* [Think your tawny moor is true]

Arnold, Samuel, 1740–1802
Colman, George, 1762–1836
1794
Theatre vocal
CHWJA/19/03:23

> A song from George Colman the younger's play *The mountaineers*, as performed at the Theatre Royal, Haymarket, in 1794, with music by 'Dr [Samuel] Arnold'.

The wedding day

Hook, Mr (James), 1746–1827
1784

Vocal

CHWJA/19/03:24

> BUCEM lists this several times, including a single edition by S. A. and P. Thompson titled 'What virgin, or shepherd, in valley or grove (The Wedding Day)' (sung by Mrs Kennedy) and one in a collection of Hook's songs sung at 'Vauxhall Gardens etc.', both from 1784.

The Marseilles march

Rouget de Lisle, Claude Joseph, 1760–1836

1792

Military vocal

CHWJA/19/03:25

> A publication by John Bland of 'The Marseilles march' is listed in the Stationers' Register on 23 October 1792, 'as sung by the Marseillois going to battle …' with words beginning 'Ye sons of France awake to glory'. However, Austen's version has words in French. An edition with French words is listed on 2 November 1792 published by Joseph Dale, with the title 'Marche des Marseillois or French Te Deum'.

Arietta veneziano [La biondino in gondoletta]

Lamberti, Antonio, 1757–1832 (lyricist)

Vocal

CHWJA/19/03:26

> The words of this song were written by Antonio Lamberti, and the tune may have been written by Johann Simon Mayr although according to RISM it has been variously attributed to at least two other composers. It was later arranged by many composers including Giovanni Battista

Perucchini, Beethoven and Reynaldo Hahn. It survives as a popular Italian song.

Somebody
Folk vocal
CHWJA/19/03:27

First line: 'Were I obliged to beg my bread'. No composer given. The words of this song are similar, though not identical, to those in the 1790 publication by J. Bland but the melody is different. The melody in Austen's MS has not been located anywhere else.

The heaving of the lead [For England when with fav'ring gale]
Shield, William, 1748–1829
Pearce, William, active 1785–1796
1792
Theatre vocal
CHWJA/19/03:28

'It formed part of a little opera called, "Hartford Bridge: or, The Skirts of a Camp", acted at Covent Garden Theatre in 1792. The music was "selected and composed" by William Shield, and it is generally considered that this musician wrote the air in question. The words are by the author of the libretto, William Pearce.'[2]

Captivity [My foes prevail, my friends are fled]
Storace, Stephen, 1762–1796
Jeans, Joshua
1793
Vocal

CHWJA/19/03:29

> This appears to have been copied from J. Dale's edition of 1793 titled 'Captivity: a ballad supposed to be sung by the unfortunate Marie Antoinette during her imprisonment in the Temple. The words by the Revd. Mr Jeans ... & sung by Sign[or]a. Storace & Mrs Crouch. Set by Stephen Storace.'

Queen Mary's lamentation [I sigh and lament me in vain]

Giordani, Tommaso, 1733 (?) –1806 (arranger)

1782

Folk vocal

CHWJA/19/03:30

> The melody is a Scottish air which was also set by several composers, including Giordani, Haydn and Corri. The melody and partial bass part in the MS match the parts in the full score for voice and string quartet first published by Preston in 1782, 'Sung by Sigr Tenducci at the Pantheon. The instrumental parts by Sigr Giordani.' Giusto Ferdinando Tenducci was a castrato soprano resident in London.

The poor little gypsey – Dr Arnold

Arnold, Samuel, 1740–1802

Colman, George, 1762–1836

1801

Theatre vocal

CHWJA/19/03:31

> A song from Colman and Arnold's musical farce *The wags of Windsor* (1801). Austen's MS closely matches the score available online at the Library of Congress.

From *The mountaineers* [When the hollow drum has beat to bed]

Arnold, Samuel, 1740–1802

Colman, George, 1762–1836

1794

Theatre vocal

CHWJA/19/03:32

> A song from George Colman the younger's play *The mountaineers*, as performed at the Theatre Royal, Haymarket, in 1794, with music by 'Dr [Samuel] Arnold'.

Duet from *The mountaineers* [Faint and wearily the way-worn traveller plods uncheerily]

Arnold, Samuel, 1740–1802

Colman, George, 1762–1836

1794

Theatre vocal

CHWJA/19/03:33

> A song from George Colman the younger's play *The mountaineers*, as performed at the Theatre Royal, Haymarket, in 1794, with music by 'Dr [Samuel] Arnold'.

Collin's ode on the death of Thomson – J. W. Calcott

Callcott, John Wall, 1766–1821

Collins, William, 1721–1759

Vocal

CHWJA/19/03:34

> Funeral ode in six sections, a setting of William Collins's 'Ode occasion'd on the death of Mr Thomson' (1749).

Begone dull care
CHWJA/19/03:35

1793
Vocal duet

>No composer given. First registered at Stationers' Hall in 1793, published by Longman and Broderip.

The mansion of peace – by Mr Webbe
Webbe, Samuel, 1740–1816

A Lady

1780

Vocal

CHWJA/19/03:36

>Several editions in library catalogues, the first dated 1780 and published in Dublin. The 1790 London edition adds 'Words by a Lady'.

The match girl
1790

Vocal

CHWJA/19/03:37

>Gammie and McCulloch cite a London edition from c. 1790, music by 'A Lady', words by 'T. H.'. However, RISM has a reference to an MS source tentatively dated to 1750, with incipit matching this tune.

Songs [Scrapbook of manuscript and printed vocal and keyboard music, c. 1775 – c. 1810 – Catalogue number CHWJA/19/07]

[I ha'e laid a herring in sa't]

1790

Folk vocal

CHWJA/19/07:02

> On Traditional Tune Archive the earliest date given is 1776, with this version dated at 1790.

[Theme and variations]

Instrumental

CHWJA/19/07:08

> No composer given – unidentified melody.

[How imperfect is expression some Emotions to impart]

1772

Theatre vocal

CHWJA/19/07:09

> This song has been attributed by some to Charles Dibdin. However, according to Frank Kidson it is not by Dibdin but is originally a French song first published in London in 1772. The song was originally sung by Mrs Abington in *Twelfth night.*

Susan [O Susan, Susan lovely dear]

Vocal

Gay, John, 1685–1732 (lyricist)

CHWJA/19/07:10

No composer given. The lyrics are extracted from John Gay's 1719 poem 'Black-eyed Susan'. Another MS of this song appears later in the same book.

Why tarries my love?
Leeves, W. (William), Rev., 1748–1828
Blamire, Susanna, 1747–1794
1784
Vocal
CHWJA/19/07:12

> In some editions this song is attributed to the author of 'Auld Robyn Gray', W. Leeves, with the earliest date given by the British Library 1784. The words appear as 'The carrier pigeon' in the collected works of Susanna Blamire.

Silent sorrow: Song from *The stranger* – the words by R. B. Sheridan Esqr., the air by the Duchess of Devonshire
Cavendish, Georgiana Spencer, Duchess of Devonshire, 1757–1806
Sheridan, Richard Brinsley, 1751–1816
1798
Theatre vocal
CHWJA/19/07:13

> *The stranger* was a play based on *Menschenhass und Reue* (Misanthropy and Repentance) by the German playwright August von Kotzebue (1761–1819). It opened in London in 1798. The song appears in Act 4, scene 1.

Appendix 2

Song in *La fée urgèle* – Phillidor [Ah! que l'amour est chose jolie]

Duni, Egidio, 1708–1775

Favart, M. (Charles-Simon), 1710–1792

1765

Theatre vocal

CHWJA/19/07:14

> This is not by 'Philidor' (François-André Danican Philidor, 1726–1795) as Austen has written on her MS, but by Egidio Duni. The opera was first performed in Paris in 1765. The libretto, by Charles-Simon Favart, is based on Voltaire's *Ce qui plaît aux dames* and Chaucer's *The Wife of Bath's tale*. This Ariette is for soprano.

[Laisse la sur l'herbette]

Pollet, Benoît, 1753–1823 (?)

1810

Vocal

CHWJA/19/07:18

> University of Oxford Library holds a chanson by Benoît Pollet with the same first line, lyrics by 'Mr B***', titled 'Le Refus', estimated date given in their catalogue of 1810. The tune and words of this edition are the same but the accompaniment is different from the MS.

Goosey goosey gander, where shall I wander

Wesley, Samuel, 1766–1837

1800

Children's vocal trio

CHWJA/19/07:21

The MS is similar to Wesley's setting of the nursery rhyme as recorded in another MS by RISM. Wesley's 'Goosy Gander: a favorite glee' was published in London by R. Birchall c. 1800.

Hither love thy beauties bring

Krumpholtz, Jean-Baptiste, 1742–1790
Rannie, John
Vocal
CHWJA/19/07:25

> The words in Austen's MS, set to a different melody, are found in a collection of songs by John Ross, *A second set of nine songs with an accompaniment for the piano-forte or harp* (London, Longman & Broderip c. 1796), with words by 'Mr Rannie'. The tune is from the Romanza of J.-B. Krumpholtz's harp concerto Opus 9, no. 6 and was used for the song *The nuns complaint from Mrs Robinson's Novel of Vancenza … the music by Krumpholtz* (London, Preston & Son, c. 1794). No other source for the combination of these words and this melody has been found.

Ellen the Richmond primrose girl – R. Spofforth

Spofforth, Reginald, 1770–1827
Pearce, William, active 1785–1796
1800
Vocal
CHWJA/19/07:26

> British Library suggests a publication date of 1800 for this edition.

Glenviddich strathspey

Marshall, William, 1748–1833

1781

Dance instrumental

CHWJA/19/07:27

> This tune is attributed to William Marshall in the Traditional Tune Archive, with an earliest date of 1781.

The chosen few

Dance instrumental

CHWJA/19/07:28

> No composer given – unidentified melody.

The Egyptian love song [Sweet doth blush the rosy morning]

Harington, Henry, 1727–1816

1778

Vocal duo

CHWJA/19/07:31

> The MS closely follows the version published by Longman, Lukey and Broderip who traded under that name in about 1778. Printed score is subtitled 'From Potiphar's wife to young Joseph, translated from an Oriental essay on chastity – for 2 voices – Mr Harington'.

The prayer of the Sicilian mariners

Jones, Edward, 1752–1824

1785

Vocal duo

CHWJA/19/07:32

Manuscript closely follows the version in Edward Jones's *A miscellaneous collection of French and Italian ariettas; adapted with accompaniments for the harp or harpsichord.* BUCEM suggests a publication date of 1785. Words begin 'O sanctissima! O piissima dolce virgo Maria'. A Sicilian source for this hymn has not been positively identified but it has since become widespread as a tune for several hymns and the anthem 'We shall overcome'.

Air Russe – arrangée par Crotch

Crotch, William, 1775–1847

1800

Instrumental

CHWJA/19/07:33

> Published source not identified. A possible source (not yet checked) is J. & W. Crotch's *Familiar airs for the piano forte* (1800).

Duet in *the Siege of Belgrade*: sung by Mr Banister jun. and Sig'ra Storace [Tho you think by this to vex me]

Storace, Stephen, 1762–1796

Cobb, James, 1756–1818

1791

Theatre vocal duo

CHWJA/19/07:34

> Duet for Lilla and Leopold from Act 3, scene 3 of Storace's 1791 opera *The siege of Belgrade*. Libretto by James Cobb.

Appendix 2

A song from *the Siege of Belgrade* [How provoking your doubts]

Storace, Stephen, 1762–1796

Cobb, James, 1756–1818

1791

Theatre vocal

CHWJA/19/07:37

> Song for Leopold from Act 3, scene 1 of Storace's 1791 opera *The siege of Belgrade*. Libretto by James Cobb.

Song in *the Siege of Belgrade* [The sapling oak]

Storace, Stephen, 1762–1796

Cobb, James, 1756–1818

1791

Theatre vocal

CHWJA/19/07:39

> Song for Anselm from Act 1, scene 3 of Storace's 1791 opera *The siege of Belgrade*. Libretto by James Cobb.

[Since then I'm doom'd]

Baudron, Antoine Laurent, 1742–1834

Bickerstaff, Isaac, 1735–1812

1792

Theatre vocal

CHWJA/19/07:40

> Song from Isaac Bickerstaff's 1792 play *The spoilt child*, with music based on Baudron's aria 'Je suis Lindor' from the music included in the first performance of Beaumarchais's *Le barbier de Séville* (1775). The melody is slightly changed from Baudron's aria – i.e. the second note (in D major) is a G rather than an F sharp. Baudron's

melody is best known for Mozart's piano variations on it (K. 354).

Cossack dance

Dance instrumental

CHWJA/19/07:41

No composer given – unidentified melody.

As I was walking

1796

Folk vocal

CHWJA/19/07:42

No composer given. The tune and words (though indistinct in the MS) are similar to 'He's dear to me tho' he's far frae me', first published anonymously in 1796.

O Susan, Susan lovely dear

Gay, John, 1685–1732 (lyricist)

Vocal

CHWJA/19/07:43

No composer given. The lyrics are extracted from John Gay's 1719 poem 'Black-eyed Susan'. Another MS of this song appears earlier in the same book as 'Susan'.

Pauvre Jacques

Marie Antoinette, Queen, consort of Louis XVI, King of France, 1755–1793 (attrib.)

Travenet, Jeanne-Renée de Bombelles, marquise de, 1753–1828 (attrib.)

1789

Vocal

CHWJA/19/07:44

> No composer given. Many arrangements of this tune are recorded in RISM and other indexes, in different keys. In some the tune is attributed to Queen Marie Antoinette and the words to the Marquise de Travenet (1753–1828), or vice versa.

[Sure 'twould make a dismal story]

Arnold, Samuel, 1740–1802
Andrews, Miles Peter, d. 1814
1780
Theatre vocal duet
CHWJA/19/07:45

> 'From the medley opera *Fire and water* [1780] … . Of the whole opera, only this song and the libretto were ever published.'[3]

Loose sheets (CHWJA/19/11 and CHWJA/19/12)

Glee Robinhood

Mornington, Garrett Colley Wellesley, Earl of, 1735–1781
Vocal ensemble
CHWJA/19/11 (single loose sheet)

> Manuscript possibly in hand of Eliza de Feuillide, Jane Austen's cousin and her brother Henry's first wife. Music appears to match Lord Mornington's glee 'Here in cool grot' but the words are different: 'By greenwood tree or mossy cell, we merry maids and archers dwell, in quiet here from wordly strife we pass a gay and rural life …'.

Duo des deux savoyards [De votre or que pourrais-je faire]

Dalayrac, Nicolas-Marie, 1753–1809

1789

Theatre vocal duo

CHWJA/19/12 (single loose sheet)

> Manuscript possibly in hand of Eliza de Feuillide, Jane Austen's cousin and her brother Henry's first wife. Duet from Dalayrac's opera *Les deux petites Savoyards*, first performed in Paris in 1789. Incomplete copy. Gillaspie suggests that the last 34 bars of this incomplete MS were copied by Austen, continuing her cousin's MS.[4]

Savage Dance

Dance instrumental

CHWJA/19/12

> Manuscript possibly in hand of Eliza de Feuillide, Jane Austen's cousin and her brother Henry's first wife. Composer and source unidentified. Dance instructions written below the music.

[Untitled volume – Catalogue number Jenkyns 03]

Waltz 1st – Clementi

Clementi, Muzio, 1752–1832

1798

Dance instrumental

Jenkyns 03:03

This waltz is no. 1 from *Twelve waltzes for the piano forte with an accompaniment for the tamburino & triangle* by Muzio Clementi, Opus 38. Entered in the Stationers' Register on 30 June 1798. (NB there is also a set of 3 Sonatinas by Clementi published as Opus 38).

Waltz 5th
Clementi, Muzio, 1752–1832
1798
Dance instrumental
Jenkyns 03:04

This waltz is no. 5 from *Twelve waltzes for the piano forte with an accompaniment for the tamburino & triangle* by Muzio Clementi, Opus 38. Entered in the Stationers' Register on 30 June 1798. (NB there is also a set of 3 Sonatinas by Clementi published as Opus 38.)

Waltz 2
Clementi, Muzio, 1752–1832
1798
Dance instrumental
Jenkyns 03:05

This waltz is no. 2 from *Twelve waltzes for the piano forte with an accompaniment for the tamburino & triangle* by Muzio Clementi, Opus 38. Entered in the Stationers' Register on 30 June 1798. (NB there is also a set of 3 Sonatinas by Clementi published as Opus 38.)

[God save the king]
Bach, Johann Christian, 1735–1782
1763

Instrumental

Jenkyns 03:06

> A simple arrangement of 'God save the king', with one variation followed by a repeat of the theme indicated by da capo. No composer or title given. This is the theme and first variation of the final movement of Johann Christian Bach's harpsichord concerto Opus 1, no. 6 (1763).

Sonata – Sigr. Haydn

Haydn, Joseph, 1732–1809 1792

Instrumental

Jenkyns 03:08

> This is Haydn's sonata Hob. XVI/35, first published in 1780. It was published in London c. 1792.

Overture to La buona figliuola – Sigr. Piccini

Piccinni, Niccolo, 1728–1800

1767

Theatre instrumental

Jenkyns 03:09

> Piccinni's 1760 opera *La buona figliuola* is based on Samuel Richardson's 1740 novel *Pamela*. An incomplete print version of this arrangement of the overture, published by Robert Bremner in 1767, appears in the collection of Elizabeth Austen (née Bridges).

Lesson

Jones, John, 1728–1796

1761

Instrumental

Jenkyns 03:10

Appendix 2

From Volume 1 of John Jones's *Lessons for the harpsichord*, published in London in 1761. Two movements. In the printed score they are marked 'Allegro' and 'Tempo di Minuet'. John Jones was organist at St Paul's Cathedral 1755–1796.

Tambourin

Dance instrumental

Jenkyns 03:11

> Unidentified – no composer given.

Rondeau

Garth, John, 1721–1810

1768

Instrumental

Jenkyns 03:12

> This is the first part of the Rondeau (Allegro) from the first of John Garth's *Six sonatas for the harpsichord, piano forte, and organ with accompanyments for two violins, and a violoncello*, Opus 2, London, 1768.

Sonata

Instrumental

Jenkyns 03:13

> Unidentified keyboard sonata in E flat major, in three movements: 1. Allegro, 2. Andante, 3. Allegretto/ Andantino.

Air varié par M. Blattman Dufeuille

Blattman, P. P. (Pierre Philibert Dufeuille), d. 1821

Instrumental

Jenkyns 03:14

This is a set of 5 variations on the song 'Dieu d'amour en ce jour' from André-Ernest-Modeste Grétry's opera *Les mariages Samnites*. There are published variations on this tune by several other composers, including Mozart (K. 352/374c). A print version of this set of variations has not been identified. The composer is the harpist Pierre Philibert Dufeuille, known as Blattman.

Duo [Little Jack Horner]
Children's vocal duo
Jenkyns 03:15
> No composer given, and this version of the nursery rhyme has not been identified

Trio [Who comes there? A grenadier]
Children's vocal trio
Jenkyns 03:16
> No composer given, and this version of the nursery rhyme has not been identified

Duo [I'll sing a song of sixpence]
Children's vocal duo
Jenkyns 03:17
> No composer given, and this version of the nursery rhyme has not been identified.

How gentle was my Damon's air – Dr Arne
Arne, Thomas Augustine, 1710–1778
Dalton, John, 1709–1763 (lyricist)
1797
Theatre vocal

Jenkyns 03:18

> This recitative and aria are from Act 3 of Thomas Arne's setting of John Milton's masque *Comus* (1634), adapted by John Dalton for the London stage in 1738. The lyrics of this piece are by Dalton. The *Piano-forte magazine* Volume III, no. 2 (c. 1797) included an arrangement for piano of *Comus* from which this MS may be copied.

Sweet Echo sweetest nymph

Arne, Thomas Augustine, 1710–1778

Milton, John, 1608–1674

1797

Theatre vocal

Jenkyns 03:19

> This aria is from Act 1 of Thomas Arne's setting of John Milton's masque *Comus* (1634), adapted by John Dalton for the London stage in 1738. The lyrics of this piece are from Milton's original text. The *Piano-forte magazine* Volume III, no. 2 (c. 1797) included an arrangement for piano of *Comus* from which this MS may be copied.

By the gaily circling glass

Arne, Thomas Augustine, 1710–1778

Dalton, John 1709–1763

1797

Theatre vocal

Jenkyns 03:20

> This song is from Act 1 of Thomas Arne's setting of John Milton's masque *Comus* (1634), adapted by John Dalton for the London stage in 1738. The lyrics of this piece are by

Dalton. The *Piano-forte magazine* Volume III, no. 2 (c. 1797) included an arrangement for piano of *Comus* from which this MS may be copied.

Epitaph [Forgive blest shade the tributary tear]

Callcott, John Wall, 1766–1821

1795
Vocal ensemble

Jenkyns 03:21

> The earliest recorded edition of this work, held by University of Oxford Library, is included on page 4 of *The Fryar of orders gray* (see Jenkyns/02:22). The full title is: 'Epitaph in the church yard of Brading in the Isle of Wight. Set to music as a glee for 2 trebles and a bass', by J. W. Callcott.

The request [Tell me babbling echo why]

Vogler, Gerard

1780
Vocal

Jenkyns 03:22

> Several editions of this song are listed on library catalogues, the earliest by Preston and Son with an estimated date of 1780.

Song from Burns [Their groves of sweet myrtle]

Burns, Robert, 1759–1796 (lyricist)
Folk vocal

Jenkyns 03:24

> No composer given, and this version of the tune has not been identified among the various printed settings.

However, another copy of the song with this melody is held in the manuscript collection of Mary Elizabeth Egerton (1782–1846) of Tatton Park.

Deh prendi un dolce amplesso amico

Mozart, Wolfgang Amadeus, 1756–1791

Mazzolà, Caterino, 1745–1806

1791

Theatre vocal duo

Jenkyns 03:28

> This is the 'duettino' from Act 1 of Mozart's opera *La clemenza di Tito*, first performed in Prague in 1791. Several printed versions of this duet appear in London from about 1800 onwards. The lyrics are by Caterino Mazzolà, who adapted a libretto by Pietro Metastasio for Mozart's opera.

Megan oh oh Megan ee – Michael Kelly

Kelly, Michael, 1762–1826

Lewis, M. G. (Matthew Gregory), 1775–1818

1798

Theatre vocal ensemble

Jenkyns 03:29

> Song for tenor and chorus in *The castle spectre: a dramatic romance in five acts* by Matthew G. Lewis, music by Michael Kelly. Sung by the character Motley. In the libretto, the word is 'megen', while Austen has written 'megan'. It is not the name of any of the characters and appears to be a nonsense word. First performed at the Theatre Royal, Drury Lane, in 1797. Score published 1798.

The spectre song [Lullaby, lullaby, hush thee my dear]

Kelly, Michael, 1762–1826

Lewis, M. G. (Matthew Gregory), 1775–1818

1798

Theatre vocal

Jenkyns 03:31

> This short song appears in Act 1, scene 2 of *The castle spectre: a dramatic romance in five acts* by Matthew G. Lewis, music by Michael Kelly. First performed at the Theatre Royal, Drury Lane, in 1797. Score published 1798.

Music from the oratory while the ghost appears – Jomelli

Jommelli, Niccolò, 1714–1774. Kelly, Michael, 1762–1826 (arranger)

Lewis, M. G. (Matthew Gregory), 1775–1818

1798

Theatre instrumental

Jenkyns 03:32

> Music from *The castle spectre: a dramatic romance in five acts* by Matthew G. Lewis, music by Michael Kelly. First performed at the Theatre Royal, Drury Lane, in 1797. Arranged from the chaconne in Niccolo Jomelli's divertimento in E flat major.

Jubilate on the ghost's retiring

Kelly, Michael, 1762–1826

Lewis, M. G. (Matthew Gregory), 1775–1818

1798

Theatre vocal ensemble

Jenkyns 03:33

> Chorus from *The castle spectre: a dramatic romance in five acts* by Matthew G. Lewis, music by Michael Kelly. First performed at the Theatre Royal, Drury Lane, in 1797. Score published 1798.

Ne vous repentez pas mon pere

Monsigny, Pierre-Alexandre, 1729–1817

Sedaine, Michel-Jean, 1719–1797

1777

Vocal trio

Jenkyns 03:34

> Trio from Act 3, scene 9 of *Félix, ou, L'enfant trouvé*, music by Monsigny; words by Sedaine. First performed 1777.

The babes in the wood

Children's vocal

Jenkyns 03:35

> No composer given. A different arrangement of the tune published under the title 'Sweet babes in the wood' by B. Carr's Music Repository in Philadelphia.

Dickery dickery dock

Children's vocal duo

Jenkyns 03:36

> No composer or arranger given. This rhyme first appeared as 'Hickere, dickere dock' in 1744 in *Tommy Thumb's pretty song book*. The version 'Dickery, dickery dock' appeared in 'Mother Goose's melody' c. 1765. The tune in Austen's MS is the familiar one still used today.

See saw saccaradown
Children's vocal duo
Jenkyns 03:37
> No composer or arranger given. A different setting of this nursery rhyme appears in James Hook's *Christmas box* (1797).

The death of poor Cock Robin
Welsh, Thomas, approximately 1780–1848
Children's vocal
Jenkyns 03:38
> A version very similar to Austen's was published by B. Carr's Musical Repository in Philadelphia, attributed to 'Master Walsh of Drury Lane Theatre'. Thomas Welsh was a boy soprano and composer at Drury Lane Theatre in the 1790s. The words appeared in *Tommy Thumb's pretty song book* (c. 1744) but may be much older.

[Hushaby baby]
Children's vocal trio
Jenkyns 03:39
> No composer or arranger given. A different setting of this nursery rhyme appears in James Hook's *Christmas box* (1797).

[Cock a doodle doo]
Children's vocal trio
Jenkyns 03:40
> No composer or arranger given. J. Dale published *Cock a doodle doo: a favorite duet or trio for two or three voices* in London in 1797. There is also a setting of this nursery rhyme in James Hook's *The fairing: a collection of juvenile songs*

published by Preston & Sons c. 1800. Neither of these scores has been viewed for comparison.

Duo [Tell tale tit]
Children's vocal duo
Jenkyns 03:41

> No composer or arranger given or identified. J. Dale published *Tell tale tit: a favorite duett for two voices adapted for juvenile performers* in London in 1797. This has not been sighted for identification.

Irish air [Lost is my quiet]
Opie, Amelia, 1769–1853 (lyricist)
1790
Folk vocal
Jenkyns 03:42

> This is not the famous duet by Henry Purcell but an arrangement of the tune 'Ye banks and braes of Bonny Doon' set to words by Amelia Opie, first published in London around 1790 by Preston & Son.

Seaton clifts
Hayes, Phil. (Philip), 1738–1797 (arranger)
1785
Vocal
Jenkyns 03:43

> Several editions of *To thy cliffs rocky Seaton adieu. Adieu to Seaton Cliffs. ... The words & melody ... by a Gentleman of Oxford, at whose request Dr P. Hayes added a bass and the accompaniments* were published in London and Dublin around 1785. 'Clifts' is Austen's spelling of 'cliffs'.

Appendix 2

Address to sleep

Cartwright, Edmund, 1743–1823 (lyricist)

Vocal

Jenkyns 03:44

> First line: 'Sleep, though death thou dost resemble'. No
> composer given and this song has not been traced in
> any other collections or libraries. The text is Edmund
> Cartwright's 'imitation' or translation of a Latin poem,
> 'Ad somnum', of uncertain origins.

Morning hymn [and Evening hymn] – Thos. Shell

Shell, Thomas, d. 1801

Ken, Thomas, 1637–1711 (lyricist)

1801

Religious vocal ensemble

Jenkyns 03:45–46

> Anthem or hymn for SATB interspersed with sections for
> solo duet or trio. Thomas Shell was a musician based in
> Bath. This was probably published as part of his *Twenty
> new psalms*, printed by G. Steart, 1801. The words begin
> 'Awake my soul and with the sun' and 'Glory to thee my
> god this night' and have been set by many composers.

Free mason's song

1801

Vocal

Jenkyns 03:47

> This song appears to be copied from *A tour through Germany:
> particularly along the banks of the Rhine, Mayne, etc.* by Wilhelm
> Render (London, 1801), where it is given as a 'specimin
> of a German masonic song, which is adopted in all the

lodges in the Empire'. Words begin 'Come brothers sing with me' ('Laszt uns ihr Brueder'). German title is 'Freymaeurer Lied'.

Love and wine
Hiller, Johann Adam, 1728–1804
Weisse, Christian Felix, 1726–1804
1801
Vocal
Jenkyns 03:48

> This song appears to be copied from *A tour through Germany: particularly along the banks of the Rhine, Mayne, etc.* by Wilhelm Render (London, 1801). In the printed version the German words are given with an unattributed English translation. German title is 'Liebe und Wein'.

Rhenish wine
Vocal
Claudius, Matthias, 1740–1815 (lyricist)
Jenkyns 03:49

> This song appears to be copied from *A tour through Germany: particularly along the banks of the Rhine, Mayne, etc.* by Wilhelm Render (London, 1801). No composer given. German title is 'Rheinwein Lied'; lyrics begin 'With ivy crown'd behold' ('Bekränzt mit Laub den lieben vollen Becher').

Love my Mary dwells with thee
Stevenson, John, 1761–1833 (arranger)
Moore, Thomas, 1779–1852
1809

Vocal duo

Jenkyns 03:50

> A song of this title is held in several editions by the British Library, with the earliest publication date given as 1809 (based on a watermark): 'a favorite duet, the music selected from the ancient ballads, with an accompaniment for the piano forte, by Sir John Stevenson ... The words by Thomas Moore. London: at I Powers'. John Power, publisher of Moore's *Irish melodies* (arranged by Stevenson) moved from Dublin to London in 1807–1808. This song does not appear to be included among the 8 volumes of Moore's *Irish melodies*, published between 1808 and 1834.

Here's the bower

Moore, Thomas, 1779–1852 (words and music)

1807

Vocal

Jenkyns 03:51

> No composer given, but in early editions both words and music are attributed to Thomas Moore. The first publication listed in JISC is 1807 by 'I. Power, London'.

Oh giovinetti

Casti, Giovanni Battista, 1724–1803 (lyricist)

Theatre vocal

Jenkyns 03:52

> The words with slight differences appear in Giovanni Battista Casti's libretto to Giovanni Paisiello's opera *Il re Teodoro in Venezia* (1784). However, this is not Paisiello's setting of these words, which appears in another of Austen's

manuscript books under the title 'Duo du Roi Theodore', translated into French as 'Filles charmantes'. The variation in Austen's version from 'giovinette innamorate' to 'giovinetti innamorati' changes the gender of these two words from the feminine to the masculine.

The wreath you wove

Moore, Thomas, 1779–1852 (attrib.)

1803

Vocal

Jenkyns 03:53

> No composer given. Two early editions listed in JISC are titled 'The wreath you wove, a ballad by Thos Moore', dated London c. 1803 and 1804 (J. Power). These editions have not been sighted for comparison with Austen's MS. Various contemporary and later editions have music by other composers. However, the melody in Austen's MS is different from all these and has not been identified. In his journal Moore referred to this 'song' as 'one of my juvenile productions'.

Fly not yet

Carolan, Turlough, 1670–1738

Moore, Thomas, 1779–1852

1807

Folk vocal

Jenkyns 03:54

> This song is in Volume 1 of Moore's *Irish melodies*, arranged by Sir John Stevenson, published by W. & J. Power in Dublin and London in 1807. The melody is O'Carolan's 'Hugh Kelly' or 'Planxty Kelly'.

Venetian ballad [Spazza camin]

Children's vocal

Jenkyns 03:55

> No composer given. An arrangement of this song is included in E. S. Biggs's *Six Venetian airs*, published by Birchall. Austen's words and melody are slightly different and the arrangement is quite different, so it is clearly not copied from this source

In the dead of the night

Arnold, Samuel, 1740–1802

Hall-Stevenson, John, 1718–1785

1794

Theatre vocal

Jenkyns 03:56

> From Mrs Inchbald's *The wedding day* (first staged at Drury Lane in 1794). The words appear in *A collection of poems in six volumes, by several hands*, Volume 6, 1770, by John Hall-Stevenson, translated from the third Ode of Anacreon, Greek lyric poet of the sixth century BCE.

Eveleen's bow'r: Irish melody

Stevenson, John, 1761–1833 (arranger)

Moore, Thomas, 1779–1852

1807

Folk vocal

Jenkyns 03:57

> This song is in Volume 2 of Moore's *Irish melodies*, arranged by Sir John Stevenson, published by W. & J. Power in Dublin and London in 1807.

Hindoo girl's song

Biggs, E. S. (Edward Smith), d. approximately 1820

Opie, Amelia, 1769–1853

1800

Vocal

Jenkyns 03:58

> E. S. Biggs's 2nd set of *Hindoo airs*, of which this is no. 3, is listed in the *German Museum* magazine for July 1800 as a new publication. The title details are 'A Hindustani girl's song, 'Tis thy will, and I must leave thee, Adapted by Mr Biggs', and a note attributes the words to Mrs Opie. Austen has written 'Mrs Curwen' on her manuscript but there appears to be no composer, poet or performer of that surname in this period.

Rob Roy Macgregor: strathspey

Dance folk instrumental

Jenkyns 03:59

> No composer given. This tune is different from versions of 'Rob Roy Macgregor' found online. A tune of this name is listed (with other titles included in this MS book) in Goulding, D'Almaine, Potter & Co.'s *Select collection of country dances, waltzes, &c for the piano forte*, no. 41 (1816), held by the British Library. This score has not been sighted for comparison.

Meg Merrilies

1816

Dance folk instrumental

Jenkyns 03:60

> This appears to be copied from Goulding & Co.'s *Select collection of country dances, waltzes, &c for the piano forte*, no. 38 (1816).

Musette variée by L. Von Esch

Esch, Louis von, d. 1829.

1804

Instrumental

Jenkyns 03:61

> Published by Broderip & Wilkinson and entered at
> Stationers' Hall on 12 April 1804.

The Sicilian dance

1816

Dance folk instrumental

Jenkyns 03:62

> This tune appears in other anonymous MS sources in
> RISM, and is the basis of variations by composers includ-
> ing John Ross, G. Masi and Charles Horn. None of the
> scores viewed matches the arrangement in Austen's MS.
> The Traditional Tune Archive gives three instances of
> this tune plus useful commentary. 1816 is the earliest date
> identified, although the tune may be older. Other titles
> are 'Mignonette' and 'Royal Albert'.

On ne sauroit trop embellir – Holst

Holst, Matthias, 1769–1854 / Méhul, Étienne, 1763–1817

1802

Instrumental

Jenkyns 03:63

> A printed edition of this set of variations by Matthias
> Holst has not been located in any libraries or collections,
> although Holst published several sets of variations on vari-
> ous tunes. Étienne Méhul's opera (or 'comédie mêlée de
> chants') *Une folie* was first produced in Paris in April 1802.

The queen of Prussia's waltz

Himmel, Friedrich Heinrich, 1765–1814

Dance instrumental

Jenkyns 03:64

> This tune is variously attributed to Prince Louis Ferdinand of Prussia and W. A. Mozart but the attribution to Himmel is most common.

The Campbells are coming: air

Dance folk instrumental

Jenkyns 03:65

> The melody, though not found in this form elsewhere, is similar in harmonic structure and length to the unharmonised version on p. 43 of Thomas Wilson's *Companion to the ball room* (1816), perhaps transcribed from memory and harmonised.

The young May moon

Moore, Thomas, 1779–1852 (lyricist)

1813

Folk instrumental

Jenkyns 03:66

> The song 'The young May moon' is in Volume 5 of Moore's *Irish melodies* (1813), where the air is named as 'The Dandy O!' However, this is quite different from and much simpler than the Stevenson arrangement and is for piano solo. This arrangement has not been located elsewhere

Drops of brandy

Dance folk instrumental

Jenkyns 03:67

The melody appears in various versions in the Traditional Tune Archive (without accompaniment), usually described as an Irish slip jig.

Cawdor fair

Dance folk instrumental

Jenkyns 03:68

> The melody is very similar to the nursery rhyme 'Sing a song of sixpence'. An arrangement of 'Cawdor Fair' was published in a collection titled *Miss Platoff's wedding, to which are added the favorite dances of 1813, as performed at his annual ball, George Street assembly rooms the 9th March* by Nathaniel Gow. This has not been sighted for comparison.

Andante – Zwingmann

Zwingmann, Johan Nicolaus, b. 1764

Instrumental

Jenkyns 03:69

> The two variations match the first and third in *Zwingmann's air with variations with additions for these numbers* published in Baltimore in 1817. Very few other traces of his work remain. Originally from Germany, Johan Nicolaus Zwingman or Zwingmann worked in London from the early 1790s until at least 1807.

The Waterloo

Dance folk instrumental

Jenkyns 03:73

> A 'Waterloo dance' is listed on the back page of Goulding, D'Almaine, Potter & Co.'s *Select collection of country dances, waltzes, &c for the piano forte*, no. 38 (1816), among the

Appendix 2

contents of no. 36 along with other titles matching those among Austen's MSS. However, this volume has not been sighted for comparison with Austen's MS and this tune has not been found elsewhere.

Notes

INTRODUCTION

1 Samantha Carrasco, *The Austen family music books and Hampshire music culture, 1770–1820* (Unpublished thesis, Southampton University, 2013), p. 33. Online. eprints.soton.ac.uk/466879/. Accessed 21 August 2022.

2 Robert K. Wallace, *Jane Austen and Mozart: classical equilibrium in fiction and music* (Athens: University of Georgia Press, 1983, p. 260.

3 Wallace, *Jane Austen and Mozart*, p. 261.

4 Jeanice Brooks, 'In search of Austen's "missing songs"', *Review of English studies*, 67:282 (2016), p. 916. DOI: 10.1093/res/hgw035.

5 Robert Toft, *Heart to heart: expressive singing in England 1780–1830* (Oxford: Oxford University Press, 2000), p. 15.

6 Gillian Dooley, 'Jane Austen: the musician as author', *Humanities*, 11:3 (2022), p. 73. DOI: 10.3390/h11030073.

7 Hermione Lee, '"Taste" and "tenderness": moral values in the novels of Jane Austen', in R. T. Davies and B. G. Beatty (eds), *Literature of the romantic period 1750–1850* (Liverpool: Liverpool University Press, 1976), p. 82.

8 Jon Gillaspie (afterwards Nessa Glen), 'Music collections in the Austen family with especial reference to the Rice music manuscripts' (unpublished report, c. 1990), p. 30.

Notes

9 Gillian Dooley, '"There is no understanding a word of it": musical taste and Italian vocal music in Austen's musical and literary world', *Persuasions*, 43 (2021), p. 89.

10 James H. Johnson, *Listening in Paris: a cultural history* (Berkeley: University of California Press, 1995), p. 3.

11 Nicholas Mathew, *The Haydn economy* (Chicago: University of Chicago Press, 2022), p. 156.

12 Michael Burden, 'Pots, privies and WCs: crapping at the opera in London before 1830', *Cambridge opera journal*, 23:1–2 (2012), p. 32. DOI: 10.1017/S0954586712000018.

13 Burden, 'Pots, privies and WCs', p. 32.

14 Brooks, 'In search', p. 916.

15 Joanne Wilkes, 'Jane Austen as "Prose Shakespeare": early comparisons', in Marina Cano and Rose García-Periago (eds), *Jane Austen and Shakespeare: a love affair in literature, film and performance* (Cham: Palgrave Macmillan, 2019), p. 29.

16 Caren Zwilling, *The original songs in Shakespeare's plays* (St Albans: Corda Music Publications, 2015), p. 21.

17 Lesley Peterson, Introduction, in Jane Austen, *Sir Charles Grandison*, Lesley Peterson, Sylvia Hunt et al. (eds) (Sydney: Juvenilia Press, 2022), p. xv.

18 Gillian Dooley, 'A most luxurious state: men and music in Jane Austen's novels', *English studies*, 98:6 (2017), p. 604. DOI: 10.1080/0013838X.2017.1322386.

19 Susan Allen Ford, '"My name was Norval": *Douglas*, elocution, and acting in *Mansfield Park*', *Persuasions*, 43 (2021), p. 136.

20 William Shakespeare, *The merchant of Venice*, Act V, scene 1.

21 Patrick Piggott, *The innocent diversion: music in the life and writings of Jane Austen* (London: Cleverdon, 1979).

22 See the Note on sources at the end of the book for explanations about accessing and searching the music collection online.

23 Carrasco, *The Austen family music books*.

1 THE JANE AUSTEN MUSIC MANUSCRIPTS

1 To view the collection online, visit the Austen family music books page at Internet Archive. archive.org/details/austenfamilymusicbooks. There is a detailed physical description of most of the collection in Samantha Carrasco's thesis *The Austen family music books*.

Notes

2 Kathryn L. Libin, 'Daily practice, musical accomplishment, and the example of Jane Austen', in Natasha Duquette and Elisabeth Lenckos (eds), *Jane Austen and the arts: elegance, propriety, and harmony* (Bethlehem: Lehigh University Press, 2014), p. 10.

3 Carrasco, *The Austen family music books*, pp. 271–367.

4 Percy Scholes in *The Oxford companion to music*, 10th edition (London: Oxford University Press, 1970), describes a pot-pourri as 'a composition that consists of a string of favourite tunes with the slightest connecting links and no development' (p. 822).

5 Roger Fiske, *Scotland in music* (Cambridge: Cambridge University Press, 1983), p. 3.

6 On 16 September 1813 Austen wrote to Cassandra from London: 'Fanny desires me to tell Martha that Birchall assured her there was no 2d set of Hook's Lessons for Beginners, & that by my advice, she has therefore chosen her a set by another composer. I thought she wd rather have something than not' (*Letters*, p. 224).

7 On 2 December 1815 Austen wrote to Cassandra, 'I have not Fanny's fondness for Masters, & Mr Meyers does not give me any Longing after them' (*Letters*, p. 303).

8 'Samuel Arnold (1740–1802)', Naxos composers information archived online at https://web.archive.org/web/20070314153116/http://www.naxos.com/composerinfo/2252.htm. Accessed 15 November 2022.

9 James D. Brown and Stephen S. Stratton, 'Samuel Arnold', in *British musical biography* (New York: Da Capo Press, 1971), pp. 14–15.

10 Penny Gay, *Jane Austen and the theatre* (Cambridge: Cambridge University Press, 2002), p. 52.

11 Gay, *Jane Austen and the theatre*, p. 53.

12 Sheridan was not the translator of the Kotzebue play, and the song would have been an insertion into the play, whether or not it was written for the purpose.

13 See for an extended discussion of this song G. Dooley and Umme Salma, 'The Hindoo girl's song: a shady story from British India', *South Asian review*, 43:3–4 (2022), pp. 333–47. DOI: 10.1080/02759527.2022.2040084.

14 Percy Scholes, 'Suite (1)', in *The Oxford companion to music*, p. 992.

15 Jeanice Brooks, 'Making music', in Kathryn Sutherland (ed.), *Jane Austen: writer in the world*, (Oxford: Bodleian Library, 2017), p. 43.

16 Todd Gilman, *The theatre career of Thomas Arne* (Newark: University of Delaware Press, 2013), p. 224.

Notes

17 Allison Thompson, *Dances from Jane Austen's assembly rooms* (Author, 2019), p. 50.

18 Scholes, 'Waltz', *The Oxford companion to music*, p. 1110.

19 Thompson, *Dances from Jane Austen's assembly rooms*, pp. 30ff.

20 Erin Helyard, *Clementi and the woman at the piano: virtuosity and the marketing of music in eighteenth-century London* (Liverpool: Liverpool University Press, 2022), p. 90.

21 Thompson, *Dances from Jane Austen's assembly rooms*, p. 34.

22 Scholes, 'Périgourdine', *Oxford Companion to Music*, p. 783.

23 Resource information for CHWJA/19/07 at Internet Archive.

24 Quoted in Gillian Dow, 'Theatre and theatricality; or, Jane Austen and learning the art of dialogue', *Persuasions*, 43 (2021), pp. 120–1.

25 Dow, 'Theatre and theatricality', p. 122.

26 *The nuns complaint from Mrs Robinson's novel of Vancenza ... the music by Krumpholtz* (London, Preston & Son, c. 1794).

27 John Ross, *A second set of nine songs with an accompaniment for the piano-forte or harp* (London, Longman & Broderip, c. 1796).

28 Resource Information for Jenkyns 03 at Internet Archive.

29 Resource Information for Jenkyns 03 at Internet Archive.

30 The Jenkyns volumes are indexed in a Handlist by Jon A. Gillaspie (now Nessa Glen), prepared in 1987. The handwriting identifications in that handlist occasionally seem to me to be mistaken – although I admit that it is often difficult to be certain.

31 See the page for Matthias Holst on IMSLP, including links to facsimiles of his compositions such as 'The nightingale' and various sets of variations. https://imslp.org/wiki/Category:Holst%2C_Matthias. Accessed 15 November 2022.

32 Erik Routley, *A short history of English church music* (London: Mowbray, 1997), pp. 37–8.

33 Adrienne Bradney-Smith, 'Brushes with ebony and ivory: some musical instruments of Jane Austen's time', *Sensibilities*, 40 (June 2010), pp. 14–15.

34 'Thomas Shell', *Janet Shell*. Online https://janetshell.co.uk/ts3.html. Accessed 23 August 2022.

35 Le Faye, 'Fanny Knight's diaries', p. 20.

36 Gillaspie (afterwards Glen), 'Music collections in the Austen family', p. 56.

37 This information comes from Gillaspie/Glen's unpublished document 'Music collections in the Austen family'.

Notes

38 Ian Gammie and Derek McCulloch, *Jane Austen's music* (St Albans: Corda Music Publications, 1996), p. 37.

39 Piggott, *The innocent diversion*, p. 153.

40 Wallace, *Jane Austen and Mozart*, p. 250.

2 JANE AUSTEN'S MUSICAL RELATIONSHIPS

1 Jeanice Brooks, 'Making music', in Kathryn Sutherland (ed.), *Jane Austen: writer in the world* (Oxford: Bodleian Library, 2017), pp. 38, 40.

2 Rosemary Richards and Julja Szuster (eds), *Memories of musical lives* (Melbourne: Lyrebird Press, 2022), p. 3.

3 I note, however, that Paula Byrne takes this literally. She believes that, as the Opera House had recently been renovated, 'Austen's sympathy for Cassandra's double disappointment was … equally distributed between seeing the new Opera House and seeing the great Mrs Jordan' (Paula Byrne, *The genius of Jane Austen* (London: William Collins, 2017), p. 71).

4 An earlier version of this section was published in *Jane Austen's regency world*, 110 (Mar./Apr. 2021).

5 Jan Ladislav Dussek, *Variations on Shepherds I have lost my love* (Dubin: Hime, n.d.), IMSLP. Online. https://imslp. org/wiki/Variations_on_'Shepherds%2C_I_have_lost_my_love'_(Dussek%2C_Jan_Ladislav). Accessed 8 July 2022.

6 Ros Oswald, 'A reputation Chard', *Jane Austen's regency world*, 115 (Jan./Feb. 2022), pp. 38–44.

7 Caroline Austen, *Reminiscences* (Guildford: Jane Austen Society, 1986), p. 22.

8 I am grateful to Lesley Peterson for illuminating discussions on this and many other points.

9 See Deirdre Le Faye, 'Fanny Knight's diaries: Jane Austen through her niece's eyes', *Persuasions occasional papers* 2 (1986).

10 Julienne Gehrer (ed.), *Martha Lloyd's household book: the original manuscripts from Jane Austen's kitchen* (Oxford: Bodleian Library, 2021), p. 21.

11 Le Faye, 'Fanny Knight's diaries', p. 18.

12 Thompson, *Dances from Jane Austen's assembly rooms*, p. 74.

13 Brooks, 'Making music', p. 44.

14 Birchall, one of the leading music publishers in London at the time, who also ran a music circulating library, seems to have been wrong about this. James Hook – a popular composer of the time – had

indeed produced two sets of lessons under the title *Guida di musica*. The first (Opus 37) appeared in around 1785 and the second part (Opus 81) was published by Bland and Weller in December 1796. This publication is listed in Michael Kassler, *Music entries at Stationers' Hall 1710–1818* (Farnham: Ashgate, 2004), on 30 December 1796 (p. 320).

15 Gehrer (ed.), *Martha Lloyd's household book*, p. 3.

16 Caroline Austen, *Reminiscences*, p. 13.

17 Caroline Austen, *Reminiscences*, p. 13.

18 Steventon auction notice in the *Reading Mercury*, held at Jane Austen's House Museum, Chawton.

19 Austen family music books. Internet Archive. Online. https://archive.org/details/austenfamilymusicbooks

20 Elizabeth Boardman, 'Mrs Cawley and Brasenose College', *The brazen nose*, 38 (2003–2004), p. 63.

21 Boardman, 'Mrs Cawley', p. 63.

22 Boardman, 'Mrs Cawley', p. 64.

23 See the information page for the Austen family music books on Internet Archive.

24 These two books are 'CHWJA/19/1 – Manuscript of keyboard and vocal music, copied c. 1750 –c. 1755 with later additions' and 'Jenkyns 01 – Manuscript of keyboard and vocal music, copied c. 1754–1760 with later additions'.

25 Brooks, 'Making music', p. 42.

26 Brooks, 'Making music', p. 43.

27 Steventon auction notice in the *Reading Mercury*, held at Jane Austen's House, Chawton.

28 E. J. Clery, *Jane Austen, the banker's sister* (London: Biteback Publishing, 2017), p. 131.

29 Clery, *Jane Austen*, p. 132.

30 Caroline Austen, *Reminiscences*, p. 29.

31 Valerie Grosvenor Myer, *Obstinate heart: Jane Austen: a biography* (London: Michael O'Mara, 1997), p. 34.

32 'Godmersham Park Library', *Reading with Austen*. Online. https://readingwithaustenblog.com/godmersham-library-catalogue/. Accessed 9 July 2022.

33 Clery, *Jane Austen*, p. 247.

34 A description of these two albums can be found online in a catalogue from the rare books dealer Voewood ('Jane Austen at the piano: "She played from the manuscript, copied out by herself"' (Holt: Voewood

Notes

Rare Books, c. 2020), pp. 10–11). https://issuu.com/voewoodrare
books/docs/voewood_catalogue_2_issuu. Accessed 5 November 2022.

35 Voewood Rare Books, 'Jane Austen at the piano', pp. 10–11.

3 JANE AUSTEN AND THE MUSIC OF THE FRENCH REVOLUTION

1 This chapter was first published in *Essays in French literature and culture*, 57 (2020), pp. 151–66.

2 Warren Roberts, *Jane Austen and the French Revolution*, 2nd edition (London: Athlone, 1995), p. 3.

3 Kathryn Sutherland, 'Women writing in time of war', in Kathryn Sutherland (ed.), *Jane Austen: writer in the world* (Oxford: Bodleian Library, 2017), p. 106.

4 Nicola McLelland, 'The history of language learning and teaching in Britain', *The language learning journal*, 46:1 (2018), p. 7. Online. DOI:10.1080/09571736.2017.1382052.

5 Noël Riley, *The accomplished lady: a history of genteel pursuits c. 1660–1860* (Huddersfield: Oblong Books, 2017), p. 36.

6 James Austen, 'National difference of character between the French and English – plan proposed for improving each', *The loiterer*, 10 (Saturday 4 April 1789). Online. www.theloiterer.org/loiterer/no10.html. Accessed 10 October 2022.

7 Lucy Worsley, *Jane Austen at home: a biography* (London: Hodder and Stoughton, 2017), p. 71.

8 Mary Spongberg, 'Jane Austen, the 1790s, and the French Revolution', in Claudia L. Johnson and Clara Tuite (eds), *A companion to Jane Austen* (Chichester: Wiley, 2009), p. 274.

9 Sutherland, 'Women writing in time of war', p. 106.

10 Sutherland, 'Women writing in time of war', p. 112.

11 Roberts, *Jane Austen*, p. 9.

12 Paul F. Rice, *British music and the French Revolution* (Newcastle upon Tyne: Cambridge Scholars, 2010), p. ix.

13 See Rice, *British music and the French Revolution*, pp. 163–4, 176ff. I differ from Rice in his assumption that 'supposed to be sung …' implies that Jeans and Storace were attempting to pass this song off as a composition by Marie Antionette. I believe that 'supposed' in this case means simply 'imagined'.

14 Stephen Storace, *Captivity: a ballad* (London: J. Dale, 1793). British Library Music Collections DRT Digital Store G.1277.a.(44.). Online.

Notes

http://explore.bl.uk/BLVU1:LSCOP-ALL:BLL01018749536. Accessed 15 November 2022.

15 Spongberg, 'Jane Austen, the 1790s, and the French Revolution', p. 280.

16 Spongberg, 'Jane Austen, the 1790s, and the French Revolution', pp. 279–80.

17 Alain-Jacques Tornare, 'L'histoire de "Pauvre Jacques"', *Pauvre Jacques*. Online. https://pauvrejacques.simdif.com/l_histoire_.html. Accessed 29 September 2022.

18 Jeanice Brooks has written extensively on this song in her article 'In search of Austen's "missing songs"', *Review of English Studies*, 67:282 (2016), pp. 914–45. DOI: 10.1093/res/hgw035.

19 Both these editions are listed in Kassler, *Music Entries at Stationers' Hall*, pp. 184, 185.

20 Rice, *British Music and the French Revolution*, pp. 373–4.

21 Guillaume François Mahy, *Justification de M. de Favras* (Paris: Potier de Lille, 1791), p. 165.

22 'Thomas de Mahy, marquis de Favras', Wikipedia. Online. https://en.wikipedia.org/wiki/Thomas_de_Mahy,_marquis_de_Favras. Accessed 29 September 2022.

23 Translation: 'A troubadour from Béarn, his eyes streaming with tears, sang to his mountain companions, in a refrain which caused alarm, Louis the son of Henri is imprisoned in Paris' (Author's translation).

24 Mahy, *Justification*, p. 167.

25 Freya Johnston, 'Galloping girl', *Prospect magazine*, April 2017, p. 31. Online. https://www.prospectmagazine.co.uk/magazine/jane-austen-galloping-girl. Accessed 10 October 2022.

26 Mary Poovey, 'From politics to silence: Jane Austen's nonreferential aesthetic', in Claudia L. Johnson and Clara Tuite (eds), *A companion to Jane Austen* (Chichester: Wiley, 2009), p. 260.

27 Roberts, *Jane Austen*, p. 8.

4 'These happy effects on the character of the British sailor'

1 This is an edited version of a chapter in Heather Dalton (ed.), *Keeping family in an age of long distance trade, imperial expansion, and exile, 1550–1850* (Amsterdam: Amsterdam University Press, 2020), pp. 239–59.

2 Mark Philp, *Resisting Napoleon: the British response to the threat of invasion 1797–1815* (Aldershot: Ashgate, 2006), p. 173.

Notes

3 Patricia Yu Chava Esther Lin, *Extending her arms: military families and the transformation of the British state, 1793–1815* (Unpublished thesis, Berkeley: University of California, 1997), p. 18.

4 Philp, *Resisting Napoleon*, p. 174.

5 George Hogarth, 'Memoir of Charles Dibdin', in *The songs of Charles Dibdin* (London: Davidson, 1848), p. xxxi.

6 Gillian Russell, *The theatres of war: performance, politics and society 1793–1815* (Oxford: Clarendon Press, 1995), p. 101.

7 Niklas Frykman, 'Seamen on late eighteenth-century European warships', *International review of social history*, 54 (2009), p. 70.

8 Caroline Jackson-Houlston, '"You heroes of the day": ephemeral verse responses to the Peace of Amiens and the Napoleonic Wars, 1802–1804', in Mark Philp (ed.), *Resisting Napoleon* (Aldershot: Ashgate, 2006), p. 191.

9 Jackson-Houlston, '"You heroes of the day"', p. 184.

10 James Davey, 'Singing for the nation: balladry, naval recruitment and the language of patriotism in eighteenth-century Britain', *The mariner's mirror*, 103:1 (2017), p. 44.

11 Russell, *The theatres of war*, p. 100.

12 Scholes, 'Shanty', in *The Oxford companion to music*, p. 946.

13 Davey, 'Singing for the nation', p. 176.

14 Philp, *Resisting Napoleon*, p. 176.

15 Russell, *The theatres of war*, p. 105.

16 Isaac Land, *War, nationalism and the British sailor, 1750–1850* (New York: Palgrave Macmillan, 2009), pp. 45, 50, 52.

17 Land, *War, nationalism and the British sailor*, pp. 94–5.

18 Davey, 'Singing for the nation', p. 60.

19 Hogarth, *The songs of Charles Dibdin*, pp. xxx–xxxi.

20 Joanne Begiato (Bailey), 'Tears and the manly sailor in England, c. 1760–1860', *Journal for maritime research*, 17:2 (2015), p. 127.

21 Hogarth, *The songs of Charles Dibdin*, pp. xxx–xxxi.

22 This song, along with many other details of Flinders's life, is discussed in detail in my book *Matthew Flinders: the man behind the map* (Adelaide: Wakefield Press, 2022).

23 Davey, 'Singing for the nation', pp. 45, 47.

24 Land, *Nationalism and the British sailor*, p. 95.

25 Carrasco, *The Austen family music books*, p. 167; Russell, *The theatres of war*, p. 101.

26 Begiato, 'Tears and the manly sailor', p. 118.

Notes

27 Davey, 'Singing for the nation', p. 35.

28 A 'carfindo' is a member of the carpenter's crew.

29 Quoted in William Kitchiner, *The sea songs of Charles Dibdin: with a memoir of his life and writings* (London: Whittaker, 1823), p. 21.

30 Martha Vandrei, '"Britons, strike home": politics, patriotism and popular song in British culture, c. 1695–1900', *Historical research*, 87:239 (November 2014), p. 694; Philp, *Resisting Napoleon*, p. 177.

31 Hogarth, *The songs of Charles Dibdin*, p. xxvi.

32 Hogarth, *The songs of Charles Dibdin*, p. 228.

33 Carrasco, *The Austen family music books*, p. 176.

34 Sutherland, 'Women writing in time of war', p. 112.

5 JANE AUSTEN, THOMAS ARNE AND GEORGIAN MUSICAL THEATRE

1 Gilman, *The theatre career of Thomas Arne*, pp. 2–3.

2 Gilman, *The theatre career of Thomas Arne*, p. 1.

3 Gilman, *The theatre career of Thomas Arne*, p. 4.

4 Gilman, *The theatre career of Thomas Arne*, p. 2.

5 Douglas Murray, '*Persuasion* as opera and song cycle: a librettist's tale', *Persuasions*, 43 (2022), p. 99.

6 Michael Burden, 'Pots, privies and WCs', p. 28.

7 *Don Juan; or, The libertine destroy'd: A tragic pantomimical entertainment, in two acts. Revived under the direction of Mr. Delpini. The songs, duets and choruses, Mr. Reeve. Music composed by Mr. Gluck* (London: Longman and Broderip, c. 1789).

8 Paula Byrne, *The genius of Jane Austen* (London: William Collins, 2017), p. xi.

9 Byrne, *The genius of Jane Austen*, p. 52.

10 John Cunningham, 'The reception and re-use of Thomas Arne's Shakespeare songs of 1740–1', in B. Barclay and D. Lindley (eds), *Shakespeare, music and performance* (Cambridge: Cambridge University Press, 2017), p. 135. DOI:10.1017/9781316488768.010.

11 Gillen D'Arcy Wood, *Romanticism and music culture in Britain, 1770–1840* (Cambridge: Cambridge University Press, 2010), p. 120.

12 Wood, *Romanticism and music culture*, p. 120.

13 Janine Barchas and Kristina Straub, 'Jane Austen's Shakespeare', *Shakespeare and beyond*. Online. Folger Library, 2016. https://shakespeareandbeyond.folger.edu/2016/08/12/jane-austen-william-shakespeare/. Accessed 1 October 2022.

Notes

14   Wood, *Romanticism and music culture*, p. 120.

15   Michael Burden, 'Imaging Mandane: character, costume, monument', *Music in art*, 34:1/2 (2009), p. 107.

16   Burden, 'Imaging Mandane', p. 107.

17   Burden, 'Imaging Mandane', p. 107.

18   'The Argument' and the libretto are printed in the accompanying booklet to Thomas Arne, *Artaxerxes: An English Opera* reconstructed and edited by Peter Holman [Sound recording] (London: Hyperion, 2009).

19   Michael Burden, 'Imaging Mandane', p. 108.

20   Gilman, *The theatre career of Thomas Arne*, p. 5.

21   *The British poets: including translations.* Volume LX: 'Hill, Cawthorn, Bruce' (Chiswick: Whittingham, 1822), p. 40. Google Books. Online. www.google.com.au/books/edition/The_British_Poets/hboDAAAAQAAJ?hl=en&gbpv=1&pg=PP1&printsec=frontcover. Accessed 14 October 2022.

22   Gilman, *The theatre career of Thomas Arne*, p. 313.

23   Thomas D'Urfey, 'A Scotch song', in *Wit and mirth; or, pills to purge melancholy*, Volume 3 (London, 1719), pp. 88–9.

24   Gilman, *The theatre career of Thomas Arne*, p. 288, note 100.

25   Paul F. Rice, 'The secular solo cantatas of Thomas A. Arne (1710–78)', *The phenomenon of singing*, 2 (1999), p. 198. https://journals.library.mun.ca/ojs/index.php/singing/article/view/675/0. Accessed 1 October 2022.

26   *Cymon and Iphigenia: a cantata set by Mr Arne* (London: Thompson and Co., c. 1753). Online. British Library. http://access.bl.uk/item/viewer/ark:/81055/vdc_100054482513.0x000001#?c=0&m=0&s=0&cv=0. Accessed 1 October 2022.

27   Rice, 'The secular solo cantatas', p. 198.

28   Paul F. Rice, *The solo English cantatas and Italian odes of Thomas A. Arne* (Newcastle upon Tyne, Cambridge Scholars, 2020), p. 85.

29   Gilman, *The theatre career of Thomas Arne*, p. 113.

30   Gilman, *The theatre career of Thomas Arne*, p. 327.

31   'Nymphs and shepherds', *The Brent, or English Syren* (London: Bladon, 1765), p. 231.

32   The aria can be found on page 33 of the full score of Thomas Arne, *The masque of Alfred* composed by Mr Arne. IMSLP. Online. https://imslp.org/wiki/The_Masque_of_Alfred_(Arne%2C_Thomas_Augustine). Accessed 1 October 2022.

Notes

33 Gilman, *The theatre career of Thomas Arne*, p. 394.

34 Rice, *The solo English cantatas*, pp. 65–7.

35 Gilman, *The theatre career of Thomas Arne*, p. 77.

36 Gilman, *The theatre career of Thomas Arne*, p. 77.

37 Gilman, *The theatre career of Thomas Arne*, p. 77.

38 Gilman, *The theatre career of Thomas Arne*, p. 84.

39 *The whole of the music in Milton's Comus: a masque, in two acts; as revived at the Theatre Royal Covent Garden, 1815, composed by Dr. Arne & Handel, with additions by Bishop, newly arranged, with a piano forte accompaniment by Henry R. Bishop* (London, D'Almaine & Co., n.d.).

40 See information on the musical settings of the poem at 'Yes, I'm in love, I feel it now', *The LiederNet archive*. Online. https://www.lieder.net/lieder/get_text.html?TextId=17402. Accessed 1 October 2022.

41 Rice, *The solo English cantatas*, p. 214.

42 Cunningham, 'The reception and re-use', pp. 133–4.

43 In fact, I was unaware of all the other settings until I curated a programme of music for *The Tempest* in 2011.

44 Barchas and Straub, 'Jane Austen's Shakespeare'. The playbill for this performance of *Merchant* is used to illustrate their article.

45 Gilman, *The theatre career of Thomas Arne*, p. 13.

46 Gilman, *The theatre career of Thomas Arne*, p. 15.

47 Gilman, *The theatre career of Thomas Arne*, p. 5.

48 Piggott, *The innocent diversion*, p. 153.

49 Gilman, *The theatre career of Thomas Arne*, p. 16.

50 Deborah Rohr, *The careers of British musicians 1750–1850: a profession of artisans* (Cambridge: Cambridge University Press, 2001), p. 154ff.

6 JANE AUSTEN AND BRITISH SONG

1 Gammie and McCulloch, *Jane Austen's music,* p. 37.

2 Fiske, *Scotland in music*, p. ix.

3 Fiske, *Scotland in music*, p. x.

4 Fiske, *Scotland in music*, p. 2.

5 Fiske, *Scotland in music*, pp. 78–9.

6 Helyard, *Clementi and the woman at the piano: virtuosity and the marketing of music in eighteenth-century London*, p. 167.

7 I discuss music in *Pride and prejudice* in detail in 'Jane Austen: the musician as author.

Notes

8   This section was first published as 'A red, red rose' in *Jane Austen's regency world*, Jan.–Feb. 2011.

9   Elaine Bander, '"O leave novels": Jane Austen, Sir Charles Grandison, Sir Edward Denham, and Rob Mossgiel', *Persuasions*, 30 (2008), p. 202.

10 Robert Burns, 'Their groves o' sweet myrtle', *Burns country*. Online. www.robertburns.org/works/531.shtml. Accessed 3 October 2022.

11 Gillaspie (afterwards Glen), 'Music collections in the Austen family with especial reference to the Rice music manuscripts', p. 31.

12 Brooks, 'In search', p. 921.

13 Brooks, 'In search', p. 920.

14 Brooks, 'In search', p. 924.

15 Untitled preface, *A selection of Irish melodies with symphonies and accompaniments by Sir John Stevenson and characteristic words by Thomas Moore* (London: J. Power, 1807), n.p.

16 Una Hunt, *Sources and style in* Moore's Irish melodies (London and New York: Routledge, 2017), p. 35.

17 Thomas Moore, *Memoirs, journal, and correspondence of Thomas Moore: Diary*, Volume 7 (London: Longman, 1856), p. 291. Online. Google Books. www.google.com.au/books/edition/Memoirs_Journal_and_Correspondence_of_Th/OpEVAAAAYAAJ?hl=en&gbpv=1&printsec=frontcover. Accessed 31 August 2022.

18 Dooley and Salma, 'The Hindoo girl's song', pp. 333–47.

19 Peter F. Alexander, '"Robin Adair" as a musical clue in Jane Austen's *Emma*', *The review of English studies*, 39:153 (1988), pp. 84–6.

20 Colleen Taylor, 'Austen answers the Irish question: satire, anxiety, and Emma's allusory Ireland', *Persuasions*, 38 (2016), pp. 218–27.

21 'Eileen Aroon': Annotations. Traditional Tune Archive. Online. https://tunearch.org/wiki/Annotation:Eileen_Aroon_(1). Accessed 31 August 2022.

22 'Ye banks and braes': annotations. Traditional Tune Archive. Online. https://tunearch.org/wiki/Annotation:Ye_Banks_and_Braes. Accessed 31 August 2022. The *Traditional tune archive* is a treasure trove of such information.

23 Carrasco, *The Austen family music books*, p. 127.

24 William Jackson, *Observations on the present state of music in London* (Dublin, 1791), pp. 29–30. Online. Google Books. www.google.com.au/books/edition/Observations_on_the_Present_State_of_Mus/KGZRiIo-ojIC?hl=en&gbpv=0. Accessed 28 August 2022.

Notes

25 Fiske, *Scotland in music*, pp. 78–9.

26 Gammie and McCulloch, *Jane Austen's music*, p. 37.

27 Gammie and McCulloch, *Jane Austen's music*, p. 5.

28 For a discussion of where Austen stood in the debate between Italian virtuosity and English virtue, see my article '"There is no understanding a word of it"', pp. 88–98.

7 Juvenile songs and lessons

1 An earlier version of this chapter was published in *Persuasions on-line*, 41:1 (2020). Online. https://jasna.org/publications-2/persuasions-online/vol-41-no-1/dooley/. Accessed 5 October 2022.

2 Carrasco, *The Austen family music books*, pp. 144ff.

3 Jane Austen, *Frederic and Elfrida*, Peter Sabor, Sylvia Hunt and Victoria Kortes-Papp (eds) (Sydney: Juvenilia Press, 2015), p. x.

4 I am relying on Sutherland and Johnson's suggested chronology of composition of the various items in their edition of the *Teenage writings*.

5 Jane Austen, *Three mini-dramas*, Juliet McMaster, Lesley Peterson et al. (eds) (Sydney: Juvenilia Press, 2006), p. 35, n. 59.

6 Samantha Carrasco, *The Austen family music books*, p. 167.

7 Russell, *The theatres of war*, p. 101.

8 Karen L. Hartnick, Introduction, in Jane Austen, *Henry and Eliza* (Sydney: Juvenilia Press, 2015), p. xiii.

9 Mary Spongberg, 'Jane Austen and *The history of England*', *Journal of women's history*, 23:1 (2011), p. 70.

10 G. K. Chesterton, Preface, Jane Austen, *Love and freindship and other early works now first printed from the original MS* (London: Chatto and Windus, 1922), p. xv.

8 Marianne and Willoughby, Lucy and Colin

1 This chapter was first published in Susan Petrilli (ed.), *L'immagine nella parola, nella musica, e nella pittura* (Milan: Mimesis, 2018), pp. 239–55.

2 Oliver Goldsmith, 'Preface to the beauties of English poetry, first published in the year MDCCXLVII (1747)' in *Miscellaneous works of Oliver Goldsmith*, Volume IV (Edinburgh: Chambers, 1833), p. 294.

3 Thomas Seccombe, 'Lesser verse writers', in A. W. Ward and A. R. Waller (eds), *The Cambridge history of English literature*, Volume IX (Cambridge: Cambridge University Press, 1912), p. 173.

Notes

4 Ian Ousby, 'Tickell, Thomas', in *The Cambridge guide to literature in English*, revised edition (Cambridge: Cambridge University Press, 1993), p. 942.

5 David Atkinson, 'William and Margaret: an eighteenth-century ballad', *Folk music journal*, 10:4 (2014), p. 497.

6 Byrne, *The genius of Jane Austen*, p. 132.

7 Byrne, *The genius of Jane Austen*, p. 145.

8 Kathleen Fowler, 'Apricots, raspberries, and Susan Price! Susan Price!: *Mansfield Park* and Maria Edgeworth,' *Persuasions*, 13 (1991), p. 28.

9 Margaret Anne Doody, 'Turns of speech and figures of mind', in Claudia L. Johnson and Clara Tuite (eds), *A companion to Jane Austen* (Malden, MA: Wiley-Blackwell, 2009), p. 173.

10 Rodney S. Edgecombe, 'Change and fixity in *Sense and sensibility*', *Studies in English literature, 1500–1900*, 41.3 (2001), p. 620.

11 John Wiltshire, *Jane Austen and the body* (Cambridge, Cambridge University Press, 1992), p. 45.

12 Wiltshire, *Jane Austen and the body*, p. 44.

13 Doody, 'Turns of speech', p. 170.

14 The words 'groan'd' and 'shook' are reversed in the musical setting, perhaps for aesthetic reasons.

15 John Wiltshire, *The hidden Jane Austen* (Cambridge: Cambridge University Press, 2014), p. 7.

CONCLUSION

1 Gillian Dooley, Kirstine Moffat and John Wiltshire, 'Music and class in Jane Austen', *Persuasions on-line*, 38:3 (2018). Online. https://jasna.org/publications-2/persuasions-online/volume-38-no-3/doolley-moff at-wiltshire/. Accessed 2 October 2022.

2 Seven works based on Irish music by J. B. Cramer are listed in the bibliography of Una Hunt's article 'The harpers' legacy: Irish national airs and pianoforte composers', *Journal of the Society for Musicology in Ireland*, 6 (2010–2011), p. 28.

3 Gillian Dooley, 'Musicianship and morality in the novels of Jane Austen', *Sensibilities*, 40 (June 2010), p. 37.

4 Caroline Austen, *Reminiscences*, p. 22.

5 John Essex, *Young ladies conduct* (1722) quoted in Helyard, *Clementi and the woman at the piano*, p. 80.

Notes

6 For a detailed discussion of the harp in Jane Austen's time, see Mike Parker's article 'Tidings of my harp', *Jane Austen's regency world*, 44 (Mar./Apr. 2010), pp. 35–9.

7 This situation is discussed at length in Gillian Dooley, '"Her own more elegant and cultivated mind": Anne Elliot and music', in John Wiltshire and Marcia Folsom (eds), *Approaches to teaching* Persuasion (New York: Modern Languages Association, 2021), pp. 80–5.

8 Quoted in Deirdre Le Faye, *Jane Austen's 'outlandish' cousin: the life and letters of Eliza de Feuillide* (London: British Library, 2002), p. 49.

9 Geoffrey Lancaster, *The First Fleet piano: a musician's view*, Volume 1 (Canberra, ANU Press, 2015), p. 90.

10 Carrasco, *The Austen family music books*, p. 57.

11 Gammie and McCulloch, *Jane Austen's music,* p. 7.

12 Brooks, 'In search', p. 914.

13 Thomas Dibdin, *Of age tomorrow: a musical entertainment in two acts etc.* (London: Barker and Sons, 1805), p. 9.

14 Carrasco, *The Austen family music books*, p. 32.

15 An edition of 'The wife's farewell, or No, my love no' published by Kelly himself and listed on the British Library catalogue specifies that it was 'Written by M. G. Lewis'.

16 Brooks, 'In search', pp. 938–9.

17 Wallace, *Jane Austen and Mozart*, p. 260.

18 Katherine R. Larson, *The matter of song in early modern England: texts in and of the air* (Oxford: Oxford University Press, 2019), p. 207.

Appendix 2

1 I have not included a link to the University of Southampton Library Catalogue as sites such as this change their addresses from time to time. It should always be possible to search for 'Southampton University Library' and find a link to their catalogue on their website. I will endeavour to keep the information about searching within the catalogue up to date on my Jane Austen's Music website, accessed by searching 'Jane Austen's Music sites'.

2 Alfred Moffat and Frank Kidson (eds), *English songs of the Georgian period* (London: Bayley and Ferguson, n.d. [c. 1900]), p. 184.

3 Gammie and McCulloch, *Jane Austen's music*, p. 29.

4 Gillaspie (afterwards Glen), *Music collections in the Austen family*, p. 29.

Note on sources

With the exception of the following primary sources, references are included in footnotes and listed in the References section.

Primary sources – printed works

Given the nature of this book there are several printed works which are cited very frequently. Accordingly I will refer to these sources in the following editions, using the abbreviated title or initials provided, followed by a page number, in parentheses in the text. I have retained the idiosyncratic spelling and punctuation in all quotations, without interrupting the flow by adding '(*sic*)' unless not doing so would cause confusion.

The novels of Jane Austen, 3rd edition, edited by R. W. Chapman (Oxford University Press, 1932–1934, reprinted 1988)
E *Emma*
MP *Mansfield Park*

Note on sources

NA	*Northanger Abbey*
P	*Persuasion*
PP	*Pride and prejudice*
SS	*Sense and sensibility*

Family record – W. Austen-Leigh, R. A. Austen-Leigh and Deirdre Le Faye, *Jane Austen: a family record* (British Library, 1989)

Letters – *Jane Austen's letters*, collected and edited by Deirdre Le Faye, 3rd edition (Oxford University Press, 1995)

Memoir – J. E. Austen-Leigh, *A memoir of Jane Austen and other family recollections* edited by Kathryn Sutherland (Oxford University Press, 2002)

MW – *The works of Jane Austen: Volume 6: Minor works*, edited by R. W. Chapman (Oxford University Press, 1954, reprinted 1988)

TW – *Jane Austen, Teenage writings*, edited by Kathryn Sutherland and Freya Johnston (Oxford University Press, 2017)

Austen family music books online

Another major source of information for this work is the digitised collection of Austen family music books at the Internet Archive, as well as the individual catalogue records for the collection on the University of Southampton library catalogue, each of which includes a link to the individual item online.

The catalogue numbers of most items in the collection begin with either 'Jenkyns' or 'CHWJA/19', depending on their current custodianship, followed by an album number and an item number. These numbers are now the standard identifiers for this collection.

Links to the catalogue records are liable to change, so, rather than cite each piece of music when mentioned in the text, I refer readers to the University of Southampton library catalogue, where all the music is indexed in detail. The URL is currently southampton.on.worldcat.org/. If this link does not work, search 'Southampton University Library' and look for a link to the library catalogue.

A library catalogue search on the phrase 'Austen family music books' combined with title keywords or names should bring up the required item with associated information and a link to the facsimile online. The current catalogue interface (as at October 2022) prompts for a password, offering an alternative option to 'continue as guest' to access only the library holdings. The latter alternative should be chosen.

To access the Internet Archive collection directly for browsing in the facsimile albums, visit the Austen family music books page at archive.org/details/austenfamilymusicbooks.

For more information on the cataloguing project and tips for searching, see my Jane Austen's Music site at sites.google.com/site/janeaustensmusic/austen-family-music-books.

Music history references – abbreviations

BUCEM – British union catalogue of music

RISM – Répertoire international des source musicales. Online. https://opac.rism.info/. Accessed 16 October 2022

Note on sources

IMSLP – International Music Score Library Project. Online. https://imslp.org/wiki/Main_Page. Accessed 16 October 2022

JISC – Joint Information Systems Committee. Online. www.jisc.ac.uk/. Accessed 21 October 2022

Bibliography

Alexander, Peter F. '"Robin Adair" as a musical clue in Jane Austen's *Emma*', *The review of English studies*, 39:153 (1988), pp. 84–6.

Andrews, Miles Peter. *Fire and water! A comic opera in two acts, performed at the Theatre-Royal in the Hay-Market* (Dublin, 1790). Online. Eighteenth Century Collections Online. Accessed 16 December 2017.

Arne, Thomas. *Artaxerxes: an English opera*, reconstructed and edited by Peter Holman [sound recording], London, Hyperion, 2009.

Arne, Thomas. *Cymon and Iphigenia: a cantata set by Mr Arne*, London, Thompson and Co., c. 1753. Online. British Library. http://access.bl.uk/item/viewer/ark:/81055/vdc_100054482513.0x000001#?c=0&m=0&s=0&cv=0. Accessed 1 October 2022.

Arne, Thomas. *The masque of Alfred*. IMSLP. Online. https://imslp.org/wiki/The_Masque_of_Alfred_(Arne%2C_Thomas_Augustine). Accessed 1 October 2022.

Atkinson, David. 'William and Margaret: an eighteenth-century ballad', *Folk music journal*, 10:4 (2014), pp. 478–511.

Austen family music books. Internet Archive. Online archive.org/details/austenfamilymusicbooks. Accessed 15 November 2022.

Austen, Caroline. *Reminiscences*, Guildford, Jane Austen Society, 1986.

Austen, James. 'National difference of character between the French and English – plan proposed for improving each', *The loiterer*, 10 (Saturday

Bibliography

4 April 1789). Online. www.theloiterer.org/loiterer/no10.html. Accessed 11 October 2022.

Austen, Jane. *Frederic and Elfrida*, Peter Sabor, Sylvia Hunt and Victoria Kortes-Papp (eds), Sydney, Juvenilia Press, 2015.

Austen, Jane. *Sir Charles Grandison*, Lesley Peterson, Sylvia Hunt et al. (eds), Sydney: Juvenilia Press, 2022.

Austen, Jane. *Three mini-dramas*, Juliet McMaster, Lesley Peterson et al. (eds), Sydney, Juvenilia Press, 2006.

Austen, Jane. *The works of Jane Austen*, R. W. Chapman (ed.), Oxford: Oxford University Press, 1933–1969.

Bander, Elaine. "'O Leave Novels': Jane Austen, Sir Charles Grandison, Sir Edward Denham, and Rob Mossgiel', *Persuasions*, 30 (2008), pp. 202–15.

Barchas, Janine and Kristina Straub. 'Jane Austen's Shakespeare', *Shakespeare and beyond*. Online. Folger Library, 2016. https://shakespeareandbeyond.folger.edu/2016/08/12/jane-austen-william-shakespeare/. Accessed 1 October 2022.

Begiato (Bailey), Joanne. 'Tears and the manly sailor in England, c. 1760–1860', *Journal for maritime research*, 17:2 (2015), pp. 117–33.

Boardman, Elizabeth. 'Mrs Cawley and Brasenose College', *The brazen nose*, 38 (2003–2004), pp. 58–65.

Bradney-Smith, Adrienne. 'Brushes with ebony and ivory: some musical instruments of Jane Austen's time', *Sensibilities*, 40 (June 2010), pp. 14–23.

The British poets: including translations. Volume LX: 'Hill, Cawthorn, Bruce', Chiswick, Whittingham, 1822. Google Books. Online. www.google.com.au/books/edition/The_British_Poets/hboDAAAAQAAJ?hl=en&gbpv=1&pg=PP1&printsec=frontcover. Accessed 14 October 2022.

Brooks, Jeanice. 'In search of Austen's missing songs', *Review of English studies*, 67:282 (November 2016), pp. 914–45. DOI: 10.1093/res/hgw035.

Brooks, Jeanice. 'Making music', in Kathryn Sutherland (ed.), *Jane Austen: writer in the world*, Oxford, Bodleian Library, 2017, pp. 37–55.

Brown, James D. and Stephen S. Stratton. *British musical biography*, New York, Da Capo Press, 1971.

Burden, Michael. 'Imaging Mandane: character, costume, monument', *Music in art*, 34:1–2 (2009), pp. 107–36.

Burden, Michael. 'Pots, privies and WCs: crapping at the opera in London before 1830', *Cambridge opera journal*, 23:1–2 (2012). DOI: 10.1017/S0954586712000018.

Bibliography

Burns, Robert. 'Their groves o' sweet myrtle', *Burns country*. Online. www. robertburns.org/works/531.shtml. Accessed 3 October 2022.

Butler, Marilyn, *Jane Austen and the war of ideas*, revised edition, Oxford, Clarendon Press, 1987.

Byrne, Paula. *The genius of Jane Austen*, London, William Collins, 2017.

Carrasco, Samantha. *The Austen family music books and Hampshire music culture, 1770–1820*. Unpublished thesis, PhD, Southampton, University of Southampton, 2013. Online. eprints.soton.ac.uk/466879/. Accessed 21 August 2022.

Chesterton, G. K. Preface, in Jane Austen, *Love and freindship and other early works now first printed from the original MS*. London, Chatto and Windus, 1922, pp. ix–xv.

Clery, E. J. *Jane Austen, the banker's sister*, London, Biteback Publishing, 2017.

Cunningham, John. 'The reception and re-use of Thomas Arne's Shakespeare songs of 1740–1', in B. Barclay and D. Lindley (eds), *Shakespeare, music and performance*, Cambridge, Cambridge University Press, 2017, pp. 131–44. DOI:10.1017/9781316488768.010.

Davey, James. 'Singing for the nation: balladry, naval recruitment and the language of patriotism in eighteenth-century Britain', *The mariner's mirror*, 103:1 (2017), pp. 43–66.

Dibdin, Thomas. *Of age tomorrow: a musical entertainment in two acts etc.*, London, Barker and Son, 1805. [N.b. printed on demand by British Library Historical Print Editions in 2022.]

Don Juan; or, The libertine destroy'd: A tragic pantomimical entertainment, in two acts, revived under the direction of Mr. Delpini, The songs, duets and choruses, Mr. Reeve, Music composed by Mr. Gluck, London, Longman and Broderip, c. 1789.

Doody, Margaret Anne. 'Turns of speech and figures of mind', in Claudia L. Johnson and Clara Tuite (eds), *A companion to Jane Austen*, Malden, MA, Wiley-Blackwell, 2009, pp. 165–84.

Dooley, Gillian. 'Anna with variations', *Jane Austen's regency world*, 110 (Mar./Apr. 2021), pp. 44–7.

Dooley, Gillian. '"Her own more elegant and cultivated mind": Anne Elliot and music', in John Wiltshire and Marcia Folsom (eds), *Approaches to teaching Persuasion*, New York, Modern Languages Association, 2021, pp. 80–5.

Dooley, Gillian. 'Jane Austen and the music of the French Revolution', *Essays in French literature and culture*, 57 (October 2020), pp. 151–66.

Bibliography

Dooley, Gillian. 'Jane Austen: the musician as author', *Humanities*, 11:3 (2022). DOI: 10.3390/h11030073.

Dooley, Gillian. 'Juvenile songs and lessons: music culture in Jane Austen's teenage years', *Persuasions on-line*, 41:1 (2020). Online. https://jasna. org/publications-2/persuasions-online/vol-41-no-1/dooley/.

Dooley, Gillian. 'Marianne and Willoughby, Lucy and Colin: betrayal, suffering, death and the poetic image', in Susan Petrilli (ed.), *L'immagine nella parola, nella musica, e nella pittura*, Milan, Mimesis, 2018, pp. 239–55.

Dooley, Gillian. *Matthew Flinders: the man behind the map*, Adelaide, Wakefield Press, 2022.

Dooley, Gillian. 'A most luxurious state: men and music in Jane Austen's novels', *Englishstudies*, 98:6 (2017). DOI: 10.1080/0013838X.2017.1322386.

Dooley, Gillian. 'Musicianship and morality in the novels of Jane Austen', *Sensibilities*, 40 (June 2010), pp. 36–52.

Dooley, Gillian. 'A red, red rose: Jane Austen and Robert Burns', *Jane Austen's regency world* January–February 2011, pp. 49–52.

Dooley, Gillian. '"There is no understanding a word of it": musical taste and Italian vocal music in Austen's musical and literary world', *Persuasions*, 43 (2021), pp. 88–98.

Dooley, Gillian. '"These happy effects on the character of the British sailor": family life in sea songs of the late Georgian period', in Heather Dalton (ed.), *Keeping family in an age of long distance trade, imperial expansion, and exile, 1550–1850*, Amsterdam, Amsterdam University Press, 2020, pp. 239–59.

Dooley, Gillian, Kirstine Moffat and John Wiltshire. 'Music and class in Jane Austen', *Persuasions on-line*, 38:3 (2018). Online. https://jasna.org/ publications-2/persuasions-online/volume-38-no-3/doolley-moffat-wiltshire/. Accessed 2 October 2022.

Dooley, Gillian and Umme Salma. 'The Hindoo girl's song: a shady story from British India', *South Asian review*, 43:3–4 (2022), pp. 333–47. DOI: 10.1080/02759527.2022.2040084.

Dow, Gillian. 'Theatre and theatricality; or, Jane Austen and learning the art of dialogue', *Persuasions*, 43 (2021), pp. 111–27.

D'Urfey, Thomas. 'A Scotch song', in *Wit and mirth; or, pills to purge melancholy*, Volume 3, London, 1719, pp. 88–9.

Dussek, Jan Ladislav. *Variations on Shepherds I have lost my love* (Dublin, Hime, n.d.), IMSLP. Online. https://imslp. org/wiki/Variations_on_'Shepherds%2C_I_have_lost_my_love'_(Dussek%2C_Jan_Ladislav). Accessed 8 July 2022.

Bibliography

Edgecombe, Rodney S. 'Change and fixity in *Sense and sensibility*', *Studies in English literature, 1500–1900*, 41.3 (2001), pp. 605–22.

'Eileen Aroon': Annotations. Traditional Tune Archive. Online. https://tunearch.org/wiki/Annotation:Eileen_Aroon_(1). Accessed 31 August 2022.

Fischer, Lewis R. and Helge Nordvik (eds). *Shipping and trade, 1750–1950: essays in international maritime economic history*, Pontefract, Lofthouse, 1990.

Fiske, Roger. *Scotland in music*, Cambridge, Cambridge University Press, 1983.

Ford, Susan Allen. '"My name was Norval": *Douglas*, elocution, and acting in *Mansfield Park*', *Persuasions*, 43 (2021), pp. 128–42.

Fowler, Kathleen. 'Apricots, raspberries, and Susan Price! Susan Price!: *Mansfield Park* and Maria Edgeworth', *Persuasions*, 13 (1991), pp. 28–32.

Frykman, Niklas. 'Seamen on late eighteenth-century European warships', *International review of social history*, 54 (2009), pp. 67–93.

Gammie, Ian and Derek McCulloch, *Jane Austen's music*, St Albans, Corda Music Publications, 1996.

Gay, Penny. *Jane Austen and the theatre*, Cambridge, Cambridge University Press, 2002.

Gehrer, Julienne (ed.). *Martha Lloyd's household book: the original manuscripts from Jane Austen's kitchen*, Oxford, Bodleian Library, 2021.

Gill, Ellen. *Naval families: war and duty in Britain, 1740–1820*, Martlesham, Boydell & Brewer, 2016.

Gillaspie, Jon A. (afterwards Nessa Glen). 'Handlist of Austen family music (manuscript and printed) in the possession of Mr H. L. Jenkyns', unpublished report, 1987.

Gillaspie, Jon A. (afterwards Nessa Glen). 'Music collections in the Austen family with especial reference to the Rice music manuscripts', unpublished report, c. 1990.

Gilman, Todd. *The theatre career of Thomas Arne*, Newark, University of Delaware Press, 2013.

Giordani, Tommaso. *Colin and Lucy, a favorite English ballad* by Mr. Tickell, set to music by Signor Giordani, London, Dale, 1783.

Glen, Nessa, *see* Gillaspie, Jon A.

'Godmersham Park Library', *Reading with Austen*. Online. https://readingwithaustenblog.com/godmersham-library-catalogue/. Accessed 9 July 2022.

Bibliography

Goldsmith, Oliver. 'Preface to *The beauties of English poetry*, first published in the year MDCCXLVII (1747)', in *Miscellaneous works of Oliver Goldsmith*, Volume IV, Edinburgh, Chambers, 1833.

Gustar, Andrew. 'The life and times of Black-ey'd Susan: The story of an English ballad', *Folk music journal*, 1:4 (2014), pp. 432–48.

Hartnick, Karen L. Introduction, in Jane Austen, *Henry and Eliza*, Sydney, Juvenilia Press, 2015.

Helyard, Erin. *Clementi and the woman at the piano: virtuosity and the marketing of music in eighteenth-century London*, Liverpool, Liverpool University Press, 2022.

Hogarth, George. 'Memoir of Charles Dibdin', in *The songs of Charles Dibdin*, London, Davidson, 1848, pp. xv–xxxii.

Hunt, Una. 'The harpers' legacy: Irish national airs and pianoforte composers', *Journal of the Society for Musicology in Ireland*, 6 (2010–2011), pp. 3–51. Online. https://musicologyireland.com/jsmi/index.php/journal/article/view/75. Accessed 24 October 2022.

Hunt, Una. *Sources and style in Moore's* Irish Melodies, London and New York, Routledge, 2017.

Jackson, William. *Observations on the present state of music in London*, Dublin, 1791. Online. Google Books. www.google.com.au/books/edition/Observations_on_the_Present_State_of_Mus/KGZRiIo–ojIC?hl=en&gbpv=0. Accessed 28 August 2022.

Jackson-Houlston, Caroline. '"You heroes of the day": ephemeral verse responses to the Peace of Amiens and the Napoleonic Wars, 1802–1804', in Mark Philp (ed.), *Resisting Napoleon: The British response to the threat of invasion 1797–1815*, Aldershot, Ashgate, 2006, pp. 184–91.

Johnson, James H. *Listening in Paris: a cultural history*, Berkeley, University of California Press, 1995.

Johnston, Freya. 'Galloping girl', *Prospect magazine*, April 2017, pp. 30–2. Online. www.prospectmagazine.co.uk/magazine/jane-austen-galloping-girl. Accessed 10 October 2022.

Kassler, Michael. *Music entries at Stationers' Hall 1710–1818*, Farnham, Ashgate, 2004.

Kelly, Helena. *Jane Austen, the secret radical*, London, Icon Books, 2016.

Kitchiner, William. *The sea songs of Charles Dibdin: with a memoir of his life and writings*, London, Whittaker, 1823.

Krumpholtz, J. B. *The nuns complaint from Mrs Robinson's novel of* Vancenza, London, Preston & Son, c. 1794.

Lancaster, Geoffrey. *The First Fleet piano: a musician's view*, Canberra, ANU Press, 2015.

Bibliography

Land, Isaac. *War, nationalism and the British sailor, 1750–1850*, New York, Palgrave Macmillan, 2009.

Larson, Katherine R. *The matter of song in early modern England: texts in and of the air*, Oxford, Oxford University Press, 2019.

Le Faye, Deirdre. 'Fanny Knight's diaries: Jane Austen through her niece's eyes', *Persuasions occasional papers*, 2 (1986).

Le Faye, Deirdre. *Jane Austen's 'outlandish' cousin: the life and letters of Eliza de Feuillide*, London, British Library, 2002.

Lee, Hermione. '"Taste" and "tenderness": moral values in the novels of Jane Austen', in R. T. Davies and B. G. Beatty (eds), *Literature of the romantic period 1750–1850*, Liverpool, Liverpool University Press, 1976.

Libin, Kathryn L. 'Daily practice, musical accomplishment, and the example of Jane Austen', in Natasha Duquette and Elisabeth Lenckos (eds), *Jane Austen and the arts: elegance, propriety, and harmony*, Bethlehem, Lehigh University Press, 2014, pp. 3–20.

Lin, Patricia Yu Chava Esther. *Extending her arms: military families and the transformation of the British state, 1793–1815*, unpublished thesis, Berkeley, University of California, 1997.

Mahy, Guillaume François. *Justification de M. de Favras*, Paris, Potier de Lille, 1791.

Mathew, Nicholas. *The Haydn economy: music, aesthetics, and commerce in the late eighteenth century*, Chicago, University of Chicago Press, 2022.

'Matthias Holst'. IMSLP. Online. https://imslp. org/wiki/Category:Holst%2C_Matthias. Accessed 14 October 2022.

McLelland, Nicola. 'The history of language learning and teaching in Britain', *The language learning journal*, 46:1 (2018), pp. 6–16. Online. DOI: 10.1080/09571736.2017.1382052.

Moffat, Alfred and Frank Kidson (eds). *English songs of the Georgian period*, London, Bayley and Ferguson, n.d. (c. 1900).

Moore, Thomas. *Memoirs, journal, and correspondence of Thomas Moore: Diary*, Volume 7, London, Longman, 1856. Online. Google Books. www.google.com.au/books/edition/Memoirs_Journal_and_Correspondence_of_Th/OpEVAAAAYAAJ?hl=en&gbpv=1&printsec=frontcover. Accessed 31 August 2022.

Murray, Douglas. '*Persuasion* as opera and song cycle: a librettist's tale', *Persuasions*, 43 (2022), pp. 99–110.

Myer, Valerie Grosvenor. *Obstinate heart: Jane Austen: a biography*, London, Michael O'Mara, 1997.

Bibliography

'Nymphs and shepherds'. *The Brent, or English siren*, London, Bladon, 1765, p. 231.

Oswald, Ros. 'A reputation Chard', *Jane Austen's regency world*, 115 (Jan./Feb. 2022), pp. 38–44.

Ousby, Ian. 'Tickell, Thomas', in *The Cambridge guide to literature in English*, revised edition, Cambridge, Cambridge University Press, 1993, p. 942.

Parker, Mike. 'Tidings of my harp', *Jane Austen's regency world*, 44 (Mar./Apr. 2010), pp. 35–9.

Philp, Mark. *Resisting Napoleon: the British response to the threat of invasion 1797–1815*, Aldershot, Ashgate, 2006.

Piggott, Patrick. *The innocent diversion: music in the life and writings of Jane Austen*, London, Cleverdon, 1979.

Poovey, Mary, 'From politics to silence: Jane Austen's nonreferential aesthetic', in Claudia L. Johnson and Clara Tuite (eds), *A companion to Jane Austen*, Chichester, Wiley, 2009, pp. 251–60.

Rice, Paul F. *British music and the French Revolution*, Newcastle upon Tyne, Cambridge Scholars, 2010.

Rice, Paul F., *The solo English cantatas and Italian odes of Thomas A. Arne*, Newcastle upon Tyne, Cambridge Scholars, 2020.

Rice, Paul F. 'The secular solo cantatas of Thomas A. Arne (1710–78)', *The phenomenon of singing*, 2 (1999), pp. 196–205. Online. https://journals.library.mun.ca/ojs/index.php/singing/article/view/675/0. Accessed 1 October 2022.

Richards, Rosemary and Julja Szuster (eds). *Memories of musical lives: music and dance in personal music collections from Australia and New Zealand*, Melbourne: Lyrebird Press, 2022.

Riley, Noël. *The accomplished lady: a history of genteel pursuits c. 1660–1860*, Huddersfield, Oblong Books, 2017.

Roberts, Warren. *Jane Austen and the French Revolution*, revised edition, London, Athlone, 1995.

Ross, John. *A second set of nine songs with an accompaniment for the piano-forte or harp*, London, Longman & Broderip, c1796.

Routley, Erik. *A short history of English church music*, London, Mowbray, 1997.

Russell, Gillian. *The theatres of war: performance, politics and society 1793–1815*, Oxford, Clarendon Press, 1995.

'Samuel Arnold (1740–1802)'. *Naxos classical composers*, archived online at Wayback Machine. https://web.archive.org/web/20070314153116/http://www.naxos.com/composerinfo/2252.htm. Accessed 9 October 2022.

Bibliography

Scholes, Percy (ed.). *The Oxford companion to music*, 10th edition, London, Oxford University Press, 1970.

Seccombe, Thomas. 'Lesser verse writers', in A. W. Ward and A. R. Waller (eds), *The Cambridge history of English literature*, Volume IX. Cambridge, Cambridge University Press, 1912.

Selection of Irish melodies with symphonies and accompaniments by Sir John Stevenson and characteristic words by Thomas Moore, London, J. Power, 1807.

Spongberg, Mary. 'Jane Austen and the *History of England*', *Journal of women's history*, 23:1 (2011), pp. 56–80.

Spongberg, Mary. 'Jane Austen, the 1790s, and the French Revolution', in Claudia L. Johnson and Clara Tuite (eds), *A companion to Jane Austen*, Chichester, Wiley, 2009, pp. 272–81.

Storace, Stephen. *Captivity: a ballad*, London, J. Dale, 1793. British Library Music Collections DRT Digital Store G.1277.a.(44.) Online. http://explore.bl.uk/BLVU1:LSCOP-ALL:BLL01018749536. Accessed 14 October 2022.

Sutherland, Kathryn. 'Women writing in time of war', in Kathryn Sutherland (ed.), *Jane Austen: writer in the world*, Oxford, Bodleian Library, 2017, pp. 97–117.

Sutherland, Kathryn and Freya Johnston. Introduction, in Jane Austen, *Teenage writings*, Oxford, Oxford University Press, 2017.

Taylor, Colleen. 'Austen answers the Irish question: satire, anxiety, and *Emma*'s allusory Ireland', *Persuasions*, 38 (2016), pp. 218–27.

'Thomas de Mahy, marquis de Favras'. *Wikipedia*. Online. https://en.wikipedia.org/wiki/Thomas_de_Mahy,_marquis_de_Favras. Accessed 29 September 2022.

'Thomas Shell'. *Janet Shell*. Online. https://janetshell.co.uk/ts3.html. Accessed 23 August 2022.

Thompson, Allison. *Dances from Jane Austen's assembly rooms*, Author, 2019.

Tickell, Thomas. *Lucy and Colin: a song, written in imitation of William and Margaret*, in *The tea-table miscellany or, a collection of choice songs, Scots and English*, Allan Ramsay (ed.), Volume 1, London, Millar, 1750, pp. 349–51.

Toft, Robert. *Heart to heart: expressive singing in England 1780–1830*, Oxford: Oxford University Press, 2000.

Tornare, Alain-Jacques. 'L'histoire de "Pauvre Jacques"', *Pauvre Jacques*. Online. https://pauvrejacques.simdif.com/l_histoire_.html. Accessed 29 September 2022.

Bibliography

Vandrei, Martha. '"Britons, strike home": politics, patriotism and popular song in British culture, c. 1695–1900', *Historical research*, 87:239 (November 2014), pp. 679–702.

Voewood Rare Books. 'Jane Austen at the piano: "She played from the manuscript, copied out by herself"' in Voewood catalogue 2, Holt, Voewood Rare Books, c. 2020, pp. 10–11. Online. https://issuu.com/voewoodrarebooks/docs/voewood_catalogue_2_issuu. Accessed 5 November 2022.

Wallace, Robert K. *Jane Austen and Mozart: classical equilibrium in fiction and music*, Athens, University of Georgia Press, 1983.

The whole of the music in Milton's Comus: a masque, in two acts; as revived at the Theatre Royal Covent Garden, 1815, composed by Dr. Arne & Handel, with additions by Bishop, newly arranged, with a piano forte accompaniment by Henry R. Bishop, London, D'Almaine & Co., n.d.

Wilkes, Joanne. 'Jane Austen as "Prose Shakespeare": early comparisons', in Marina Cano and Rose García-Periago (eds), *Jane Austen and Shakespeare: a love affair in literature, film and performance*, Cham: Palgrave Macmillan, 2019, pp. 29–50.

Wiltshire, John. *The hidden Jane Austen*, Cambridge, Cambridge University Press, 2014.

Wiltshire, John. *Jane Austen and the body*, Cambridge, Cambridge University Press, 1992.

Wood, Gillen D'Arcy. *Romanticism and music culture in Britain, 1770–1840*, Cambridge, Cambridge University Press, 2010.

Worsley, Lucy. *Jane Austen at home: a biography*, London, Hodder and Stoughton, 2017.

'Ye banks and braes': annotations. Traditional Tune Archive. Online. https://tunearch.org/wiki/Annotation:Ye_Banks_and_Braes. Accessed 31 August 2022.

'Yes, I'm in love, I feel it now', The LiederNet archive. Online. www.lieder.net/lieder/get_text.html?TextId=17402. Accessed 1 October 2022.

Zwilling, Caren. *The original songs in Shakespeare's plays*, St Albans: Corda Music Publications, 2015.

Illustration credits

Acknowledgements

It is hard to know where to begin in thanking the many people who have helped me on my decades-long (and ongoing) project of thinking about and investigating Jane Austen and music. I could begin with the supervisor of my Honours thesis at Flinders University, the late Humphrey Tranter, who helped me shape my ideas about music in Austen's novels, or further back to Pat Wenger, my high-school English teacher, who asked a question in class that sparked my interest in music in *Pride and Prejudice*. More recently, there is Vincent Megaw, professor of archaeology at Flinders University and music-lover, who alerted me to the Austen music collections in 2007 and suggested I organise a concert drawing on that repertoire.

Then there are all the musicians I have performed with in the past fifteen years – too many to name, but I must acknowledge the London-based harpist Mike Parker, whom I met in Bath in 2010 and who has taught me much about the music of the period. I have been very lucky, also, to have wonderful

Acknowledgements

associate artists in Adelaide – Fiona Macaulay on piano and Christine Morphett on harp among several others.

I must also acknowledge the encouragement and collegiality of Jeanice Brooks from Southampton University, who enabled me to undertake the project of cataloguing the Austen family music collections. Her colleagues in the library, including John Dover, Julian Ball and Jenny Ruthven, have also been most helpful over the years.

Fellow Austen scholars have also made enormous contributions to my scholarly work. Many are, of course, mentioned in the bibliography but I have been personally in touch with several, including John Wiltshire, Kirstine Moffat, Emma J. Clery and Lesley Peterson, who have stimulated me to think in new ways about various aspects of Austen and music. I also have to thank two dear friends – Frances White and Helen Healy – who read and made very useful comments on the book in draft form. It is a true mark of friendship to provide this kind of support and I am deeply grateful.

And finally, to all the volunteers who run the many Jane Austen societies and festivals all over the world and who have provided venues for me to air my ideas and my performances, a huge vote of thanks for all the work you do in fostering the informed admiration of the great Jane Austen, musician and author.

Index

Index

Index

Index

Index

Index

violin, 227
Vogler, Gerard, 277

Webbe, Samuel, 46, 190, 261
Weisse, Christian Felix, 284
Welsh, Thomas, 281
Wesley, Samuel, 59, 264–5

Whitehead, William, 152, 191
Wildman, James, 83–4
Williams, Helen Maria, 66

'Yellow hair'd laddie, The', 231

Zwingmann, Johan Nicolaus, 291

EU authorised representative for GPSR:
Easy Access System Europe, Mustamäe tee 50,
10621 Tallinn, Estonia
gpsr.requests@easproject.com